Barbara Michaels is the bestselling author of *Shattered Silk*, *Search the Shadows*, and numerous other suspense-thrillers. She was born and raised in Illinois and received her Ph.D. in Egyptology from the University of Chicago. A frequent reviewer for the *Washington Post Book World*, Ms Michaels has also served as a judge for the Edgar Awards given by the Mystery Writers of America. She currently lives in Frederick, Maryland.

Also by Barbara Michaels in Bantam Books

SHATTERED SILK
SEARCH THE SHADOWS

BARBARA MICHAELS

SMOKE AND MIRRORS

BANTAM BOOKS
TORONTO • NEW YORK • LONDON • SYDNEY • AUCKLAND

Pilgrim's Way by John Buchan. Copyright © 1940 by John Buchan. Copyright renewed © 1968 by Susan Charlotte, Lady Tweedsmuir. Used with kind permission of A. P. Watt Ltd on behalf of the Rt. Hon. Lord Tweedsmuir of Elsfield CBE.

The quote on page 360 is taken from John F. Kennedy's Inaugural Address: January 20, 1961.

SMOKE AND MIRRORS

A BANTAM BOOK   0 553 17694 3

Originally published in Great Britain by Judith Piatkus (Publishers) Ltd

PRINTING HISTORY
Piatkus edition published 1989
Bantam Books edition published 1990

Bantam Books are published by Transworld Publishers Ltd.,
61–63 Uxbridge Road, Ealing, London W5 5SA,
in Australia by Transworld Publishers (Australia) Pty. Ltd.,
15–23 Helles Avenue, Moorebank, NSW 2170, and in New
Zealand by Transworld Publishers (N.Z.) Ltd., Cnr. Moselle
and Waipareira Avenues, Henderson, Auckland.

Printed and bound in Great Britain by
BPCC Hazell Books
Aylesbury, Bucks, England
Member of BPCC Ltd.

To Grace Peterson

One of the great ladies of the book
  business
And my dear friend

"Politics are almost as exciting as war, and quite as dangerous. In war you can only be killed once, but in politics many times."

> —Winston Churchill,
> *Remarks* (1920)

"You have all the characteristics of a popular politician: a horrible voice, bad breeding, and a vulgar manner."

> —Aristophanes,
> *The Knights* (424 B.C.)

"Politics is still the greatest and the most honorable adventure."

> —John Buchan, Lord Tweedsmuir,
> *Pilgrim's Way* (1940)

PROLOGUE

THEY CAME *to him every night. They never moved; they never spoke. They just stood there, by the side of the bed, their grave dark eyes fixed on his face. One of the smaller ones clung for support to its mother's skirt. The smallest of them lay cradled in her arms.*

She didn't look at all the way he remembered her. She looked old—scant graying hair, wrinkled cheeks—the way she might have looked if she had lived out her natural life, prematurely aged by poverty and hard work. He had never seen . . . the others. (Don't use the words, don't even think them: the little ones, the children.) The images he saw bore no resemblance to reality, they had shaped themselves from the dark ectoplasm of guilty nightmare. But those cobweb forms were stronger than sleeping pills or liquor or any of the other means by which he had sought oblivion. Shadow shapes, stronger than steel or stone. There was no way he could prevent them from coming.

Every night he lay paralyzed and helpless, waiting for it

to happen. It was always the same, and oddly beautiful—a bright ruffle of gold around the hem of her ragged skirt. That was when he woke, sweating and struggling for breath and thanking God for sparing him the final horror. But the night breeze seemed to carry a faint, grisly scent, and there was always the fear that one night he might not wake in time.

Chapter One

THE FACE was thirty feet high. Dark hair crowned it, like a hillside streaked with snow. The yard-long lips curved gently, with just the hint of a smile. The eyes were mesmerizing, not only because of their size; by some trick of setting they seemed to stare straight at the viewer, demanding his attention.

Erin turned the wheel slightly; she had been drifting dangerously close to the shoulder of the road. The billboards must be new. She had not noticed them before. They should have been hard to miss; but the eyes and their complex interconnections with brain and nervous system have a disconcerting habit of seeing only what concerns them. Until recently Erin had had only the mildest interest in politics, much less a local Senate race.

She wondered who had designed the advertisement, if that was the right word. But it was just that, an ad designed to sell a product—in this case not so much a person as a carefully packaged image. Rippling folds of red and white framed the giant face, stars floated on an azure background. The printed message, in glaring crimson, was short and simple: ROSEMARY WHITE MARSHALL FOR U.S. SENATE. No doubt the anonymous designer had calculated to the letter how many syllables an average reader could absorb while approaching the billboard at so many miles per hour.

Traffic was heavy, as it always was, even on Saturday. The Virginia suburbs of Washington had expanded rapidly over the past decade; housing developments, huge office complexes, and gargantuan shopping centers funneled tens of thousands of cars daily onto the highways. The traffic issue was a hot one in local politics, with one candidate pointing out the increased prosperity such growth had brought and another pandering to the fury of frustrated commuters who spent hours inching along the crowded roads on their way to and from work. Not until after she had passed the Dulles Airport exit was Erin able to relax at the wheel of her borrowed car. Traffic patterns and routes were unfamiliar to her, and she had not been behind the wheel of a car for almost a year. Fran, who liked to cultivate an impression of carefree affability, was in actual fact extremely selfish about her property, and the car was a prized possession. Only a very special occasion—and one from which, Erin thought uncharitably, Fran hoped to profit—had prompted her generosity on this occasion.

Fran was Erin's roommate, and at times her pet peeve. A friend . . . well, they certainly had not been friends in high school. It was not a question of active dislike back then, just of paths that seldom crossed. Their senior-class yearbook entries made their differing life-styles explicit. Fran's toothy grin appeared on every other page; as a cheerleader, member of the debating society and a dozen other clubs, as "most popular" and "most likely to succeed Joan Rivers." There were four pictures of Erin, in addition to the official senior photo. She had been editor of the literary magazine, a library aide, a member of the choir, and winner of the award for highest senior-class average grade. When they ran into one another at their class reunion five years later, they both had to squint surreptitiously at one another's name tags. It was pure accident that they had started talking.

Or so Erin believed at the time. To Fran, there were no such things as accidents. It was Fate—Karma—that had brought them together. It was Meant to Be. Fran had a way of encouraging people to talk—one of the reasons why she had been voted "most popular"—and Erin had been in a particularly vulnerable state of mind that day. She had talked, all right—spilled her guts, in fact—and Fran had made the right responses: sympathy for the recent death of Erin's father, interest in her plans, helpful suggestions.

"Suggestions" was probably too weak a word. As soon as Erin mentioned that she was thinking of moving to a larger city, where jobs in her field were easier to find, Fran began babbling about Karma. What a coincidence! Her roommate had just left and she was looking for someone to share her apartment in the Washington suburbs. It was a Sign, that was what it was. New York? You're crazy, love, do you know what a one-room hovel in Manhattan would set you back? Do you have any idea what they pay editorial assistants? And talk about your mean streets—you'd be mugged or raped, or both, within a day. Listen, sweetie, there are thousands of magazines and newsletters and house organs published in D.C. . . .

Erin finally got a word in. "Thousands?"

Fran grinned and ran a careless hand through her fashionably tousled hair. "Hundreds, at least. Honestly, Erin, this is too perfect. I mean, you have to get out of this hick town. You said your mother is all set, living with your aunt and sharing expenses, but you can't stay there, you'll go crazy with two old ladies bitching at you all the time about cleaning your room and getting home by midnight."

Erin was feeling guilty and disloyal for complaining about her aunt's nagging and her mother's helplessness, but Fran's shrewd assessment struck a nerve; her lips curled, and Fran was quick to exploit her emotions. "They can't help it," she said kindly. "You know mothers. But that's no way for you to live. We can have a great time. And I know we'd get along. Just look at us, we're exact opposites. We complement one another perfectly. Yin and Yang, Laurel and Hardy. I'm Scorpio, you're Aquarius—''

"Gemini," Erin said.

"What? Oh." Fran dismissed this minor error with a wave of her hand. "Same thing."

The more Erin thought about the idea, the more it appealed to her. She had only dim memories of the years she had lived in Virginia, but the memories were all happy ones. She told Fran she'd think about it and let her know; and when she got home to face her aunt's probing questions about where she had been and why she was so late and how many beers she had drunk, the decision was made. It pleased everyone. Her aunt wasn't quite rude enough to say so, but her first, unguarded reaction to the news made it very evident that she would be delighted to see the last of Erin. Even her mother adjusted to the idea more readily than Erin had expected—so readily that Erin felt a little hurt.

"Well, but darling, you'd have to leave home sometime, everyone does, and at least you won't be alone—I know Mrs. Blenkinsop slightly, she was on the Library Committee with me, and she seems very pleasant, I'm sure her daughter must be a suitable companion for you—of course I would rather you were going to a home of your own, but you'll surely meet someone soon, there are lots of nice young journalists and congressmen in Washington."

Erin saw no reason to correct the numerous misapprehensions in this naive speech. Her mother was right about one thing—at least she wouldn't be alone. The transition to independence would be eased by someone who knew the ropes, the shortcuts, the pitfalls to be avoided. There were advantages for Fran too. She had found the ideal roommate—one who was too meek to complain or criticize.

On the whole they got on better than one might have expected. Fran had been right about how different they were, even in appearance. Fran was short and dark and rounded; Erin was six inches taller, with strawberry-blond hair and, in her opinion, a figure embarrassingly flat fore and aft. (She got no sympathy from well-rounded Fran about that.) Fran dressed in clothes she fished out of bins at Goodwill and local thrift shops; Erin's blouses, pants, and skirts were color-coordinated, and she never appeared in public with a button missing or a hem that sagged. Erin's room was immaculate; Fran's was a cheerful confusion of discarded garments, magazines, and newspapers heaped onto the perpetually unmade bed. Fran had dozens of friends; after almost a year in Washington, Erin had made none.

Fran couldn't understand it. "I can't figure you out, Erin. Is it insecurity or conceit that keeps you from opening up to people? You don't go anyplace or do anything—"

"That's not true."

"Well, maybe it's a slight exaggeration." Fran studied Erin with a speculative look the latter had come to loathe; she knew it often heralded one of Fran's forays into amateur psychoanalysis. "I guess losing your dad was traumatic," Fran mused. "According to that article I read last week, the death of a parent rates nine and a half on a scale of ten, and you were always his little girl—"

"Shut up, Fran," Erin said.

Fran was not offended. "At least you're learning to talk back. Must be my good influence."

Erin had to admit Fran was correct. What she could not admit, even to herself, was that Fran's offhand comment about her father had also struck home. She still dreamed about him several times a week, and often woke crying.

Her job was a disappointment. Fran had helped her find it, on the staff of the newsletter of a national merchandising organization. Erin had not minded starting out in a secretarial position, but after months of typing and filing and making coffee, with no prospect of the promotion she had been promised, she began to feel put upon. Fran listened sympathetically if impatiently to her complaints. "If it bores you, quit. There are other jobs; hell, there's always McDonald's. That bastard isn't going to promote you, not if he can find a man for the job, he's nothing but a goddamn chauvinist. Look what happened last month with the associate-editor job. You said the guy who got it had only been there six weeks."

"He does have a wife and a couple of children," Erin said. "He needs the money more than—"

"Jesus H. Christ! If you insist on walking around bent over, somebody is going to accept the invitation and kick you in the butt."

"I don't want to sound like some strident women's libber—"

"No, you're going to go on being one of those mealy-mouthed 'please-kick-me-because-I'm-a-woman' types."

When she was passed over the second time—for yet another man—Erin didn't mention it to Fran, but stored-up resentment boiled within her all week, and by Saturday night she was in a very sour mood.

For a wonder Fran was not going out, or entertaining friends. Erin knew what that meant, and as they settled down in front of the TV, she wondered what masochistic impulse kept her from excusing herself and retiring to her room with a book. Fran was a news freak. She could sit unblinking and absorbed through endless repetitions of the same information, including the weather. First came the local news, then the network news, followed in due course by the late-night news— one program at ten and another at eleven. On weekends the program was varied slightly by the addition of a number of talk shows and public-information broadcasts, not to mention political specials, of which there were an inordinate number during the fall of this particular election year.

Fran settled down with a tray that held a huge bowl of chili, accompanied by chunks of cheese and half a box of saltines. She was always trying to diet, but on Saturday night before the tube she didn't even try. "I need all my strength to yell at Novak," she explained.

Fran yelled at all of them—Novak, Sidey, McLaughlin, Will. She even yelled at Sam Donaldson, her idol, when she thought he wasn't forceful enough. Once, during one of Fran's verbal attacks on Morton Kondracke, Erin had been moved to protest. "They can't hear you, you know. Why do you waste all that energy?"

Fran wiped her perspiring brow. "It relieves my pent-up rage. Oh, hell, Kondracke, you limp wimp, why don't you tell him he's a carbuncle on the backside of journalism?"

At first Fran couldn't believe Erin failed to share her passion. "Not interested in politics? What the hell do you mean? How can anybody not be interested in politics? These people are running your life. Don't you care what they think—what they do?"

"They never say what they think and they never do what they say they're going to do," Erin said. "What's the point?"

"Huh," said Fran, for once at a loss for words.

Despite her lack of interest, Erin couldn't help absorbing some information. Washington was a political town. It was a trite truism, one to which she would have acquiesced without giving it much thought; but she had never really comprehended what it meant until she had moved to the area. There was only one subject that interested metropolitan Washington more than politics, and that was the Redskins. Mercifully Fran wasn't a football fan. Erin would have seriously considered moving out if she had been forced to watch football as well as political discussions.

Fran polished off her chili and trotted into the kitchen to prepare the next course. Erin slumped lower in her chair and pushed the salad around her plate. She had spent all morning cleaning the apartment; it wasn't her turn to do it, but things had gotten to such a state she couldn't stand it any longer. Then she had accompanied Fran to a newly opened thrift shop in Alexandria. The store had lived up to its principles by failing to install air-conditioning, and the internal temperature had been in the high nineties. Erin was tired. She wanted to sit and stare mindlessly at something that required absolutely no effort, physical or mental. There was a forties' musical on cable, and Channel 4 had a comedy sitcom about two guys and two girls who shared an apartment, an abandoned baby, and a cute chimpanzee. But the TV was Fran's, and Fran picked the programs, and Fran had chosen to watch a debate on one of the public-broadcasting stations. The District of Columbia had no voting representation in Congress—as its residents were constantly pointing out—but the suburbs of the city were in both Maryland and Virginia, so the congressional races in those states concerned a large percentage of the viewing audience.

Fran returned with a huge bowl of popcorn just as trumpets heralded the celebration of the democratic process. She thrust the bowl at Erin.

"Here. Eat up and pay attention. You'll be voting for some of these characters—Virginia Tenth District congressional race, and a senator."

Erin saw no reason to mention that she hadn't registered to vote. Fran seemed fairly calm at the moment; why stir her up? The popcorn was excellent, a little too salty, but dripping with butter. When Fran went off her diet she went all the way.

Erin reached for her mending and let her mind drift away from the TV as she concentrated on making the stitches neat and tiny. The object was a black lace dress she had rescued from a carton of miscellany at the thrift shop. Fran insisted on dragging her along on her cheapie shopping trips; she had that variety of enthusiastic self-confidence that tries to impose its tastes on unwary friends. Usually Erin managed to resist the two-dollar sweaters ("Real cashmere—those stains under the arms will wash out") and the limp, out-of-style skirts. The stains never did wash out, and the skirts could never be remodeled or mended or revived. But the dress had caught her eye, torn and crumpled as it was, because it was obviously of good quality, and the rents were mendable by someone with her skill at sewing. Besides, it only cost five dollars. The expensive wardrobe her father had given her was beginning to wear out, and she certainly couldn't afford to replace it. Might as well get used to thrift shops and Sears instead of designer labels.

Fran nudged her. "This is it. The Senate race. Are you watching?"

"Yes," Erin said absently.

The encounter wasn't a debate in the formal sense; a moderator asked questions, which the opponents answered. Erin rather liked the looks of Senator Bennett, the Republican incumbent, but she knew better than to express her views, for Fran's opinion of the gentleman and all his works was outspokenly profane. He was a fine-looking man with a profile that resembled one of the more high-minded Roman emperors. Though he had obviously been schooled in public speaking, enough remained of the soft Virginia accent to make his slow, deep voice very easy on the ear.

His opponent was a congresswoman making her first bid for the Senate. The fact that she was a woman would have been enough to win the loyalty of Fran, a self-proclaimed and defiant feminist. Erin had another, more personal reason for being interested in Rosemary White Marshall. She let her sewing fall to her lap and watched.

Marshall was in her early fifties and, Erin thought, she looked every day of it. Her eyes were her best feature, large, dark, and wide-set, but makeup didn't hide the fan of fine wrinkles at the corners of her lids, or the deeper lines bracketing her mouth. When she smiled, which she did frequently, the lines curved into softer shapes, but her face was that of an affectionate grandma, not a mover and shaker of world events. Who, after all, would want a senator with dimples? Her soft pink suit and the ruffles framing her chin increased the grandmotherly image; she wore no jewelry except pearl earrings and a wide gold wedding band.

I'd have recognized her, Erin thought. She's changed a lot, but the resemblance is there.

At first Bennett dominated the debate; his booming voice sounded forceful and confident next to Marshall's soft alto. He took the offensive, reminding the audience of the worthy causes he had supported and the admirable legislation he had introduced. Among the latter was a day-care bill; and all at once, Marshall, who had been smiling and dimpling at the camera, interrupted.

"Now that's just so sweet," she said loudly.

The inappropriate comment caught Bennett off guard. His brief second of hesitation gave Marshall her chance. Her smile continued to dazzle, but it had turned predatory, lips curled back, teeth bared: Grandma transformed into the wolf.

"So sweet of Senator Bennett and his friends to jump onto the bandwagon. Better late than never, one presumes, but I only wish they had chosen to take this stand five years ago, when I introduced a child-care bill in the House. The companion bill in the Senate was defeated, thanks in large part to the tireless filibustering of Senator Bennett here. He was

all in favor of six-hundred-dollar toilet seats for the Defense
Department, but supporting the needs of America's children—oh, no, that would have been a waste of taxpayers'
money! Now, five years later, child care is a national disaster,
so desperate that even my myopic opponent has been forced
to take notice. Ten and a half million children under six who
are cared for by people other than their parents! Neglect,
child abuse, physical and emotional torture. . . ."

Bennett couldn't défend himself, she never gave him a
chance; the soft but surprisingly íncisive voice went on and
on, barely pausing for breath. The questioner had to interrupt
her to explain that they were out of time, whereupon she
apologized, with the prettiest smile imaginable. "I just get
carried away when I think about children being in danger. As
a mother and grandmother . . ."

Fran was beside herself. "Isn't she great?"

"She dresses nicely," Erin said. "That soft pink—"

"Oh, for God's sake, I wasn't talking about her looks!
Didn't you hear what she said? She ran rings around that old
fart Bennett. He's the most reactionary, bigoted—"

"How could you tell? I didn't hear him commit himself to
anything except God, motherhood, and a strong national defense."

"Hell, everybody's in favor of a strong defense. Marshall
has fought Pentagon waste and overspending for years. Bennett gets hundreds of thousands in campaign contributions
from military contractors; you think he's about to bite the
hands that feed him by questioning their bills?"

"I think a person's appearance is very important," Erin
said, reaching for her sewing.

"If you aren't the most . . ." Fran stopped and then went
on, grudgingly, "You're right, actually. Politics is more appearance than substance these days. You can bet her staff has
calculated every nuance, down to the diameter of her earrings. I guess the results must appeal to the greatest number
of potential voters, but I'd like to see her show a little more
pizzazz—funky earrings, a plunging neckline."

"I don't know anything about politics, but I know enough
about clothes—and about people—to know that would be di-

sastrous. She's not a young girl. Older women should dress conservatively, like ladies. I admit that pink is a little bland. With her coloring she could wear more vivid shades—turquoise or bright coral. It would come over better on television too, I'll bet.''

"Maybe you ought to write and tell her all about it," Fran said sarcastically. Her fingers scraped the bottom of the bowl, gathering the last stray kernels.

"Maybe I will," Erin said. Sometimes Fran's superior manner rankled. "Mother's been nagging me about getting in touch with her."

If she hoped to impress Fran, she succeeded. The latter's eager questions made it easy for her to appear cool about the relationship—which wasn't, in her private opinion, worth bragging about. Her mother and Rosemary White had once been close friends; "but it was years ago—they were in college together." The correspondence had deteriorated into little more than an exchange of Christmas cards and family photos, but Rosemary had written a lovely letter of condolence after the death of Erin's father.

"Written? In her own hand?" Fran asked breathlessly.

"You don't type condolence letters."

"I do. When I write them at all." Fran considered the matter. "My God, this is exciting. Why didn't you tell me you knew her?"

"I don't. And I don't understand why you're so thrilled. She's just another politician. Washington is full of them."

"She's not just another politician. She's a comer. No question about it. With a little luck she could be the first woman President. Not now—maybe in ten years. If she wins this fall . . . ''

"According to McLaughlin and Novak, she hasn't a prayer," Erin said. "All the commentators I've heard seem to favor the other candidate, Mr. Bennett."

"Popularly known as Buzz the Buzzard," said Fran. "You haven't read the latest polls, I guess. It's true that when she first agreed to run, nobody gave her a chance. Bennett's entrenched, he's been in the Senate for fifteen years. But after the flap about him and that girl . . ."

"I heard about it," Erin admitted. "But I didn't think it would make much difference. Everybody seems to be doing it."

Fran grinned. "You're more cynical than I thought. No, honey, everybody isn't doing it, and the ones that do do it are careful not to get caught. Buzz got caught with his pants all the way down to his ankles, and he'd been so damned self-righteous about his moral virtues that it hit him harder than it would have hit someone else. Then there's his wife. She's very popular with his constituents—the sweetest little old honeypie you'd ever want to meet. . . . Oh, hell, let's not talk about that, let's talk about Rosemary. She's my idol—"

"I thought your idol was Sam Donaldson."

"It's his eyebrows," Fran said dreamily. "They do something to me."

Erin had no comment to make on this but she wouldn't have been allowed to make it in any case. Fran sat bolt upright. "Hey. Hey! There's your answer!"

"Answer to what?"

"Your job problem. The campaign is heating up and she's still the underdog; she'll want all the people she can get. Why don't you ask her to hire you?"

"Her? Who?" Erin stuttered. "Her? You must be crazy. Why should she give me a job? I don't know anything about politics, or running a campaign, or—"

"You could give her advice on how to dress," Fran said, grinning. "No, but seriously. You're a crackerjack typist, and not entirely devoid of brains. That combination is rarer than you might suppose."

"Yes, but—"

So in the end—as she might have expected—she wrote the letter. Withstanding Fran's manic enthusiasm was like trying to remain stationary in a gale-force wind. Erin could do it—but only when the wind wasn't blowing in the direction she wanted to go anyhow. Not that she agreed with Fran's tirades about gender discrimination, but passing her over in favor of a less qualified applicant, male or female, just wasn't fair. The job was a dead end; high time she faced the fact. And it had been rather exciting to see Rosemary Marshall, after all the stories she had heard from her mother. Actually running for the Senate . . . The job, supposing she could get it, had to be more interesting than what she was doing.

The answer took a week to reach her. It sounded as if it had been written by an aide—cool, rather businesslike—but it did not propose a business appointment. Instead, she was invited to lunch the following Saturday. Directions to Rosemary's home near Middleburg were included. Fran was thrilled at this evidence of friendly interest. She had even made the ultimate sacrifice of offering the loan of her car, pointing out that it would be almost impossible to get to Middleburg any other way. Erin had accepted with thanks, and tolerated with relative good humor Fran's frenetic attempts to decide what she should wear; but she wasn't convinced the invitation was a good omen. She had not asked for friendship, she had applied for a job. This might be a way of turning down the application without overt rudeness to the offspring of an old friend.

She would soon know. The road had narrowed and the tight-packed dwellings of suburbia had dwindled to isolated houses. She was in the country now.

From time to time she caught glimpses of the distant mountains. That was what they called them here, mountains; a westerner would have laughed at the idea of using that word to describe the tree-covered, gentle mounds of the Blue Ridge. In the bright morning light they were more green than blue, with a few patches of pale color to break the monotony—soft yellow and muted orange, the beginning of the autumn change. It was late September, and unusually hot for that time of year. At least that was what Washingtonians claimed. They were, as Erin had learned, given to exaggeration.

Gilbert's Corners, where Routes 50 and 15 intersected, boasted a stop light and little else. Four miles to Middleburg. Seized by a sudden attack of stage fright, Erin pulled off the road. She didn't have to refresh her memory of the route she had been directed to take; she had memorized it. Instead she twisted sideways and looked into the rearview mirror.

It was too small to give her an overall view of her anxious

face. She started at the top and worked down. Frown lines
scarring her forehead—smooth them out, relax. Narrowed
gray-green eyes—open wide, look interested and optimistic.
There was nothing she could do about her nose. It was hopelessly plebeian, snubbed and freckled like a plover's egg. Not
that she had ever seen a plover's egg, but that was the conventional literary image. . . . She stretched her mouth and
stroked on additional lip gloss. Her hair was her biggest problem; both fine and thick, its reddish-blond waves refused to
stay confined in a neat coil. I should have had it cut, she
thought, and reached for the pins. A glance at the clock on
the dashboard warned her against that move; better to be on
time and slightly disheveled than late—and probably just as
disheveled. Short of a coat of varnish, there was no way she
could confine the floating wisps. In the humid heat, hair spray
turned sticky and gluey. Erin's tailored wool suit was uncomfortable as well as somewhat inappropriate, but she had had
little choice; her summer-weight clothing was hopelessly out
of style, or too casual. The pale-green classic suit had lived
up to the saleslady's claim, and Erin was determined to look
professional. Fran had hooted at the suit, the white blouse
with its soft bow at the throat, and the simple pumps—"You
look like little Miss Manners"—but Erin had remained ob-
durate.

A chorus of whistles and howls from a passing pickup
brought the frown back to her face. Chauvinist rednecks . . .
Realizing what she had thought, she was surprised at herself.
She'd been listening to Fran yelling about men too much. Nor
was "redneck" a good choice, the young men were potential
voters, and for all she knew, they could be Harvard Ph.D.s.

She waited until another truck had passed—did everyone
in rural Virginia drive rusty-blue pickups?—before pulling
back onto the road. Soon she was in the outskirts of Middleburg. Handsome dignified houses, set back from the road,
low stone or white-painted fences preserving their privacy.
Then the town itself—elegant shops, eighteenth-century
houses and inns. She made a left turn and was soon in the
country again; white fences outlined rolling pastureland where
horses grazed on grass yellowed by the summer heat. Occa-

sionally the chimneys and rooflines of mansions could be seen over the trees that enclosed them in smug aloofness. Fran had given her a crash course on the notables of the Middleburg area: actors and football players, publishers and presidents. John F. Kennedy had spent only a single weekend at his retreat at Wexford before the fatal trip to Dallas; the estate had passed through several hands before Reagan stayed there during the presidential campaign of 1980. The region's most glamorous resident had been Elizabeth Taylor, when she shared the heart, hand, and home of Senator John Warner. Taylor had gone on to greener pastures, but another of Hollywood's not-so-youthful glamour queens had recently moved in to replace her on the local scene, if not in the hearts of her fans and those who had found her outspoken comments on the political world enormously refreshing.

Erin drove slowly, watching for the turn. She found it, though not without difficulty; there was no sign except for a small country-road marker. The new road was well maintained and fairly straight, but it was barely wide enough for two cars. She met only one vehicle—sure enough, another pickup.

The first sign of habitation appeared as a break in the tangled vegetation to the left, marked by a pair of stone pillars. It couldn't be the Marshall place; according to the directions she had received, it was on the right-hand side, and there was still another mile to go. The people who lived out this way certainly cherished their privacy. The clustering greenery lining the road appeared to be impenetrable.

As soon as she had received the invitation, Erin had begun cramming on the subject of politics in general and Rosemary White Marshall in particular. Even Fran had been impressed at her industry, though her compliment might have been phrased more politely: "The one thing you do know is how to study."

The Marshalls didn't have as much money as some of the other residents of the area, but their social and political lineage was impeccable. There had been a Marshall in state or national politics for almost two hundred years, and Rosemary's husband Edward had held the House seat to which she

succeeded upon his death—the so-called "widow's game,"
which until recently had been a woman's easiest entry into
politics. The Marshalls were aristocrats of Ole Virginny, but
Ed Marshall had married beneath him; Rosemary's father had
been a postal clerk from Arlington, her grandfather, a la-
borer. These biological details were stressed in her campaign
literature; the monied, old-boy network might be useful in
raising funds and collecting favors, but the average voter was
more impressed by a picture of Granddad in overalls, brandishing a hammer.

Erin glanced at the odometer. Almost there. Another break
in the underbrush, this time on the right. This must be it. As
she had been promised, the gate was open. It was no impressive construction of wrought iron between massive gate-
posts, but a simple wooden farm gate. Beyond was the
driveway, graveled but not paved, with ominous ruts and pot-
holes breaking its surface. The house was a good quarter mile
from the gate. Erin stopped and stared.

She had expected a stately mansion, along the lines of
Twelve Oaks or Tara—a white-pillared monument to the Old
South set in green velvet lawns, or a graceful gem of Federal
architecture like Monticello. The house was big enough, and
white enough, but there wasn't a pillar to be seen, and the
wings and additions that shot out from it, apparently at random, robbed it of any claim to architectural purity. To the
south and east of the grounds the land rose in an enclosing
semicircle of heavily wooded hills. The land to the north was
open field, sloping down to a little river—a run, as they called
them here. No blooded horses cropped the pasture; the fields
had gone wild, Queen Anne's lace and burdock and the blue
of wild gentian mingling with knee-high grass.

Erin took her foot off the brake and proceeded at a cautious
crawl. The driveway really was a disgrace. The closer she got
to the house, the more evidences she saw of—not neglect
exactly, but certainly not the impeccable maintenance one
would have expected to find in an estate with the imposing
name of Fairweather. The house needed a coat of paint. The
lawn had been cut but not raked; a series of flower gardens
to the left of the driveway, running to the edge of the pines,

were weedy and carelessly tended. The bright profusion of blooms seemed to consist mainly of zinnias, petunias, and marigolds—the cheapest, most easily maintained of all annuals.

So maybe the Marshalls weren't rich. Money was the manure of politics, according to Fran, and a campaign could do nasty things to a candidate's cash flow, especially if he or she was running against a popular, well-funded incumbent. A thirty-second TV spot cost more, and was more important, than a coat of paint.

The drive divided as she neared the house. The left-hand portion, narrower and even more rutted, led toward a clutter of outbuildings. Erin took the right-hand turn, which circled the house and ended in a sunbaked stretch of bare ground. She pulled up beside one of the cars parked there and turned off the engine.

It was no wonder she had received no coherent impression of the house; what she had seen before was only one side of it. This was the front, the formal entrance, but the adjective was screamingly inappropriate for what she beheld: Victorian Gothic at its best, or worst, with the wonderful indifference to coherence that had marked some of the more entertaining examples of the genre. A stately tower, with a shingled cupola; a long porch or veranda, stretching all the way across the front and curving giddily around the corner; windows of all shapes and sizes, some perfectly ordinary rectangles, others arched and framed in gingerbread. It might have looked impressive if the material had been stone, but white clapboard just didn't do the job. The bits and pieces of furniture scattered the length of the veranda were an eclectic blend of rickety wicker and modern plastic. There was even a porch swing, hanging from rusted chains. The cushions on sofas, chairs, and swing matched only in the degree to which the varied fabrics had faded. And most of the cushioned surfaces were occupied, though not by people. The motionless mounds appeared to be cats—of all sizes, colors, and shapes. At least a dozen of them.

Even in the few moments she had sat there, the interior of the car had warmed up considerably. She rolled the window down, but only a cautious two inches. Fran might be thrilled at pointing out a stain on the upholstery as having been made by one of Rosemary Marshall's cats. On the other hand, she might not.

Through the opened window Erin heard a sound she had not been aware of earlier, and her hand stopped on its way to the handle of the door. If it wasn't the furious baying of a gigantic hound, that was certainly what it sounded like. Not one hound—two or more. None of the cats had so much as flicked a whisker; it was probably safe to assume the dogs were chained or caged. Probably . . .

As she hesitated, the front door opened and a man came out onto the porch. (Though surely they called it a veranda in Ole Virginny?) He shouted at the top of his lungs, "Knock it off, will you? I heard you!"

The dogs stopped barking, so Erin deduced the remarks had not been directed at her. She got out of the car and walked toward the house. The newcomer trotted down the stairs and met her with a broad smile and an outstretched hand.

"Didn't anybody warn you about the dogs? It's okay, they're locked up."

Her modest two-inch heels raised her to a height of five-nine, only a little shorter than he. Her eyes were level with the tip of his nose—a particularly fine-cut, narrow nose, she couldn't help noticing. Fran would have noticed his eyebrows—thick, dark, splendidly arched. Any female with functioning eyesight would have noticed his build; his jeans fit like a second skin over lean hips and thighs, and his thin blue cotton shirt clung to shoulders that were almost disproportionately broad. His sleeves had been rolled to the elbows, baring muscular brown forearms, and the hand he extended was crisscrossed by scratches, presumably feline in origin.

"Hey, don't you listen to the weather forecast? Take off your jacket, why don't you, you must be roasting."

The hand, which she had mistakenly believed she was supposed to shake, had actually touched her shoulder before she stepped back, her face stiffening. "No, thank you. I'm quite comfortable."

"Oh, come on. You don't have to impress us, we're a casual lot—"

"So I observe."

He was a very good-looking man, with thick, unruly dark hair and brown eyes fringed by curling lashes. It was obvious that he was only too well aware of the effect those eyelashes—and his other attributes—made on impressionable females. Instead of being intimidated by her frosty tone, he grinned even more broadly.

"Okay, melt if you want. I was just trying—"

"I believe Mrs. Marshall is expecting me. My name is Erin Hartsock."

"I believe she is," the other agreed. "How do you do, Ms. Hartsock? Or do you prefer Miss?"

"As a matter of fact—"

"My name is Nick McDermott. I prefer Nick." He seized her limp hand and pumped it vigorously, continuing to hold it as he started for the house. His grip was firm enough so that Erin would have had to struggle to free herself. She had no intention of doing so, it would have been undignified, but she raged inwardly as she trotted to keep up with his long strides. From his confident manner she assumed he must be someone important, someone she dare not risk offending, but she resented him all the more because he looked so cool and comfortable in his shirtsleeves while her blouse was sticking to her perspiring body.

He led her up the stairs and across the porch, stepping over and around sprawled cats with practiced unconcern. The cats were equally unconcerned; one rolled over onto its back and stretched lazily, but none of the others stirred.

Nick opened a screened door and motioned her inside. The interior of the house was dark and shady, and cooler than the out-of-doors, but it was obviously not air-conditioned. At first, eyes blinded by the transition from bright sunlight to cool gloom, she could make out very few details. There were no windows in the vestibule; the only light came from the door behind her. Matching doors on either side were closed; a third door, straight ahead, opened onto a long hallway. Here a ceiling fixture glowed softly, showing stairs on the left and more closed doors on the right. "Offices," Nick said, gesturing but not pausing. "We go this way. . . ."

Past the stairs, straight down the hall, to another door, of heavy oak shining with varnish. He threw it open.

Light at last—floods of sunlight from wide windows on two adjoining walls. An ancient window air conditioner, clacking and grumbling, lowered the temperature somewhat. It was a big room, high-ceilinged and paneled in dark wood; and the furnishings suggested that it served a variety of functions. Sofas, tables, and chairs formed a social "grouping" in front of a massive brick-and-marble fireplace; one end of the room contained office equipment: filing cabinets, a desk, tables covered with books and papers; the other end had been fitted up as a dining area. The long table held cups, some used, some clean; boxes of sugar and artificial sweetener; plastic stirrers; and the oversized coffee maker without which, as Erin was to learn, no political campaign could function. Built-in bookcases flanked the fireplace; the shelves were piled high, not only with books but with office supplies, magazines, and . . . knitting bags? Yes, unquestionably knitting bags; one had tipped over onto its side and spilled a tangle of bright-red yarn onto the shelf.

Erin was always nervous when she had to meet a group of strangers; she had developed a cowardly habit of focusing on some inanimate object or piece of furniture instead of meeting eyes that might be critical or curious or unwelcoming. On this occasion she found herself stupidly wondering how the yarn had got into such a tangle. Perhaps one of the cats . . .

She gave herself a mental slap and forced herself to concentrate on the people in the room. If things worked out as she hoped, these were the men and women she would be working with—or for. Her chances of getting the job weren't very good if she stood gawking like a shy teenager.

There were three of them: an older man, balding and incredibly rumpled, wearing horn-rimmed glasses that looked too small for his broad, heavy-featured face; a woman, whose graying brown hair was coiled into a heavy bun at the back of her neck; and a young black man.

The latter appeared to be about the same age as her guide, in his late twenties or early thirties, but he was taller and more slightly built. His aquiline features and precisely shaped mouth were as attractive as Nick's, but more refined. The word "patrician" came to Erin's mind; if he had worn ruffles at his throat and a sword at his side he might have posed for a portrait of a Gentleman of Aristocratic Lineage. His attire was just as formal, if more contemporary—a well-cut three-piece suit and a carefully knotted tie.

". . . Joe Esler, campaign manager and Grand High Monkey-Monk," Nick was saying. The older man hoisted his posterior an inch off the seat of his chair and nodded at her. "And Jeff Ross, our legal counsel. At least that's his official title; like all the rest of us, he does a little bit of everything. He's also Joe's aide, assistant, and intellectual superior."

Joe chuckled, and Jeff allowed himself a tight, brief smile. With a start of chagrin Erin realized she had missed hearing the older woman's name while she dithered about yarn. When would she ever learn . . .

"And then there's me," said a voice from the far end of the room. "Or, more properly, 'I.' Unfortunately, grammatical precision sounds pompous and incorrect, accustomed as we have become to the vulgarities of common usage."

A man rose from behind one of the desks. He was so tall, and he moved so deliberately, that it seemed to take him forever to get all the way up to his full height. It was no wonder he had blended into the furniture; he was all one color, a faded grayish buff, from his close-cropped hair to his khaki pants. His glasses had gold rims; a toothbrush mustache of the same shade as his hair blended with the bookish pallor of his face.

"Hello. I'm Will."

"Sorry," Nick exclaimed. "I didn't see you."

"People don't," Will murmured.

"It's your own fault, Will," the woman said in a brisk, no-nonsense voice. "You must learn to assert yourself if you want to be noticed. Please sit down, Erin. Rosemary will be here in a few minutes, she's on the telephone."

She was knitting as she spoke; a virtuoso performance, for

the pattern was complex and she kept her eyes fixed on Erin as the wool looped unhesitatingly over and under the needles. So she was the knitter—and a fanatical one, if she had several projects underway at the same time. The afghan on which she was working was a fisherman's knit in pale-cream wool, with a complex cable pattern.

"I hope you had no difficulty following my directions?" she asked.

Erin shook her head. "No, ma'am."

It had been years since she had called anyone "ma'am." Her use of it now was unplanned and spontaneous, perhaps because this woman conjured up images of stern schoolteachers and Victorian governesses. She was big-boned and heavy-set, and dressed with a sobriety that suggested a uniform: white shirtwaist blouse, brown tweed skirt, and flat-heeled walking shoes. The courtesy was well received; the woman's stiff features relaxed, and she nodded pleasantly. "That's good. I'm glad you have your own car."

"It isn't mine, actually," Erin admitted. "My roommate lent me hers."

"Oh, really? Dear me. That presents a difficulty. There is no way of getting here by public transportation, you know. And you must understand that we really can't afford to hire additional staff. We depend to a large extent on volunteers. Running a political campaign is very expensive, especially when—"

"For God's sake, Kay, Rosemary is the one who makes the decisions about hiring," Joe growled. "Get off the girl's back. Relax, kid, you aren't on trial. How about a drink?"

Kay didn't bother to conceal her annoyance; she frowned at Joe, and Nick, glancing from one to the other, burst into rapid speech. "Good idea. What'll it be, Erin? Sherry, Chablis, beer, gin, bourbon? Normally we're a sober lot, but Saturday is supposed to be our day off."

"Just a soft drink, if you have it," Erin said cautiously.

Kay nodded approvingly. "Very sensible. Nick is joking, of course. During this stage of the campaign we work seven days a week. And although some people claim they are not

affected by alcohol, I am convinced it lowers one's efficiency.''

The criticism was obviously aimed at Joe, whose glass was
filled to the brim with a dark amber liquid. Erin would have
been willing to bet it wasn't sherry.

Joe's only response was to raise the glass to his lips and
take a long swallow. Kay continued to glower, Jeff stared at
his own glass, which appeared to contain tonic or mineral
water, and Nick whistled loudly and tunelessly as he rummaged through a miscellaneous collection of bottles in a cab-
inet behind the table. Erin could feel the tension in the air.
It was only to be expected, she supposed. These people were
the inner circle, those responsible for the day-by-day running
of the campaign; to a large extent success or failure depended
on their efforts. The older woman—Kay—must be Rosemary's personal secretary, or perhaps her aide. Not only was
there tension between them, there was a measurable degree
of jealousy as they jockeyed for position and influence.

Nick handed her a glass. ''Behold the Star Chamber,'' he
said. For a startled moment Erin wondered if she had spoken
aloud, his comment matched her thoughts so closely. ''The
powers behind the throne, the Cardinals Richelieu, the *ém-
inences grises*. Except me. I'm nobody. They let me hang
around because I do the chores nobody else wants to do.
Polish shoes, de-flea dogs, scrub floors—''

''Wrong,'' said Joe, with a rumble of laughter. ''We let
him hang around because he's so goddamned handsome.
Gives the girls a thrill. Right, Kay?''

''Don't tease the boy, Joe,'' Kay said gravely. ''Nick is
one of our dedicated volunteers, Erin. He acts as media consultant, speech writer—''

''And court jester.'' Jeff spoke for the first time. He may
have meant it as a joke, but he didn't smile, and the look
Nick gave him was visibly devoid of amusement.

''He keeps our spirits up,'' Kay said, with another of her
decisive little nods. ''That's very important.''

Nick did find this amusing; he rolled his eyes and grinned
at Erin. She couldn't decide whether Kay was unaware of the
nuances, or determined to pretend they did not exist.

The door behind her opened. Erin didn't have to turn to know who had entered; Rosemary Marshall's presence was mirrored on the faces of the men who faced her, in very different but equally visible ways. A heightened awareness, a stiffening of pose—and something more, a kind of reflected glow.

Erin turned in time to see her hostess lunge forward. "Goddamn it! Catch him, Joe, Nick—somebody—"

"He" was a cat, though at first Erin saw only a mottled blur, heading at full speed for the nearest place of conceal-ment—the sofa. After being flushed out from under it he ric-ocheted around the room, from the mantel to the back of Joe's chair, to the table, and then beneath it. She joined in the chase—the peremptory voice had been as compelling as a direct order—and it was she who fished the cat out from un-der the tablecloth. As soon as he realized he was fairly caught he melted, hanging limp from her hands and giving her a look of pained reproach. He appeared to be a tabby of inde-terminate age and considerable bulk. Opening massive jaws and displaying a set of sharp white fangs, he emitted a small soprano mew of protest.

"Give him to me," said Nick, red-faced with exercise and laughter. "He's shedding on you. He does it on purpose."

Deliberately or not, the cat had left fuzzy souvenirs all over her palms and fingers. Erin dusted them off as Nick cradled the animal in his arms.

"Out." Rosemary gestured vigorously. "Get him out, Nick. Damn the creature, he lurks like Dracula. I didn't see him until he was on his way through the door."

The ice had definitely been broken. Rosemary was laugh-ing and even Jeff's austere face had softened into a half-smile.

The first thing that struck Erin was the distinguished con-gresswoman's size. Somehow she had gotten the impression that Marshall was much taller. In the flesh she appeared al-most diminutive, a scant inch over five feet tall, and her in-formal clothes made her look even tinier. She wore faded, baggy jeans, a man's shirt that flapped loosely over generous hips, and a pair of dirty sneakers. Her hair had been pulled back into a ponytail, and a smudge of ink marked her chin.

Erin knew she was staring, rudely and openly. She couldn't help it. The contrast between the sophisticated candidate and this sloppy specimen, dressed like a street person and swearing like a farmhand, was too much for her. Rosemary was quite accustomed to being stared at. She smiled—the practiced candidate's smile Erin had seen on the tube—and said, "You're Erin, of course. You look so much like your mother."

Erin began, "People say I look more like—"

"Not the way she is now; the way she looked in college. Oh, Lord. I don't know whether that makes me feel eighteen again, or a hundred and eighteen."

For a moment she appeared to be about to embrace Erin, but she changed her mind and stepped back. "You'll want to wash your hands. God knows what rubbish bin that damned animal has been rooting in."

"I'll show her." Kay put her knitting aside. "And Rosemary—please watch your language. Someday one of those words will slip out during a speech or a debate—"

"A little 'damn' never hurt anybody," Rosemary said defiantly. "Oh, well, I suppose you're right. You always are."

A door near the long table opened onto a passageway that led to a butler's pantry and kitchen, with a half-bath next to the latter. Erin emerged from the bathroom in time to meet Kay coming from the kitchen with a large cut-glass bowl of shrimp salad. She asked if she could help.

"Thank you, but I have everything under control. We wait on ourselves weekends; Rosemary prefers it that way. You go and sit down."

Rosemary had taken Kay's place on the sofa, as well as her knitting. She wasn't as skillful as Kay; she had to watch her hands, but it didn't keep her from talking.

"I won't appear on the same platform with that sleazeball, Joe; no way. Tell him thanks but no thanks. Be tactful, as only you can be. . . ."

Seeing Erin she broke off and motioned at the place beside her. Joe wasn't willing to abandon the topic, however.

"Damn it, Rosie, you need his endorsement. Those union votes—"

"You're out of touch with modern politics, Joe," Rosemary interrupted. "Unions don't vote as blocs—if they ever did. The last election . . . " She dropped the knitting and snapped her fingers. "Will?"

Will had blended back into the scenery. An apparently disembodied voice replied promptly, "Split all the way down the line from President to county council. Rosemary got sixty-one percent last time."

"Thanks, Will." Rosemary snapped her fingers again. "I love doing that," she murmured.

"Power mad," said the distant voice of Will.

"Talk about being out of touch with political reality!" said Joe, who had not appreciated Rosemary's criticism. "Last election you were the incumbent in a district you've owned for over a decade. This is the Senate, dammit. Buzz Bennett owns that seat the way you own yours."

"Never mind that now," Rosemary said firmly. "We have a guest, and I'm sure political strategy bores her. How is your mother, Erin?"

But it was impossible in that house and that time to keep off the subject of politics. They served themselves from the dishes Kay had placed on the table—shrimp salad, hot rolls, iced tea—and before long Joe had returned to the forbidden subject. "So maybe he can't deliver the votes he thinks he can; we can use his organization and his people, for canvassing, direct mailings—"

"His idea of a direct mailing is a quick and dirty," Rosemary retorted, biting into a roll with a ferocity that implied she would have preferred to sink her teeth in someone's jugular. "Even if I'd stoop to those tactics, they do more harm than good."

Erin found herself on one of the wide, cushioned window seats, with Nick beside her. "All this is so much Greek to you, I suppose," he said.

Torn between resentment at his patronizing tone and genuine curiosity, Erin yielded to the latter. "What's a quick and dirty?"

"Something that accuses the other candidate of a charge that is either false or impossible to refute. Even if he can prove it's a lie, the damage is done; people remember the accusation longer than the refutation.''

"Oh.''

"You didn't tell me you knew Rosemary way back when.''

"It was my mother who knew her.''

"Before you were born?''

"Well—before and after. We lived in Richmond until I was two.''

"And then you moved to—''

"Indianapolis.''

"I thought the accent was midwestern," Nick said. "So you haven't seen Rosemary since?''

"No.'' It was beginning to sound, and feel, like an interrogation.

"Nobody ever tells me anything, but I get the impression this isn't a purely social call. Kay was right, you know; our cash flow is a muddy trickle. If you're looking for a job—''

"I don't know that that's any of your business, Mr. McDermott.''

"Nick. It could be my business. I wear a lot of different hats; you might end up working for me if you—''

"Excuse me.'' Erin rose. "I'm going to have a little more salad.''

After helping herself, she went to join the others. The job wasn't so important to her that she was willing to be quizzed by a lowly volunteer, how ever many hats he wore. He had no right to pry into her background. Hadn't Joe said it was Rosemary who would make the decision?

She looked at Rosemary—feet on the coffee table, hair straggling—and hoped her feelings about this peculiar interview didn't show on her face. It was so wildly different from the way she had pictured it—a stately mansion, a handsomely furnished office, Rosemary rising with quiet dignity from behind a mahogany desk, wearing something elegant and tailored. . . . Surely this was not a typical political campaign, or a typical candidate. Why did Rosemary allow these people, her subordinates, to treat her the way they did? Well, not Nick or Jeff, they were polite enough, but even they didn't demonstrate the deference a congresswoman ought to command, and the other pair were downright rude at times.

Kay was the next one to engage Erin in a private conversation—not difficult, since the argument between Joe and Rosemary had risen in volume and the others were listening, putting a word in now and then when they could make themselves heard. Kay's questions were even more searching than Nick's had been, but this time Erin felt she could not refuse to answer. She wasn't sure of Kay's precise position, but the older woman obviously held a high-level job. Perhaps Rosemary had deputized her to conduct the job interview.

Erin had barely begun to describe her background when Kay surprised her by saying, "I knew your father, years ago, when he handled some of Congressman Marshall's legal work. We were sorry to hear of his death. Cancer, wasn't it?"

"Yes. I didn't realize you—"

"You yourself have had no legal training?"

"No. I majored in English."

"No experience in the law? Not even in your father's office—part-time, perhaps?"

"I did work for him one summer." Erin realized that legal experience would have been a plus, but honesty compelled her to continue. "It was just routine. Typing and filing."

"I see." Kay's eyes dropped to her work. She executed a series of complex stitches and then looked at Erin. "What made you decide to leave Indianapolis? I would have thought your mother would want you near her, especially now."

The not-so-implicit criticism put Erin on the defensive. "She's living with my aunt. There was . . . there wasn't as much money as we had thought. We had to sell the house, and Aunt Ann was living alone, she never married, and she was glad to have Mother, they've always been close. I didn't feel . . . They didn't really need me. . . ."

Kay's gaze was cool and unwavering. A wave of resentment filled Erin, not so much against Kay as against herself. It did not occur to her—then—that the questions had no real bearing on her qualifications for a job. She only knew she was telling Kay far more than she needed to know, and when she went on her voice was brusque to the point of rudeness.

"I need the money—for myself and for Mother. I thought I could earn more here."

"I see." Kay's voice matched hers. "But why Washington? Why not Chicago, New York?"

It was another question that had no short, simple answer. Erin explained about Fran and the apartment and the job opportunities; Kay listened with an expression that suggested none of it made any sense or answered the question. "I suppose," Erin said finally, "it was partly because the area wasn't entirely strange to me. It was years ago that I lived in Virginia, but I liked it, and—and . . ."

She stammered into silence as she realized the other voices had stopped and that they were all looking at her. Rosemary frowned.

"All right, Kay," she said. "If you don't mind, I'll talk to Erin myself."

The others took the hint. Jeff was the first to leave, after a coolly courteous "Nice to have met you, Miss Hartsock." Joe's comment was more friendly: "See you around, kid." Nick followed him out, with no more than a nod at Erin. She wondered if she had offended him, and decided she didn't care if she had. Kay remained firmly planted in her seat until Rosemary asked pointedly about some letters that had to go out that day; then she moved slowly, stopping to look back at Rosemary as if she were hoping to be asked to remain.

When the door closed after Kay, Erin expected Rosemary to begin questioning her. Instead she turned and called loudly, "We give you leave to depart, Will."

Erin had forgotten he was there. He rose slowly, fixing Rosemary with a critical stare. "Now it's the royal 'we.' I do urge you to consider what you are about to do, Miss Hartsock. It's dangerous enough to get involved with this gang of rampant individualists, but a boss suffering from delusions of grandeur—"

"Go away, Will," Rosemary said.

Will winked solemnly at Erin and ambled out.

Ten minutes later Erin left the house. There was no one in sight, except for the scattered cats. Two kittens—a tabby and a gray-and-white—were chasing a leaf, but the rest were asleep, forming furry puddles on the chairs or sprawled in drowsy stupor across the worn floor.

The car was as hot as an oven. Erin took off her jacket and then—after **a** wary glance to make sure no one was looking— struggled out of her panty hose.

Thus refreshed, she was able to think more clearly. It had happened so fast she felt a little dazed. A series of rapid-fire questions from Rosemary—none of them personal, all of them relating to her experience, expectations, and salary requirements—had relieved her of any need to explain or elaborate. Nor had Rosemary deliberated over her decision.

"I can't offer you any more than you are presently earning, and I certainly can't promise you job security. I'm not even sure at this point precisely what I will ask you to do. It depends to a certain extent on you—your interest, your willingness to turn your hand to whatever may be asked of you. To an even larger extent, however, your job depends on factors over which none of us has any control. The only thing I can promise you is that you won't be bored. If you are willing to take a chance—"

Erin had committed the social solecism of interrupting in her eagerness to accept.

As she sat mopping her perspiring face she wondered why she had been so eager. Rosemary was unquestionably an attraction; she had been charming and friendly, even insisting Erin call her by her first name. It was exciting to be on first-name terms with someone you had seen on television. But was that ephemeral reward worth the risk of finding herself unemployed after only a few weeks or months? What would happen to Rosemary's staff if she lost the election? Rosemary would be out of a job too. She had given up her House seat in order to run for the Senate.

I must have lost my mind, Erin thought. At least I could have told her I wanted to consider it for a day or two. . . . And then a sudden, uncharacteristic burst of recklessness overwhelmed her. Why the hell should I consider it? Fran is always telling me I'm too chicken, too conservative. Why not take a chance for once? I'm young and healthy and capable. I can find another job if I have to; there's always McDonald's!

And if Rosemary does lose, I won't be the only one looking for work. They'll all be unemployed, including her.

She put the car in gear and turned the air-conditioning on full blast. It made enough noise to drown out the sounds that were coming from the house, but she glanced into the rearview mirror in time to see Kay come running out onto the porch, with a speed that contrasted sharply with her usual deliberate movements. Erin stopped the car. But apparently Kay didn't want her; the older woman came to a halt at the top of the stairs and stood gazing, but she didn't motion or call.

After a moment Erin drove on. She had forgotten the incident by the time she reached the highway.

Chapter Two

ERIN STARED at the letter in disgust. It had been written on coarse brown paper torn off a grocery bag and the ballpoint pen had scored deeply into the rough surface.

"Problem?"

She looked up to see Nick standing by her desk. He was usually around; she had been working for a week, and so far he hadn't missed a day. She was not vain enough to suppose that she was the attraction. The office, just outside the District in Arlington, was Rosemary's headquarters, the space having been donated—like so many other things—by an admiring constituent who hadn't been able to rent the store anyway. It had the look of all temporary offices: paint hastily applied, wires and extension cords running every which way, cheap hired desks and office chairs. From the walls Rosemary Marshall's face looked down in endless repetition, surrounded by draped red-white-and-blue bunting. The acoustics were terrible: phones shrilling, word processors humming, typewriters clicking, blended into a dull roar of sound.

For once she didn't mind Nick's assumption of authority. Wordlessly she handed him the paper. He scanned it in a glance, his lips curling.

"Cute. Can't spell very well, can he?"

"He knows the two essential four-letter words."

"Probably from seeing them scrawled on walls." Nick dropped the letter and dusted his fingers fastidiously. "File it under *S*, as usual."

"*S* for 'sicko'?" Erin placed the letter in the designated basket. Incoming letters were sorted by type: contributions, requests for help or for information, complaints, and so on. Since Rosemary was both candidate and, until the end of her term, congresswoman as well, it was not always easy to determine into which category a particular letter might belong, but Rosemary was insistent on keeping them separate. Letters that dealt with constituents' problems were forwarded to her office on the Hill, and that office in turn sent campaign mail to Arlington. Erin had been given the sorting job only that morning. It was a step up from typing lists, for it required some discrimination—and, as she had already learned, one could not be too squeamish.

"Or 'shit,' " Nick said. There were half a dozen other sheets of paper in the *S* file; he picked one up and began to read it. His face was as mobile as an actor's; eyebrows, lips, and cheek muscles twitched in sympathy with his emotions.

"Why does she keep them?" Erin asked.

"What would you do with them?"

"Throw them away. Burn them—"

"Oh, everybody gets letters like these," Nick said absently. Then he realized what he had said, and laughed. "All public figures, I mean. They develop a certain thickening of the skin. But crap like this can't be ignored. There are a lot of loonies in the world, and thanks to the NRA, too many of 'em own guns."

"But surely no one would—" She broke off, not needing Nick's quizzical sidelong glance to tell her she was being naive. People would; people had.

She shivered and Nick looked at her. "Maybe you'd rather do something else."

"Of course not! I can handle it. You're the one who's making a big thing of it!"

Nick pretended to cower. "Please don't hit me, lady, I was just trying to be a little gent. I keep forgetting you feminists don't like it."

"I am not a feminist. I hate that word."

"Why? What's wrong with being a feminist? High bloody time you were, isn't it?"

"I do not want to discuss the subject," Erin said frostily.

"Right, right. Nothing to discuss. Self-evident. Anything you say. No, but seriously—I wasn't trying to put you down; I encountered a couple of equally foul offerings when I was sorting mail, and I'm not too proud to admit they made me sick at my stomach."

The confession made Erin feel a good deal more kindly toward him. "You sorted mail?"

"Lady, I've tackled most everything," Nick said in a John Wayne drawl. "I wasn't always the big shot you see today. Only one year ago I was as insignificant and humble as you; a mere cipher in the majestic numbers of politics, a cog in the bureaucratic wheel. . . . "

"Then you must have something more important to do," Erin said, unable to refrain from smiling.

"My day wouldn't be complete without a quick glance through the shit file," Nick said. "This guy doesn't know his Bible very well. The number of the beast is 666—no way you can get Rosemary's name to fit that—and said beast is specifically designated as male."

The letter he held was almost a manuscript—eight single-space typewritten pages. "It was incoherent throughout," Erin said. "Why are the religious-fundamentalist people down on her?"

"She's against prayer in the schools and public funding for private schools. Both hot issues in rural Virginia." Nick tossed the letter aside. "That one wasn't so bad. 'Whore of Babylon' seems to be the strongest epithet. What's this?"

It was the last letter in the basket—typed, like the one he had discarded, but containing only two lines. Erin glanced at it.

"I wasn't quite sure what to do with it. At first I thought it might be from some undetected criminal, asking for reassurance; but it's not a question, is it?"

The message was short and simple. "There is no statute of limitations for murder."

Nick departed somewhat abruptly, taking the *S* file with him. He mumbled something that sounded like "right to life," and Erin puzzled over it briefly, wondering if some new in phrase had replaced "see you around" and "so long." Then the light dawned. Of course, that must be the meaning of the ambiguous letter—another way of calling Rosemary Marshall a baby killer, a favorite epithet of right-to-lifers.

She had worked her way through most of the letters when one of the volunteers brought the morning delivery, and an involuntary moan escaped her when she saw the bulk of it. The other girl's smile was not untouched with malice; Erin was one of the few in the office who was getting paid, and she knew she was an object of envy.

Steeling herself, she returned to the attack. There were no more anonymous outpourings in the first dozen envelopes, only a letter written more in sorrow than in anger that wanted to know why Rosemary didn't find herself some nice fella and settle down, instead of chasing around the state doing stuff "wemin" wasn't meant to do. After brief consideration, Erin decided not to consign it to the *S* file. "Mrs. Dick Milhauser" had signed her name, and she didn't sound threatening. Was there, Erin wondered, a form letter for such impertinent and irrelevant inquiries?

As she studied it, the door of an inner office opened and Joe ambled out. From the corner of his mouth a cigar emerged at a jaunty, FDR angle. He stopped by Erin's desk, removed the cigar, looked around as if searching for an ashtray, found none—there were "No Smoking" signs all over the office—and put it back in his mouth.

"Let's go out for coffee."

"There's a coffee maker back there." Erin started to rise. "Would you like me to—"

"I said 'out.' " Joe took her arm and led her to the door,

giving her barely time to snatch her purse from where it hung over the back of her chair.

That should do it, Erin thought. The people who had been sucking up to her would increase the suction; the ones who resented her would have even greater cause. If Rosemary Marshall was the White Goddess of the volunteers, Joe was her High Priest, and although he was matey enough with the others, cracking jokes and slapping backs and bottoms, such a sign of favor to an individual was rare.

The coffee shop down the street was crowded, since it was getting on toward lunchtime. The place was popular with Rosemary's supporters, being convenient to headquarters; they were easy to identify, since they all sported huge "Marshall for Senator" buttons. Joe stopped by a table occupied by a pair of them. "You guys through?" he asked.

By a strange coincidence, they were just going. Joe pulled out a chair. Catching Erin's critical eye, he gave her a broad grin. "When you've got it, flaunt it."

"What's *it*?" Erin asked.

Joe looked down at his stomach and brushed cigar ashes off the bulge of his shirt. His tie was beyond such first aid; the stains appeared to be coffee. "It ain't my good looks," he admitted.

Erin laughed. Elbows planted on the table, forehead gleaming with perspiration, he nevertheless had a certain charm. He must have been a good-looking man once, she thought, with the unconscious condescension of youth. Before he let himself go.

Joe planted his cigar in an ashtray. "Do you mind my smoking?" he asked, in a voice whose suddenly cultured accents fell oddly on her ear.

"No, that's okay. My father smoked cigars. I like the smell."

"Rosemary told me about him. Was he ill long?"

"It was lung cancer," Erin said.

She looked at his cigar, and Joe acknowledged the unspoken lecture with a grimace. "Yeah. We always assume it will happen to the other guy. I'm sorry. Must have been tough— for you and your mother both."

"Tougher for Dad," Erin said, reaching for the cup the waitress had brought. She was reluctant to break down in public, though the sympathy in Joe's voice had touched depths of grief she had believed were decently buried. But she found herself talking freely, describing her father's anger—"Why me, God?"—and her mother's collapse into teary helplessness. "She's angry too—angry with Dad for dying—but she can't admit it."

Joe nodded. "That's a normal reaction. I suppose he handled all the financial matters. That's a heavy load to have dumped on you without warning or advance preparation."

"There was time. He tried to go over things with her, once he realized . . . But she couldn't handle it. Most of it fell to me. That sounds disgustingly self-pitying, doesn't it? But it was a shock to find out there was so little money left. No savings, no annuity, only a minimal amount of insurance. Mother still refuses to accept the fact that her life-style has to change, we'd always lived comfortably—too comfortably, I realize now. We had to sell the house, there was a huge mortgage—and both cars. . . . Oh, you don't want to listen to this. I'm sorry."

"No sweat, honey. Is your mother all right financially? Rosemary wouldn't want—"

Erin felt her cheeks flame. "Please don't say anything to Mrs. Marshall! We're fine—we really are—and I wouldn't want her to think . . . Promise you won't."

"Okay, I promise. But she has her little ways of finding things out. If you need any advice—legal or financial— remember I'm not as stupid as I look."

Joe frowned, but not at her; turning, she saw Jeff threading his way through the tables toward them.

"I might have known I'd find you feeding here," he said, taking one of the empty chairs and putting his briefcase under it. "Hi, Erin. How are things going?"

Except for occasional glimpses as he passed in and out of the office, Erin had not seen him since their first meeting at the house in Middleburg. He was dressed with the same formality as before, but the smile that warmed his sharp features made him look like a different man—a much more attractive one. Erin was too dazzled to do more than murmur a reply and smile back at him. He had even remembered her name.

"When did you get back?" Joe asked.

"A couple of hours ago. Rosemary was exhausted; I persuaded her to rest this morning, she's got a speech later, and then that fund-raiser this evening."

Erin knew that Rosemary had been on a tour of southern Virginia, making a dozen speeches in two days. According to the polls she was in good shape in the northern counties, but she was still far behind her opponent in the rural areas. "How did it go?" she asked.

"Not bad." Jeff's tone was the same he had used with Joe—equal to equal, without condescension. "Nobody's better at working the shopping malls and the grocery stores. By the time she gets through exchanging recipes with the old ladies and telling the young ones how to handle diaper rash—"

"Never mind the diaper rash," Joe grunted. "What about that direct-mail list we were promised?"

Jeff glanced at Erin. She reached for her purse. "I'd better get back—"

"It's okay," Jeff said, with another dazzling smile. "I wasn't being cagey, I just didn't know how much of this boring stuff you'd want to hear." He summoned a waitress with a wave of his hand. "Have you had lunch? Joe lives on coffee and Danish, it would never occur to him to offer you food fit for humans."

"Hey, it is lunchtime, isn't it?" Joe glanced at the watch strapped to his hairy wrist. "Make mine a double cheeseburger and fries. Erin?"

Lunch with the two top men in Rosemary's campaign was too heady an invitation to refuse. Fran would be green with envy. . . . Though admittedly the Columbia Café didn't sound as impressive as Duke Zeibert's or one of the other restaurants favored by top politicians. As she ate a decidedly wilted chef's salad, Erin comforted herself with the knowledge that she was already more savvy about politics than her starry-eyed roommate. This was what it was about, in reality—too much coffee and too little time, conversations about money and mailing lists and little old ladies in shopping malls. No glamour, just plain hard work.

The conversation that ensued wasn't boring, though some of it was incomprehensible. Key wards and swing wards, maxing out, hard money versus soft money. . . . During a brief lull in the talk when Joe had bitten off a larger bite of cheeseburger than was easily manageable, she ventured a question. "What does that mean—to go where the ducks are?"

Joe's cheeks still bulged, so it was Jeff who answered. "That's just one of those colorful phrases old-time political hacks like Joe enjoy using. Don't waste valuable time and money in areas that are unwinnable, or that you're already sure of."

"Oh. You mean, concentrate on swing wards." Jeff's eyes shone with what she took to be amusement; she added, "Did I say something stupid? I thought a swing ward—"

"I wasn't laughing," Jeff protested, and then proceeded to do just that. "I apologize, Erin; it's just that you sound so knowledgeable, and you look . . . well, you don't look like a politician. Most of 'em look like Joe."

Joe, still speechless, rolled his eyes in sardonic commentary. Jeff went on, "You've got the idea. A swing ward, as you obviously know, is one that can go either way and that therefore may pay off in terms of votes for your candidate if you play it right. The ones you go after are those with a large number of non-registered and uncommitted voters. It's unlikely you can get a die-hard, longtime Democrat or Republican to change his commitment unless your candidate does something brilliant or the other guy does something abysmally stupid."

Joe's Adam's apple bulged alarmingly as he swallowed. "Like old Buzz's fling with his floozie. God bless him. . . . Let's get back, time's a-wasting."

Snatching up the check, he headed for the cash register. Jeff helped Erin out of her chair. "When Joe's finished, everybody's finished," he murmured.

*   *

THE WORKDAY was drawing to a close, and Erin was tallying the checks that had come in the mail, when a burst of hilarity from the other end of the room made her look up. It was Nick again, going through his daily routine of entertaining the troops. The overwhelming majority of them were female, which might have had something to do with Nick's dedication. Most of the volunteers seemed very young to someone who had reached the advanced age of twenty-three; but there was a sizable sprinkling of middle-aged women among them, and to give Nick his due, he was as popular with the senior citizens as with the girls. He was particularly attentive to one white-haired old lady who lost no opportunity of proclaiming her age: "Eighty-four last birthday, and still with it!" She leaned heavily on a cane when she walked, but she never missed a day, and her vocabulary would have made a truck driver blush.

Watching Mrs. Watson flirt outrageously with Nick, who responded in kind, Erin wondered why there were so few men among the volunteers. Many women worked these days, and children kept others homebound, but the proportion was still out of balance. Was it because of Rosemary Marshall's strong support for so-called women's issues? That might have been a factor, but from what she had learned, the same thing was true of other candidates, including those who thought a graceful compliment was to tell women that without them men would still be walking around in skin suits. Perhaps the true explanation was that women, unlike men, were accustomed to working without pay. Funny that the idea had never occurred to her before, even after watching her mother and her mother's friends provide free labor for most of the charitable, cultural and social services of the town.

She grinned as she watched Nick plant a smacking kiss on Mrs. Watson's cheek and dodge the playful swipe of her cane. He might resent the term "court jester," but she was beginning to understand that it was an important job. Volunteers were a vital part of a campaign, especially one as poorly financed as Rosemary's. Keeping up morale could make a difference; and Nick did it superbly. It wasn't all calculation on his part, either. He was obviously delighted by the spunky old lady. When he came toward Erin she greeted him with a smile so warm he blinked.

"Hi," he said.

"Hello again. Sorry, I have no more goodies for you. This afternoon's mail was astonishingly unperverse."

"Please don't think I am attracted to you only by your collection of obscenities," Nick said.

"Oh, no. I assumed it was my efficiency, intelligence, and graciousness."

"Graciousness?" Nick hoisted a hip onto the edge of the desk and considered her thoughtfully. "You probably have bushels of it, but you haven't dumped much on me. Why don't you like me?"

"I don't even know you," Erin protested, taken aback by the blunt question.

"That's easily remedied. I'm available. Lunch, dinner, breakfast. . . . Tonight's out, though, I have to work. Unless . . ." His face brightened. "Hey, that's an idea. Want to go to a football game?"

"I thought you said you had to work."

"I do. I'm covering the game."

"You're a reporter?" Nick nodded. "But the Redskins aren't playing tonight—or are they? I don't follow sports closely."

"You're absolutely right," Nick said seriously. "The Redskins are not playing tonight. And if they were, I would not be attending the game. About the only way to get tickets to regular season games is to inherit them. As for covering the game—who do you think I work for?"

The gleam of sardonic amusement in his eyes told Erin her first assumption was undoubtedly wrong. "Not the *Post*?"

"The Washington *Post* is one of the country's major newspapers," Nick said. "I should be so lucky. You behold before you the sports editor of the Loudon County *Daily Sentinel*. At least I was as of this morning. My boss isn't too happy about my political activities."

"Conflict of interest?" Erin hazarded.

Nick shook his head. "Not exactly. It would be hard, even

for me, to insert a political opinion into a story about a high school football game. It's a question of time. Working two full-time jobs is taking its toll. Especially," he added in a lighter tone, "of my social life. So how about going to the game with me? You can point out the niceties I might miss. I'll even buy you dinner. The affair is being catered by the ladies of the Boosters Club and some of 'em bake a great apple pie."

"Thanks, but no thanks. I hate football."

"Oh, come on. This isn't your ordinary boring major-league game. The Vikings are playing their arch rivals, the Demons of St. Joseph's Academy. It will be the thriller of the year. The Vikes are really up for this one, they got knocked out of the play-offs last year by St. Joe's. And"—he paused for effect—"during the time-outs I'll tell you everything you ever wanted to know about politics. Including the definition of a swing district."

"Jeff told you? I suppose I asked him some dumb questions, but I didn't think he would laugh at me behind my back."

"Oh, hey, it wasn't like that. Everybody knows you haven't had any political experience, you made no secret of that; he wasn't making fun of you, he was impressed by your intelligence and quickness to learn. . . ." Nick broke off. "What am I doing defending a rival?" he demanded dramatically. "Never mind Jeff, I'm just as knowledgeable as he is, and I'm almost as good-looking. I can teach you a lot, baby. What do you say?"

"Well . . ." Erin told herself it would be foolish to refuse. Keeping on good terms with coworkers was only common sense. Nick could be irritating, bossy, chauvinist (that word again!), but he did have his moments. "Why not?"

Nick dropped to one knee, snatched her hand, and raised it to his lips. "Thank you. Thank you! The gracious enthusiasm of your response overwhelms me. You have made my day. Your ineffable condescension—"

"Oh, get up! I have to finish adding up these checks."

"I go, but I will return. In half an hour?"

"Okay."

Erin went back to work, fully aware of the curious, amused, and frankly envious stares that had been focused on them. She couldn't help wondering about the reason for his persistence. Nick might be one of those men whose interest is piqued by a woman's indifference, but he would never be hard up for female companionship—not around campaign headquarters, at any rate. Talk about your ready-made harems. . . . And surely it was not a coincidence that she had been favored, that same day, by attention from both Joe and Jeff. Rosemary must have passed the word: "Give the kid a pat on the head, I can't be bothered."

Rosemary made her appearance shortly before five-thirty. She looked like Her Majesty paying a flying visit to the workhouse, swathed in rainbow chiffon, white-gloved to the elbow, glittering with jewelry. The man who was with her wore tails and carried a top hat and stick. His brown hair, worn in a vaguely old-fashioned style, with a dip or wave on one side, showed not a trace of gray, and his sharp-cut features would have been attractive if the curve of his long thin lips had not resembled a perpetual sneer instead of a smile. He surveyed the cluttered room and the motley assortment of volunteers with an air of looking down, not from his actual height of six-two or -three, but from the lofty peaks of Olympus. There was something vaguely familiar about him, but Erin couldn't remember where she had seen him.

Looking like a daintily dressed doll next to her tall escort ("Send no money now, the Fund will bill you only $79.98 per month"), Rosemary made the rounds, smiling impartially on all and addressing an occasional greeting to a favored and flattered worker. Erin received the greatest mark of favor—a full pause, an outstretched hand, and a friendly "How is it going?"

"Fine," Erin answered. "Some of the letters are—uh—very interesting."

Rosemary's escort laughed. "Is that what you've been doing, you unfortunate infant? My commiseration. You may find them interesting now, but I assure you, the maudlin outpourings of the illiterate public will soon pall."

He reached for the *S* basket. Erin wasn't surprised that he had selected that one; his low, murmurous laugh had given her the necessary clue to his identity. Philips Laurence, commentator, columnist, and moderator of a television talk show, and the man for whom Fran reserved her choicest epithets. He called himself a neoconservative; Fran called him, among other things, a Fascist reactionary. What on earth was he doing with Rosemary Marshall, when he opposed almost every issue she supported?

"Your love of the common man is notorious, Philips," Rosemary said. "Didn't your mother ever teach you it's rude to read other people's mail? If you dare quote any of those letters—"

"Hate mail isn't worth quoting," Laurence said lazily. "Most consist of a nice derangement of epithets and a singular paucity of imagination." He tossed the letters carelessly onto the desk.

They fluttered and fell in a disorderly pile; Erin made a grab for a sheet of paper that was about to slide off the desk. Rosemary bent over to study one of the papers more closely.

"There is no statute of limitations . . . " she began. "Good God. What's that all about?"

"Nick said something about right-to-lifers," Erin offered.

"I suppose that's it." Rosemary grimaced.

"My poor darling." Laurence put his arm around her. "You're too sensitive. The effusions of clods like this writer aren't worth your notice. Philips will get rid of the nasty thing." Using only the tips of his fingers, he folded the letter and tucked it into his pocket. "See? All gone."

"Throw it in the wastebasket," Rosemary said shortly.

"And contaminate the office? I'll find a handy trash can outside."

"Philips, you can be a real pain in the posterior sometimes," Rosemary snapped. "Stop treating me like a frail little southern lady."

"But, darling, you are."

"Like hell I am. Where's Joe? I told him to be ready at five-thirty."

The office door opened and Joe emerged. He looked mildly exasperated, probably because someone had forced him to stop working and get dressed up. The results were splendid; he wore a tuxedo that fit him reasonably well, he was freshly shaved, brushed, and combed; there was not even a cigar in evidence. Nick followed him out. Catching Erin's eye, he went through an extravagant pantomime, clasping his hands and fixing an adoring gaze on Joe's back, then wiping his brow and staggering, as if to suggest that the effort of producing the resplendent effect had worn him out.

Rosemary's lips quivered, but she kept her face straight. "Very nice, Joe. You really can look like a gent when you try."

Joe came to a dead stop and fixed a stony glare on her escort. "What the hell is he doing here?"

"Now, Joe—"

"It's all right, Rosemary," Laurence said gently. "I'm well accustomed to Joe's diamond-in-the-rough manners. Sorry to spoil your evening, old chap, but I'm attending this function too."

"So long as you paid," Joe grunted. "Come on, Rosemary, shake a leg."

Instead of offering his arm he grabbed hers and towed her toward the door at a pace that made her break into an undignified trot. Laurence followed, smoothing his gloves onto his fingers with voluptuous care. He was smiling smugly, as well he might; his cool control had made Joe look like an ill-bred boor. Surely there was something stronger than political antipathy there. . . .

Nick joined her at her desk, but continued to glower at Laurence's retreating form until the door closed behind it. How much of *his* antipathy was personal? Erin wondered. His dedication to Rosemary and/or the causes she supported was obviously intense, but there was more to it than that; he looked like an overprotective father who harbored the direst suspicions about his daughter's date.

"Talk about your unholy alliances," he muttered.

"You mean Rosemary and Mr. Laurence?"

"Who else? Haven't you read his column—watched his show?"

"Uh . . . occasionally. I gather he's a trifle conservative."

"He's so right-wing he'll drive all the way around the block rather than make a left turn. You didn't see today's column, where he said the homeless should thank God they're freezing on the streets of an American city instead of living in a one-room apartment in Moscow?"

"He didn't say that."

"Oh yes, he did." Nick glowered even more darkly. "I can't believe people take that jackass seriously. And I can't figure out why he's supporting Rosemary. I guess it's like they say—politics makes for strange bedfellows."

"Or the reverse?"

It took him a few seconds to understand what she meant. "Good God, no!" he exclaimed indignantly. "At least . . . I hope to hell not."

"Why? She's a woman, not a two-dimensional campaign poster."

"Well, yeah, sure, I guess. . . ." The idea seemed never to have occurred to him. "But not . . . Look, Erin, it's nothing like that. You don't understand the way these things work in Washington. You can call somebody a Comsymp and a lecherous cretin in public—Laurence has done it—and invite him out for a drink afterward, and he'll say, sure, why not? It has to be that way. If politicians took insults personally, there'd be bleeding bodies all over Capitol Hill."

"I don't think I'd be so detached," Erin admitted.

"I'm not very good at it myself. I hate people who have the goddamn gall to disagree with me!"

Erin laughed and after a moment Nick's scowl faded into a sheepish grin. "Which is why I'm an enthusiastic volunteer instead of an up-and-coming political reporter. Ah well, I'm learning; I haven't slugged Laurence yet, and believe me, that has required considerable self-control. My car's over there. . . . Damn. Another parking ticket."

"At least they didn't tow you."

"There is that. Wait a minute. The door sticks some. . . ."

The door looked as if it were about to fall off. The car was an ancient Dodge whose original green had faded to a dusty indeterminate gray. Nick wrenched the door open, helped

Erin in, and, after a prolonged struggle, managed to shut it again.

The drive was hair-raising, in every sense of the word. The window on Erin's side wouldn't close. Nick was apologetic. "The part costs sixty bucks, and that doesn't include labor. I meant to look for it in a junkyard, but I haven't had time. . . . Oh, hey, sorry about that. The catch on the door to the glove compartment doesn't hold very well. . . ."

Perched on a sagging bench in the bleachers, watching the Vikings devastate their hapless opponents from St. Joe's, Erin realized with some surprise that she was enjoying herself. Her supper had consisted of a country ham sandwich and a Coke; the portly person seated next to her was the father of the Vikings' quarterback, and whenever he bounded to his feet to cheer a completed pass, the plank seat slapped Erin's posterior. But the night air was cool and crisp, the ham sandwich was excellent, and the portly person's enthusiasm was rather touching. Nick kept running back and forth from the seat beside her—to the bench, to the trailer manned by the mothers of the Boosters Club.

During halftime she joined him on the sidelines, at his request. Among the people to whom he introduced her, with transparent pride, was a sports reporter from a local TV station. "What are you doing out here?" Nick asked. "Thought you'd been promoted to news reporting."

"Dave called in sick," the round-faced youth explained morosely. "You know how it is. Listen, you got any openings for a media man in the campaign?"

"We haven't got any openings, period. Here." Nick reached in his pocket. "Have a button."

The youth allowed Nick to pin the campaign button to his shirt. "Keep me in mind, okay?"

"Yeah, sure, old buddy. Gotta run now; Erin is dying to meet some of the players."

"I'm not, you know," Erin remarked, as he led her away.

"Never pass up an opportunity to do some work for your candidate," Nick said. "Some of the players are eighteen and they all have relatives who vote—or should. Smile and look pretty—that won't be hard—and tell them all how wonderful Rosemary Marshall is.''

Most of the players were too concerned with the game to listen to Nick's political lecture. Those who did promised him—leering amiably at Erin all the while—that, sure, they'd vote for Marshall, why the hell not? Only one objected. He was an extremely large eighteen-year-old, who would have made two of Nick. Instead of being intimidated by the bulk looming over him, Nick fell on him like a piranha on a whale. ''How can you vote for a man who helped promote Virginia's massive resistance to integration when he was in the state legislature and who said, as recently as 1984, that he had no regrets about doing it?''

The large young man was no match for Nick in rhetoric; when it dawned on him that he was losing the argument, he cocked an enormous fist and Erin prudently retreated behind one of the other players, a rangy black youth who had been introduced as the star tight end. He was pleased to see her, but showed no desire to prevent the imminent annihilation of Nick; in fact, he and the other players cheered the debaters on. Erin was relieved when the coach finally intervened with a firm ''Knock it off, you guys. We got a game to play. Carson, don't waste your energy. Get the hell outta here, Nick, what's the idea of bugging my guys?''

''They're ahead twenty-one to zip,'' Nick reminded him. ''Great job, Coach; how about an interview?''

''Later, maybe. Get lost.''

''Right.'' Nick seized the ham-sized fist of his antagonist and shook it vigorously. ''Great talking to you, bro. That's what this country is all about, right? Honest disagreement and discussion, the heart of democracy. You just think over what I said—''

Erin took him firmly by the arm and led him away. They were followed by the jeers and cheers of the players.

''Why do you do that?'' she demanded.

''Do what?''

''Argue with people like that boy. His mind, what there is of it, is made up. You're supposed to go where the ducks are, aren't you?''

Nick stopped, and in full view of all the spectators, under the glaring lights, seized her in a fervent embrace. "You're awfully cute," he said.

Up to that point Erin had found his exuberance entertaining. Why the compliment roused such sudden, violent annoyance she could not have said; a few weeks ago she would have accepted it with a modest simper. Instead she jabbed her elbow into Nick's midsection and snapped, "Don't patronize me!"

"I didn't. I wouldn't! If you want to tell me I'm the sexiest man you've ever met, go right ahead; I won't take offense."

"Oh, yeah?"

"Yeah. I said you were cute and you are cute, by God. I didn't say, and didn't mean, that you were not also intelligent, capable, worthy of respect—"

"You implied as much. That's what 'cute' means to men like you. Cute and dumb."

"Not true." Infuriatingly Nick's lips curved into a smile. "Hey, have you been reading Rosemary's speeches?"

"I can take offense at rudeness without help from Rosemary."

"Sure you can," Nick said. "But listen, you ought to read the one she gave a couple of years ago when she spoke in support of her day-care bill. I'll get you a copy. Though it loses something in the mere reading; Rosemary's a great speaker, and she's improving all the time. Even television doesn't capture her quality completely. Tell you what, next time she gives a major speech maybe you'd like . . ."

It was difficult to quarrel with a man who blandly ignored your complaints and launched into a lecture. Erin let him escort her to her seat in the bleachers.

As soon as the second half started he was off again, after presenting her with a piece of apple pie. The pie lived up to his praise, but the paper plate on which it reposed wasn't very sturdy, and the gyrations of the quarterback's adoring dad sent trickles of sticky amber juice cascading onto Erin's skirt. Philosophically licking her fingers, she was seized by a fit of the giggles, as she remembered Fran's envious comments. "Politics is the most glamorous business in the world.

Mixing with the rich and famous—gorgeous clothes, beautiful people, caviar and champagne . . . ''

Caviar and champagne . . . Well, there was something to be said for limp chef's salad and homemade apple pie too. It all depends on the ambience, and the company.

* *

BY THE FOLLOWING morning her opinion of Nick had undergone another switch, back to the negative side. He had accepted her invitation to come in for a cup of coffee and had stayed till 2 A.M. arguing politics with Fran. She would like to have believed he had lingered in the hope that Fran would go tactfully to bed and leave them alone, but she had already learned enough about Nick to recognize the hope was delusory. Nick would rather argue than eat, or sleep, or . . . anything else.

She could cheerfully have murdered Fran, who had committed the unforgivable sin of being bright-eyed, alert, and witty while she sat like a lump of suet. She couldn't have gotten a word in even if she had had anything intelligent to contribute; Fran and Nick were a perfect match in loquacity and detailed knowledge of political issues. They agreed on practically everything, including the dazzling wonderfulness of Rosemary Marshall. And after Nick had left—remarking calmly that he still had a story to write—Fran had raved on and on about him. "Talk about your fringe benefits! Of course, if you're really crazy about the guy I wouldn't dream of horning in, but after all, you just met him. . . .''

The unspoken assumption being that if Fran wanted him, she could get him.

Erin pushed the stack of mail aside and stood up, avoiding the eagle eye of Mrs. Patterson, the office manager. Patterson was a soured virgin of ninety-seven (Nick's description) who clearly believed Erin was badly hung over after a night of sinful dissipation. To hell with Patterson; she needed coffee.

The coffee urn and accompanying amenities—which included a soft-drink machine and an unpredictable selection of doughnuts and pastries—were concealed behind a screen at the back of the room. Erin filled a cup and stood by the

table as she sipped; she was in no hurry to return to her desk
where she would be overlooked by Mrs. Patterson's critical
eye. All at once she heard her own name, uttered in tones
that rose distinctly over the usual background noises.

"Erin! Where the hell has she gotten to?"

Erin made haste to present herself. There was no mistaking
Joe's bass roar.

"I was just getting a cup of coffee," she began.

Joe slung his coat jacket over one shoulder and wrenched
at his tie. His face looked as if he had shaved in the dark or
a thick fog; patches of unattended bristles marked his jutting
chin. "Bring it to my office, I want to talk to you. Get me a
cup too. Cream and sugar." Without waiting for an answer
he swung on his heel and stamped toward his office.

Erin's hands were unsteady as she filled the cup according
to his specifications. The milk looked a little peculiar; she
hoped it hadn't gone sour, Joe was obviously in a foul mood
already. Had she done something to anger him, or committed
some ghastly blunder with the mail? In spite of Joe's kindness
to her she was a little afraid of him; she had seen him reduce
one of the typists to tears for committing a minor error.

The office door stood open. Joe was speaking on the phone,
and Jeff stood by the desk. Joe gestured to Erin to close the
door; while she was trying to work out the logistics of obey-
ing his order while holding a Styrofoam cup in either hand,
Jeff came to her assistance. She thanked him, and murmured
an apology. "I didn't know you were here. Would you like
some coffee?"

"No, thanks. Haven't you heard that fetching coffee for
the boss is a feminist issue?"

The edge in his voice surprised Erin and increased her
nervousness. She racked her brain trying to remember
whether she had said something to Nick that might have
sounded critical of Rosemary, the issues, the world in general. . . .

Joe slammed the telephone into the cradle. "We're trans-
ferring you to home base," he said. "Kay managed to mash
her hand last night—the right hand, of course—she can't type,
or tie Rosie's hair ribbons, or whatever the hell else she does.

Better get out there as fast as you can; Kay's in one of her states.''

Erin felt as if the hinges on her jaw had given way. "I don't understand," she gasped.

"What don't you understand? English?"

"You mean . . . Do you want me to go to Middleburg?"

"For Christ's sake!" Joe bellowed.

"Cool it, Joe." Jeff smiled encouragingly at Erin. "Give her a chance to assimilate it."

"So what's to assimilate? Most people would consider this the biggest break of their lives."

"No doubt she is speechless with joy," Jeff said sarcastically. "People like to be asked, Joe. Asked, not told."

The expression on Joe's face as he considered this astonishing idea was almost comical. "That's not it," Erin said quickly. "Of course I'll go. I just wondered why—"

"I told you, Kay's crippled herself. Caught her hand in the car door, for God's sake. Broke a couple of fingers. Do you want to go, or don't you?"

"Of course. I'll leave right away. Should I tell Mrs. Patterson, or—"

She stopped; Joe's face was crimson, and he looked as if he were about to explode with exasperation. Initiative, Erin told herself; display a little initiative, woman. When a man like Joe gave an order, he expected the orderee to work out the details. Such as how she was going to get to Middleburg without a car.

"Yes, sir," she snapped. "Right away, sir."

She didn't hear Jeff follow; he walked like a leopard. But his hand reached the knob before hers, and after he had ushered her out he said in a low voice, "Don't mind Joe, he's in a bad mood. Things are a little tense all around."

"He talks as if the poor woman broke her hand on purpose," Erin muttered.

"Things are a little tense," Jeff repeated. "I'll explain to Mrs. Patterson. You'd better go home first and pack a bag in case they want you to stay overnight."

"Thanks," Erin said gratefully. His quiet, calm manner

was as helpful as the practical suggestions Joe hadn't bothered to offer. "Is there . . . I suppose there's a bus?"

"To Middleburg?" His elegantly shaped eyebrows shot up. "Oh, that's right, I remember you said you didn't own a car. No problem. I'll drive you. I have to go out there anyway. Why don't you go home and pack, and I'll pick you up in . . . say an hour and a half?"

The office was in Falls Church, only twenty minutes away from the apartment, but by the time she had waited for the bus and walked the distance on either end, she had very little time to spare. She made it, just barely, running breathlessly out the door only seconds before Jeff arrived. He acknowledged her promptness with an approving smile, and got out to take her overnight bag and stow it in the backseat. The contrast between his immaculately tended though modest Camaro, and the wreck Nick drove was ludicrous. The backseat of Nick's car looked like a traveling office, heaped with boxes of campaign literature, newspapers, and miscellaneous debris. Jeff's contained only his briefcase. Even the car keys reflected the personality of their owners. Nick's chain held over a dozen keys, held together by twists of plastic ties; Jeff's key ring was a polished curve of heavy silver in the form of a stylized fish.

"That's good-looking," Erin said, indicating the ornament.

"Thanks." Jeff wasn't the man to waste time on meaningless courtesies, especially when, as seemed apparent from his frowning look, he was preoccupied with more important matters. Erin waited until the lines on his forehead had smoothed out before she ventured to speak again.

"Can I ask a question?"

"Sure. Sorry if I sounded a little brusque. I was thinking about a sentence in a speech I'm working on for Rosemary."

"I thought Nick was the official speechwriter."

"There is no official speechwriter," Jeff snapped. He gave her a rueful sidelong smile. "There I go again. Sometimes the way this campaign is being run gets to me. We all have official titles, but they don't mean anything, except in Joe's case—and a campaign manager is supposed to be a jack-of-all-trades, in charge of everything. Not that political campaigns are ever models of organization, I've heard the process described as lurching from one crisis to the next. But this one . . .''

He shook his head. ''As for the speechwriting, we all take a shot at it. Rosemary reworks every word herself, but she's very good about listening to other ideas. So feel free, if the urge strikes you, to become the next Schlesinger.''

''I wouldn't dare.''

''Why not? Erlichman began as a baggage handler for Nixon's 1960 campaign—though that may not be a career you'd care to emulate. And I know of one political writer who was writing speeches for Robert Kennedy two days after he began work as a junior-grade assistant. But you wanted to ask me something. What was it?''

''You've already answered it,'' Erin said. ''I was going to ask whether things were always this frantic.''

Jeff seemed quite at ease, now that he had let off a little steam. ''Actually, they get worse,'' he said, smiling. ''The closer we get to election day, the more frantic the pace. A lot of people who go into that voting booth make up their minds, or change them, at the last minute. The polls are increasingly accurate in predicting the outcome—some would say they affect the outcome—but there are always the famous exceptions. Something can happen at the last minute to change the whole picture.''

''Like Rosemary's secretary breaking her hand?''

''Oh, that. A minor contretemps. Kay doesn't like to admit it, but she can be replaced.''

''But why by me?''

''That's the question I thought you were going to ask,'' Jeff said. He was silent for a moment. It was not a pause of uncertainty, but of someone coolly considering all the pros and cons before issuing a statement. Then he said, ''I don't ordinarily gossip about people, but you're being tossed into the thick of this situation, so you have a right to know some of the problems you'll be facing. Kay is Rosemary's secretary. Period. She's had the job for years, and by all accounts she has handled it well. Lately, though, she's aspired to giddier heights—aide, executive assistant. And that job she cannot handle."

"Why not?"

"It's hard to explain. And," Jeff added, in a burst of unexpected candor, "it makes me feel like a petty-minded lout to criticize Kay; I'm fond of her, and she's always been nice to me. But she just doesn't have it. The imagination, the political savvy, the subtlety . . . Oh, hell, I have to say it—the brains. She can't accept that, of course. But it makes things very awkward, especially when Kay tries to usurp the functions of the office she doesn't hold. She's always snipping at Joe, which doesn't improve his inequable temper. If Rosemary weren't such a sentimental sucker she'd retire Kay and give the job to someone younger and more flexible."

"Kay seemed perfectly competent the day I met her," Erin said. What she didn't say, because it was not her place to do so, was that Kay had been a little too competent, too quick to assume authority. She hadn't even asked the right questions.

"She's not senile," Jeff said. "I didn't mean to imply that. But she's slowing down; it's become more apparent even in the past few days. Being personal secretary to a person like Rosemary involves more than typing and filing. You have to be tactful, quick to react in a crisis, a generally soothing influence. Kay's performance this morning, when she realized she was temporarily out of commission, was indicative. She carried on like a maniac; Rosemary had to soothe her, instead of the other way around. She wouldn't shut up until Joe agreed to send you out to the house."

"Then this was Kay's idea?"

"I guess so," Jeff said disinterestedly. "But it was okay with Rosemary; she said something about keeping it in the family. As I said, she's a sucker for sentimental relationships. If I were you, I'd be careful not to complain about Kay to Rosemary, no matter what dumb thing she does. Rosemary isn't stupid, she won't blame you for goofing if it isn't your fault, but she'll like you better if you take the 'full-responsibility' route."

"Thanks," Erin said gloomily. "I don't get it, though. Why would Kay want me, of all people?"

"Oh, that's obvious, I should think. She doesn't consider you a threat. Some of the other secretaries could replace her. You—forgive me—you couldn't. Not with your lack of experience. Don't get any grand ideas about your job, you're just another pair of hands—Kay's hands—doing exactly what she tells you to do."

Chapter Three

IF ERIN HAD entertained any remaining illusions about her promotion, they would have been stripped away by the manner in which Kay received her. She and Jeff had barely gotten out of the car when Kay rushed out of the house and down the porch steps. She stumbled on the steps; Jeff, who had apparently feared just such an accident, dropped Erin's bag and leapt forward to catch the older woman.

"What're you trying to do, break a leg to match your hand?" he asked, setting her back on her feet.

Kay looked ten years older than she had the previous Saturday. Her hair had been bundled into an untidy wad at the back of her head, her face was sunken, and her eyes looked odd and unfocused. Her right arm had been strapped to her body, probably to keep her from waving it in agitated gestures.

"What took you so long? The work is piling up. I can't even . . . " She brushed a lock of straggling hair from her face and then pressed her hand to her forehead. "Those darned pills are too strong, I feel funny. I didn't want to take them, but Rosemary insisted.''

"Well, of course you have to take them," Jeff said easily. "If you'd let me drive you to the hospital last night, after it happened, instead of waiting till this morning—''

"I thought it was only bruised." Kay's lips turned down like those of a sulky child. "Don't just stand there, Jeff, Rosemary wants to see you right away. You're late.''

"We came as fast as we could. I suggested Erin pack a suitcase.''

"I should hope so. This isn't any nine-to-five job, she'll be staying. I've had a room prepared for her. I suppose I'd better show her, but she'll have to get right to work. Hurry, both of you.''

She turned back to the stairs, holding the rail with her good hand. Jeff gave Erin a meaningful glance and followed Kay, ready to steady her if she stumbled again. Once inside, he disappeared into the office and Kay fussily directed Erin to the stairs. Erin wondered what on earth she would do if Kay fell. Drop the suitcase, grab the rail, and hope for the best, she supposed; Kay outweighed her by at least fifty pounds.

Fortunately she was not called upon to put her plan into effect. Kay's steps were slow but firm; she paused to catch her breath on the landing, and then proceeded up another flight of stairs to the third floor. "Here we are," she panted, opening a door. "This will be your room.''

Erin's image stared back at her from a mirror opposite the door. If she had come into the room at night and seen the reflection, she probably would have yelled and backed out again; the streaked worn surface distorted her features hideously, and patches of silver had worn off, giving her face a leprous look. The mirror and the dresser to which it was attached stood between two windows. They were dormers; the roof slanted sharply down on that side of the room. A braided rug covered part of the worn floor. The narrow single bed was part of a suite, matching the dresser and a chest of drawers; it had once been pretty furniture, with an inlaid design of formalized flowers and leaves, but some of the inlay had fallen out and the veneer was flaking.

Kay dropped heavily onto the bed, producing a squawk of rusting springs that boded ill for the future sleeper. She pressed her hand to her heaving chest and waited for her breathing to slow, while Erin examined her new quarters. There wasn't much left to examine—a big, ugly wardrobe on the wall to her right, a few chairs, and a closed door in the left-hand wall. Life was certainly strange, she thought philosophically. Here she was, translated in less than a day from her small apartment to the dwellings of the rich and famous. But this wasn't exactly the setting she had pictured.

"My room is next door," Kay said. "We'll be sharing the bath, it's across the hall. I hope you don't mind being way up here; the stairs are no problem for a young thing like you, and it will be convenient for me to have you close by, in case I need help dressing."

So she was expected to act as Kay's maid, as well as her office assistant. Jeff had tried to warn her, and Erin knew she had no legitimate cause for complaint. Hadn't Rosemary stressed flexibility and willingness to lend a hand? Erin didn't mind performing personal services for other people, she had done a great deal of it for her mother, who took a certain rueful pride in her own lack of domestic talent. Erin had been glad to sew on buttons, arrange hair, carry trays, and smooth pillows when her mother took to her bed with a cold or flu.

She couldn't object to assisting an elderly woman, her superior in rank, who was temporarily incapacitated. Nobody had promised her a rose garden—or anything else. She was lucky to be getting a salary, and she suspected she owed that to the streak of sentimentality in Rosemary that Jeff had stressed. She ought to be grateful—but the situation was depressingly reminiscent of the one that had characterized her other job.

She reminded herself that Kay really did need her help, and that she ought to understand. She had broken her wrist once, in high school, when an overenthusiastic teammate had whacked her with a hockey stick, and she remembered all too well how madddeningly helpless one could be with an arm out of commission. Even such simple tasks as tying a shoelace became impossible. She wondered, though, why such a kindly person as Rosemary Marshall would expect an older woman to climb two flights of steep, narrow stairs.

Kay seemed to read her mind. "Rosemary wanted me to move down to the second floor," she said defensively. "She's been after me to do that for years. But we're short on staff—as always—and the guest rooms ought to be kept ready for important visitors. I'm perfectly capable of climbing a few stairs."

"Of course." Erin put her suitcase down. Adjust, she told herself. Be flexible. And for God's sake, try to be cheerful about it. "But it's hard to do some things with only one arm. Like fixing your hair. Would you like me to see whether I can't anchor your chignon a little more securely? It seems to be coming loose."

"We ought to get right to work."

"It will only take a minute. I'm very good at doing people's hair—honestly. Why don't you sit here, in front of the mirror? Then you can tell me if I do something wrong."

The idea obviously appealed to Kay; after only a little persuasion, she went to get her comb and brush. She didn't invite Erin into her room, but she left the door open, and Erin could see it had been furnished with a degree of comfort and ruffled charm that made her room look even shabbier. Which was only as it should be, of course. Quite obviously hers was seldom if ever occupied; the days of big, live-in household staffs were long past. If anything, Kay's room was overcrowded and overdecorated, but that was a question of personal taste. Maybe she enjoyed her aerie at the top of the house and preferred the privacy it afforded. What did she do up here, all alone by herself—entertain gentlemen friends who ascended to her window by means of a rope ladder? Indulge in orgies of pot smoking or Scotch? Erin smiled to herself. If there were orgies of any kind, they probably featured chocolate bars and dirty books—though Kay's definition of the latter, she supposed, would be more PG than X-rated.

She placed one of the straight chairs in front of the dresser, and Kay sat down. After taking out pins and combs Erin began to brush the long, graying hair, deliberately prolonging the process as she saw the lines in Kay's face fade and soften. "My, that feels good," Kay said dreamily.

"Do you always wear your hair in a bun?" Erin asked. "I mean, a chignon?"

Kay's shoulders heaved with silent laughter. " 'Bun' is the right word, honey. I get fancied up for special occasions—I know what's proper—but the good old common bun is the real me."

Her voice was a little slurred, and her eyes were drowsy and unfocused. Finally Erin stopped brushing and began to twist the heavy hair into a neat coil. In another minute Kay would topple gently off the chair; she was already listing visibly to one side.

"How does that look?" she asked.

Kay opened one eye and contemplated her reflection. " 'Most as neat as I could do it myself. Rosie tried, but she just ain't no good at it. . . ." And then, in a loud angry voice that made Erin jump, she said, "Goddamn this lousy hand anyhow!"

Erin's fingers fumbled as she stared in shocked disbelief. She had heard that people under the influence of analgesics or anesthesia sometimes came out with uncharacteristic, even obscene, remarks, but the change in Kay's accent and vocabulary was so dramatic as to be almost frightening.

"Just one damn thing after another," Kay muttered. "They say things allus come in threes, but I swear to God there's been so many. . . . Like she was cursed or somethin'. She'd say that was crazy, but I dunno, seems like it ain't natural somehow. . . . So many accidents . . ."

"What on earth are you talking about, Kay?"

The speaker had come unobserved and unheard; her voice startled Erin so that the hairpin she was holding stabbed into Kay's scalp.

"I'm so sorry," Erin exclaimed. "Did I hurt you?"

"My fault," Rosemary said. "I shouldn't have crept up on you. Kay, how do you feel?"

Kay did not turn. From the direction of her gaze Erin realized she was looking at Rosemary's reflection in the mirror, as Rosemary was looking at hers.

"What was I talking about?" Kay asked. "I was half asleep. . . . "

"You were talking a lot of nonsense," Rosemary said.

"She was fixing my hair," Kay muttered.

"And very nice it looks too. Thank you, Erin, that was kind. Perhaps you can persuade her to rest, and let you take over. She's out of her head from those pills, she isn't used to them."

The suggestion that anyone could take over Kay's work acted like a shot in the arm. Her slumped shoulders straightened and when she spoke it was in the well-bred, unaccented voice Erin had heard before. "Don't be silly, Rosemary; I'm quite all right. I won't take so many of the pills next time. I can't rest, I have to show Erin what to do."

"There's no reasoning with you," Rosemary said. She put an affectionate hand on her old friend's shoulder. It was a gentle touch, it couldn't possibly have jarred the injured hand; it must have been the expectation of pain that made Kay cringe away.

*   *

KAY WAS CRISPLY businesslike as she showed Erin around. The change in her manner was so extreme Erin almost fancied she must have imagined that brief, frightening metamorphosis.

The former library had been converted into offices. Makeshift partitions divided it into one large room and several smaller cubicles, and the flat, featureless surface of the newer walls looked odd compared with the dark wooden paneling and casemented windows of the older ones. Kay had her own cubicle, as did Joe, when he was there. Rosemary's office had not been altered, it was a pleasant room next to the library, with deep window seats and a fireplace. The furnishings were old and somewhat masculine in character—leather chairs, engravings of animals and birds on the walls, a dark geometric print covering cushions and windows.

"This was Congressman Marshall's office," Kay explained in a hushed voice. It was an odd way of putting it, Erin thought; the use of the past tense told her that Kay was referring, not to Rosemary, but to her husband. "It's just as it was in his time. Nothing has been changed, not even the curtains. Oh, they've been replaced, of course, fabric fades so badly in sunlight. But it's the same print."

She closed the door quietly, as upon a shrine.

She went on to explain that although it was convenient for Rosemary to maintain an office in her home, the practice had certain disadvantages. "Especially when, as in this case, we are running a campaign from here. It's a rather unusual arrangement, in fact, but Rosemary prefers it that way, and thanks to telecommunications and computer hookups we can keep in touch with our workers elsewhere. Rosemary has several offices in her district, like the one in Arlington; in other cities where offices have been opened for the Democratic presidential campaign, we share the space and the personnel to some extent, but of course the presidential race gets most of the money and almost all the press. Rosemary refuses to let her office on the Hill be used for campaign practices, she's made a big point of refusing to use taxpayers' money for that purpose, and it certainly does go over well with the voters."

She introduced Erin to the office workers. There were only four of them—and Erin couldn't help noticing the balance; two men, two women; two blacks, two whites. She made a conscious effort to remember their names. Jan Berger, a stocky, sober-faced blond boy who didn't look a day over sixteen; Anita Valdez, raven-haired and conspicuously plain, with a long thin nose like a heron's beak; Jackson Price, who looked like an ebony version of the linebacker who had engaged in political dispute with Nick, except for his shrewd dark eyes; and Christie Johnson, office manager and political aide—titles she was careful to emphasize when she acknowledged the introduction. Christie was several inches taller than Erin and made rather a point of looking down on her. She was also devastatingly attractive, with features as chiseled as those of a Benin bronze head, and a lean athlete's figure. She wore tight designer jeans and a shirt that might as well have had a designer's name on the pocket; it was cunningly cut to look both sexy and businesslike. All the workers except Christie were part-time volunteers, political-science and government majors from various universities who were earning credits as well as practical experience, and whose training made them more valuable than the average enthusiastic amateur. Christie was the only true professional; as Erin was to learn, she had been one of Rosemary's aides on the Hill. Obviously Christie wasn't afraid of taking a chance, but on the other hand, she had little to lose. If the campaign was successful, she would have taken a giant step up the ladder, ending as aide to a senator rather than a representative.

Kay took Erin into her own cubicle and put her to work. By late afternoon she was hard-pressed to hold on to her sympathy for the invalid. Kay's increasing discomfort, as the medication wore off, was discernible in her tense muscles and tight lips, but surely, Erin thought, pain couldn't be entirely responsible for her alarming lack of organization. Erin barely had time to finish one task before Kay told her to stop doing it and do something else. Though she was familiar with several different kinds of computers, Kay's was new to her, and Kay's instructions only confused her more. If Kay was testing her ability to perform under pressure, she wasn't doing very well. But she felt sure that wasn't the reason for Kay's brusque manner. Circumstances had forced Kay to open her private files to a stranger, and admit someone else into the world of sensitive information she had taken pride in handling herself. She had to do it, but she resented the necessity, and her innocent assistant, bitterly.

Rosemary finally came to the rescue, appearing in the doorway to announce it was quitting time. "Five o'clock, you poor wage-slaves."

"Since when has five o'clock been quitting time in this office?" Kay demanded. "I want Erin to finish typing these memos, and then she can—"

"Never mind the memos." Rosemary reached over Erin's shoulder and punched the break key. Kay let out a gasp of outrage.

"Now you've lost that one. Honestly, Rosemary!"

"I haven't lost it, it's somewhere in the metal innards of that contraption. And if I have, so what?" Rosemary looked tired, her nose shiny as a mirror and her lipstick blurred.

"Close up shop, I said. Erin hasn't even had time to unpack, and I need you to help me. I have to get dressed."

This time she had taken the right approach. "Oh, the fund-raiser," Kay said. "Yes, you'd better hurry."

"Another one?" Erin asked incredulously.

"One of many." Rosemary leaned against the desk and passed a grubby hand over her face. "The curse of the candidate. The food is boring, the company is boring, the speeches are boring. But without them we couldn't operate. I don't get a lot from the PACs. . . . You do know what a PAC is, don't you?"

"Yes, of course." Mercifully, that was one of the political terms she did know. "Political Action Committees. They were set up by various groups—business, labor, special interests such as education, conservation, animal welfare—"

"Don't forget women," Rosemary interrupted, her lip curling. "It drives me crazy to hear women referred to as a special-interest group, but it's common usage. Half the god-damn population of the country . . . All right, Kay, all right, no more cussing. Your definition is technically correct, Erin, but in actual fact PACs were set up to get around the laws limiting the amount of individual campaign contributions. If I could afford it I'd refuse to take PAC money, even from organizations whose aims I would ordinarily support. . . . Kay, what the hell are you doing? I don't have much time."

"I have to lock up," Kay said. "There are important papers in my desk, you know. It wouldn't do to leave them lying around."

Rosemary's hands clenched, but she said nothing, only watched in stoic silence as Kay fumbled with keys and locks.

"But aren't PAC contributions limited too?" Erin asked.

"Yes—by federal law. But some states have no reporting requirement, and others allow contributions over the federal limit. In theory this money is supposed to be used only to benefit local candidates and parties, but a lot of it is diverted out of state. Oh, it's too complicated to explain in a few minutes; ask Joe to explain the difference between hard and soft money. Or Nick; he adores showing off his expertise to attractive young women. Kay, if you don't stop, I swear I'll go to the Sheraton looking like this.''

Erin followed at a modest distance; but when she would have continued up the stairs to the third floor Kay stopped her with a sharp question. ''Where are you going? I'll need you to do some pressing.''

''We didn't hire her to be a maid of all work, Kay,'' Rosemary protested.

''You didn't hire me as a maid, either. I'm not ashamed to help out in any way I can, and neither should Erin be.''

''I'm not. Anything I can do, of course.''

She wasn't sorry to have a chance to see Rosemary's private quarters, and possibly—dream on, she told herself—make a few modest suggestions about clothes. Rosemary's request for Kay's assistance might have been a tactful means of getting her secretary away from her desk and onto her bed for the rest she needed, but if Kay was her adviser on wardrobe and makeup, Erin could understand why Rosemary looked a little dowdy.

Rosemary's bedroom wasn't really a letdown, or a surprise. Erin had grown accustomed to the casual life-style and organized chaos that characterized both the candidate and the campaign. The room had been beautifully decorated and furnished with fine antiques, dominated by a mahogany highboy and canopied bed. The color scheme was blue and white, restful if unimaginative. But the clutter was indescribable. Papers covered every flat surface, books lay in untidy heaps; a television set glared from one corner and an IBM Selectric on a table by the window proved that Rosemary shared her generation's suspicion of word processors.

Adjoining the bedroom was a dressing room, with clothes hanging from open racks and shoes neatly aligned. It contained an ironing board and sewing supplies—everything needed to keep a wardrobe in repair. To Erin it seemed beautifully organized, but Kay began apologizing for its condition. ''I just don't know what I'm going to do, things are in such a mess, and the girls don't know how to take care of them—''

Rosemary cut her short. "I'm going to take a quick shower. Stop fussing, Kay, everything looks fine. Pick out a dress. The aqua or the rose, I think."

When she came out of the adjoining bathroom, modestly wrapped in a cotton robe, Erin was passing the iron carefully over a smooth stretch of rosy-pink silk, while Kay breathed anxiously down the back of her neck and asked for the fifth time if she was sure she hadn't set the iron too high.

"It's fine, great, perfect," Rosemary said impatiently. "Leave it, Erin. Kay, you go lie down on my bed. You can supervise this massive undertaking and we'll carry out your orders. Erin, would you get the jewelry boxes? They're in the second drawer of the wardrobe. What do you think, Kay— the pearls or the gold earrings and necklace?"

Kay settled herself and watched complacently as Erin trotted back and forth, helping Rosemary into her dress, hanging up the robe, locating the jewelry and carrying it to the dressing table where Rosemary sat. As the boxes were opened and their glittering contents displayed, Erin wondered where Rosemary kept her good jewelry, and why she wasn't wearing any of it. These ornaments were all fake—faux, to be more elegant—although they were expensive and in excellent taste. The pearls, on which Kay decided (against Erin's judgment), were obviously cultured.

She helped Rosemary fasten the clasp and watched while she inserted the matching earrings with quick, impatient fingers.

"You've torn a nail," she said hesitantly.

"Oh, shit, so I have." Rosemary glanced guiltily in the mirror. "Sorry, Kay, it just slipped out. . . ." But Kay's eyes had closed and she made no comment. Rosemary let out a little breath of relief. "Is she asleep?"

"I think so."

"Good." Rosemary picked at the broken nail.

"Don't do that," Erin exclaimed involuntarily. "Oh, I'm sorry, I didn't mean to sound . . . Would you let me?"

"With pleasure." She held out her hand. "Do you really like to do this sort of thing?" she asked curiously, as Erin carefully trimmed the mutilated nail. "Or are you just being polite? You don't have to—do it, or be polite about it. I'm quite accustomed to looking after myself. And," she added with a smile, "I get the impression, from the way you've been looking at me, that you don't think I do it very well."

"You always look nice," Erin murmured.

"Nice, she says." Rosemary leaned back in her chair and ran her fingers through her hair. She had taken out the pins that held it in its regal, upswept coiffure, and it stood out around her face like Medusa's snakes. "Nice is, I'm afraid, the safest option for a lady candidate. Nice and neat and well-groomed. I wish television had never been invented. I spend more time thinking about how I look than what I'm going to say; the damned political process has become a beauty contest." Then she burst out laughing, muting the sound into a rich chuckle in deference to the sleeper. "Erin, you have the most transparent face. I know exactly what you're thinking: if that woman doesn't stop pawing at her hair, I'm going to scream! Just hand me that brush, will you please?"

She was easily persuaded to let Erin do the brushing and pin the thick, heavy locks into a becoming shape. "You look lovely," Erin said, when the job was done. "You really do."

Rosemary glanced casually into the mirror. "Rich but not gaudy? But not too rich, nobody will give me money if I look prosperous. Thanks, Erin. I'd better run; Joe will be here any minute and patience is not one of his virtues." She reached for the lacy stole Erin had laid out for her and then paused, glancing at the sleeping woman. "Maybe I ought to wake her and help her into her own bed."

"Would you like me to stay with her?" Erin asked.

"Would you? That is kind. I'm afraid she may be disoriented—from the pain and the medication—when she wakes. She could fall, or stumble. . . ." Rosemary bit her lip. "Poor Kay, she's hating this, that's why she's so brusque and impatient. I hope you weren't offended by the way she spoke to you. It's not like her, she's usually not so—so peremptory."

Erin rather doubted that; but if Rosemary allowed her secretary to scold her like a naughty child, she, Erin, was in no position to complain.

"Honestly, I don't mind a bit. I only hope I can help out.

This is all new to me, but I'll do my best, and it's all so—so interesting.''

The speech sounded stilted and too, too sweet, but apparently Rosemary didn't think so; she reached out and touched Erin's cheek in a gesture as affectionate as it was unexpected. "You're a darling. Your mother said you were, but naturally I assumed she was a little prejudiced. . . . I was wrong. Just relax, take it easy. I'll send someone up to relieve you soon.''

Her departure left the room feeling strangely empty. Erin was beginning to understand, not only why Rosemary was a successful politician, but why she commanded such devotion from her staff. How much of that charm had been calculated? It was alarmingly effective. In less than an hour Rosemary had managed to make her feel as if she really were one of the family—an intimate friend, a confidante. Yet what had she really said? Nothing Erin didn't know, or could not easily have surmised. A graceful apology, some self-deprecating humor, a few casual compliments—and that quick, warm touch on the cheek.

She glanced at Kay, whose mouth had dropped open. From it came a series of sounds that the dignified secretary would indignantly disavow if anyone had accused her of snoring. Erin grinned. Kay's efforts equaled those of her father, and he had been a champion snorer, audible through a closed bedroom door.

She looked around the room wondering how to occupy herself for the next . . . however long it might be. There was no dearth of things to do: a television set, countless books and papers, and even one of the ubiquitous knitting bags on the blanket chest at the foot of the bed. A folded afghan lay beside it. Erin unfolded it and placed it carefully over the sleeper.

She wandered to the window, feeling like Cinderella as she saw Rosemary sweep down the porch steps on Joe's arm. I have to hand it to her, Erin thought admiringly; when she's in her public persona, she can make even that insipid pink dress look regal. The car was a limousine—hired for the occasion, one presumed. The uniformed driver helped them in, got behind the wheel, and the long black vehicle moved smoothly away. As smoothly as it could, considering the condition of the driveway.

The gray-blue shadow of the house lengthened as Kay continued to snore. Christie emerged into view, got into her car, and drove off. There were several other cars in the parking areas, including Nick's unmistakable old Dodge.

Erin didn't want to turn on the TV, for fear of waking Kay, but as the dusk deepened she ventured to switch on a lamp and, greatly daring, to investigate some of the papers lying around. Newspaper clippings and magazine articles, lists of contributors, notes for speeches . . . She recognized Nick's vigorous sprawling hand, and a neat, precise script that could only be Jeff's—if the theories of orthographers were indeed correct. His ideas were as ordered and as passionless as his handwriting, Erin thought, as she read. A good point, the one he had made about verification of nuclear testing, but there must be a more emphatic way of phrasing it. . . .

She was absorbed in the notes when there was a gentle tap on the door. Opening it, Erin put her finger to her lips, but the newcomer—Jeff—only smiled, and said in a normal speaking voice, "Whew, what a racket! I had no idea she snored like that. Sorry to have left you on duty so long; I was talking to a particularly long-winded constituent." He glanced at the papers she had left on the table beside her chair, and his smile broadened. "Couldn't you find anything better to read? You must have been desperately bored."

"Oh, I'm so sorry—maybe I shouldn't have looked at them—"

Jeff's smile shut down behind tight-set lips. "For God's sake, Erin, stop apologizing for everything! You have a perfect right to read any garbage you find lying out in the open. If I had anything to hide . . ." He stopped, and then said lightly, "You sure don't need me yelling at you, do you? Let's get something to eat. I'm grumpy and I'll bet you're starved as well as bored."

"What about Kay?"

"Time she got up anyway." Jeff bent over Kay and called her name.

He had to repeat it several times before she stirred and

groaned. "Oh, dear . . . What? Who is it? I was resting my eyes. . . . Where's Rosemary?"

"Long gone." Jeff put his arm around her and helped her to sit up. "Supper is ready; do you want to come downstairs, or shall I bring you a tray in your room?"

"Of course I'll come down." Kay yawned widely. Her eyes slid sideways, with an unpleasant suggestion of slyness. She gestured to Jeff, who bent obediently so she could whisper in his ear. "Who's that?" she hissed. "What's she doing here?"

Jeff's brows drew together, but he mastered his surprise and said calmly, "You know Erin. You asked me to bring her here to help you—"

"You don't have to tell me who she is. She's Roy Hartsock's little girl. I dreamed about her. The strangest dream . . . You shouldn't have let me sleep so long. I never take naps."

She swung her feet onto the floor and stood up. Jeff tried to take her arm, but she shook him off. "I wish you'd stop treating me like an invalid. I'm just a little groggy from sleep, that's all. Perfectly normal. No, wait, Jeff, I have to clean up this mess before I go downstairs. Rosemary's room—"

"I'll do it," Erin said. "You go ahead."

She had already picked up after Rosemary; there was nothing left to do but smooth the rumpled spread and fold the afghan, but she was glad of a few moments alone. What was the matter with everyone? First Jeff's outburst, so uncharacteristic of him, even though he had apologized with the grace only he could employ; then Kay's memory lapse. There had to be something seriously wrong with her. Maybe, Erin thought more optimistically, it was only the medication she was taking. Sometimes drugs affected people in odd, unexpected ways.

When she left the room she heard Kay's voice from the hall below. It was as brisk and peremptory as ever. Whatever the cause of her confusion, the spells didn't last long.

The commons room, as she had learned to call it, was deserted except for Jeff and Kay, who had entered just before her. The door to the kitchen was open; Erin heard voices, first Nick's, raised in poignant protest, followed by a woman's rich laughter.

"Is Nick still here?" Kay asked, lowering herself carefully onto the sofa.

"Is the Pope Catholic?" Jeff's tone was caustic. "He's always here when it's time to eat."

Kay reached for the knitting bag, and then made a sound that, in another woman, would have shaped itself into a hearty "damn." "This is driving me crazy. I can't even . . . Erin, do you know how to knit?"

Erin decided it was time to draw the line. Politely but firmly she said, "I used to, but I've forgotten everything except the basic stitches. I certainly couldn't do anything as complicated as that."

"This is a very simple pattern," Kay insisted. "That's why I selected it; we all work on it from time to time. Rosemary agrees with me that it's relaxing and therapeutic."

Jeff came to the rescue. "Cut it out, Kay. Since when has knitting been one of the job requirements around here? We *don't* all work on the cursed thing. Erin, you should have heard Joe when Kay suggested he learn to knit. Come to think of it, I'm glad you didn't hear him. Susceptible as I am to her charm, I too have thus far resisted the opportunity to broaden my skills. In fact, the only sucker in the crowd is—voilà, he comes."

"Hard upon his hour," Nick agreed. "What am I being accused of now? Ah, my adored one." He rushed at Kay. "I would have been at your side and wakened you with a kiss, but this jealous swine prevented me. How are you feeling, gorgeous?"

Kay's tight lips curved into a smile. "Don't you dare touch me, Nick. You don't know your own strength; it's like being hugged by a gorilla."

Arms ostentatiously behind him, Nick leaned over her and gave her a delicate peck on the cheek. "Only your fragile condition keeps me from crushing you in a passionate embrace. Hi, Erin."

"Hi."

"Now, what's the problem?" Nick went on. "The famous—the notorious—knitting! Allow me to step into the breach. Untainted as I am by the slightest tinge of male chauvinism, I had no hesitation at adding this skill to the others for which I am so highly commended."

Jeff said something rude under his breath and retreated to a chair, where he picked up the newspaper and hid behind it. Nick grabbed the knitting bag with such ardor that balls of wool rolled in all directions. Kay exclaimed, "Oh, Nick, be careful. You've ripped out that last row—"

"No problem, love." Nick began clumsily to pick up the dropped stitches. He hammed it up, eyes crossed and tongue protruding in fierce concentration as he crooned an absurd litany of inappropriate terms. "Hook one, skip one, knit some, drop one . . . oops. . . ."

The appearance of the cook carrying a covered casserole put an end to Nick's performance. She was a middle-aged black woman, with the round, comfortable figure that becomes a chef.

"You shouldn't have stayed so late, Sarah," Kay said. "We could have managed."

"I figured that with you not feeling so good I should do a little extra."

"That was very kind, and I'm sure Miss Rosemary will appreciate it. Run along, now; I'm sure you must have something else to do this evening. Sarah is very active in her church," Kay added, glancing at Erin. "This is Miss Hartsock, Sarah."

Everything she had said grated just a little; even the studied pleasantness of her voice was the tone of a lady of the manor to a servant. Nothing that any reasonable person could possibly object to, but . . . The introduction was the last straw. Erin stood up. "My name is Erin," she said clearly. "Please let me help, Sarah; I should have offered before."

"It's all done, honey, thanks just the same. Nick, you gonna bring in those plates, or aren't you finished messing up that poor old afghan?"

Nick squashed the knitting back into the bag. "You cut me to the quick, madam. I will carry your plates, or anything else your little heart desires, but note that I do it with my spirits crushed and my ego deflated.''

"That'll be the day," Jeff said, as Nick followed the cook toward the kitchen.

Supper was a simple meal—a spaghetti casserole and a tossed salad, with a plate of rich homemade brownies for dessert. Nick was the only one who ate with any appetite; and even he ate left-handed while he scribbled on a pad of paper.

"How does this sound?" he asked through a mouthful of salad. " 'The citizens of Virginia deserve a representative who is not only honest but honorable; whose personal life is as unblemished as her political record.' ''

"Aren't you being too subtle?" Jeff asked, with a twist of his well-cut lips. "Why don't you just run the famous photo of Buzz emerging from the motel room, next to a shot of Rosemary with her granddaughter?"

"Negative campaigning tends to backfire," Kay said seriously.

"I'm not suggesting she keep referring to 'my opponent the adulterer,' '' Nick argued. "But that little error really hurt old Buzz, in the districts where he has the strongest support. We don't want the voters to forget it. They have short memories."

"They aren't likely to forget it, with Miz Marylou turning up at every rally looking as if her li'l ol' heart was broken," Jeff said.

"Yeah, that's the truth, isn't it?" Nick agreed. "If I were Buzz, I'd lock her in her room and tell the press she has a bad case of flu. It's the duty of every good political wife to play the loyal long-suffering spouse, but Miz Marylou looks more suffering than loyal."

"Poor thing," Kay murmured. "She's worked so hard for him, and she was so in love. I remember their wedding. When she looked up at him and said, 'I will,' her face just glowed."

"Do you know her?" Erin asked.

"Oh, yes. When you've been in politics as long as I have, you get to know everybody—especially in your own part of the country. She's some distant relation of Eddy's—Congressman Marshall's—I believe.''

"The good old First Families of Virginia,'' Jeff murmured.

There was a brief, rather uncomfortable pause. Then Nick said, "Oh, well. If he can't see how she's hurting him, I'm sure not the boy to point it out. 'Personal and professional integrity . . .' ''

After they had finished eating, he and Erin cleared the table, while Jeff settled down with a stack of computer printouts. Kay turned on one of the television sets—there were three of them in the room—and Jeff looked up. "Oh, no, Kay—not one of your glitz, glamour, and sleaze shows! I hate that garbage.''

"There's not much else I can do,'' Kay said sulkily. "Unless Erin needs me to help her finish those memos she was typing—"

A joint grumble of protest from the men stopped her. "Lay off the lady, Kay,'' Jeff said. "She's been hard at it all day.''

"Right,'' Nick agreed. "She needs a break. Come on, Erin, let's take a walk.''

"It's pitch-black dark out,'' Kay objected.

"But the moon is full,'' Nick intoned in a sepulchral voice. "You wouldn't want her to miss seeing me turn into a werewolf.''

Kay laughed and made no further objections. Erin would have accepted an invitation from a genuine werewolf—anything to get out of the house for a while. She accompanied Nick through the kitchen and into an enclosed glassed-in porch. The windows were opaque with darkness; not only was the promised moon missing, but not a star was visible.

"Damn, nobody turned on the lights,'' Nick muttered. "Wait a minute. . . .'' A battery of floodlights came on, bathing the area in garish brilliance. Erin could see only a wide stretch of grass bisected by a brick walkway that stretched off into the dark.

Nick collapsed heavily onto the steps. "Whew. I hope you didn't mind my pressing invitation; I had a feeling you needed to get away from Kay.''

''You were right.'' Seeing his drooping shoulders and general air of collapse, she asked, ''I expect you're tired, after your late night.''

''Nah, I'm used to that. What wears me out is being so relentlessly, tirelessly funny all the time.'' Erin laughed, but Nick only shook his head gloomily. ''Jeff was right, that's my most useful role—court jester. All those massive egos in constant conflict generate a lot of tension. I make 'em laugh. Ha, ha.''

''But you do lots of things,'' Erin said. ''Wasn't that a major speech you were working on at supper?''

Nick straightened up and beamed at her. ''I love a little sympathy and appreciation. That wasn't a speech, but it was major—a mail-out we're preparing. You're absolutely right, you wonderful woman, they couldn't get along without me. Jack-of-all-trades and master of none. . . . I'd better go and see what Sam is up to. He's supposed to be in charge of security around here. If you want a hearty laugh, wait till you meet our security guard.''

''Everything seems so casual,'' Erin said as they walked along the brick path. ''I expected—oh, I don't know; a guard at the gate, and someone at the house to check IDs and screen visitors.''

''That's not Rosemary's style. Her accessibility is one of the reasons why she's so popular with her constituents, and this relaxed, seemingly casual life-style goes over very well. 'See, she can't get her lawn mowed either, or afford a new coat of paint on the house.' Which,'' Nick added, ''is in fact the case. And there's really no need for tight security. She gets lunatic letters, like the ones you saw, but no more than other representatives, and a really effective security system would cost— Careful, the bricks are uneven back here. There's a gate. . . . Well, at least the old coot has switched on the lights in the stableyard.''

There were three lights, one on a post in the middle of a paved area, the other two on buildings that ran in parallel rows flanking it. Those on the right appeared to be garages or workbuildings; a row of smaller, separate structures on the left-hand side looked like cottages. As they approached these, a door opened and a man's figure appeared, silhouetted against the glow inside. A rattle of what sounded like automatic rifle fire made Erin start.

"Hey, Sam, don't shoot," Nick bellowed. "It's me."

"Nick?" The quavering voice was that of an old man. "What you doin' out in the dark? You lucky I didn't shoot you at that."

"Don't worry, he doesn't have a gun," Nick murmured. "That was the TV you heard. We're just taking a walk, Sam. Nice night."

"Nice night, my foot. Too hot. And it's comin' on to storm. Who's that you got with you?"

Nick performed the introductions. Sam was completely bald, and apparently very nearsighted; he thrust his withered face so close to Erin's that she could feel his breath. He greeted her with old-fashioned courtesy: "Welcome, young lady," he added, "you may's well let them dogs out, Nick. I was just gonna do it, but so long as you're here. . . ."

"Okay. Get back to your cops and robbers, Sam."

The old man retreated and slammed the door.

"See what I mean?" Nick asked.

"He's sweet."

"Sure he's sweet. And so decrepit a faint breeze would bowl him over. Another one of Rosemary's sentimental attachments; he's been with the family for a million years and she thinks his feelings would be hurt if she hired somebody to assist him. Here, take my hand, it's pretty dark back this way."

The dogs were penned in a run behind the garage. The first sight of them made Erin cling more tightly to Nick's hand; a pillar lamp cast a dim glow and made the huge bodies hurling themselves at the chain-link fence look formidable.

"You aren't afraid of dogs, are you?" Nick asked casually, opening the gate.

After slobbering messily over Erin, from her face to her feet, the dogs gamboled off, baying wildly.

"Retrievers," Nick sneered, wiping his wet forearm on his shirt. "They are the most useless excuses for watchdogs I've ever seen. I suggested Dobermans—"

"They sounded fierce." One of the dogs was running around in circles, baying like the hound of the Baskervilles.

"That's all they do. Look at that furry idiot, chasing his own tail. Thinks he's a cat."

"Don't they chase the cats?"

"They chase the cats? It's the other way around."

He led her across the dew-wet grass to a bench in the shadow of a group of white pines. When they sat down, one of the dogs joined them, collapsing onto Erin's foot. The white hairs of his muzzle glimmered palely, and she bent down to pat his head.

"He's old, isn't he?"

"Ten years old. This is Samson. The other one is Tiny. He's four, but he's mentally retarded. Thinks he's a puppy."

Head down, tail thrashing, Tiny followed some arcane unseen path across the lawn.

As the panting breath of the old dog quieted, other sounds became audible—small, sly rustles of movement made sinister by one's inability to identify their causes. As her eyes continued to adjust to the darkness Erin began to see shapes moving noiselessly from the shadows. The cats were on the prowl.

One pale fuzzy shape strolled toward the dog. Tiny welcomed it with a sharp bark and pounced, then yelped and backed off, pawing at his nose. The cat walked away as leisurely as it had approached.

"It's very . . . peaceful," Erin said. The word wasn't entirely appropriate. Bathed in the merciless glare that showed all the imperfections of flaking paint and splintered trim, the house looked like a tiny island of life besieged and about to be overwhelmed by towering walls of darkness. Clouds massed like attacking armies overhead and along the horizon.

"Sure is," Nick said, not hearing the note of uncertainty in her voice. "Rosemary is lucky her home is so close to D.C.; she doesn't have to maintain two residences. It's a long commute, though."

"Is this her husband's family home?"

"Yes. Ed Marshall's family used to own half Virginia, but they lost everything in the War Between The States except a town house in Richmond and this place. It was just a farm then; a brief period of questionable prosperity (there were nasty rumors about illegal investments) resulted in the architectural abortion you see before you.''

''You know a lot about the Marshalls.''

''I should. My aunt was the Marshalls' housekeeper till she retired some years ago. How do you think I got my foot in the door?''

''I thought you were a volunteer. Anybody can volunteer, can't they?''

''Sure. I assure you it wasn't my family connections that got me my present munificent salary of zero a year. What it got me was noticed, so that when I did come through in a clutch situation, people were watching.''

''What did you do, rescue Rosemary from a mad dog?''

Nick chuckled. ''You'll never guess. I won my spurs baby-sitting.''

''What?''

''You heard me. The Lord works in mysterious ways. . . . They came for a visit last spring—Rosemary's daughter and her husband, and the kid. Kevin and I hit it off right away, he's an antique car buff and a fiery liberal. Elizabeth—the little girl—reminds me of Rosemary, she's funny and spunky and cute as a tick. I like kids, and being creatures of rare discernment, they adore me. Before they left I was 'Uncle Nick,' and the most popular guy on the block.''

Erin was about to express incredulity when she remembered that she had won a friendly smile and a pat on the cheek by offering to baby-sit Kay.

''I guess it can happen,'' she said doubtfully.

''Take my word for it. Of course,'' Nick added modestly, ''I was doing a superb job in every other way. I was also one of the first to volunteer, way back before the primary, when nobody gave her a prayer. They thought she was crazy to give up a sure House seat for a long shot. The local party supported her opponent in the primary—a well-heeled, well-connected realtor who suffered from delusions of grandeur. We beat the pants off the sucker, but it took Buzz's half-witted performance to make people sit up and take notice.

We're on a roll now, contributions picking up, endorsements from some key people, but it's still up for grabs.''

"Baby-sitting aside, I can see why you're so highly esteemed,'' Erin said. "To jump feet first the way you did, into what looked like a hopeless cause—''

"I wasn't doing anything important anyway. The truth is, I'm what you might call a late bloomer. I screwed around with a lot of things—a little PR work, courses in business administration, before I decided to follow in the footsteps of Edward R. Murrow and Dan Rather. It didn't take me long to realize that that path was a bit crowded—a regular traffic jam. As a matter of fact, I quit my job today.''

"Your job at the paper? Why? Too many high school football games?''

"Too little time. The next few weeks are crucial. Rosemary hasn't got the financial backing Buzz commands; he had raised a million bucks by the middle of the summer. He can afford to pay a big staff, and a team of expensive media consultants. Rosemary has me.''

"But Nick, that's really . . . What are you going to live on?''

"Oh, I'll get by. And don't get the wrong idea about how noble I am. This is a gamble, but if it pays off I'm in the catbird seat. Even if we lose, I'm making useful contacts and—I hope—impressing them with my brilliance and dedication.''

The branches over them swayed in a sudden gust of wind. "Storm's about to break,'' Nick muttered. "I hope Rosemary doesn't stay in town too late, these roads can be murder when they're flooded.''

The comment was more revealing than he realized, and Erin thought she knew the real reason for the dedication he boasted about. Only a fool would have hitched his career to a star as low in the sky as Rosemary's had been, and Nick was no fool. He was undoubtedly an idealist, but sympathy for the causes Rosemary supported wasn't the reason either. It was Rosemary herself who had won him over. A young man's platonic devotion to an older woman whose profession (if not her face and figure) was the quintessence of glamour.

Shades of the Round Table and the ideals of chivalry . . . She liked him all the better for it, though Nick would have scoffed if she had compared him with Sir Lancelot—and maybe that wasn't the most appropriate comparison, come to think of it. There were all those rumors about Lancelot and Guinevere.

A fat, warm raindrop splashed on the back of her hand. "We'd better go in," Nick said.

"I haven't seen you turn into a werewolf," Erin protested. "No moon."

There was a moon, though; Erin saw it over her left shoulder as they crossed the lawn toward the house. The clouds closed over it again even as she looked: a monstrous, swollen globe of tarnished silver, with a single shadow of dead branch piercing it like a spear through a knight's shield.

*   *

LATE THE FOLLOWING morning Erin snatched a moment to call Fran. "I won't talk long," she began. "I know your boss doesn't like you to get personal calls—"

"Never mind him," Fran cut in. "I've been dying to hear from you. Tell me everything!"

"There isn't much to tell."

"Oh, for God's sake! You're there, right in her house— have you seen her? What's she doing? What are *you* doing?"

Erin was tempted to tell her, if only to shatter Fran's illusions about politics, which now seemed to her hopelessly naive and infantile. She had spent a restless night with the connecting door between her room and Kay's ajar, listening to the snores and groans and squeaking springs as the older woman tossed and turned. Kay hadn't settled down until almost dawn, but she had been up and raring to go shortly after seven. Erin had helped her dress, arranged her hair, made both beds, dusted and swept. She had not seen Rosemary at all that day.

She managed to cut into Fran's raptures long enough to explain why she had called. "I'm going to try to get a ride in this evening so I can pick up some more clothes. I'm not sure when, everyone is so busy—"

"No problem. I'll bring you whatever you need. I'd love to."

Erin didn't doubt that. Her need was an answer to prayer. If it hadn't happened, Fran would have found some other excuse to come for a visit.

"What do you want? The black lace formal, of course. What else?"

Erin pictured herself making Kay's bed in black lace and ruffles. "Never mind the formal. I need everyday clothes— jeans, tops, underwear. . . . What am I saying? You can't come, Fran. I can't invite you, not without asking permission. . . ."

She might as well have protested to the wind. Fran assured her she didn't need directions, she knew the way, and then hung up without so much as a good-bye.

Erin went in search of Kay, who was no more inclined to listen to her than Fran had been. When she finally got her point across, the old woman thought for a moment and then nodded. "I suppose that would be best. I can't see any other way of arranging it. You should have brought more than an overnight bag. Didn't Joe explain the situation? Well, never mind, there's no sense in crying over spilt milk. Tell your friend to come ahead, there's no one here who can drive you, and no extra car to lend you. Except mine . . . but I really can't spare you today."

Erin had already heard a few jokes about Kay's precious Mercedes, for which she had been saving all her life, and which she refused to entrust to anyone else. "She ought to lend it to you, since she can't drive right now," Nick had remarked at breakfast, when Erin explained her problem. "But she won't even let me behind the wheel—can you imagine that, superb driver that I am? I wish I could take you, but I have to go to Richmond and I don't know when I'll be back."

The others had also scattered on various errands, which left Erin to the tender mercies of Kay. The older woman seemed sharper, in every sense of the word—efficient and in control as well as sharp-tongued and critical. Though Erin was the chief victim, the other workers also felt the brunt of Kay's disapproval, and during the brief lunch break—sandwiches and coffee in the commons room—Jan muttered sourly. "The old witch is in a foul mood today."

"Sssh." Christie gave him a warning look. Kay had gone to the kitchen to talk to Sarah about supper—and, Erin thought, to get *her* back up too. There was no way Kay could have overheard the complaint; it was the presence of an outsider, Erin, that had prompted Christie's warning.

"She's probably in a lot of pain," said Jackson.

"I'll bet she's not taking those pills," Anita said shrewdly. "She was so out of it yesterday—" She broke off as the distinctive click of Kay's heels sounded along the passageway.

Erin knew they all shared her hope that Kay would rest after lunch, but none of them had the nerve to suggest it, and Kay went doggedly on, wearing herself out and driving everybody crazy. The afternoon crawled by, with no end in sight; she would be through for the day when Kay released her, and not before. She was taking notes on voter breakdowns, by age, gender, and occupation, when Christie poked her head in the door.

"Excuse me. Erin, are you expecting company by any chance? There's someone at the door asking for you."

Her curt, critical tone was another reminder that Erin was the new kid on the block, and no more popular with Rosemary's possessively adoring staff than she deserved to be. The others were beginning to unbend a little—Jackson had even asked her whether she wanted sugar in her coffee at lunch—but Christie remained aloof. Once Erin would have assumed, smugly and simplemindedly, that Christie was just jealous of the attention Jeff and Nick were lavishing on another woman. She knew better now. People like Christie were more interested in power than in passion or popularity. But how could Christie possibly believe that she, Erin, was any threat to her ambitions? In training, experience, and education, if not in actual talent, her qualifications were so inferior to Christie's it was laughable.

Fran had not been invited in. Erin found her sitting on the porch steps with a cat on her lap and several others nudging for attention. Animals adored Fran, probably because she didn't particularly care for them. But these were Rosemary Marshall's cats, and therefore worthy of attention.

She jumped to her feet at the sight of Erin, spilling the lap-sitter ignominiously onto the ground. "Hi. Is she here?"

Erin didn't have to ask who "she" was, nor did she feel obliged to answer. Eyeing the two big suitcases, she exclaimed, "What did you do, pack everything I own?"

"It's better ⊍ have too much than not enough. You never know what will come up, and you have to be prepared."

Fran had to be pushed toward the stairs; she eyed the closed doors longingly and asked question after question. "Which is her office? Is Nick here? What a great portrait! Do you suppose it's her husband?" Even the sight of Erin's unpretentious room didn't dim her enthusiasm. "Imagine being right here, in her own house," she exclaimed.

"Servants' quarters."

"Listen, kid, I'd sleep in a closet." She opened the adjoining door. "Is this her room? It's just the way I expected it would look!"

"Frilly and feminine and pink?" Erin inquired sarcastically. "Get the hell out of there, Fran; that isn't Rosemary's room, it belongs to her secretary, and you have no business prying."

"Oh." Fran closed the door. "Where is *her* room?"

"Never mind, you aren't going to see it. This isn't the historic-homes tour."

Feeling like a sheepdog herding a recalcitrant ewe, she escorted Fran down the stairs and headed her off when she tried to turn into the second-floor corridor. Kay was waiting at the foot of the stairs.

"Oh, there you are," she said. "I couldn't think where you'd gotten to."

Erin had no choice but to introduce Fran, adding, "You remember, I told you she had volunteered to bring my clothes."

"Certainly I remember. How do you do, Fran." She bestowed a gracious smile on the potential voter and apologized for not offering her hand.

"Oh, gosh, that's a terrific shame," Fran exclaimed. "Erin said you'd had an accident, but I didn't realize how bad it

was. Gosh, that's just terrible. Especially right now, with the
campaign heating up and you so important to Rosemary . . .
Oh, gee, I should call her Mrs. Marshall, but honestly, I'm
such an admirer of hers, I feel as if she's a friend, you know?
I just wish there was something I could do to help.''

The performance was so outrageously saccharine, Erin expected Kay to be as revolted by it as she was. Kay only smiled
more warmly; of course she couldn't know that ''gee'' and
''golly'' were foreign to Fran's normal vocabulary.

''You're very kind. I presume you're one of our volunteers?''
Caught flat-footed, Fran looked her interrogator straight in
the eye and lied. ''Yes, ma'am. But if there's anything I can
do for you personally—I mean, I can imagine how awful it
must be for you, your hand and all. . . .''

Feeling her self-control about to give way, Erin said firmly,
''Thanks, Fran, I appreciate your help. I know you're in a
hurry to get back, so—''

''Oh, no, I haven't a thing to do this evening,'' Fran assured her.

Erin glowered at her, and Kay said pleasantly, ''We certainly can't let you make that long drive back to town without
at least offering you some refreshment. It's about that time, I
believe.''

It was exactly that time, a little after five-thirty. Fran must
have left work early in order to arrive at the conventional cocktail
hour. She probably thinks we sit around swilling sherry and
Chablis every afternoon, Erin thought disgustedly. She didn't
quite have the nerve to appear at suppertime. . . .

But she managed to stay for the meal, such as it was. The
intimate little dinner of the previous evening had been an
aberration; Sarah's usual custom was to provide a cold buffet,
in order to accommodate the unpredictable schedules and increasing work load. People wandered in and helped themselves to the covered dishes of salads and cold cuts, and
expelled cats that had invaded the room—when they could
catch them. From five to eight, and sometimes later, there
was usually someone in the room eating and/or drinking.

It was exactly the casual ambience in which Fran shone.
Though visibly disappointed not to find Rosemary, and to

learn that she was not likely to return for several hours, she flattered the women, flirted with the men, and kept at a safe distance from Kay, who was inclined to ask embarrassing questions about her fictitious volunteer work.

It only required one look at Will to tell her he wasn't worth cultivating. After mumbling a vague greeting and fussing nervously with his glasses he sank back into obscurity behind his desk.

Erin was praying Fran would get bored and go home when Nick's appearance put an end to that hope. In Erin's opinion his greeting was far more enthusiastic than their brief acquaintance justified. Before long they were engaged in an animated discussion, and a couple of the others had joined them. Only Christie remained aloof; arms folded, eyes calculating, she watched the laughing, chattering group with a cynical smile. Erin was forced to sit with Kay, who couldn't manage her food with only her left hand; cutting Kay's cold turkey into ladylike bites, she watched her roommate winning all hearts and tried to think of reasons why she shouldn't kill her.

Fran lingered up to, but not quite beyond, the point of rudeness. The others had drifted away, and Nick was beginning to drop hints about work that awaited him before she gave up.

"I guess I'd better be going," she said to Kay. "I know how busy all you people must be, and I just want to thank you for letting me stay. I'll never forget this."

Erin leaped to her feet. "I'll walk you to the car."

"Talk about how to speed the parting guest," Fran said as soon as the door had closed behind them. "You could have let me go on being sweet and winsome for a few more minutes; that gorgeous man might have offered to see me to the door."

"That," said Erin, "was the most disgusting demonstration of bullshitting I've ever seen."

"Oooh!" Fran clapped her hand to her heart. "How shocking. You said a dirty word! What's come over Miss Prim and Proper? Once away from my restraining influence—"

Erin kicked the screen door open and propelled Fran out with more force than was strictly necessary. Recovering from the burst of giggles that had interrupted her last sentence, Fran went on, "You're a fine one to talk. Sitting there sweet as pie cutting up the old lady's food and looking demure. What kind of an act is that?"

"It's no act," Erin said slowly. "At least it wasn't, once upon a time. . . ."

"That's true. Sweetness and light come naturally to you. Well, maybe someday you'll grow up. Listen, kid, there's something I want to talk to you about. A proposition you can't refuse—"

This time the interruption came from one of the cats, whom Fran had attempted to push aside with her foot. The animal retaliated with a snarl and a swipe of a clawed paw. Fran swore and clutched her ankle.

"I haven't time to talk now," Erin said, noting that the cat in question was a lean, gray tom. She must remember to give him a piece of chicken later. . . .

"No, this isn't the time or place," Fran agreed. "I'll call you. We'll have lunch." She got in the car and turned the key; Erin's reply, a vigorous negative, was lost in the roar of the engine. Fran put her head out the window.

"What did you say?"

"Never mind. Good-bye, Fran."

"Say rather au revoir," Fran retorted, grinning. "You haven't seen the last of me. I have only begun to fight."

"I suggest you start by signing on as a volunteer," Erin said sarcastically. "A post-dated finding, so to speak."

Fran only laughed heartily. "I had already planned to be at local headquarters first thing Saturday morning. Bye, bye, sweetie."

When Erin returned to the house she found Nick at the door, about to evict a cat. He held the door for her, then eased the intruder out. "Fran gone?" he asked.

"Yes."

"She's quite a character," Nick said admiringly.

"Yes."

"Did you get those clothes and things you wanted?"

"Yes." The repeated monosyllables sounded childish and sullen. She added, "Fran brought them. That's why she was here."

"Oh. I wondered."

"Oh, I see. You wondered. You assumed, I suppose, that I had the nerve to invite a friend to someone else's house for purely social purposes?"

"What the hell is the matter with you? A person asks a simple question or makes a harmless remark. . . ."

He stopped, obviously expecting an apology or an explanation, but Erin was in no mood for either. She found it hard to admit to herself, much less to Nick, how sharply Fran's assessment of her character, or lack thereof, had stung.

"Oh well, that's okay," Nick said, after a prolonged pause. "I understand. It's been a long day for you. Kay isn't the easiest person in the world to get along with, even when she's in a good mood. Come on, let's sit down and swing for a while. Nothing like an old-fashioned porch swing to induce a gentle, relaxed frame of mind, possibly even conducive to a touch of equally old-fashioned and respectable dalliance."

It wasn't so much the fact that he took her agreement for granted, coolly seizing her arm and pulling her toward the swing; it was a number of irritations, from his unfortunate choice of words like "old-fashioned" and "respectable" to the insulting assumption that all she needed to put her in a better humor was a little kissing and fondling.

"I have to go in," Erin said, pulling away. "Go and—and swing yourself."

Nick followed her without further comment; he appeared to be more perplexed than angered, and she really didn't blame him for failing to understand her reaction. She was just beginning to understand it herself.

When she entered the commons room she saw Jeff sitting next to Kay, listening to her with the grave, courteous attention he always showed her.

"I didn't know you were back," Nick remarked. "How long have you been here?"

"I arrived about an hour ago. Hearing sounds of uncouth revelry coming from this room, I went straight to the office."

"The way you avoid harmless social activities is just plain unhealthy," Nick declared, throwing himself into a chair. "All work and no play makes Jeff a dull boy. I thought you were going straight home from the Hill."

"What is this, an inquisition?" Jeff demanded, frowning. "I brought those reports out for Rosemary to look over."

Nick cowered, covering his head with his arms. "Sorry, sorry, boss, sorry. I was just making conversation."

"Huh." Jeff relaxed. "Hello, Erin. I'd have greeted you properly if this clod hadn't started yakking. I was just telling Kay about the Buzzard's latest gaffe."

"I heard about it." Nick rubbed his hands together with an evil smile. "I've already started composing responses."

"What was it?" Erin asked.

Jeff chuckled. "You won't believe this. He was making a speech this afternoon in Warrenton, and after a lot of stupid remarks about giving the ladies the respect and admiration that is their due, he said, 'But we don't want to see a senator in hot pants, now do we?' "

"How vulgar," Kay murmured.

"Vulgar? It's beautiful!" Nick exclaimed. "He actually said 'hot pants'? Oh, boy, oh, boy—"

"You can't do it, Nick," Jeff warned.

"I don't have to. The phrase itself is enough. What speech-writer came up with that gem?"

"It's outdated," Erin said critically.

"It's also plagiarized." Will's head appeared over the stack of papers like that of a wary rabbit emerging from its hole. "Spiro Agnew said that about Abzug, back in 1972. Or was it 1971?"

"Who cares?" Nick demanded gleefully. "You mean we can get him on plagiarism as well as sexism, vulgarity, and remarks degrading to women?"

"I do think a statement might be justified," Will said mildly.

"You're damn right, Will." Nick reached for a pad of paper.

The statement didn't go together as quickly as it ought to have done because of the suggestions, some from Will, most from Nick, that reduced all of them except Kay to helpless laughter. "I can't see why you find it so amusing," she de-

clared indignantly, after a particularly unprintable idea of
Nick's that made even Jeff whoop with unseemly laughter.
"Senator Bennett ought to be ashamed of himself. Rosemary
never wore hot pants in her life, and she certainly wouldn't
be ill-bred enough to wear them to the Senate."

"Exactly." Jeff wiped the tears from his eyes and patted
her hand. "That's exactly what we're going to do, Kay—make
him ashamed of himself."

"Maybe he's trying to imply that he's so uninterested in
women he doesn't even notice what they're wearing," Erin
said. "Or not wearing."

"Oh, Lord, it is tempting, isn't it?" Jeff shook his head.
"Can't do it without being coarse, though."

"What about something like 'Senator Bennett's contempt
for women extends even to their attire,' " Erin suggested.
" 'As the quintessential symbol of sexism in fashion . . .' "

"That's not bad." Nick began scribbling. "Go on, Erin,
keep talking."

They were still hard at work when the frantic barking of the
dogs announced the arrival of Rosemary. She looked tired and
irritable; Joe, who had accompanied her, tossed his coat in the
general direction of a chair and loosened his tie before proceeding with what was obviously a continuing argument.

"I tell you, I don't trust him. He's got something up his
sleeve, or he wouldn't be playing footsie with you. Why is
he giving you all this support?"

"I can think of several possibilities," Rosemary said. She
batted her eyelashes and simpered.

Joe replied with a single emphatic word that made Kay turn
to him in indignant reproof. "Oh, shut up, Kay," he snarled,
before she could speak.

Rosemary's flirtatious smirk turned to a scowl. "Watch
your damn mouth, Joe," she snapped, taking the seat next to
Kay and putting an arm around her. "I don't trust Philips
any more than you do, but it's just possible that I know him
a little better. He's perfectly dependable where his own self-
interest is involved. He's had it in for Buzz Bennett ever since
Buzz did that ghastly takeoff on him at the Press Club Dinner.
I know, everybody is supposed to be a good sport about those

things, but Philips—well, let's face it, Philips is not a good sport, and that was a particularly devastating imitation.''

Joe's eyes gleamed with reminiscent pleasure. ''Yeah. I loved every second of that routine. Of course old Buzz never wrote it himself—''

''No, he hired that young man from Boston U—the one whose Nixon record sold so well. That's not the point, nor does it matter *why* Philips is so supportive. I can use his support and I will, as long as it lasts—which, given Philips's reputation, may not be very long. You may not like it, Joe, and I certainly don't, but the brutal truth is that political analysts like Philips do affect public opinion. They don't exactly distort the facts, but by careful selection and interpretation they can make a saint look like Jack the Ripper and turn a catastrophe into a triumph.''

''Not to mention the equally brutal fact that a lot of idiots believe everything they read in the paper,'' Joe agreed sourly. ''Okay, okay. You're right, I'm wrong. But you know something? I don't hate many people in this business, but I really do hate that son of a bitch.''

''You amaze me,'' Rosemary exclaimed, and the last of the tension dissolved as they all laughed at Joe's look of surprise.

''Did you hear about Buzz's latest?'' Nick asked.

''Yeah, it was on the late news,'' Joe answered, reaching for a cigar. ''We heard it in the car coming home.''

''We've been working on a statement,'' Jeff said.

''Good. Let's hear what you've got.''

''Hold on a minute,'' Rosemary begged, sagging against the cushions. ''Or ten, or maybe even fifteen? I need to unwind before we go back to work. I haven't even had a chance to ask Kay how she's feeling, or say hello to Erin. Hello, Erin. Kay, how's the hand?''

Kay began to talk, recounting in laborious detail all the problems that had arisen that day, and how she had handled them. Rosemary listened patiently, her eyes half closed.

''Anything to eat around here?'' Joe asked. ''I'm starved; don't know why it is, but I never seem to get any food at those damn receptions.''

''It's because you talk all the time,'' Nick said.

The same was probably true for Rosemary, Erin realized. She followed Joe to the kitchen, where she found Will filling a plate with cold turkey and salad.

"Hey, leave some for me," Joe said. "You've been noshing all evening."

"This is for Rosemary," Will said. "I don't suppose she got anything to eat at that bash, she never does."

"How should I know? I'm not her mama," Joe grunted.

"Would she like coffee?" Erin asked, as Joe dived headfirst into the refrigerator and began rummaging.

"A glass of milk, I think," Will answered. "Much more healthful."

Rosemary accepted the food with a smile of thanks and began to eat, slowly at first and then with increasing appetite. "Thanks, Will. That was just what I needed. Five more minutes, Joe, and I'm all yours—you lucky devil."

"Not that damned knitting," Joe grumbled, as she reached for the bag.

"Two rows, Joe."

She reached into the knitting bag and then recoiled with a muffled cry, jerking her hand out of the bag and dislodging an object that fell to the floor at her feet. "God! What is it?"

At first Erin thought, as Rosemary must have done, that the small, shapeless bundle was a mouse or some other creature. But it didn't move; it lay where it had fallen until Nick gingerly picked it up.

"It's just a bundle of rags," he announced, relieved. "No, wait a sec. It looks like . . ." He turned it over and held it up, and its true character became apparent: a shapeless body wrapped in dusty cloth, a crude painted face, strands of black yarn for hair. . . .

"It's a doll," Nick said in a puzzled voice. "Cinderella? It's covered with ashes."

Like the others, Kay had leaned forward to stare at the thing. Nobody noticed what was happening until she slid to the floor in a dead faint.

Chapter
Four

"SON OF A BITCH!" Joe snatched the cigar from his mouth and hurled it across the room. "Down four points!"

The cigar landed on a pile of newspapers. Erin pounced like a cat, only to find that the disgusting object was thoroughly dead.

The others hadn't turned a collective hair. "I wish you wouldn't be so confounded dramatic," Jeff said crossly. He plucked the computer printouts from his superior's clenched fist and smoothed them out. "There's a three-point margin of error and you know we anticipated a slight drop; the last poll was taken right after Bennett's escapade hit the fan. He was bound to bounce back."

"Goddamn stupid voters," Joe grumbled. "Memories like sieves and brains like mush."

"I thought we weren't supposed to refer to voters that way," Nick said.

"You aren't. I can say anything I want." But Joe sounded less irate; he took a sip of coffee and recovered the printouts from Jeff. "Could be worse," he admitted, perusing them. "Allowing for the margin of error . . ."

Erin had had another bad night. Kay had made light of her collapse: "Faint? Nonsense, I just lost my balance. So stupid of me. . . ." But Erin had felt she ought to leave the door open again, and although Kay had slept like a rock, thanks to the sleeping pill Rosemary insisted upon, she had snored mercilessly. Erin had crept downstairs at daybreak to find Nick and Jeff hunched over the table in the commons room plotting their counterattack on Bennett. She had ignored Nick's unsubtle hints about breakfast, but hunger finally drove her to the kitchen and it seemed rude to cook for herself and not the others. Joe turned up shortly afterward, so she made bacon and eggs for him too.

"Yeah, it's about what we expected," he said finally. "Southside and the upper Valley. Bennett country. We'll have to make another swing south. Danville, Martinsville, Harrisonburg, Roanoke . . ."

"The TV spots are due to start next week," Nick said.

"Should have been this week."

"You know why it wasn't this week." Nick was on the defensive. "We didn't have the money. Then Rosemary objected to the format—"

"Okay, okay," Joe grunted.

Realizing she was unneeded and probably unwanted, Erin stacked the dishes and went upstairs to see if she could do anything for Kay. She found Kay up and looking for trouble. Her hair straggled down her back and she had thrown a robe around her shoulders. "There you are," she snapped. "I couldn't think where you'd got to."

The criticism and its corollary—that she should have stayed in her room awaiting Kay's commands—was infuriating, but Erin bit back the reply that had sprung to her lips. She mustn't let newly aroused sensibilities affect her judgment. Kay wasn't Nick; Kay could, and probably would, get her fired if she talked back. It was not until that moment that Erin realized, with genuine amazement, how desperately she wanted to keep her job. It involved unpleasant duties like waiting on Kay and putting up with her rudeness, but it also included times like that exhilarating hour the night before, when they had huddled around the table laughing themselves silly and plotting the downfall of Buzz Bennett.

"I brought you some coffee," she said stiffly.

"Oh." Kay had the decency to look embarrassed. "Sorry I snapped at you; I just hate being dependent on other people. I can't even do my hair by myself, and my room is a mess, and there's such a lot of work to do. . . ."

Erin couldn't help thinking that it would have been easier to keep the room tidy if Kay had not been so addicted to little ruffled pillows and framed photographs and countless china, glass, and stuffed ornaments. At her suggestion Kay sat down at the dressing table and sipped her coffee while she straightened the room. Kay watched her every move and made helpful suggestions. "That cushion with the cat on it goes on the chaise, not the chair. Just push that picture of Mr. Kennedy a little to the right—no, I mean the left. . . . You'd better strip the bed and remake it. I didn't do a very neat job."

After she had brushed and arranged Kay's hair, Kay graciously dismissed her, and Erin made her escape. The others were hard at work on a tall stack of Sunday newspapers. Knowing she lacked the knowledge to assist in selecting pertinent articles and editorials, she stole the comic sections and retreated to Will's desk. An interlude with "Doonesbury" and "Bloom County" refreshed her. When Kay appeared, she was able to ask, quite pleasantly, what the other woman wanted for breakfast. She knew Kay was about to ask, or order, her to prepare something, and it gave her a small sense of satisfaction to play volunteer instead of servant.

Kay ordered a soft-boiled egg—"Exactly four minutes, Erin, I can't stand runny eggs—" and added, "Rosemary just has juice and coffee and a piece of toast. You might see if there are any of those muffins of Sarah's left. Warm them in the oven, the microwave makes them soggy."

It wasn't only the way she said it, it was what she said! Erin was washing dishes, amid a violent splashing of suds, when Jeff came to the kitchen in search of more coffee.

"Hey, you don't have to do that," he exclaimed. "Just stack them. Or, if you want to be truly noble and acquire

Sarah's heartfelt thanks, rinse them and put them in the dishwasher.''

"I wouldn't leave a mess like this for Sarah," Erin said.

Jeff put his hand on her shoulder. "I don't know what we did to deserve you. Everything is in such a state of chaos around here, we don't say thanks as often as we should, but believe me, we do appreciate what you're doing—and you."

His warm fingers moved to the curve between her neck and shoulder. "Mmmm," Erin murmured. "That's nice."

"You're all tensed up." His other hand found the corresponding muscles on her left shoulder and moved in slow rhythm. "Relax. There. How's that?"

"Lovely."

She was sorry when he took his hands away—for reasons she was in no mood to analyze. When he stepped back away from her she felt oddly chilled.

"Have you ever considered running for office yourself?" she asked, smiling at him over her shoulder.

"Who, me? I've got better sense."

The brief intimacy was gone and neither of them tried to recapture it. Erin thought he looked a little self-conscious. Afraid she would mistake his kindness for something else?

"I'll bring the coffee when it's ready," she said.

"Thanks."

She made fresh coffee and carried the pot into the commons room just as Rosemary entered. She was wearing a demure dark-navy print dress with a lace collar, a navy hat with a veil, and white gloves.

"What's that in aid of?" Joe asked. "You don't have to get all gussied up for me."

"I had someone a little higher up in mind," Rosemary said, rolling her eyes heavenward. "It's Sunday, in case you've forgotten. I'm going to church."

"Church? Church!" Joe's voice rose. "For Christ's sake, Rosie—"

"Precisely," Rosemary agreed. She stripped off her gloves. "Is there any . . . Oh, thanks, Erin. I hope these louts thanked you properly for feeding them—if it was you, which I assume it was, since Joe can't cook and Jeff won't eat unless someone shoves a plate in front of him, and Nick's culinary talents run to omelettes bulging with unseemly vegetables.''

Her attempt to distract Joe didn't work. "You can't go to church," he bellowed. "Have you seen the latest polls? We need to plan another series of speeches—"

"Later."

"Not later, now. There isn't time—"

"Goddamn it, Joe!" Rosemary slammed the empty juice glass down on the table. "Don't tell me what I can and can't do! I missed last week and the week before—"

"So what?"

"So what about my image?" Rosemary's voice was higher in pitch, but even more penetrating than Joe's. "You're always bellyaching about images. It's important—"

"Not as important as that five-point drop—"

"Four," Jeff murmured.

Erin was the only one who heard him. Rosemary's cheeks were crimson with rage; she looked magnificent, like a miniature Medea. The argument climaxed in a ringing crash as Rosemary picked up the empty juice glass and heaved it into the fireplace.

Silence fell like a pall.

"Well, for God's sake," Joe said. "If you feel that strongly about it, why didn't you say so?"

Rosemary told him to do something that was anatomically impossible. Kay gasped, Joe hooted with laughter, and everybody relaxed.

Rosemary caught Erin's eye. "Excuse my language," she said primly.

"I'll—uh—make toast," Erin muttered, and fled.

Nick followed her to the kitchen. "Are you okay?" he asked.

"What kind of prude do you think I am?" Erin demanded.

"A cute, adorable, innocent kind of prude." He slipped his arms around her and kissed her on the ear.

"Stop that!"

"It's okay," Nick mumbled into her neck. "I'm listening. If somebody comes—"

"I don't care about that." She wriggled away from him

and stood at bay, her back to the counter. "I mean, I do care about having people catch me behaving like an adolescent jerk, but that wasn't— How dare you talk to me that way?"

Nick flung his arms wide and looked hurt. "What did I say?"

"Cute, innocent, adorable . . ."

"Ah." Nick tugged thoughtfully at a lock of hair. "Sexism again. And who was it, a short while ago, who yelled when I said she was a feminist? Make up your mind."

"How about you making up your mind? One minute you talk to me like a human being, you expect some evidence of intelligence—and the next minute you're grunting into my ear and calling me cute."

Nick considered the speech. "You may have a point."

"Huh?"

"Don't look so surprised. I am not impervious to reason, or so damned arrogant I can't admit I was wrong."

"Oh. Well . . ."

"It's true I haven't got my emotions straight on this liberation bit," Nick continued. "I mean, injustice to anybody—black, white, or purple; male, female, or other—gets my blood boiling. But when it comes to personal relationships I seem to have trouble figuring out how to behave. Vive la différence, right? Maybe my problem lies in—"

"Oh, Nick, knock it off. I don't want to discuss your psychological problems, I want to make sure Rosemary eats something. And you're standing in front of the toaster."

Nick turned, plucked the toast from the slots, and reached for the butter. "You looked so shocked," he said, chuckling, "when Rosemary pitched the glass into the fireplace. You better get used to scenes like that. She has a quick temper, and Joe gets her madder, faster, than anybody else."

"I don't blame her. It wasn't so much what he said—though that was bad enough—bossy, arrogant man!—it was his tone of voice."

"He's noted for it," Nick said. "He's been fired by more candidates than any other guy in the business. He's brilliant, but he gets people's backs up. Do you want to go to church?"

The abrupt change of subject caught Erin by surprise. "Not especially."

"The church is worth seeing. It's an historic building that Ed Marshall helped to restore and reconsecrate. He's buried in the cemetery there."

"Oh, really? Is it the traditional family burial ground?"

"I don't think so." Obviously Nick had never given the matter much thought and didn't intend to do so now. He added, "Rosemary tries to go every week. Makes a great impression on the voters."

"Don't you people ever do anything without calculating its effect on the voters?"

"Rosemary's reasons for going to church are her own business," Nick said. "But sometimes good politics simply consists of doing the right thing. Did you ever think of that?"

"No."

"Think about it then. Honest to God, Erin, a person can get too cynical!"

"Sez who? Does she visit her husband's grave?"

"I don't know. Why don't you come along and find out?"

"Maybe I will. I'll ask Kay if it's all right."

Kay pondered the question as solemnly as if she had been asked to pronounce on some issue vital to national policy, but Rosemary interrupted her discussion with Joe long enough to nod approval. "A sweet innocent young girl will add a nice touch, won't she, Joe? 'Rosemary Marshall Helps American Youth Find Jesus. . . .' "

"Smart ass," Joe said amiably.

Suspecting that Rosemary's remark had been intended as a tactful hint as well as a dig at Joe, Erin selected a demure Laura Ashley print with a high neck and long sleeves. In lieu of a hat—an article of clothing she did not possess—she pinned a black satin bow onto her head. When she joined the other women on the porch, Kay looked her over from head to foot (low-heeled plain black pumps) and indicated she would pass. "I don't suppose you have a handkerchief. Young women never seem to carry handkerchiefs. Here, I brought an extra."

She always has to find something to correct, Erin thought,

accepting the linen square. But this time Kay's criticism didn't irritate her; it was reminiscent of all the grandmas and maiden aunts she had ever met, more amusing than annoying.

Nick, looking immensely dignified in a three-piece gray suit, drove up in one of the cars and got out to help the women in. Kay and Rosemary sat in the back; Erin joined Nick in the front seat. The car was an Oldsmobile—nothing flashy like a Cadillac or Lincoln, Erin thought cynically. Image, always the image.

Nick drove impeccably, back straight, both hands on the wheel, eyes front. When he spoke it was out of the corner of his mouth. "You look terrific. That's a pretty dress—if you don't mind my sounding like a sexist pig."

"If you don't know the difference between an acceptable compliment and a sexist remark, you'd better start learning," Erin retorted in the same undertone. "You look adorable yourself. I rather thought you'd appear in a chauffeur's uniform, though."

"Heaven forfend," Nick said piously. "We're just folks, we don't go in for fancy touches like that. Did you ever hear the story about the jar of caviar that defeated an incumbent senator from North Carolina? His opponent waved it at the voters and bellowed, 'Cam eats Red Russian fish eggs that cost two dollars! (Weren't those the good old days?) Do you want a senator who's too high and mighty to eat good old North Carolina hen eggs?' "

Erin's laughter was echoed by Rosemary's; leaning forward, the congresswoman said, "Tell her about Vic Meyers, Nick."

"Who was he?" Erin asked. "Should I know?"

"Not really," Nick said. "He ran for mayor of Seattle back in 1932. But he carried on the wildest political campaign of all time. He used to drive around town on a beer wagon, making speeches at street corners; once a wheel came off, and Vic fell out of the wagon, along with two kegs of beer. Whereupon he yelled, 'Drink is my downfall; vive le downfall!' "

"I'd love to do something like that," Rosemary said wistfully. "Tell her about the Gandhi stunt, Nick."

"No time, we're almost there," Nick said. "It wouldn't look right for us to arrive at church howling with laughter."

The church was as attractive as Nick had promised, and under ordinary circumstances Erin would have admired the rural setting, the simple dignity of the small red brick building and slender white spire, and the quiet graveyard sheltered by overhanging boughs of oak and maple and pine. As they made the turn and the church came into view, Nick let out an exclamation. "Something's happened. Rosemary, did you—"

"No. Stop here, Nick."

He had no choice. The crowd at the gate had spilled out into the drive and a van with prominent blue lettering blocked the way. Almost as prominent, in the forefront of the spectators, was a young man carrying a video camera with a portapak slung over his shoulder.

Nick leapt out of the car and ran around to the opposite side in a noble but futile effort to interpose himself between Rosemary and the camera. After only the briefest of pauses she had let herself out; a candidate couldn't enjoy the luxury of avoiding cameras, even when she had no idea of what was happening. Erin didn't know either, but she hurried to join Rosemary. Something about the atmosphere—the looks on the faces of the spectators, the agitated bleats of the tall, stooped man who appeared to be the minister—made her suspect that Rosemary was going to need all the support she could get.

"What's the idea, Paul?" Nick demanded.

The cameraman was the TV reporter Erin had met at the football game, back on his regular straight news beat. He twisted agilely around Nick and pointed the camera at Rosemary. "Mrs. Marshall, have you heard—"

The minister pushed him aside. "Oh, Mrs. Marshall, I am so very sorry! I wouldn't for the world have allowed—"

Cameraman, pastor, and Nick gyrated in a bizarre dance, babbling in counterpoint, until Rosemary said crisply, "It's all right, Nick—Mr. Jones. Young man, I'll be happy to answer questions later, but you'll have to wait until after the service. This is a church, not a political rally."

"Yes, ma'am, sorry, ma'am, but I guess you don't know."
His voice took on its professional tone. "This is Paul Dubermann for Channel 22. Mrs. Marshall, the cemetery here
was vandalized last night, and your husband's grave was the
main target. Would you mind telling our viewers . . ."

For a moment no one moved. Then Nick lunged at camera
and cameraman.

"Nick!" Rosemary's voice stopped him as if he had run
into a wall. She held out an imperious hand. "Give me your
arm, please. Mr. Jones?"

With Nick on one side and the pastor on the other, she
walked toward the cemetery. It made an effective tableau—
the small woman between her two tall escorts—but Erin felt
sure Rosemary was restraining Nick, not leaning on him for
support. The cameraman trotted alongside; the watchers,
murmuring sympathetically, fell back to let them through.

It wasn't until Erin started to follow that she realized Kay
stood frozen, her face as gray and rigid as the granite markers
in the grassy graveyard. She touched the older woman's arm.
"Are you all right?"

"What?" Kay turned a ghastly face to her. "Oh my
God. . . . Did he say—desecrated?"

"Why don't you get back in the car, Kay? There's no need
for you to see—"

"No. No. Rosemary will need me."

Erin made no further attempt to dissuade her, but she
wished Kay weren't so determined to be helpful. It wouldn't
help Rosemary if she collapsed or had hysterics—a distinct
possiblity if the images conjured up by the word Kay had
repeated turned out to be accurate. Coffins dragged out of the
earth, broken bodies, scattered bones. . . . She felt her stomach twist at the idea, and it would be much worse for Kay
than for her. Kay had clearly idolized Edward Marshall. . . .

To move from the side of the church toward the brick wall
behind the graveyard was to move forward in time—from the
worn marble slabs of the late eighteenth century to the ornate
monuments of the mid-nineteenth, and finally to the simple
granite markers of the recent past. The place was beautifully
tended; the grass was trimmed, the flowers fresh. None of

the stones was tilted or fallen. The black blotch on one grave stood out like blasphemy made visible.

Only blackened cinders and charred sticks remained of what had been burned. Smoke had stained the pale-gray stone, like dark fingers clawing at the name of Edward Marshall; a deformed, palm-shaped blotch covered the modest epitaph that described him as beloved husband, devoted father, and loyal servant of Virginia.

Kay's breath caught in a harsh hiss when she saw the grave, but Erin sensed her relief. Bad as it was, this was not the horror she had feared.

As they joined the others, Erin heard Mr. Jones say, ". . . no idea, until this—this—this person arrived a few minutes ago. Had I but known, I would certainly have warned you—"

"Yes, that's quite all right," Rosemary said. "Please don't distress yourself, Mr. Jones. No permanent damage appears to have been made."

The cameraman edged cautiously closer to Rosemary. "Would you care to make a statement?"

"There is very little one can say." Rosemary faced the camera. "Except to express pity for the person who could do such a terrible thing. I hope the police find him and give him the help he obviously needs."

She started to turn away, but the tireless tracker of news was not ready to give up. "Do you think there is a political motive behind this?"

"Certainly not," Rosemary said sharply. "The perpetrator is obviously mentally ill."

"What do you think—"

"You'll have to excuse me," Rosemary interrupted. She raised a gloved hand to hide her eyes. "This has been—this has come as quite a shock, surely you understand. . . . I've already kept the other worshipers waiting too long. Mr. Jones, may I. . . ."

The pastor moved to her side; as his body hid her, briefly, from the camera, she turned a dry-eyed, furious glare on Nick and whispered, "Cool it, Nick. Why don't you take Kay home and come back for me?"

"I'm staying," Kay said quietly.

Rosemary's lips shaped a word she dared not utter. "Erin," she said, with a meaningful look at Nick.

"Yes, ma'am," said Erin.

The two older women moved toward the church, escorted by the pastor. The cameraman's attempt to follow them was thwarted by Nick, who placed a large, heavy hand over the camera lens.

"Go right ahead," said the prospective victim, baring his teeth. "A little violence always films well."

"Son of a . . . gun," said Nick. "Okay, Erin, unhand me, I'm not going to do anything either of us would regret. Where'd you get this, Paul?"

"Get what?"

"You know what I mean. You must have gotten a tip from someone. Who, when, how? Come on, pal," he added with a smile that convinced neither of his listeners. "Fair exchange. I don't break your nose, you tell me what I want to know."

"You guessed it," the other admitted. Rosemary had disappeared; he lowered the camera from his shoulder. "Anonymous phone call, about half an hour ago."

"This isn't big enough for the nets, of course." Clearly Nick didn't believe that himself.

The other man grinned. "You've got to be kidding."

"Yeah. Who called—man or woman?"

Dubermann hesitated, and Nick abandoned threats for reasoned argument. "Come on, old buddy, you've got the story. Man or woman?"

Dubermann shrugged. "Oh, well, why not? Man."

"Accent?"

"Local redneck, replete with ain'ts and—er—four-letter adjectives," the other said, with a glance at Erin. "Sounded authentic, but you never know."

"No, sir, you shore don't, 'cause it ain't all that goddamn hard to fake," said Nick caustically. "Well. Thanks. Lay off her, will you? You've got plenty already."

Dubermann smiled sweetly.

He was persuaded not to turn on the camera while Nick

poked distastefully in the burned rubbish. "I already looked," Dubermann said. "Looks like sticks and leaves and stuff like that; no significant remains."

"The cops won't thank you for messing up the evidence," Nick muttered, messing it still more. "You have called them, haven't you?"

"No time. I barely made it myself."

"Yeah, sure. Half the fun of this business is being the one to break the news to the victim. Why don't you go find a phone and break it to the police?"

"What, leave the scene of the crime?"

"Hey, it is a crime, isn't it?" Nick exclaimed sarcastically. "I have an excuse for failing to report it—I'm escorting the distraught widow. What's yours?"

"Hmmm. Guess I'd better. Don't do anything newsworthy till I get back."

He loped off, hugging the camera.

With the van gone, Nick was able to park directly in front of the gate. He and Erin sat at the back of the church rather than parade down the aisle to the front pew where Rosemary sat with Kay. The church was almost full. A touching demonstration of piety, or an example of the public's interest in celebrities? Rosemary often attended services, and perhaps there had been time for the news to spread, locally at least. . . . With such thoughts to preoccupy her, Erin didn't derive much spiritual benefit from the service. Mr. Jones was not at his best, whatever that might have been. He cut the congregation's responses off more than once and rushed through his sermon in a rapid mumble.

Rosemary was forced to run a gauntlet on her way through the vestibule. The people who stopped her to express their indignation and sympathy were all friends and neighbors, with the kindest of motives, but it obviously cost Rosemary considerable effort to linger. As soon as she decently could, she made for the door. When she saw who was waiting outside, she stopped with a muffled exclamation and yanked her veil down over her face. Not only had Dubermann returned to his post, camera at the ready, but two uniformed police officers were with him.

"Lean on me and look frail," Nick muttered.

In what might have passed for modified mourning, face veiled and head bowed, Rosemary looked like a new-made widow instead of a woman who had received a minor, if unpleasant, shock. The effect on the policemen was exactly what Nick had hoped; they readily agreed to his suggestion that they come to the house later instead of subjecting Rosemary to the torment of a public inquisition, and by escorting her to her car they frustrated Dubermann's further efforts at photography and interrogation.

Once in the car and underway, Rosemary pulled off her hat and sank back against the cushions. "God," she muttered.

Kay patted her hand. "As soon as we get home you go up and lie down. I'll talk to the police—"

"No, you won't," Rosemary snapped. "Oh, Lord, Lord, Lord! Wait till Joe hears about this."

The rest of the drive passed in silence. After they had passed through the gates, Nick stopped the car.

"I'll close them and put up the chain. The boys of the press should be along pretty soon."

"Surely not," Erin exclaimed.

Rosemary's voice was dry and controlled. "When Jim Wright pushed Fauntroy around the Capitol in a wheelbarrow after losing a bet on a Redskins-Dallas game, he got full network coverage. Sunday is a slow news day. They'll be here."

*   *

ERIN HAD BELIEVED she was growing accustomed to the bizarre life-style of a candidate for public office, but the remainder of the afternoon showed her she had a thing or two yet to learn. The press did show up—all the Washington television stations, plus newspaper and press services. Nick had not barred the gates to keep them out, as she had innocently supposed, but only to sift the news people from ordinary curiosity seekers. The press was welcomed in, served food and drink—mostly the latter—and entertained by Nick and

Jeff, while Rosemary, closeted in conference with Joe and Will, prepared a statement.

Erin was kept busy serving drinks and making sandwiches. She expected to pass unnoticed, but she was foolish enough to tell the truth when a reporter asked her if she had been at the church. Instantly she found herself besieged, and was only rescued by the appearance of Rosemary, poised and cool, wearing a smile that contained exactly the proper blend of friendly welcome and pained distress.

The hounds and the cameras converged on Rosemary; Erin didn't need Nick's scowl and peremptory gesture to know this was her opportunity to escape. She locked herself in the bathroom next to the kitchen and cowered there until she heard Nick's voice.

"It's okay, they're gone."

When she emerged, the hallway was empty. She found Nick in the commons room, hands on his hips, staring disgustedly at the wreckage—empty glasses, crumbs, crumpled napkins, scraps of paper, cigarette butts and ashes.

"Why do we bother with these slobs?" he demanded.

The question was obviously rhetorical, and Erin didn't bother to answer it. "I'm sorry," she began.

"What for?" Nick yanked his tie off and stuck it in his pocket.

"For talking to that reporter. I should have kept out of the way, but he started asking me questions and it seemed rude not to answer—"

"Oh, that. You couldn't have done anything else. Have you ever been on television before?"

"They won't use that! I didn't say anything important—"

"None of us did. None of us ever does. But you're a helluva lot prettier than Kay and I."

He picked up a glass, looked helplessly around the room, and put it back on the table.

"I'll clean up," Erin said. "You probably have something more important to do."

"I should get in there," Nick muttered, gesturing in the direction of Rosemary's office. "If you're sure you don't mind—"

"No, I don't mind. But, Nick—"

"Hmmm?" He was already at the door.

"Never mind, you're busy."

"We'll talk later," Nick said, and went out.

As she washed glasses and emptied ashtrays and vacuumed the carpet, Erin's mind was free to wander, and the tracks her thoughts followed were not strewn with roses. The physical disorder was only a pale reflection of the emotional invasion that had taken place. An hour's work, and all signs of the former would be obliterated (except for a few rings on the coffee table—hadn't the press ever heard of coasters?). The other, deeper intrusion left worse scars, and it had no limits. Nothing in a candidate's past was sacrosanct or private, not any more. Ancient infidelities, misdemeanors, and even simple errors of judgment—all had been dragged into the light of day, discussed and dissected, served up as the butt of humor and of sermonizing.

Not that Rosemary's misfortune fell into any of those categories; she was a victim, not a villainess. In fact, the incident would probably win sympathy for her, if it was handled properly. And Rosemary knew how to handle it. She was a past master at making the most of "free media," as opposed to the political advertising she couldn't afford to buy. The object was to get your name and face before the public, as often and as prominently and as cheaply as possible. This particular story would have been a candidate's dream, except for its grisly associations. . . .

The idea that struck Erin was so ugly she stopped short, letting go of the vacuum handle. Surely not. Surely no one— not even Joe, who had been heard to say that no trick was too underhanded, no publicity stunt too low . . .

The vacuum cleaner buzzed angrily, and she began pushing again. No. Rosemary wouldn't tolerate anything so disgusting as desecrating her husband's grave.

Then who had done it, and for what unimaginable reason? Rosemary had denied there could be a political motive. Naturally she would; they all played that game. "I am certain my opponent would never stoop. . . ." In this case she was probably right. Bennett was too seasoned a campaigner not to know such a trick would only rebound to Rosemary's advantage.

The perpetrator had to be some anonymous lunatic. That was the only sensible explanation.

She didn't stop working until the room was spotless and the papers had been neatly stacked. The rest of the afternoon dragged. She was afraid to leave the house, for fear some enterprising newsman might be lurking; the sight of the knitting bags made her shudder, as she remembered the ugly little doll.

There was another bizarre incident. Two of them, seemingly pointless, apparently meaningless, in twenty-four hours? They seemed to have nothing in common, though, except their very lack of purpose. The only result of the first episode had been Kay's fainting spell, and she had denied there was any causal relationship, had insisted a child must have hidden the little bundle of rags in her yarn. Children, playing games. . . . Sam's grandchildren visited him occasionally; Mary Ann, one of the cleaning women, had a little girl. Possible, but unconvincing. Yet the alternatives were literally unimaginable. She couldn't think of any.

It was late in the day when the others began to drift in, Rosemary and Joe from her office, Kay from her room, Jeff from wherever he had been, and Nick from outside. He was in shirtsleeves, tieless and windblown; his flushed face and quick breathing suggested he had been working off the frustrations of the day in violent physical exercise. It wasn't until he went to the television that Erin realized why they had come together. On Sunday the news began at six, an hour later than was the case on weekdays.

Nick switched on all four sets. An old movie on one channel, football games on two of the others, golf on the fourth.

"Not on yet," Nick announced unnecessarily.

"What's the score?" Joe planted himself in front of one of the sets. A pile of writhing bodies broke up into individual players mouthing obscenities at each other and the referee.

"Dunno." Nick didn't have to ask which game he was concerned about. "They're playing in San Diego, aren't they? Damn!" A score had flashed on the screen. "Down by ten."

Rosemary had collapsed onto the couch. She had changed into slacks and an oversized white shirt, and her lipstick had worn off, except for a rim of red around her full lower lip. "Who's the good fairy who cleaned up the mess?" she asked.

"Had to be Erin," said Jeff, smiling. "I think she deserves a drink, don't you?"

"We all do," Joe announced, eyes glued to the screen. "Damn it, Gibbs, what kind of call is that, running the ball on third and five?"

"He made it," Nick said. "First down."

"Still a stupid call."

Nick passed out cans of beer to everyone but Kay, who accepted sherry. The 'Skins tied it up with a last-minute field goal, and the game went into overtime. But nobody watched. The six-o'clock news had begun on Channels 5 and 7.

Erin had hoped and believed Nick's judgment was in error; she gasped with surprise when her own face appeared on the nineteen-inch screen. The sound of her voice made her wince, and the content of what she had said made her cringe, but when she murmured distressfully Nick only laughed, and Joe said approvingly, "Cute as a tick and sweet as sugar. Adds a nice—" At that point Rosemary hit him with a rolled-up newspaper, and he shut up.

"Well," Joe said, when it was all over. "Not bad. Pretty good, in fact. You can't—"

"If you say, 'You can't buy publicity like that,' I'll scream," Rosemary said through clenched teeth.

"I wasn't going to say that."

"Then what . . . Oh, never mind. Erin, you handled yourself very well. You have real talent for this sort of thing. Though I'm not sure that's a compliment."

"I'll take it as such," Erin said with a smile. How could she have suspected Rosemary of setting up such a disgusting story? She added, "Watching you, I realize how much I have yet to learn. You were superb."

"She should be, she's the pro" was Joe's comment.

"I liked that touch about offering a reward," said Jeff.

"Joe's idea," Rosemary said briefly. "Is anyone else hungry? I could eat a horse on the hoof."

"I'll go and see—" Erin started to get up. Rosemary waved her back into her chair.

"You've done more than your share already. Why don't we send out for pizza or Chinese or something?"

After some wrangling they decided on Chinese, and Nick called the restaurant to place the order. As soon as he put it down, the phone rang. It was a private line, never used for business purposes, and when Nick heard the voice on the other end he looked both surprised and annoyed. "It's for you," he said, handing the phone to Erin.

"You looked great on TV," Fran said. "How does it feel to be a celebrity?"

"How did you get this number?" Erin demanded. "It's private and unlisted."

"Oh, I copied the number when I was there," Fran said without shame. "Don't worry, I won't bug you, but this is an unusual occasion. I mean, what an awful thing! How is she? What do you think. . . ."

Erin was painfully conscious of the listeners as Fran rambled on. Rosemary had picked up a paper and was politely pretending to read it, but Joe and Nick stared in critical silence. Finally she cut Fran off with a brusque "That's crazy, Fran. I have to hang up now. Don't call me, I'll call you. Good-bye."

Obviously an apology was called for, but it infuriated her to have to make it on behalf of Fran, who wasn't in the least repentant.

"I'm sorry about that. It was my roommate, the one who was here yesterday. I'll warn her about using that number again. She's such a fan of Rosemary's—"

"Not your fault," Nick said. "What's crazy?"

"I beg your pardon?"

"You said, 'That's crazy.' "

"Oh, that." Erin laughed. "She thinks we—you—have a poltergeist."

"Poltergeist?" Kay repeated blankly.

Evidently she was the only one who didn't know what the word meant. "Doesn't fit," Joe said, masticating his cigar. Nick grinned and shook his head. Rosemary frowned and shook her head. Jeff rolled his eyes in sardonic, silent commentary; and from Will's lair in the corner came a soft, pedantic voice that made Erin turn and stare. How long had Will been there? She hadn't seen him come in.

"The word means 'racketing spirit' in German. Phenomena include objects flying around the room without visible means of locomotion, fires starting without apparent cause, raps and knocks, furniture moving—"

"Doesn't fit," Joe repeated. "The fire in the graveyard was caused by a weirdo with a match. And nobody except us knows about . . ." His eyes focused on Erin.

She knew she was suspected of something, but she didn't understand what it could be until Nick spoke up in her defense.

"Don't glare at Erin, Joe. I was the one who told Fran about the other fires. I don't even remember how the subject came up, but I didn't think it was important."

"Were there other fires?" Erin asked.

"Two," Jeff said. "Nothing major. The first one occurred—when was it, Nick? A week ago, Saturday, I think. A wastebasket. We thought it was started by one of Joe's filthy cigars."

"It wasn't," Joe said. "But it wasn't a goddamn poltergeist either. Your roommate sounds a little loony, kiddo."

There was a general murmur of agreement. Then Jeff said, "Actually, the great majority of the poltergeist cases that have come under investigation were proved to have been caused by human agents. Children playing tricks."

"Correct," said Will. "The little dears were incredibly skilled at sleight of hand. Like any good stage magician, they knew how to distract the audience's attention from what they were doing—pointing with one hand while they used the other to tug on a thread or strike a match."

"Kids," Joe muttered. "Can't stand 'em myself."

"Not always kids," Jeff said. "Sometimes the perpetrator was an adolescent or young adult. Emotionally disturbed, of course."

The silence that followed was distinctly uncomfortable.

Erin had the feeling that they were all carefully not looking at her.

Then Nick said briskly, "I'll go pick up the food. Want to come along for the ride, Erin?"

The dogs were out. They fell on Erin with howls of rapture, and when Nick opened the car door, Tiny shoved past him and climbed into the passenger seat. He had to be hauled out, protesting vehemently, and he made another attempt, this time on the driver's side, when Nick got out to open the gate. After he had closed the gate both dogs sat in the drive baying dismally as they drove away.

The dogs' antics amused Erin, but not enough to make her forget what was on her mind. She was trying to think how to introduce the subject—and whether to mention it at all—when Nick said suddenly, "Damn that bastard Joe. Did you see him leer when I asked you to come with me?"

"I didn't notice."

"Maybe I'm too self-conscious. But I'm getting tired of all the jokes about me and the women on the staff, and what a stud I am—or think I am. I mean, hell, this is a job. I'm not about to risk my professional status by fooling around."

Distracted though she was, Erin couldn't let that pass. "Then you'd better stop grabbing people and nuzzling them on the ear."

"That was precisely the incident to which I was indirectly referring," Nick said, with freezing dignity. "Fear not, it won't happen again."

"Oh?"

"No. From now on you'll have to eat your heart out and soak your lonely pillow with tears of remorse, unless, of course, you come groveling to me and plead with me to reconsider."

"Nick, can't you ever be serious?"

"Admit it," Nick said, laughter lightening his voice. "I'm not so bad. You could probably learn to like me if you gave yourself half a chance."

"Mmmm."

"What's the matter?"

"What? Sorry, I was thinking about something else."

"I noticed. What is it? Tell Uncle Nick."

"You'll think I'm paranoid."

"Maybe, maybe not. You'll never know unless you spit it out."

"They think I'm the poltergeist."

"Who thinks?"

"Don't tell me it didn't occur to you."

"No," Nick said. "It didn't."

The moon had not yet risen; the only light came from the car's headlights casting twin spears of brightness through the dark. Erin shivered, and Nick said, "You should have brought a sweater. My heater doesn't work too well; I was going to replace it, but—"

"You don't have to change the subject. I need to talk about it. Face it, Nick; I was here a week ago Saturday. Was that the first time anything odd happened?"

"Are you kidding? Odd is the norm in this business." After a moment he went on, "Put it out of your mind, Erin. Last night's fire couldn't have anything to do with the others. The cemetery isn't guarded, any one of a million people could have done the job. You read, every now and then, about some weird cult holding ceremonies in a cemetery—"

"By itself it doesn't mean anything." Erin was determined to play devil's advocate. "But add it to the other things. That awful little doll, for instance. Why won't anyone talk about it? A child didn't put it in the knitting bag; I've seen kids around, but they don't come in the house."

"What other explanation can there be?"

"I don't know. 'Too many accidents.' That's what she said. Kay. Not to me, it was as if she were talking to herself."

"Kay said that?" Nick came to an abrupt stop as an octagonal red sign loomed up ahead. His outflung arm caught Erin painfully across the chest, and she let out a yelp. "You didn't have to do that! I had my seat belt fastened!"

"Well, see, my seat belts aren't exactly. . . . Sorry about that. I was thinking about what you said, and forgot about the stop sign. The traffic cops around here lie in wait for me, I swear they do. I sure don't want to be stopped tonight after drinking that beer. Can't you see the headlines? 'Marshall Aide Ticketed for DWI, Beautiful Redheaded Passenger Unable to Walk Straight Line. . . . ' "

Erin thought he was trying to change the subject, but after they had turned onto the highway and were proceeding at a discreet speed toward town, he said, " 'Too many accidents.' I suppose you could call the wastebasket fire an accident; the other one was in the stableyard, day before yesterday. Another accident, but a minor one—no damage done, just a pile of dried weeds. The only serious accident that's happened recently was Kay's, when she hurt her hand. From her point of view that was one too many, I guess."

"She sounded really strange, Nick," Erin insisted. "It was the day I moved in. Day before yesterday. 'Too many accidents,' and something about things coming in threes . . . She was out of it, groggy with painkillers, it was like her mind was somewhere else. Off in outer space, or wandering in the past—"

"Oh, no," Nick exclaimed. "No, that's too far out."

"What are you talking about?"

"Too far out," Nick repeated. "But . . . that's how he died, you know. Edward Marshall, Rosemary's husband. An accident. He was cleaning his gun."

Chapter
Five

WHEN NICK SLOWED to turn into the driveway the gate stood wide open and one of the dogs—the older of the pair—lay in the middle of the road.

"Damn it," Nick exploded, coming to a crashing halt. "Who opened that gate? Samson—Samson! If he's hit—"

"He's just resting," Erin said with relief, as the old dog got lazily to his feet and ambled toward them.

"Sure, right on the road. Really intelligent animals. . . ." He got out of the car. "Inside, Samson. Move it, you furry moron. I suppose that stupid Tiny is halfway to Richmond by now."

His shout produced a crashing in the underbrush across the road, and then Tiny himself, delighted to find a friend. He hurled himself at Nick; after considerable discussion and exercise Nick got him inside the gate, the car inside the gate, and the gate closed.

"Somebody must have come after we left," he said as they

proceeded along the drive at a cautious crawl, while both dogs hurled themselves merrily at the wheels.

"More reporters?" Erin asked.

"I doubt it. My profession isn't noted for its manners, but trespass is against the law. There's only one person I can think of who would barge in without an invitation and not bother to close the gate. . . . Yep. That's his car."

Presumably he knew; Erin recognized the Mercedes insignia, but the sober dark-blue vehicle looked very much like the one that belonged to Kay.

Philips Laurence's arrival must have preceded their own by only a few minutes. He was still on his feet and in full verbal spate when they walked into the room.

". . . saw it on the evening news. Naturally I hurried right over. Why didn't you call me?"

"It would have been a waste of time, wouldn't it?" Rosemary said. "You just said you were at the races this afternoon. Thank you, Nick, Erin—put the cartons on the table and we'll help ourselves."

Reminded of their presence, and his manners, Laurence turned his peculiar smile on Erin. "Ah, the ingenue. You performed charmingly, my dear. Hello, Nick."

Nick's brusque response did nothing to lighten the atmosphere, which was stiff with interwoven currents of hostility. Joe's scowl would have soured milk, and Jeff, his head bent over his work, fairly radiated dislike. There was no sound or movement from Will's corner.

"I'll get plates and silverware," Erin said, and retreated to the kitchen.

When she came back, Laurence had arranged himself before the fireplace, one arm resting on the mantel. He looked like an advertisement from *Country Life* or *The Pink Sheet*. His coat was not pink, but it had been cut by a master tailor; riding breeches and polished boots, scarf and narrow gold stockpin completed an ensemble which should have looked affected, but which did not. He wore it with such splendid self-confidence that he could have walked down the meanest streets of Washington at midnight and not appeared improperly dressed.

Laurence was talking again—or perhaps he was still talking.

". . . crack down on these blasphemous local cults. One can't permit such things to go unpunished. You remember the case in Maryland when a group of young degenerates disinterred the body of a child and used its—"

"Never mind, Philips," Rosemary said, her face twisting in disgust.

"Yeah, for God's sake," Joe exclaimed. "You trying to spoil my appetite? Sorry we can't ask you to stay, we only ordered for seven—not knowing you were about to honor us with a visit."

Laurence responded to this demonstration of bad manners with a raised eyebrow and a knowing smile; Kay roused herself to make the proper response.

"I'm sure there's plenty, if you would care to join us, Philips. Chinese food, you know; they always send so much. . . . I'm not especially hungry."

"I am," said Joe.

His rudeness was wasted effort; Laurence simply ignored him and went on lecturing. Not only did he dominate the conversation, but he wielded his chopsticks with a skill that infuriated Nick; the latter's attempts to imitate it only succeeded in flipping sticky wads of food all over the room. Laurence was maddeningly tolerant, even when a blob of rice landed on his immaculate knee. "You're trying too hard, young fellow. One's grasp must be delicate and flexible, responsive to the slightest muscular effort. . . ."

Laurence's admirers considered him a modern Renaissance man, astonishingly well versed in all subjects. His enemies, who were legion, insisted that the information he spouted so glibly had been fed to him by a cadre of aides and had been memorized instead of assimilated. That evening he treated his listeners to a lecture on the subject of superstition. They were too tired or too courteous or—in Erin's case, too morbidly fascinated—to interrupt him.

"Some claim that these blasphemous ceremonies go back to prehistoric times, and that the masked, horned god became the Black Goat of the Sabbat, the incarnate god of evil. I remember seeing at Lascaux—''

This was too much for Will, who roused himself long enough to murmur, "What a memory you've got, Philips. The caves were closed to visitors in 1963."

"To the ordinary tourist, yes," Laurence replied smoothly. "M. Benedict, the curator, was kind enough to show me around in 1986."

Erin, who was watching Will, saw his lips shape a word that looked like "Liar," preceded by a colorful adjective; but he chose not to speak aloud, and Laurence went on.

"As I was saying . . . Whatever the origins—and I myself refuse to dignify these perversions by the name of religion—as satanism exists today it is evil, pure and simple." He smiled gently at Erin. "The word disturbs you, doesn't it? It isn't the fault of your generation that words such as good and evil, right and wrong make you more uncomfortable than the easy obscenities. In this case you can blame it on your elders and be entirely correct. The so-called science of psychiatry—an oxymoron if ever there was one—has attempted to deny the reality of spiritual sin—''

"Bullshit," Nick said suddenly. "We're afraid of words like good and evil because they're too subjective. Hitler thought the Jews were evil. Torquemada burned heretics alive in the name of God. The witch-hunters of Salem believed they were serving the good—''

"Ah, yes, the classic examples," Laurence said. "My young friend, you are heading blindly into a logical impasse. Do you consider the rape of children a morally neutral activity?''

"Of course not," Nick said. "But—''

"Do you believe that a few years in a comfortable mental institution is fitting punishment for a man who molests infants?''

"Hell, no; burn him alive," Joe shouted. "Are you running for Pope, Laurence, or are you just trying to be disgusting?''

Philips passed his hand over his waving, suspiciously brown hair. "I'm sorry if I offend the faint of heart, but it appears to me you may have a very practical need to consider these matters. They are disgusting; I couldn't agree more. Are you too squeamish to consider them dispassionately and arrive at the inevitable conclusion?''

"No, I guess I'm just too stupid," Joe said. "What conclusion, professor?"

"That someone with a corrupt soul—call it a sick mind, if that make⌐ you feel better—has selected Rosemary as the object of his hatred. The desecration of her husband's grave, the poppet in the knitting bag—"

"The what?" Kay exclaimed.

"Such a charming word for that malignant object," Laurence said. "You may be more familiar with it in its classical manifestation, an image of wax or clay which is used in homeopathic magic to inflict harm on the person it represents. A variety of materials can be used, of course; certain North American Indian tribes simply sketched the outline of the human figure in sand or ashes and then stabbed it, thereby, they believed, injuring the body of the enemy. You'll find a full discussion in *The Golden Bough*."

"Oh no, I won't," said Joe, heaving himself out of his chair. "Is there any more mo shu pork?" He kept up a loud monologue as he rummaged among the white paper containers. "If nobody else wants this egg roll, I may as well finish it. . . . Kay, don't you have a doctor's appointment tomorrow? Who's going to drive you? Somebody ate all the chow mein. . . . You ought to get some sleep, Rosemary, we've got a breakfast meeting tomorrow."

Laurence laughed. "*Sufficit*, Joe. You've made your point. Good night, Rosemary. I wanted to discuss something with you, but it's obvious I won't be allowed to carry on a sensible conversation this evening. Young Nick—Jeff—Kay, my dear lady, you do look exhausted—my apologies. . . ."

He stopped in front of Erin and stood looking down at her. Then he placed the palm of his hand on her cheek and tilted her head back so that he was looking deep into her eyes. It was a gesture as offensively intimate as an embrace, and it was much more painful than it appeared; his fingers pressed into her skin and his thumb dug into the sensitive spot at the juncture of throat and chin. *"À bientôt,"* he said, and sauntered out of the room.

Erin raised her hands to her flaming cheeks. She didn't believe for a moment that Laurence's gesture had been sensual, or even affectionate; his eyes had been as cold as pebbles and he wasn't the sort of man who would make such a blatant approach. What his reasons might have been she could not imagine; but it wasn't long before she found out.

Joe's voice was ominously calm. "Who told him about the goddamn doll?"

Erin's breath caught. There had only been seven of them present that evening, the inner circle and one outsider—herself. Laurence's gesture of intimacy had been delicately designed to suggest that there was a bond between them, and she knew she looked as guilty as a murderer caught with the smoking gun in his hand.

The room was still, Rosemary's soft voice echoed like a shout. "I did."

She opened the box on the table and took out a cigarette. It was the first time Erin had seen her smoke; deliberately she struck a match, lit the cigarette and inhaled deeply. "I did. Is there any reason why I shouldn't have?"

"Well, for one thing it apparently prompted that asinine lecture we just sat through," Joe grumbled. "What the hell made you do it?"

Rosemary exhaled a cloud of smoke that veiled her face like fog. "I just happened to mention it in the course of conversation. It was a meaningless, mildly amusing story, nothing more."

"Amusing?" Joe repeated incredulously.

"That's right," Kay said. "Leave Rosemary alone, Joe, she's had a horrible day."

For a moment no one spoke. Then Nick said, "I'll go down and close the gate. His lordship won't bother."

"Never mind, I'll do it on my way out." Joe got heavily to his feet. "Coming, Jeff?"

"Ready when you are." Jeff gathered his papers and put them in his briefcase.

Rosemary's confession had restored Erin to favor. Joe threw

her a friendly " 'Night, kid,'' and Jeff smiled. Rosemary and Kay left the room together, the former remarking, "I'll help Kay get into her jammies, Erin; you've done more than your share today.''

Erin caught Nick's eye. He shook his head; after the two women had left, he said in a low voice, "That was a tactful request for privacy. I guess they have some things to talk about.''

"So do I," Erin said.

Nick began piling dirty plates and empty cartons onto a tray, his back to her. "Why did he do that?'' she demanded. "You didn't believe—''

"Just stirring up trouble," Nick answered, without turning around. "Typical Laurence tactic. Divide and conquer.''

"It worked, didn't it? You did believe I was the one who told him. That I'm a spy, an informer—''

"Now listen, Erin—''

"You did." Erin picked up the loaded tray and started toward the kitchen. "All of you believed it. If Rosemary hadn't spoken up—''

"Goddamn it!" Nick ran after her. She slammed the tray down on the kitchen table; the towers of empty food cartons tottered and spilled. "You're getting egg foo yung all over the floor," Nick exclaimed.

"So, too bad. I'll clean it up. That's what I'm here for, washing dishes and being the scapegoat.''

Nick rolled his eyes, took a deep, quivering breath and began to count. ". . . nine, ten. Okay. Would you just listen to me for a minute? How about a friendly cup of coffee?''

"I have to clean up this mess.''

"I'll clean it up. Sit down! I mean, *please* sit down.''

She sat with folded arms, glowering, while he picked up the spilled cartons and made coffee. Then he took the chair across from her at the table.

"This way of life isn't easy to understand," he began, "but you'd better try, because things are going to get worse before they get better. Everybody is short on sleep, uptight, on the defensive. Right now Rosemary's chances of winning this race are anyone's guess. She's still behind in the polls, but she's moving up; and in these last crucial weeks some unexpected incident could make all the difference—even a careless statement, by Rosemary or Buzz.

"Buzz knows he's in trouble. He'd give what's left of his mean little soul to get something on Rosemary. The media people are always looking for a scoop, and dirt makes more interesting reading than positive news. You could pick up a nice piece of change from a number of sources if you had inside information on campaign strategy, or damaging information."

"Is there anything like that to be found?" Erin asked coldly.

"No. Our campaign strategy is about as subtle as a bulldozer, and as for damaging information . . . One of the things that attracted me to Rosemary is the fact that except for the unfortunate accident of birth that made her female, she's a picture-perfect candidate. Not too old, not too young, easy on the eyes but certainly not glamorous; good speaking voice, excellent debater—and clean as a whistle. There is literally nothing in her background that could hurt her. Devoted wife, mother, grandmother; honor student; she never gets drunk, never plays around, she even quit smoking a few years back. When the great marijuana issue arose a few years ago, some reporters asked her if she'd ever indulged, and her answer was 'No, bourbon has always been good enough for me.' "

"Wasn't that rather flippant?" Erin was in a mood to be critical.

"It was the way she said it." Nick's face had relaxed into a half-smile. "And the fact that she never drinks in public except for an occasional glass of wine. It reduced the whole business to nonsense. Oh, well, never mind that. What I'm getting at is that political spies aren't unheard of. The fact that Reagan had Carter's notes before their big debate, and knew in advance exactly what Carter was going to say, helped him enormously. It needn't be anything as underhanded as passing on strategically important information; a slip of the tongue could hurt, and people like Laurence are skilled at setting up traps for the unwary. I know you didn't tell him

about that damned poppet; but you might have, in all innocence, without realizing it could hurt.''

"How could it?"

"I can't imagine how," Nick admitted, frowning. "It doesn't
make sense, not even to Philips Laurence; his performance tonight was designed to annoy and stir up dissension and mistrust.
But I didn't fall for it, Erin. Honest. Even if Rosemary hadn't
'fessed up, I wouldn't have suspected you.''

"Why not? I'm the logical suspect—the outsider, the
stranger in your midst. How do you know I wouldn't sell
Rosemary out for cold cash?''

"My dear girl, you are talking to an experienced, hard-
headed, cynical political analyst," Nick exclaimed. "Do you
think I could be taken in by a pretty face, a gorgeous figure,
a pair of big green eyes?''

"Could you?''

"You're damned right I could." Nick planted both elbows
on the table and gazed at her soulfully. "Take me in. Please?''

"There you go again," Erin exclaimed. "Look, Nick, I
don't mind you lecturing me or even correcting me; you know
a lot more about this insane business of politics than I do,
and I want to learn. How often do I have to repeat this? How
many times do I have to tell you I only want to be treated
like—''

"Now who's lecturing?''

"Me. And you had it coming. Maybe you weren't trying
to be condescending, maybe you wanted to change the subject. Is that it? If you . . . Where are you going? Don't you
dare walk out on me in the middle of a discussion.''

"I'm just going to wash the dishes," Nick said, suiting the
action to the words. "It's a dirty trick to leave them for Sarah.
No, I do not want you to help me, I want you to sit tight and
talk to me. What's your point?''

She much preferred this tone to his flattery. "My point is
that although you may not suspect me of pulling these tricks,
someone else obviously does.''

"Laurence?''

"You saw it. That long, rambling lecture of his also had a
point, and he drove it home when he—when he touched me

in that offensive way. The disturbed adolescent, trying to cause trouble and gain attention—''

"Wait a minute.'' Nick turned, his hands dripping water. "Laurence didn't say that, Jeff did. Or Will—I forget which. And you sure as hell are no adolescent.''

"But if I had done those things it would be because I was mentally disturbed,'' Erin argued. "Not because I was in league with the powers of evil.''

Nick's eyes widened. "Hold it. I think I see what you're driving at, but if you will forgive me for saying so, your oratorical style is somewhat lacking in coherence. Nobody in his right mind could suppose—''

"That I had sold myself to the devil. That's what I said! Don't be so obtuse, Nick. Laurence isn't stupid. If there is something sinister about the fires, I am, as I pointed out, the obvious suspect. All that talk of his about black magic was just to cover up the fact that he can't think of a sensible motive. He loves showing off and sounding theatrical, he knows as well as we do that people don't . . . people . . .''

Her voice faltered as she saw the look on Nick's face.

"But they do, though,'' he said slowly. "Don't they?''

"Yes.'' Erin's eyes fell. "I guess some people do. I've read about cases in the newspaper—''

"I've read about them in *The Golden Bough*, as a matter of fact. Did you notice the way he tossed off the name, as if it were some esoteric work none of us illiterate slobs had ever heard of? I don't know why that bastard affects me the way he does; usually I'm pretty good with a snappy comeback, but I was still trying to think of one when he pulled that stunt on you.''

"You're grinding your teeth,'' Erin said. "And getting off the subject.''

"Ain't it the truth. Point is, it's barely conceivable that some religious fanatic or dabbler in black magic is trying to put a hex on Rosemary.''

"No, that's not the point. The point is, so what? I haven't read *The Golden Bough*, but I've heard Fran talk about such people—she's into spiritualism and astrology and that sort of thing—and they are as harmless as they are crazy. They can stick pins in waxen images all they want, they aren't going to hurt anyone that way. By the way—were there any pins in that doll?''

"No. Not that I noticed." Nick placed the last of the plates in the rack to drain and dried his hands.

"Damn it, Erin, I don't even want to think about this. It's disgusting, frightening, and far-out."

"You'll have to excuse my biased viewpoint, but I find the idea of a wandering lunatic more attractive than the possibility that one of us—me, for instance—is responsible."

"I see what you mean. What about Laurence? It would be just like him to focus suspicion on an innocent party in order to divert it from himself. I've never trusted the bastard. It's completely out of character for him to support Rosemary. He despises everything she stands for."

"Maybe he's in love with her."

"That's the accepted theory." Nick looked dubious. "As a self-appointed expert on the romantic passion, I can't see him as an infatuated lover. He was Ed Marshall's friend originally, and I suppose it's barely possible that he has a few decent feelings under that cynical facade—old loyalties, sentimental memories of boyhood days. . . ."

"Why not? He can't be all bad. Nobody is."

"Bless your sweet little heart. I hope you can hang on to that idea. How about more coffee?"

"No, thanks. It's late and I'm tired. Don't you ever go home?"

"I am home. I've moved into the overseer's shack, next to Sam's quarters."

"You gave up your apartment?"

"Had to, couldn't afford it. It was no problem; the furniture was rented too. I'll be on the spot from now on, so feel free to lean out your window and scream for help if the occasion arises."

"I fondly hope no such occasion does arise." But she felt a sense of relief, all the same, to know that the isolated household of women now had an able-bodied man on the premises. Sam was too old and too deaf to be of much use in case . . . In case of what? she asked herself. I sound like some feeble-witted antifeminist.

Nick hung the dishtowel neatly on the rack and came toward her. "How about a friendly good-night kiss to take the nasty taste out of my mouth and send me rejoicing to the pallet in my hovel, among the lowest and meanest of the humble servants of the mighty?"

"Not on your life." Erin ducked as he swooped upon her, arms extravagantly outstretched. "I wouldn't want to be responsible for making you break your sworn word."

"Not ready to grovel yet? Oh, well, I'll wait." He blew her a kiss from the door. "Sleep well."

Somewhat to her surprise, Erin did.

Chapter
Six

CONTRARY TO popular opinion, the Congress of the United States does not usually take four-day weekends. It is true, however, that in even-numbered years members try not to schedule important debates or roll calls on Mondays and Fridays during the autumn. One third of the Senate seats and all those of the House go up for grabs every two years, and members who aren't campaigning one time will be another. A little consideration for others makes life easier all around.

Rosemary was luckier than many of her colleagues because her home base was so close to Washington. Candidates from the West Coast spent precious hours commuting and almost as much recovering from jet lag.

By nine o'clock on Monday morning Rosemary had left the house, driven by Nick. Where they were going and what their schedule was Erin didn't know; no one had bothered to inform her. Of course she had no right to expect them to do so, but the more her involvement and expertise increased, the more she resented the routine chores she would once have accepted without question. Politics was addictive. It was also a lot less difficult to comprehend than she had supposed—complicated, maddeningly unpredictable (which only added to its fascination), but not intellectually daunting. Despite the fact that many of the processes could be reduced to charts and numbers, it was more of an art than a science—the art, some might say, of manipulating people's minds. But it wasn't that simple. The techniques of political manipulation were pretty crude, in fact, and the most consoling thing about them was that they didn't always work. Why did a candidate's populist message bring him an overwhelming victory in one state primary, and bomb everywhere else? Why was a group of voters bewitched by a candidate who offered them nothing but platitudes and a practiced actor's smile, when they turned thumbs down on another man with precisely the same attributes?

There was another, more personal reason for her let-down feeling that morning. In the cold light of day some of the ideas she had raised the night before seemed frivolous and unreal. But Nick had raised another fear, and this one was not for herself. She cared about Rosemary. She cared about all of them, in different ways. Kay was a pain, of course, but Erin was becoming accustomed to her foibles; they bothered her far less than they had at first. Even Christie seemed to be mellowing a little. The only person she didn't know much about, the real enigma of the group, was Will. Who the devil was he, anyway, and what did he do when he wasn't wandering in and out of the house? He treated Rosemary like a casual older brother, and she teased and criticized him—and obviously depended on his advice.

During lunch break she asked Jackson about him. Jackson seemed surprised that she didn't know. "He's the research honcho. Teaches history at Charlottesville. He's kind of weird—almost like a caricature of your absentminded-professor type—but he's a nice-enough guy."

He didn't know how Will and Rosemary came to be acquainted. Nor, obviously, did he care.

As luck would have it, Erin was still in the commons room finishing her lunch when Kay came looking for her. Kay could

make her feel guilty just by looking at her, and her look now
was distinctly critical. Brusquely and without preamble she
informed Erin that she would have to drive her to the doctor.
"My appointment is at one, so if you're quite finished eating . . ."

Knowing how reluctant Kay was to have anyone else driving the car, Erin wondered whether this was a signal honor
or the reverse. The wink and grin Jackson gave her, behind
Kay's back, made her suspect it was an honor nobody wanted.

She backed the Mercedes out of the garage with her foot
quivering on the gas pedal. Kay sat rigid as a poker, tense
with anxiety. "I wouldn't have asked you," she muttered,
"but the mail is picking up and you're the only one who . . .
Watch out for that rut—and don't hit the cat, do you see
him?"

Not only had Erin seen the cat, it was a good ten feet off
the driveway, squatting in the grass. In an effort to distract
Kay's attention from her driving, she said, "Rosemary seems
to be very fond of cats. How many are there?"

"Fifteen or twenty, I guess. There's a tree branch down—
you'd better go around it. . . . It was Congressman Marshall
who loved cats, actually. Rosemary doesn't really care. . . .
You're a little too far to the right, Erin, you're going to scrape
the fence. What was I saying?"

"I don't know," Erin said under her breath. She got
through the gate safely and negotiated the turn.

"Oh, the cats. Rosemary is fond of animals, of course,
but she doesn't care about them as much as Edward—
Congressman Marshall—did. Their presence is a tribute to
his memory, one might say."

Like Edward Marshall's office? For some reason Erin didn't
find the idea as touching as she ought to have done. It made
her think of Queen Victoria's morbid obsession with the relics
of her dear dead Albert—having his clothes laid out every
evening, sleeping with his nightshirt clutched in her arms.

The distraction didn't serve for long; Kay was soon pointing out fallen leaves, twigs, and pebbles, and warning her to
watch out for them. It was a beautiful autumn day, with a

brisk breeze sending clouds scampering across the blue bowl of the sky. The road was walled with tapestries of living color—scarlet and crimson and amber, the deepening gold of maple leaves. It would have been a pleasant drive if Kay had kept quiet.

Erin made it to Middleburg without damage, except to her nerves, and stopped at the blinking light in the middle of town. Flanking the intersection were the two handsome old stone structures that housed Middleburg's most popular restaurant-inns. The one on the left boasted a terrace that ran the length of the house; tables and chairs provided al-fresco dining, but on this cool day only a few fresh-air enthusiasts lingered over coffee and dessert.

"Turn left, Erin," Kay ordered.

"Right. I mean—yes, I know. There's a car coming."

"Park wherever you can find a space. There's one there. . . . No, it's next to a fire hydrant. The parking lot is down the street, but if you can find something closer. . . . It's a pity this town has become so . . . Look at that woman, did you ever see such a sight? Why anyone with a rear end like hers would wear stretch pants . . . Oh."

Her voice changed so dramatically that Erin had to look. It was not the unfortunate woman's rump that had affected Kay, however. The cause of her surprise was not hard to find. Posed and poised, halfway down the steps that led to the terrace of the restaurant, he had obviously seen them too.

"I wonder what Philips is doing here," Kay said.

"Having lunch, I suppose." Erin turned and proceeded at a decorous crawl, looking for a place to park. "Doesn't he live around here?"

"No, he lives in Maryland—Chevy Chase. There's a spot."

It wasn't the space Erin would have chosen for her first try at parallel parking someone's cherished Mercedes, and the fact that Philips was walking toward them, watching interestedly, didn't help. It took her two tries, but she finally made it without scraping the curb. As soon as she turned off the key, Laurence opened Kay's door.

"What a pleasant surprise," he said, smiling wickedly.

Kay accepted the hand he offered with a look that was

almost coquettish. It occurred to Erin that Kay was the only one of Rosemary's entourage who had never indicated dislike or disapproval of Laurence. Was it possible . . .

"Surprise, my foot," Kay said. "What are you up to, Philips?"

"Waiting for you, of course." He raised her hand to his lips.

Grudgingly Erin admitted he was one of the few men she knew who could carry off such a gesture. And he certainly knew how to dress. Ordinarily she paid little attention to men's clothing, but Laurence's was spectacularly suited to his public persona and his lean, trim figure. He would have been a good-looking man except for those cold, knowing eyes and the cynical twist of his lips. The fresh breeze had not dislodged a single lock of his hair. Erin smiled to herself as she remembered Nick's comment: "He doesn't go to a barber; his hairdresser comes to him, if you please. The same guy who does Reagan's hair—you noticed it's the same style, didn't you?"

"I had a luncheon appointment with a friend," Philips went on, retaining his hold on Kay's hand.

Her smile almost matched his in cynicism. "A useful sort of friend, I presume?"

"You wound me to the heart!" He dropped her hand to press his over the organ in question. "I lingered in the hope of seeing you. I had hoped for a little private chat."

"Oh, indeed? Well, I haven't time now, Philips. My appointment is at one."

"Yes, I know." Again they exchanged knowing smiles— almost, Erin thought, like lovers who couldn't be bothered to conceal their liaison. "Afterward, then. Come, I'll escort you to the door."

She took his arm. Erin followed; for once she didn't mind being overlooked. But when they reached the doctor's office Laurence took possession of her with the cool aplomb of an arresting officer. "I'll show Erin the sights of Middleburg, such as they are. We'll be back in half an hour."

Erin got out one word—"But"—before she was inter-

rupted. "I need your assistance in selecting a gift—for a lady.
You can't refuse, my dear."

Laurence's glance at Kay implied she was the lady in question. Her faint frown disappeared. "I'll wait for you here,"
she said, turning into the office. "Don't be long."

Outflanked and outmaneuvered, Erin had no choice but to
go with him. Like Joe, she wondered what he was up to. Was
he planning to apologize for his performance the night before? An apology was certainly called for, but she doubted
Philips Laurence was the man to make it.

Laurence's face was well known because of his television
appearances; people stared and pointed, and one woman
stopped him to ask for his autograph.

He made quite a performance of it, murmuring compliments and deprecating remarks; but as they walked away,
leaving the fan in a state of gaping adoration, he said, "I've
seen sheep with more intelligent faces."

Erin said nothing, but her reaction would have been clear
to a less perceptive student of human nature than Laurence.
With a sidelong smile he said, "You think I'm a twenty-four-
carat son of a bitch, don't you? Well, you're mistaken. It's
only twenty-two carats." While she was trying to decide
whether to respond—and what to say—he went on, in quite a
different voice, "Do you like to shop?"

Another loaded question. If she refused to accept the
stereo-typed female role, she was letting him manipulate her
into a flat-out lie.

"I do," Laurence said, without waiting for an answer.
"The truth is, there's not much else to do in Middleburg.
Oh, we have our tedious historic buildings and our boring
quaint inns, and I could lead you up and down the streets
spouting data. . . . For instance, did you know Middleburg
got its name because it is halfway between Alexandria and
Winchester? Do you care? Does it matter? I mean, for God's
sake, who ever goes to Winchester?"

"People," Erin said.

"Doubtless." He hadn't heard her; he took it for granted
she wouldn't say anything worth listening to. "But the real
tourist sights—the house where the Reagans lived during the

1980 campaign, the sumptuous mansion of Senator Warner and his much more famous wife, Elizabeth Taylor—aren't in town. So the inhabitants shop, the tourists shop, and everybody hopes that one of the famous names will shop. We have here kitchen shops with names like Cozy Cupboard and the Gingham Goose; craft shops with names like the Calico Cat and Country Cozy; innumerable restaurants, cafés, pubs, and the like; and clothing shops where you can buy the same garments you would find in D.C., but for twice the price. They all have names such as—''

He waved her gallantly into the door of a shop called the Sly Fox. "It's the hunt scene, of course," Laurence went on. "So tacky."

"Don't you hunt?" Erin asked. "You look as if you would."

"Ouch." He grinned at her. "I deserved that, I suppose. No, my dear, I do not hunt. Oscar Wilde said it best—''

" 'The unspeakable in pursuit of the inedible.' ''

"Just as I thought; you are adequately educated as well as beautiful. Go on, browse to your heart's content."

Erin turned to a rack of blouses. "What size is she?"

She had hoped to catch him off-guard, but he was too skilled at subterfuge—or perhaps he had only spoken the simple truth. "Your height, but considerably broader. One hesitates to use the word 'fat' of a lady. . . . About her size." He indicated the hovering saleswoman. It was a gratuitously cruel remark, and the woman's smile wavered.

Erin had expected the prices would be high, but the first tag she examined made her wince. Two hundred and ten dollars for a plain linen blouse?

Laurence flipped through a rack of robes and nightgowns. "Frightful," he said loudly. "Do you see anything that would melt a woman's heart, Erin? No? You have excellent taste. Let's try elsewhere."

They were followed out of the shop by two other customers and—Erin felt sure—the silent curses of the saleslady. As they emerged onto the street a breeze caught at her hair and lifted it like a bright banner; a scattering of golden leaves from a nearby tree sprinkled her head, and Laurence stopped short.

"Exquisite," he breathed. "No, don't brush them off, they suit you better than gold or gems. You're a pretty thing, Erin. Not beautiful, I lied when I said that. Not sweetly pretty, either. Pretty . . ."

The questionable compliment didn't offend Erin, perhaps because it sounded not only genuine but genuinely impersonal. He might have been talking about a statue or a painting.

"Why do you do things like that?" she demanded.

Laurence knew exactly what she meant. He laughed. "My dear, I must maintain my image. My public expects it. Think of the pleasure that women will derive from telling their friends that Philips Laurence is as rude and unpleasant as he is reported to be. What about a sweater? One can never have too many sweaters."

He stopped before a display window. Soft swirls of cashmere had been strewn with seeming carelessness over cardboard logs and paper sprays of bright-colored leaves. The colors glowed like autumn—forest green, deep gold, rusty red.

"There's nothing like cashmere," Erin said dryly.

Some of the labels were familiar—Braemar, Pendleton— and the clothes were country casual. One table was heaped with hand-knit and embroidered sweaters which the obsequious salesman assured them were one of a kind. Erin believed him; someone with a charming sense of humor had designed the patterns of marching cats with separate, swinging yarn tails, foxes sneering at panting hounds, horses engaging in inappropriate contortions, elephants trooping in solemn parade.

"Elephants sell well in this bastion of conservatism," Philips remarked, playing with the dangling trunks of the animals in question. "No donkeys? I fear Kay would never stand for the insignia of the other party. Do you think she'd like the cats?"

"They're absolutely adorable, but I can't imagine Kay wearing anything like this," Erin said. "What about a scarf?"

None of the scarves suited Laurence's refined tastes, so they left without buying anything and headed back toward the doctor's office. Bright leaves swirled and danced in the freshening wind; on the hillsides beyond, the colors of the trees burned like flames.

Laurence said unexpectedly, " 'The scarlet of the maples Can shake me like a cry Of bugles going by.' " Then he added coolly, "I memorized that piece of sentimental trash in prep school. What a pity one can't purge one's mind of childish enthusiasms."

"Isn't it just as childish to cultivate a veneer of false sophistication?"

Laurence stared at her in surprise and then burst out laughing. It was the first spontaneous demonstration of genuine amusement she had seen him display, and it warmed his austere features amazingly.

"I've heard that particular put-down before, but no one has expressed it quite so effectively," he said. "I suppose it's the contrast of your ingenuous face and your cutting words. So you do think I'm a twenty-four-carat bastard, and a hypocrite to boot? You needn't be afraid of offending me by speaking the truth."

"I'm not afraid." The statement was true. "Liking" was too strong a word for her new feeling of Philips Laurence; it would be more accurate to call it an absence of positive antipathy.

"No, I can see you aren't. Let me confess something to you, since you read me so accurately. I am genuinely and sincerely anxious to see Rosemary win this election. I'm sure the entourage has speculated about my motives?"

"Not to the exclusion of all other subjects," Erin said, in a fair imitation of Laurence's drawl.

It won her another burst of laughter. "Oh, excellent. I know they've been wondering, and suspecting me of subtly sinister designs; but they're wrong. I've known Rosemary ever since she was Ed Marshall's shy little bride. She's come a long way since then. I differ with her on many issues; but I have enormous respect for the passion and integrity with which she pursues her goals." The speech flowed so fluently that it sounded like a quote from one of his columns; but the next sentence did not. "I'll do anything I can to help her win."

"I believe you. But why? Are you . . ." Erin stopped. "None of my business."

"Am I in love with her? I've asked myself that same question, and I'm damned if I know the answer." His even voice roughened, as if with anger. Then he laughed lightly. "She has her own peculiar charm, does Rosemary. You must have felt it."

"She's very nice," Erin said.

"Ah, you haven't yet succumbed. You will. Everyone does. Even Buzz Bennett . . . Let's run in here for a moment, I can't return to Kay empty-handed."

The store was a food shop, featuring expensive gourmet goodies. Laurence wasted no time looking around; he picked up a handful of tiny gold boxes with the name of a well-known candy manufacturer, and paid cash for them.

"If you want to ingratiate yourself with Kay, this is the way to go," he said, pocketing his change.

"Godiva chocolates? Poor as I am, I think I could spring for something a little larger in size," Erin said.

"Ah, but that's the point," Laurence said cheerfully. "Kay has a deplorable tendency to pig out—isn't that the phrase?—on chocolates, and an even more deplorable tendency to gain weight. These little dainties contain only two pieces, just enough to satisfy her sweet tooth without making her feel guilty about devouring the entire box. We feed them to her one box at a time."

Kay seemed to appreciate the minuscule offering, and Laurence's broad hint that it was a token of a finer gift to come. But Erin's hunch that she, not Kay, had been his real quarry, was confirmed by the conversation that followed, over cups of tea in the Hungry Hound Café. Laurence said nothing new or confidential, he only reaffirmed his desire to help Rosemary, and his concern for how her health would stand up to the stress of the campaign. When Kay said it was time they were getting back, he didn't try to detain them.

Kay had obviously enjoyed herself. She looked like a different woman when she came out of the doctor's office, and Erin suspected that the new, lighter bandage was only part of the reason. She had applied fresh makeup, and loosened strands of hair so that they curled softly around her face. For the first part of the return trip she was silent, not even commenting when Erin wriggled the car out of the parking space, which had been constricted by a newcomer who had pulled up behind her.

I wonder if I'll ever understand people, Erin thought. Just when I think I've got someone figured out, they turn into an entirely different individual. Like the two-headed god Janus of Roman mythology, but even more complex; a dozen personalities instead of two, layer upon layer of masks. Maybe I'm the one who's naive, to suppose people are so simplistic. Or are these people more accustomed to concealment—two-faced in the slang sense of the word?

If someone had asked her to justify her conviction that Kay and Philips had once been lovers she could not have pointed to a single piece of evidence. It was more an atmosphere, a vague feeling. For the past few days Kay had been moping around the house, looking like an old woman. Now she looked her true age—and she wasn't that old. No older than Laurence, at any rate.

Kay sat up straighter. "Watch out for that branch," she said sharply.

"I see it." Erin smiled. Kay was herself again.

As soon as they walked into the office they knew something had happened. The clerks were all clustered around the door of the inner office; none of them actually had his or her ear pressed to the door, but that would not have been necessary since the raised voices could have been heard at a considerable distance.

"If you have nothing to do I can find work for all of you," Kay said loudly.

One by one they sidled back to their desks. Only Christie remained, facing her superior. "They're at it again," she said.

"I can hear that," Kay said caustically. She put her handbag down on the nearest desk. "Rosemary isn't back, is she?"

"No. It's the triumvirate. Sounds as if Joe and Nick are doing most of the yelling." Christie's smile was broad and unashamed.

Kay marched to the door and opened it. The voices stopped abruptly, but resumed as soon as she had closed it after her.

"What's going on?" Erin asked.

Christie had been more affable recently, perhaps because Erin's humble station had become so apparent. Christie didn't wash dishes or brush hair. She didn't even bring coffee to other people; they brought it to her.

Now her eyes sparkled with excitement. "There's a rumor going around that Joe was the one who leaked the story about Buzz Bennett and the Shady Lane Motel. Set him up."

Erin's face betrayed her bewilderment, and Christie was happy to display her superior knowledge. "Look, the *Times* had to get a tip from somebody; how else would they know exactly when Buzz and his floozie were going to be there? I mean, did you see that photo? They caught him in his underwear, and her right behind him, wearing even less."

Erin hadn't given the matter any thought, but she hated to admit she was as innocent as Christie thought her. "I assumed the floozie—the girl—was the one who tipped off the photographers."

"Sure, she was part of it. Got her cute little bod right out there where the cameras could catch every curve. She was paid to perform—by the same person who called the paper."

"Well, suppose that person was Joe," Erin argued. "It's a rotten, low-down trick, but all's fair in—"

The door exploded outward and Nick emerged. His face was crimson. Joe's voice followed him: "Get the hell back in here!"

Nick's reply was emphatic and of the variety that would, in earlier times, have been considered unprintable. A mild ripple of amusement ran through the avid listeners. Nick's glazed eyes focused on Christie and Erin. "Excuse me, ladies," he snarled, and stormed out of the room.

"Wow," Christie said appreciatively. "He's really pissed, isn't he? Go on after him, and see if you can find out what's going on."

"I really don't think—"

"Oh, for God's sake, don't be such a self-righteous prig." Christie gave her a shove.

Erin expected to find Nick in the kitchen; he had a thing going with Sarah, the cook, and often retreated to the comfort of motherly sympathy and muffins when things got too much for him. Nick wasn't there. Sarah was staring at the back door, which still vibrated from the fury of his exit.

"He's gonna break that door one of these days," Sarah said critically. "What's the matter with him this time?"

"I was just about to ask you the same thing."

"He didn't stop to talk," Sarah said. "Just came roaring through like a cyclone and slammed out the door."

She went back to rolling out pie crust, and Erin said, "Men! They can be so childish sometimes."

"So can women, honey."

"Got me there," Erin admitted. "Okay, I won't be childish; I'll go after him and see if I can calm him down."

"Good idea. He's gonna do himself an injury someday, banging around the way he does when he gets mad." She glanced at Erin, her eyes twinkling. "He's not so bad, you know—for a man."

As Erin crossed the stableyard the dogs howled a welcome, but she didn't stop to chat. In the pasture below the house she saw a lonely figure running wildly in circles.

By the time she reached him the circles had decreased in diameter and the run had slowed to a jog. He rolled his eyes in her direction but did not stop.

"Say it," he wheezed as he passed her.

"Say what?"

She had to wait for the answer until he came around again. "Childish. Me."

"Oh, Nick. . . ." On the next round she caught hold of him with both hands. He had taken off his coat and loosened his tie; his blue shirt showed dark patches of sweat.

"The wind is chilly," she scolded, reaching for the jacket he had flung carelessly onto a rock outcropping. "Sit down. Put this on. You'll catch cold."

She suited the action to the words, draping the garment

over his shoulders and tugging at him until he sat down beside her. Nick grinned. "I love being mothered. Do it some more."

"You don't need a mother, you need a kick in the rear. What are you doing out here, running around in circles like a mad dog?"

"Working off steam," Nick replied. His breathing was still quick and his cheeks were flushed with exercise, but his voice was calm. "More socially acceptable than punching your boss in the nose, don't you think? Do you know what that louse accused me of?"

"Setting Senator Bennett up for a photo opportunity? They're saying he was the one who did it."

"Who says? Oh, the kids in the office?" Nick swabbed his wet forehead with his sleeve. "That shows you how rumors get started. They were half-right. I accused him, he accused me. The story is all over town. I heard it from one source, he got it from another. He was steaming when he arrived and I was in no mood to take any crap from anybody. Jeff kept trying to play peacemaker and both of us turned on him. . . ." A reluctant smile twitched his lips. "That's what usually happens to peacemakers."

"Explain it to me." Erin shifted position. The rock was not the most comfortable of seats. "I thought politicians did this sort of thing all the time. Why the high moral indignation?"

"You sure do have a low opinion of us, don't you?" Nick shook his head sadly. "Wish I could say it was undeserved. But in this case it is. Oh, I admit I'd have been sorely tempted if the information had come my way. Buzz has flaunted his sexual peccadilloes for years, and believe me, some of them were pretty vile. But aside from the fact that the idea makes me sick, it's simply bad politics. If you're caught, and chances are you will be, there's a backlash of sympathy for the victim. Americans hate a snitch. Remember back in grade school, when 'tattletale' was the worst name anyone could call you?"

"I can recall a few that were worse," Erin said wryly.

"So can I, now that you mention it. But you know what I mean. It's a stupid, dangerous attitude; there are times when you are morally obligated to blow the whistle on someone, friend or foe, to prevent serious trouble. But I sure didn't see it that way in my salad days, and most Americans still feel that betrayal is worse than the crime itself. Remember Chambers and Alger Hiss?'' He was silent for a moment; then he said slowly, "I guess I shouldn't have sounded off to Joe. He's too smart to pull a stunt like that—at least he's too smart to be caught. But it really burned me when he suggested I was the one who did it.''

"What you resented, in fact, was not the insult to your integrity but the implication that you had made a stupid mistake.''

"I should resent *that*,'' Nick said. "Actually, I think I do resent it.''

"Weren't you the one who suggested I was hopelessly naive about politics? I'm learning. It's not a very pleasant process.''

"You got it.'' He slid off the flat surface of the rock and propped his head back against it, knees drawn up and head tilted back. "I admit the whole business seems pretty trivial on a day like this.''

From where they sat they could see the valley fields stretching down toward the stream and its rich green-and-gold boundary of trees. The summer crops had been garnered in; amber stubble of cornstalks, yellowing close-cropped hay glowed in the sunlight. Across the stream, figures moved slowly across a velvety square of pasture: white and bay and chestnut brown, graceful and remote as horses in a Persian miniature.

Nick uncoiled himself and stood up. "Therapy complete. I'd better go back and grovel to Joe. Then maybe we can figure out how to handle this latest mess.''

He offered his hand to Erin and pulled her to her feet. As they started up the hill he said casually, "I hear you went shopping with Laurence today. Lucky girl.''

"How on earth did you find that out? We just got back half an hour ago.''

"Kay mentioned it.'' He added with a grin, "She had to outshout both me and Joe to get a word in, but she managed.

What she actually said was that you had had a long talk with the lout, singly and together, and that he hadn't mentioned the rumor, which he, of all people, should have heard.''

"She's got a point." Erin stumbled over a rock concealed by the long grass; Nick's hand was quick to steady her. "If it's all over town, he must have heard it. He didn't say anything. Unless . . ."

"Unless what?"

"I'm starting to find sly innuendos in a simple good morning," Erin grumbled. "But he did emphasize his willingness to do anything he could to help Rosemary. Could that have been a subtle way of warning us this was about to break? Oh no, that's too silly."

"It's not silly, but it's a little obscure even for Laurence."

"I wondered at the time why he was so insistent about it," Erin mused. "Could he have meant it as a warning to me personally? 'I'll do anything I can to help Rosemary win, and you'd better not get in my way?' "

"Nah. That is silly. Unless you are a political Mata Hari in disguise—a very good disguise—you have no connection with any of these people. And you don't know a setup from a place setting."

"But I'm learning," Erin said again. The words left a sour taste in her mouth.

She still had a lot to learn, though, as she was soon to discover. Rosemary had returned, tired and cross after a long day of meetings and luncheon speeches—"Concerned Mothers for Nuclear Disarmament" and "Future Farmers of America, Northern Virginia Chapter." Erin was at her typewriter when Rosemary entered the office; her expression was so formidable that only Christie would have dared to speak to her.

"How did it go, Rosemary?"

"I expect to suffer from indigestion the rest of my life." Rosemary didn't stop; she went on to the inner office.

"She's heard it too," Christie muttered. "By the way, somebody delivered a package for you. It's on the table in the hall."

"For me? I didn't buy anything."

"Oh, really? Then it must be a present."

As Erin started out of the room someone said, "Make sure it's not ticking before you open it."

The package was not ticking. It was wrapped in glittery bronze paper stamped with little figures of running foxes, and tied with an elaborate medley of gold, russet, and green ribbons. It may have been the foxes that touched off a quiver of premonition; instead of taking the parcel to her room Erin attacked it immediately, ripping off the paper and opening the box. Inside was the sweater she had admired that afternoon. Blue cats, green cats, rosy-pink cats marched across the creamy white wool. The tiny gems in the embroidered collars winked and twinkled, and the cats' tails—some braided, some wisps of fluffy angora—swung as she held the sweater out at arms' length. The price tag had been removed, but she remembered the figure. Three hundred and ten dollars. Middleburg shops had a peculiar penchant for those extra ten dollars.

Shaken by a blend of fury, bewilderment, and shame, she didn't hear the footsteps, or realize she was not alone until Jeff said, "Very pretty. Just your colors, too."

Erin whirled around. Jeff wasn't the only one who had crept up on her; Joe and Nick were with him. Christie had wasted no time spreading the word. Or it might have been one of the others, someone who recognized the distinctive wrapping paper and wondered how a humble typist/maid-of-all-work could afford to shop at such an expensive boutique.

She waved the sweater defiantly. "Take a good look. I'm sending it back, right this minute. There's some mistake."

"No, I don't think so," Joe said. He took the cigar out of his mouth, studied it as if wondering where it had come from, and tossed it into a Sèvres bowl. "I don't think it was a mistake."

"Is there a card?" Nick's voice sounded strained.

"No," Erin said.

"Hardly necessary, is it?" Jeff caught the garment as Erin flung it away. "Not that a mere male like me would know, but I gather the price on this is about the same as the yearly income of a Third World peasant. Kay said Laurence had taken you shopping. He assumes we have enough intelligence to put two and two together, but not enough to recognize this as another of his dirty little tricks.''

Erin turned to him. "Then you don't believe—"

"Believe, hell. I *know* you aren't conspiring with Philips Laurence.''

Slumped against the wall, hairy arms folded, Joe emitted a hoarse Humphrey Bogart chuckle. "Don't be simple, sweetheart. If you were spying for Philips he wouldn't pay you off so publicly. Besides, he doesn't need a snitch inside the organization. He's got Rosemary.''

*   *

ERIN REWRAPPED the sweater in plain brown paper and addressed it to Laurence in care of the newspaper that carried his column.

The suggestion had come from Jeff: "A public slap in the face—much more effective than sending it to his home address.''

"I dunno," Nick said doubtfully. "I mean, it's certainly more effective, but it could be dangerous. Laurence doesn't like being publicly humiliated.''

'·Too bad," Erin growled. She handed the parcel to Jeff, and gave him her most caressing smile. He had jumped to her defense with a speed and certainty that made Nick's failure to do so a double affront. Come to think of it, Nick still hadn't . . . She put both hands on Jeff's broad shoulders. "Thanks, Jeff. For everything.''

Jeff blinked as if in surprise, but looked pleased. "Hey, you don't owe me. I wish I could . . . It's the least . . .''

"Good gracious me, you've got the poor chap all in a swit," Nick said caustically. "Come off it, Jeff. That aw-shucks, little-boy routine is pretty corny, don't you think?''

Jeff's expression did not change. Slowly and gently he moved away from Erin's touch and started to turn. It was the way he moved that warned her, smooth and controlled as a snake coiling before it struck. She caught at his arm.

"Jeff, don't. Nick, what are you trying to do, start trouble? Seems to me there's enough of it around here already."

The two men eyed one another challengingly. Nick was the first to back off, though he obviously hated doing it. "I was out of line," he mumbled. "Sorry. Can't imagine what got into me."

"Can't you?" Jeff's tight muscles relaxed; he even smiled faintly. "Think about it—buddy. I hate to tear myself away from one of you, but if you'll excuse me. . . . By some miracle there is no fund-raiser, speech, meeting, or conference scheduled for this evening, and I intend to make the most of what may be my last night off before the election. I am going home. If I can remember where it is."

He walked away, leaving Nick looking, and obviously feeling, foolish in the extreme. As soon as the door closed, Nick began, "Listen, Erin, I didn't mean—"

"Yes, you did! I've never been so disgusted in my life. How could you be so rude to Jeff?"

"Well, dammit, you didn't have to fall all over him!"

"I expressed my appreciation for his thoughtfulness and his trust. He spoke up for me. Unlike some people I could mention."

"Jesus Christ, how often do I have to tell you—"

"Oftener than you have. You stood there with your mouth hanging open, looking glum—"

"Glum! That was my introspective look. I was trying to figure out why Philips L. has gone to such lengths to get you in trouble. A flunky like you should be beneath his notice—"

Erin was so furious she couldn't speak. Instead she let out a wordless shriek that stopped Nick in midsentence and gave her time to catch her breath. "You've really outdone yourself, Nick McDermott! I never thought even you could get so many insults and nasty insinuations into a single speech. If you don't leave, I'll—I'll—"

"Oh, shit," Nick said gloomily. "I can't win. Go on, hit me. It'll make you feel better." He offered a tanned cheek.

"I wouldn't give you the satisfaction." Erin turned on her heel and stamped up the stairs.

Once in her room she flung herself on the bed and contemplated the iniquities of Nick while she pounded the pillow with both fists. She was still pounding when she heard someone giggle, and realized, with astonishment, that the sound came from her own throat.

But it *was* funny. A tempest in a teapot, the result of strained nerves and Nick's unfortunate habit of moving his mouth without consulting his brain, or his heart. He had them both, intelligence and compassion, and he had another talent, that of stirring people up. I enjoyed that, Erin thought disbelievingly. A good straight fight, the kind I've always shied away from.

You've come a long way, baby.

*   *

ERIN WAS LOOKING forward to an evening off too, though she had no idea what she wanted to do with it until she learned that her assumption has been erroneous. "I want to wash my hair," she bleated, as Joe handed her a thick report that had to be retyped. "And read and write to my mother and—"

"Life is tough all over, kid," said Joe.

Kay was more sympathetic than Erin had expected; the euphoria of her trip to Middleburg still lingered. "I'm sorry I can't help you, Erin. If I hadn't been so clumsy . . . I never imagined it would be as bad as this." She looked resentfully at her bandaged hand. "The fingers are healing nicely, but there's still something wrong with the thumb. You wouldn't think a little thing like a thumb could be so important."

"Ask any anthropologist," Joe said. He picked up his briefcase and stalked out.

"Goodness, he's in a bad mood," Kay muttered. "And Rosemary is even worse."

"I suppose this business about the leak has upset them."

"Oh, that." Kay shrugged. "None of us had anything to do with it, so they can't prove we did. Let's have a bite of supper and then get started on that report."

Supper was the usual buffet arrangement, with people wandering in and out as their schedules allowed. Kay allowed no lingering over coffee; they went straight to her office, and it was almost ten before she leaned back in her chair with a sigh and allowed as how she was getting too tired to think sensibly. "Just finish that last letter, Erin," she said. "Leave them and the report on Rosemary's desk. And turn off the lights when you leave."

"Yes, ma'am. Thank you, ma'am."

The sarcasm was lost on Kay. Just as well, Erin reflected guiltily, as she watched the older woman make her slow way to the door. Why should she resent Kay, when she had everything Kay wanted and was rapidly losing—youth, competence, a healthy body and a future limited only by what she could do with it?

With any luck she would still have time to wash her hair. Might as well dash off a note to her mother right now, while she was at the typewriter. She could claim, with perfect truth, that she was too busy to write a long, chatty letter. The cheerful remarks she had imagined herself writing—humorous stories about the funny things that happened during the political campaign—didn't seem appropriate. "Funny things" was right. Not the sort of funny things a depressed widow would find amusing.

She finished the last letter and the note. "Don't worry, Mom, I'm a little tired, but so is everyone else; and the job is fascinating. I had no idea . . ." Lucky her mother couldn't see her face as she fought her way out of one Freudian tangle after another. ". . . no idea how complicated politics is." Of all the stupid remarks! Doggedly she continued, "Everyone has been so kind to me . . ." Especially Philips Laurence. ". . . and I'm learning a lot." Such as how to return a bribe and avoid nosy reporters. She yanked the paper out of the machine and signed it. "Your loving daughter." Well, that was a simple statement of truth, at any rate.

Writing the string of evasions had exhausted her. She gathered up the report and the letters she had typed and went to Rosemary's office. The room was quite dark; shrubbery outside the windows obscured what little light came from moon and stars. She didn't realize someone else was there until she turned on the light and saw a form huddled forlornly in the window seat, half concealed by the long draperies.

Instantly and reflexively her hand reversed the switch, but

the image had burned itself onto her vision. Rosemary was wearing her favorite at-home costume of oversized shirt and faded jeans, and her feet were bare. Somehow the pale, dusty toes looked even more pathetic than the clear evidence of tears.

"It's all right. You can turn the light on." Rosemary's voice gave nothing away.

"I didn't know you were here."

"Why should you? I must have startled you as much as you startled me." A softer, kindlier light went on; Rosemary had reached out to turn on a standing lamp. "Kay shouldn't have kept you working so late."

Since the damage was done, Erin crossed to the desk and put the papers down. "I don't mind. I mean, she was working too. I mean . . . I'm on my way to bed right now."

She carefully avoided looking at Rosemary. "Sit down for a minute," the latter said quietly. "Unless you're too tired."

"Oh, no. But I don't want—"

"I know you don't. But I'd like to tell you why I'm blubbering here in the dark."

"You don't have to explain anything to me."

"You are the only person around here I don't have to explain myself to," Rosemary said with surprising vehemence. "Maybe that's why I'd like to. I get so tired of putting on an act—being cool and unruffled when I feel like screaming, pretending to be cheerful when I'm depressed, exhibiting a stiff upper lip when I want to cower in a corner. I have a feeling you know about that."

The words woke to aching life a nerve she had thought atrophied by now. She nodded mutely, remembering her mother's endless tears. She had wept for her husband's pain and for his loss; she had also wept for her loneliness and her fear of the future. There had been no room in that watery flood for Erin's grief.

Rosemary shifted position, edging forward so that the shadow of the draperies no longer hid her face. She was not one of those women who weep prettily (if any such really exist). Her nose was red, her eyes were swollen, and blotchy patches of pink marked her cheeks. "At least you had a noble cause for grief," she said, with a faint smile. "Do you know what I was bawling about? Today is my granddaughter's birthday. She's four. That's an important year, you know. She's a big girl now. That's what she said. It's the first birthday of hers I have missed. I always made it before, even if I had to fly out in the morning and back the same night."

Erin's eyes went to the photograph on the desk. It had been reproduced in one of Rosemary's publicity flyers: a formal photographic sitting that had gone awry and, as a consequence, had produced a uniquely charming picture. The little girl, perched on her mother's lap, had turned at the last minute to say something to her grandmother, who was seated on the couch beside her. The child's smile, and Rosemary's delighted, doting grin intensified the resemblance between them to an uncanny degree; they had the same turned-up nose and wide mouth, the same dimple, the same determined chin. Rosemary's daughter was laughing, and the young man standing behind the couch leaned forward, arms spread as if to include the three generations of womenfolk in a warm embrace. Erin had never seen such an outpouring of love and affection captured on film. It was no wonder Joe had insisted on using the picture, over—Erin had heard—Rosemary's objections.

"She's adorable," Erin said. "I don't blame you for feeling sad. Why didn't you just say the hell with it, and go?"

Rosemary drew her knees up and circled them with her arms. "It wasn't only a question of time, though God knows we're short on that. I hate—" She made a fist and brought it down on the padded cushion. "I *hate* using my kids as political symbols. It degrades the whole relationship. Kevin, my son-in-law, is one of those rare people. . . . It really was a case of not losing a daughter but gaining a son. I love them all, all three, so much. . . . Can't you see the press releases Joe would have sent out, if I had decided to go? 'Lo-o-o-ove is more important than politics,' says adoring grandmother."

"He wouldn't do that," Erin exclaimed.

"Like hell he wouldn't. He'd have me walk naked down Pennsylvania Avenue if he thought it was worth a dozen votes." A sudden spontaneous burst of laughter lit her face. "Fortunately, he knows it would have precisely the opposite effect. Sheer aesthetic horror would send hundreds of voters emigrating to Canada. Joe is furious with me because I refuse to drag the kids to fund-raisers and bake sales. I don't want them involved. Especially since . . ." She broke off and frowned at her toes.

"Why don't you fire him?" Erin asked. "Or is that a stupid question?"

"Not only is it a damned good question, it's one I've asked myself over and over." Rosemary's frown deepened. "It wouldn't be the first time Joe has been booted out in the middle of a campaign. He's abrasive, outspoken, rude—and the best in the business. Don't tell him I said so—his ego is inflated enough already—but I was enormously pleased and flattered when he offered to work for me. And the very qualities that have cost him at least three jobs, and that drive me up the wall, are the qualities that make me value him. I need him all the more because everything else about what I'm doing is unreal. Sometimes I get the feeling that Rosemary Marshall exists only as a campaign poster and a series of platitudes mouthed over and over; that if you stripped the image away there wouldn't be anybody there."

"It sounds . . . awful." The word was weak and inadequate, but Erin couldn't think of a better one. "Is it worth it?"

"That's another question I keep asking myself. But I know the answer. Maybe." Rosemary laughed mirthlessly. "I could say I wouldn't put myself through this torture if I didn't believe it was worth it, but that wouldn't be strictly accurate. Sometimes people do things out of habit, without ever questioning their motives. 'Because it's there.' I believe I can do some good; but every psychopath in history has believed that, from Alexander to Joe McCarthy. Of course they were wrong and I'm right. . . ." Rosemary's chin rested on her raised knees. "Do you know what my favorite fantasy is?" she said dreamily. "I imagine myself running a real, honest, genuine campaign—the kind that never existed, at any time in history. I'd get up there to make a speech looking just the way I do now—baggy jeans, bulging hips, no makeup—and I'd tell it like it is. I'd tell the audience that Buzz Bennett is a slimy old lecher who has cheated on his long-suffering wife for forty years—and I'd go on to say that that doesn't matter as much as the fact that Buzz would sell his vote for a champagne breakfast or a token to the local whorehouse. I'd talk about the issues. I wouldn't try to win votes by equivocating or lying or avoiding questions.

"I'd cry if I felt like crying. Candidates for public office aren't allowed to shed tears in public, you know. Remember what happened to Ed Muskie? No, I suppose you don't; you're too young. But even Pat Schroeder's supporters criticized her when she broke down after announcing she wouldn't run for president."

"President Reagan used to cry," Erin said.

"Oh, Reagan." Rosemary dismissed the President with a flip of her hand. "He can get away with anything, I don't know how he does it; it is the ultimate triumph of image over reality. Or charisma—defined as 'I don't know what the hell it is, but I wish I had it.' "

"Some people think you do."

"I hope not. I'd prefer to think my appeal is to reason rather than emotion. I'm kidding myself, of course. I have to tailor every speech to my audience, avoid issues that might offend. Joe doesn't want me to talk about women's issues. Women's issues, for God's sake!"

She broke off, with a snort of rage; and Erin said, " 'We're not a special-interest group! What's so special about our interest? We're your mothers, your sisters, your daughters, your wives. We care for your children and ours; we tend your aging parents and our own. We work in the factories and the hospitals, in the farmyards and in the shops and in the schools. We pay taxes. We don't pay as much as you do because we don't earn as much, even at the same job; but in what ways do our interests differ from yours? Don't all human beings want the same things? Don't you want peace and freedom—clean air to breathe and unpolluted water to drink? Do you care less about your children's safety and happiness than we do? Don't call us a special-interest group; and don't tell us that if it weren't for us you'd still be wearing skins and wielding clubs. Do you think so little of yourselves and so narrowly of our abilities?' ''

She couldn't remember the rest of it.

Rosemary lifted her head. ''That's the speech I made in support of the day-care bill.''

''I know. I've been doing some reading.'' Erin added apologetically, ''I didn't know much about politics when I came here, so I thought I had better try to catch up.''

''But you memorized it!''

''I didn't intend to. I guess it just sort of stuck in my mind.''

''I see.'' After a moment she swung her feet to the floor and stood up. ''Damn, I'm stiff as a board. Never curl up in a corner to brood when you're over fifty, Erin. Oh, by the way—Jeff let it slip that his birthday is next week. We're going to have a surprise party—nothing fancy, just a cake and some silly presents.''

''That's nice,'' Erin said, smiling. Rosemary really seemed to be looking forward to the event; her eyes sparkled and the traces of tears were almost gone.

''Tell Nick, and warn him not to give it away.'' Rosemary wandered over to the desk and glanced at the letters. ''Funny hats,'' she murmured, ''and balloons. And those things— what do you call them—that you blow into, and a paper strip uncurls.''

''And we all sing 'Happy Birthday.' ''

''Of course. The rest of us will have to bellow, to drown Joe's voice. He's tone-deaf and croaks like a frog.''

''I'll do my best. Well—good night.''

''Good night.''

But as she turned toward the door Rosemary said, ''Erin?''

''Yes?''

''You asked me a question a while ago: 'Is it worth it?' I think you just answered that question. Yes, it is. Thank you.''

The trained debater's voice dismissed her even as it left her speechless with gratified embarrassment. When she turned to close the door, Rosemary had seated herself at the desk and was reading the letters, her head propped on her hand.

As she climbed the stairs, Erin's mind was a welter of

confused thoughts. That's what she meant, it must have been—you, the young, the future, you make it all worthwhile by your caring. What a cliché. . . . But she put it awfully well. Hard to resist that kind of flattery. . . . "She has a peculiar kind of charm," Laurence had said. "You haven't felt it yet—but you will."

Now she knew what he meant. Not charm, something stronger. More like magic.

Chapter Seven

AFTER LISTENING to her mother endlessly bemoaning her poverty, Erin had believed no one could be more concerned with money, or the lack thereof. She had been mistaken. Money—and the lack thereof—was a constant source of anxiety to Rosemary's staff. There just wasn't enough.

Erin had read about the unending debate on campaign financing; she decided it was like the weather—everybody complained about it, but nobody did anything about it. A few people, including Rosemary, had tried, but bills limiting contributions, personal expenditures, and paid advertising had a strange habit of dying in committee or being emasculated by amendments.

Over $211 million spent on Senate races, almost $239 million on the House. Add the cost of presidential campaigns and state races, and the total became horrifying—and the implications even more so. The candidate with the most money didn't always win, but he had an edge that was difficult, if not impossible, to overcome.

Television was one of the reasons why the cost of a campaign had increased so astronomically. TV spots were the most effective method of reaching large numbers of voters. They were also one of the most expensive. (The United States was one of the few Western democratic nations to allow paid commercial political advertising; Rosemary's attempt to introduce a bill forbidding this pleasant and lucrative activity hadn't even made it to committee.) The cost of a single thirty-second spot on a local station in New York City was over $8,000. New York was the most expensive market in the country, but D.C. wasn't far behind; and since most of Virginia picked up the Washington stations, Joe had insisted they buy time on "Eyewitness News" and the others. They had saved the major effort for the final weeks of the campaign, and Rosemary had reluctantly agreed to hire a professional media firm to produce the spot. She remarked that she didn't know where the hell the money was going to come from; and Nick, trying to hide his resentment at being supplanted, said sourly that he didn't either.

"Listen, it's no criticism of you, Nick," Joe insisted. "You've done a great job. You just don't have the technical equipment—special effects, and all that jazz."

Nobody mentioned specific figures, but Erin's reading had given her some idea of the amounts involved. Fifty thousand up front, plus 15 percent of the buy (the total amount spent on radio and TV time). Or $75,000 clear. Both figures were real, from real campaigns, covering the cost of production only, not the cost of air time.

Joe had high hopes for a reception–fund-raiser that was to be given that weekend by one of Rosemary's supporters. One thousand a head was the asking price, as Joe crudely put it. He obviously hoped for more, and nobody was vulgar enough to ask how he planned to get around the laws limiting campaign contributions. There were ways. Even Erin knew that now.

The reception was being hosted by a Hollywood actress whose enthusiasm for liberal causes was as notorious as her habit of acquiring and discarding husbands. (When asked why she bothered to marry the gentlemen in question, whose tenure usually averaged less than a year, she replied that she was just an old-fashioned girl.) Her current spouse owned a beautiful mansion near Leesburg that was considered one of the showplaces of the old South, but the attraction was not so much the house and its collection of valuable antiques as the guest list, which glittered with big names from the show-biz world. Entertainment was to be provided by a famous concert pianist and the hottest new rock group, whose lead singer was one of the lady's exes.

It had never occurred to Erin that she would be asked to attend. She had taken a certain malicious pleasure in informing Fran of that fact, when her roommate called with the transparent hope of wangling an invitation, or, more accurately, a free ticket.

Fran wasn't convinced. "What do you mean, you aren't going? My God, you've got no more imagination than a goldfish. Can't you think of some way—"

"I could poison Kay," Erin said. "Was that what you had in mind? Sorry, Fran, that wouldn't do it. Anyway, I'm not interested in going."

"Now that," said Fran, "has to be a flat-out lie. Honest to God, Erin, I can't believe you. I know you aren't exactly the most forceful person in the world, but there you are, in a position where you could do yourself and your friends a lot of favors—"

"Friends like you?" Erin inquired softly.

"You wouldn't have had the nerve to write Rosemary if I hadn't pushed you."

There was too much truth in that for Erin to deny it, even if Fran had given her time to do so. "You owe me," Fran insisted. "I'd kill to go to that party. Get to work on it."

"No," Erin said.

"I have a couple of other ideas I want to discuss with you. Like, you could ask Rosemary . . . What did you say?"

"I said no. No party, no pressure, no whatever you were going to propose. I don't owe you a damn thing, Fran, especially if it means betraying the confidence Rosemary has in me. Such as it is."

"Why, Erin, I wouldn't do anything to hurt Rosemary, you

ought to know me better than that.'' Fran's voice changed.
She knew when she had gone too far. ''I was only going to
suggest . . .''

She went on and on. Erin finally hung up on her. She
despised herself as much as she despised Fran; how could
she have been such a spineless wimp as to let Fran push her
around and put her down? Even more infuriating was the fact
that Fran's eagerness had forced her to admit to herself that
she had been lying when she said she didn't care about going.

Late Friday afternoon she left the office for a much-needed
break. After pacing along the driveway to relax her stiff muscles, she sat down on the porch steps, where she was promptly
submerged in cats. The beautiful fall weather held; a haze of
warmth veiled the far-off hills, and sunlight freshened the
colors of the massed chrysanthemums in the flower beds by
the porch. They blazed gloriously—golden yellow, snowy
white, all shades of russet and rust and cinnamon. Her fingers
buried in the soft fur of the feline who had been first onto
her lap, Erin was enjoying a complete absence of coherent
thought when Nick came around the corner of the house.

He shifted a cat and sat down beside her. ''I thought you'd
be upstairs primping. Don't Newman and Redford deserve
your best?''

Erin stared. ''Who?''

The question was meaningless in itself; it led to an agitated
(on Erin's part), amused (on Nick's) exchange of query and
response, and finally Erin let herself be convinced that Rosemary really did expect her to attend the party.

''She told me to keep a fatherly eye on you,'' said Nick
clinching the argument. ''Now don't tell me you don't have
anything to wear, that's such a tired old cliché.''

''But I don't—nothing suitable. The only formal dress I
brought with me is one I bought in a thrift shop because it
was only five bucks. Every other woman there will be wearing gowns they bought from Neiman Marcus and Saks and
Garfinckel's. . . . I'll bet none of them have even heard of
Second Time Around!''

Nick dismissed this argument with a shrug. ''So what? You

don't have to go if you don't want to, but think what you'll be missing."

"Redford and Newman," Erin murmured.

"Not to mention me in tails."

"That might make it all worthwhile."

"Rented, I hardly need add." Nick stretched his legs out and leaned back, bracing himself on his elbows. "Our youth and beauty will overcome any minor disadvantages of previously owned attire. We'll make those tired, paunchy, dissipated millionaires look sick."

Two cats climbed onto his outstretched legs. Erin added the one she had been holding and retired, leaving him up to his navel in fur.

Rosemary was on the Hill and wasn't expected back till evening; when Erin located Kay, she put the question rather tentatively. Kay frowned.

"I hadn't heard anything about it. But if Nick says so, I expect he's right. I had hoped you would be able to help me with my hair. . . ."

"It looks lovely," Erin said. She had chauffeured Kay to the hairdresser earlier in the afternoon. "But of course I'll be glad to help any way I can."

"Thank you." Kay's voice was cool. "I have a few things to finish up here. Did you type those memos?"

Chastened, Erin went to her desk. Obviously Kay didn't approve of her going. So what? she thought defiantly, echoing Nick. She worked steadily until Kay came out of her office and summoned her with a curt "Leave the rest of them."

If she hadn't known she was being unfair, Erin would have suspected that Kay deliberately prolonged the process of dressing in order to shorten the time Erin could spend on herself. Kay tried on three different dresses before settling on the one Erin knew she had bought especially for the occasion.

It was not until she asked whether she should offer her assistance to Rosemary that she got an inkling of the real cause for Kay's ill humor. "She doesn't need either of us," Kay said with a short laugh. "She's got Raymond."

She pronounced it in the French fashion, with the accent on the last syllable and an exaggerated, drawn-out vowel.

Seeing Erin's blank look, she explained, "He's a hairdresser and makeup 'artiste,' as he calls himself. *The* hairdresser; does the Vice President's wife, and all the other la-di-da types. Silly business, if you ask me, but Joe said this was an important occasion and only the best was good enough. Personally I can't stand the man; silly, affected creature. . . . There's Hoboken or Brooklyn under that fake French accent of his, or I miss my guess."

"I suppose this is a special occasion," Erin said.

Kay sniffed. "I think Rosemary will just end up looking ridiculous. Her own natural style is good enough for anybody."

Another prolonged period of fussing and indecision over jewelry, shoes, an evening wrap followed, before Kay finally dismissed Erin and suggested that she had better make haste or they would have to go without her.

The fear of being late made Erin clumsier than usual, and her hair seemed to have acquired an agitated life of its own; it clung crackling to her fingers and fought every attempt to confine it in a roll or a chignon. The dress, a simple sheath of black lace over a slim underslip, could have done with a quick pressing, but Erin was afraid to take the time to look for an iron. The long tight sleeves were modest enough, but she tugged anxiously at the low-cut neckline, wondering if she was showing too much skin. She was putting on earrings, long dangles of jet and crystal, when she heard Kay's door open; with a last despairing look in the mirror she stepped into her black pumps, snatched up her knit stole and black evening bag, and bolted.

Kay didn't turn, though she must have heard Erin behind her on the stairs. Kay reached the landing and turned toward Rosemary's room just as the door of the room opened and a man came out. It could only be Raymond himself—tall and impossibly thin, a neat black short-cropped beard enlarging a jawline that without its aid would have jutted not at all. His vaguely vacuous expression hardened when he caught sight of Kay. He stopped short with a theatrical start. The two acolytes who had followed him out of the room pulled up short and stood quivering as they juggled the boxes and bags that presumably contained Raymond's tools. It would have been funny if the two girls had not been so visibly terrified, and if Raymond's faint smile had succeeded in concealing his dislike of the woman who passed him with only a brusque nod in response to his *"Bon soir, madame."*

Raymond glared at Kay's back and stuck out a long red tongue. Turning, he saw Erin, who had been watching in fascination. His distorted features relaxed and he swept down on her, cooing. "Ah, *la pauvre petite belle!* Do you attend upon the dragon? She is beyond help; even I, Raymond, can do little for her; but you, *si belle, si charmante.* . . ."

His hand swooped out, gathered Erin's loose hair and gave it a painful twist. She was too startled to protest, nor could she move without hurting herself.

Raymond snapped his fingers. One of the girls rushed to him, the bag she carried already open, her hand fumbling inside. Like a surgeon awaiting the service of an operating-room nurse, Raymond accepted the hairpins the girl slapped into his open palm, and in a few daring movements had fixed the twisted coil to Erin's head.

The girls broke into a soprano duet of admiration. Raymond smiled complacently. *"Oui, oui, c'est admirable.* I could do more, *vous comprenez,* had I the time. For you, *ma chérie,* there is no charge."

He passed on, trailed by his entourage. Erin raised a careful hand to her aching head. The pins felt as if they had been stabbed directly into her skull, but she was afraid to loosen them for fear Raymond would turn and see the sacrilege.

Rosemary emerged from her room. "Has he gone?" she asked in a stage whisper.

Erin nodded dumbly.

"He's a dreadful little man," Rosemary said. "But Joe insisted. . . . My dear, how pretty you look. I like your hair that way." Something in Erin's petrified look betrayed the truth. She began to laugh. "Don't tell me. Did Raymond . . ."

"In about thirty seconds," Erin said. "Snap, snap, swoop, pounce. . . . I'm afraid to move. Does it look awful?"

Rosemary was whooping with laughter. "If you could see your face. . . . It looks divine, *ma chérie.* Oh, dear, I mustn't laugh or my makeup will run. Every damned grain of mascara cost—''

"Here." Kay, who had followed her, produced a lace-trimmed handkerchief. She wasn't laughing. "Wipe your eyes, Rosemary. Personally, I can't see what's so funny."

"You didn't see Erin's face." Rosemary accepted the handkerchief and dabbed carefully at her eyes. "Admit it, Kay, she looks adorable, with her hair that way. Raymond may be a pompous poseur, but he knows his stuff. That's one of his favorite tricks, Erin—leaping on some unsuspecting female and transforming her with a single twist of the wrist."

"Hmph," Kay said.

"He did a wonderful job with you," Erin said.

The white streaks in Rosemary's hair lifted like wings, their contrast to the surrounding darkness subtly enhanced and shining. Upon closer examination Erin realized they really did shine; tiny flecks of glitter sparkled with the slightest movement. Bouffant puffs of black chiffon framed Rosemary's shoulders and throat; the dress itself was dramatically simple, a straight fall of satin that followed the curves of waist and hips before flaring to the floor.

"You ain't seen nothing yet," said Rosemary. With a snap of her wrist she unfurled a huge ostrich-feather fan whose soft rosy-pink color matched her lipstick. "Ta dah!"

Kay sighed loudly. "Rosemary—"

"Oh, don't be such an old poop, Kay," Rosemary said. "I look sensational and you know it. I don't look like me, but I look sensational. My face feels like a plaster mask and my girdle is killing me; if I can stand it for a few hours, you can stand looking at me."

Flapping the fan vigorously, she marched forward. "Let's do a Raymond. Fall in, please, ladies."

Kay's expression softened as her eyes followed the parading little figure. "You do look lovely," she called out; turning to Erin she added, "But I like Rosemary better the way she usually looks. This is so—so artificial."

Erin was inclined to agree; but she wondered whether Kay was referring to Rosemary au naturel, in ragged sneakers and flapping shirt, or the smooth, smiling candidate. The latter image was, in its own way, just as artificial.

Joe was waiting for them downstairs. Circling Rosemary, who posed with the fan held behind her head and her hips seductively tilted, he grunted approval. "Good. Just control yourself, and don't get cute. Where's your coat?"

"The mink is in storage," Rosemary purred. "The sable needed glazing—"

Joe slapped her on the rump. "Cool it, I said. No horsing around tonight, okay?"

"You're no fun," Rosemary said sulkily. She rubbed her hip. "That hurt."

"It'll hurt a lot more if you sound off to a contributor. Where the hell is Jeff? We should have left five minutes ago."

"I'll see if he's in the commons room," Erin offered. She didn't really care where Jeff was, or whether they were late. What she wanted was a mirror. She had a desperate, almost compulsive need to see what Raymond had done to her hair before she appeared in public.

She hadn't expected to find anyone in the room. She started and gasped when she heard the rustle of paper, like a mouse scuttling for safety. Then Will's face appeared over the barricade of his heaped desk. He adjusted his glasses, studied her thoughtfully, and then remarked, " 'Oh, she doth make the candles to burn bright.' Or, as Joe might say, you look sharp, kiddo."

"Thanks, Will, I was just . . ." A glance into the mirror over the fireplace told her the compliment was not misplaced. She couldn't see the back of her head, turn and twist as she might, but the general effect was chic as well as becoming.

Watching her pirouette, Will chuckled. "Take my word for it, or you'll have a stiff neck in the morning. Are they ready to leave?"

"I guess so. Aren't you going?"

Will glanced down at his wrinkled shirt and rolled-up sleeves. "Like this? I'm a research analyst, my dear, not a gigolo. Give this to Rosemary, will you?" He held out a sheaf of papers.

"You really should go and wish her good luck. She looks marvelous."

Will considered the suggestion, head tilted and lips pursed. "No doubt that would be the proper thing to do. Not that I necessarily endorse all forms of meaningless social courtesy, when they interfere with—"

Joe's roar sounded as if he were in the room with them. "Jeff! Son of a bitch, where have you been? Goddamn it all, now Erin's disappeared!"

Will grinned and rose to his feet. "I'll accompany you, if only to provide a buffer. I don't know what Joe's complaining about, there's plenty of time."

"I guess this is a big deal," Erin said, following him to the door. "Everybody seems high-strung tonight."

"Not me," Will said, throwing the door open and bowing her through. "Sometimes I think my massive, unconquerable calm is the only thing that keeps this covey of lunatics from . . . Yes, Joe, I mean you. Lunatic in chief."

Joe glowered at him. "Aren't you going?"

"Obviously not," Will said in a resigned voice.

"Oh. Well, did you finish that research I asked for?"

"Of course." Will handed him the papers. "I can't understand why you wanted it, but here it is. Much more important is the other data, summing up Bennett's contributions from various PACs and interest groups and equating them with his votes during the past six years."

"You carry scholarly detachment to the point of stupidity," Joe grunted, shuffling through the papers. "These people don't give a damn about Bennett's voting record, they want to see charm, glamour, and glibness. Oh—here it is. Rosie, we'll go over it in the car. Your hostess's foibles, hobbies, weaknesses. Things to talk about, things not to talk about. Don't mention anybody named Oscar, she never got one. She's becoming a little sensitive about husbands and divorce. Collects Meissen, antique dolls, stuffed teddy bears. . . ."

Rosemary took the sheet of paper from him. Her eyes were fixed on Will, who was studying her thoughtfully, arms folded, forehead corrugated. "Well, Will?"

"It's all there," Will said abstractedly. "Frivolous nonsense, in my opinion, but Joe wanted—"

"That isn't what I meant," said Rosemary, her voice dangerously quiet.

"Ah." Will nodded. "It is conventional, I believe, to reassure an individual—I would say a woman, but then I would be accused of rampant sexism—who is about to make a public appearance that his or her physical appearance meets some undefined and abstract definition of acceptability. Indeed, by the conventions of the society in which you are about to plunge, I feel certain you pass the test."

Rosemary stamped her foot. "Will, you are really a number-one pain in the—"

"Rosemary!" Kay exclaimed.

"You look lovely," Will said hastily.

"Too late." Rosemary furled her fan and tapped him rather emphatically on the nose. "Take that, you cad. Have a wonderful time with your facts and figures while we swill down champagne and devour imported caviar and mingle with movers and shakers. We'll bring you a doggy bag. Well, Joe, weren't you the one who was yelling about being late?"

She sauntered toward the door, swinging her hips and humming. " 'Oh, what a time I had with Minnie the Moocher—' "

"Cut that out," Joe shouted, following her.

The screen door slammed. As if on cue, Nick appeared from the shadows under the stairs, where he had been lurking. Erin and Will inspected him in silence. His hand went nervously to his white tie.

"Struck dumb with admiration?" he suggested hopefully.

"You look gorgeous." Erin advanced on him. "Except for that waving lock that has fallen across your alabaster brow—"

"Leave my lock alone, it's part of the effect. How's the suit fit?"

Men, Erin thought with amusement. They were much vainer than women. . . . No, that was sexist. Just as vain. She offered further compliments and reassurances, demurely received Nick's in exchange, and then said, "I take it I'm going with you."

"Oh, right." Nick fished a set of keys from his pocket. "And in style. We get the Olds; Jeff is driving Kay's car."

"Ho, ho," said Will without humor. "What's that going to do to the image, having Jeff play chauffeur?"

"Couldn't be helped," said Nick. "Kay refused to let Joe get behind the wheel of her precious. My name wasn't even mentioned."

"Run along then," Will said. "Have fun and drive carefully."

"And have her home by midnight," Nick chanted. "By the way, Will, you scored a real zip on that last one. Haven't you learned anything about women from me?"

"Have her home by midnight," Will said.

"Yes, Pop."

But after they had left the house they heard Will's voice again. "Nick."

"What?"

Light was fading and the hall behind Will was dark. They could see him only dimly, his form blurred to ghostly indefinition by the screen.

"Tell Rosemary not to bother with the doggy bag. I have to go back to Charlottesville tonight."

"Okay."

"Nick?"

"Yes, what?" Nick demanded impatiently.

"Watch out for her. Rosemary. She's in an odd mood tonight. Fey."

The indistinct shape faded from sight.

Nick drove smoothly and competently, if a little faster than the growing darkness and narrow road made expedient. "Damn Will," he grumbled. "I planned to pull off the road and spend a few minutes nibbling on your ear. You look delicious. And, of course, outstandingly intelligent, competent and well informed."

Erin was too excited to be critical.

"Dislodge one lock of this fancy hairdo and I'll run a

bobby pin into you," she said amiably. "Why do you suppose Will was worried about Rosemary?"

"She was in a giddy mood," Nick said thoughtfully. "But that's not unusual; she hates formal affairs like this one, and often lets off some steam beforehand. Nothing to worry about, she's too much of a pro to ham it up in public."

"That word he used . . ."

"Fey?"

"Yes."

"Showing off his vocabulary," Nick said, amusement coloring his voice. "It just means excited, wild."

"Now who's showing off?" Erin demanded. "I know what it means, and it means more than just excited. 'Doomed' was the original meaning. Disturbed by a premonition of approaching death."

"Oh, shit!" The car swerved. "You're a nice cheerful date, I must say. If you can't think of anything nice to say to people, keep quiet."

Nick was graciously pleased to accept Erin's apology, and for the rest of the drive they talked about less ominous subjects: Nick's frustration in not being able to rent a gibus—one of the folding top hats, which he had always yearned to play with—and the foibles of their hostess. Joe was one hundred percent right about the importance of that issue, Nick said, adding the sweeping and probably unfair generalization that people in show business were paranoid, unduly sensitive, and arrogant. "Especially this female. Her IQ and her bust measurement are roughly the same. The latest kick is the collection of dolls, so be sure you admire them if she shows them off, which she probably will, because her interest is not so much in the objects themselves as the hope that other people will desire them and envy her for possessing them."

"I'd rather see her jewels. Like that diamond necklace that's supposed to have belonged to Marie Antoinette, and the Chavez emerald."

"My dear, naive creature, you'll be lucky if she says anything other than 'Good evening, dahling,' to you. Neither of us is important enough to rate her attention."

Darkness was complete by the time they reached their destination and when Nick turned into the driveway Erin let out a low whistle. "This is more like it," she said appreciatively.

The tall wrought-iron gates were closed and the security guard checked not only the engraved invitation, but Nick's driver's license before crossing their names off a list and waving them through. The house was lit like a stage set; every window glowed, and strategically placed spots and lanterns made the scene bright as day. The theatrical effect was heightened by the architecture itself—Twelve Oaks in all its pillared purity and pride of place. "Ah 'spect Miz Melly's waitin' for us down by the barbecue pit," Erin murmured. Nick chortled appreciatively. "Wait'll you see our hostess. Miz Scarlett thirty years later."

Nick had caught up with the Mercedes a few miles back, it was directly ahead of them as they proceeded at a decorous pace along the drive. Uniformed attendants pounced as soon as they stopped moving; Nick handed over the car keys and took Erin's arm. She was disgusted to discover that her palms were wet with nervous excitement, and she clung to Nick as they climbed the stairs. The dress was a little too long and she had not had time to shorten it.

Kay and Jeff preceded them; Rosemary, disdaining Joe's arm—if indeed he had thought to offer it—seemed to be managing both skirts and fan with practiced grace. As she reached the top of the stairs the door opened; without breaking step she swept into the house, and Erin heard a shriek of feminine delight. "Rosemary, dahling! You look absolutely divine!"

Rosemary's reply was almost as shrill. "Dahling! So divine of you to do this. . . ."

Nick gave a strangled gasp of laughter, and Erin found that she was suddenly no longer nervous. "Stop it," she hissed, pinching his quivering arm.

If she hadn't known better, she would have supposed the front door opened directly into the living room. The vestibule was twice the size of a normal parlor and looked like the entrance to a museum. The only color breaking the icy whiteness of marble floors and walls were the enormous bouquets in niches at either side of the door. A cut-glass chandelier and wall sconces of crystal and silver bleached the whiteness to a purity that dazzled the eyes. She handed her humble stole to a maid, and watched Nick's chagrin at having nothing to give up—alas for the gibus—and then turned toward the open double doors beyond. Rosemary was passing through the entrance affectionately intertwined with another woman whose arm was around her waist. Erin assumed the figure in the clinging beaded silver gown was her hostess; she had thought that Juliet MacArthur was a brunette, but this woman's hair was scarlet. Not red, as in Titian-haired, but scarlet, as in Little Red Riding Hood's cloak.

The drawing room appeared to be approximately the size of the Hall of Mirrors at Versailles, and it was only one of the apartments open to the guests, who spilled out into the corridors and onto the terrace. The greedier ones clustered in the room where an ostentatious buffet had been spread along a twenty-foot stretch of damask. Nick had to identify some of the opulent dishes for Erin, and a few baffled even him. "Too small for grouse, too boneless for quail. . . . Lark? Nightingale?" The finishing touch, which sent Erin into a fit of reprehensible giggles, was an ice-sculpture centerpiece featuring the ship (of state, one surmised), a covey or bevy of eagles, and a bust of Rosemary. It had begun to melt; water dripped off the eagles' beaks and Rosemary's nose.

There were a lot of people. Erin started counting, but gave it up when she realized she was enumerating as Joe might have done: "One thousand, two thousand . . ." Were spouses included in the price, she wondered? There were a number of non-paying guests, of course; people like herself and Nick, a few journalists, and the performers. The pianist had been isolated in a small (twenty feet by thirty) room. Erin hoped he was taking advantage of the opportunity to get in some practice, since nobody stayed to listen to him. The rock group, on the terrace, was doing better. A few people gyrated in approximate time to the music.

At first she was too dazzled by the glitter and the noise, by fabulous gowns and glamorous surroundings, to take much notice of details, but as the evening went on the novelty wore off and she began to view the proceedings with an increasingly cynical eye. Nick stayed close by her side; she appreciated his courtesy, but sensed that he was as ill at ease as she, out of his element and not caring much for the new one. It wasn't until their hostess sidled up to them that she realized Nick had been seriously in error about one thing. Juliet didn't consider *him* unworthy of her attention.

"Rosemary says you're her media adviser," she said. "Isn't that just wonderful."

"Uh—yes, it is," said Nick. "And this is Ms.—"

"Lovely you could come," murmured the actress, her eyes considering and dismissing Erin in a single glance. "Why don't you come and tell me all about your job, Mr.— Oh, I just can't remember all those names; you don't mind if I call you Nick, do you?"

She drew him away. Erin turned for consolation to the caviar, but it wasn't long before Nick returned, perspiring visibly.

"That was a very succinct lecture," Erin remarked, viewing his distress with mean satisfaction.

"I was rescued by the president of GM or the managing director of Amalgamated Chemicals or some such notable." Nick mopped his bow. "Geez. She had just invited me to come look at her dollhouses."

"Is that what she calls them?"

Nick grinned. "I don't know what she calls them, but I've already had a good look."

Before long they were joined by Jeff, looking superb in a tuxedo that fit much better than Nick's rented white tie and tails. He carried a glass of champagne in either hand. Presenting one to Erin, he remarked in a low voice whose sarcasm contrasted with his fixed, pleasant smile, "Might as well drink up. Unfortunately this seems to be a very successful affair; we won't get out of here for at least another hour."

"Aren't you having *fun*?" Nick inquired.

"I endure. Anyhow, we look damned effective together, don't you think? Not only because we're young and beautiful, but as a token of Rosemary's campaign. A black, a woman, and your good old standard Anglo-Saxon male Protestant."

"Too bad I'm not gay," Nick said cheerfully.

"Too bad *I'm* not. It's so economical to double up on your token representation."

Nick refused to take offense. "You're in a cruddy mood, even for you. Has anything gone wrong?"

"Quite the reverse." Jeff drained his glass. Erin realized he had had a little too much to drink; it didn't show in his voice or his manner, only in a careful consciousness of incapacity. "Quite a successful affair."

"Don't run off," Nick said. "You're such a delightful companion this evening."

"Up yours too, pal." Jeff glanced at Erin. "Sorry, Erin. This sort of thing"—his gesture took in the ostentatious house, the rich food, the overdressed, overfed people—"gets my l'il ole liberal hackles up."

"À la lanterne," Erin suggested, smiling up into his face.

"À bas les aristos," Jeff agreed. "I'd better get back to work. Hang in there."

He walked off, steps steady, shoulders straight. "Maybe we should circulate more," Erin suggested.

"Not much we can do," Nick said. "Unless you want to let a rich industrialist pinch your bottom and offer you wealth undreamed of, which you will of course contribute to the Cause."

"From the way some of these aging females are drooling at you, you're more likely to collect than I am," Erin retorted. "Not to mention a few of the . . . Oh. Oh, Lord!"

"What's the matter?"

"When did he get here?"

"Who?" But it didn't take Nick long to locate the source of Erin's perturbation. He was several inches taller than the people around him, and he was staring straight at Erin. His narrow lips twisted when he realized she had seen him, and he raised his glass in a mock salute.

"Laurence," Nick muttered.

"He's coming over here." Erin clutched Nick's arm. "Don't leave me."

"Fear not, timid beauty, I will defend you to the death. Against what, if you don't mind my asking?"

"He must have gotten the sweater."

"So? Don't let him put you on the defensive; he's the one in the wrong, not you."

Laurence took his time approaching them, stopping to address smiles and greetings to various people. A casual observer might not have known Erin was his goal until he stood before her.

"What a nice little frock. A sweater wouldn't have been appropriate anyway, would it?"

The bland insolence of his voice brought a rush of anger that destroyed the last vestige of Erin's nervousness. "I don't take bribes," she said bluntly.

The columnist's eyes narrowed. "I should have known you'd misunderstand. You're a novice at this game and I fear your friends aren't much more experienced than you."

This was obviously directed at Nick, who resented it as fiercely as Laurence had known he would; his face darkened, but before he could retort, Laurence went on smoothly, "Contrary to what you may have heard about me, I have a generous heart. I like giving presents to deserving inferiors. If I had been trying to bribe you, dear girl, I'd have sent diamonds, not knitwear. Keep in mind; I won't charge you for the advice. And do try not to lose your sense of proportion. Ask yourself the essential question before you leap to conclusions. Have you anything I'd be willing to pay for?"

He started to turn away, but Erin was too angry to let him have the last word. "And you might ask yourself, Mr. Laurence, whether you have anything that could possibly interest any normal decent person. I wouldn't grab a rope you threw me if I were going down for the third time."

The color rushed to Laurence's face, and then drained away, leaving him as white as his stiff shirtfront. He turned on his heel and walked away.

Impulsively Erin started to follow. Nick wrapped a long arm around her waist and held her back.

"Let me go," she snarled. "I wasn't finished. That cowardly bastard hasn't even got the guts to stand and take it. I'm going to tell him—"

"Please don't," Nick said in an oddly muffled voice. "I couldn't stand it. Will you marry me?"

"What?" She stared at him and realized he was shaking all over with laughter he could barely contain.

"That was the most beautiful thing I've ever seen in my life," Nick stuttered. "And to think the first time I met you you were too prim and proper to take off your jacket. . . . You don't have to marry me if you don't want to, just let me adore you from afar."

"I'll add your application to the others," Erin said. It was a rare and unexpected pleasure to have Nick cool her temper instead of inflame it.

"Forget him," Nick said, sobering. "He isn't worth your trouble. Where's Rosemary got to, do you suppose?"

"I haven't seen her for quite a while. There's Joe, looking like a thundercloud."

"More like a tornado," Nick said. "I hope nothing has gone wrong. I'd better talk to him."

Joe stood alone; his dour expression would have frightened off anyone bent on casual conversation. The evening had taken its toll on him and his attire. His high forehead glistened with perspiration and a stain on his shirtfront had been dimmed, but not obliterated, by hasty first aid. The offending splash appeared to have had a tomato base.

He acknowledged their presence with a deeper scowl and a muttered word that might have been a greeting. "What's up?" Nick asked. "If we're not collecting, we may as well go home."

The attempt at wit was not well received. "We're collecting. No thanks to you two; every time I see you, you're stuck together like Siamese twins. Why aren't you mingling?"

"Rosemary is the star," Nick said. "We are only faint spots of light in the firmament, undetectable except by a high-powered telescope."

"Rosemary!" Joe gritted his teeth. "I knew she was in a weird mood, but she's so damned bullheaded, nobody can stop her when she. . . . Look at her. Just look at her making an ass of herself!"

Rosemary's petite size and the fact that she was always surrounded by people made her hard to locate. Following Joe's gesture, Erin recognized . . . the fan. Opened to its full size, it covered the lower half of Rosemary's face. Her eyes were fixed on the man who leaned toward her, talking and smiling so emphatically his jowls quivered. The light reflected dazzlingly from the silver streaks in Rosemary's hair and the hairless dome of her admirer's head.

"Look at her," Joe repeated. "Smirking and flirting and coming on to that lascivious old—"

"Lascivious!" Nick laughed. "A four-syllable word, no less. Who is he?"

The name Joe mentioned meant nothing to Erin, but it impressed Nick. "One of the *Fortune* Five Hundred," he murmured. "What's the problem, Joe? That's what she's here for, isn't it—to charm the cash out of those bulging pockets?"

"She's hamming it up. Making fun of him."

"He's too dumb and too horny to catch on," Nick said, his smile broadening as he watched One of the *Fortune* Five Hundred trying to look over the fan and down the front of Rosemary's dress.

"That's what I'm afraid of," said Joe, and departed without further comment.

He detached Rosemary from her admirer with brusque efficiency; leaving the hopeful one gaping. Rosemary didn't appreciate his interference. Her smile never wavered, but the purportedly playful tap of her fan on Joe's cheek produced a wince clearly visible to the fascinated observers across the room. They exchanged glances.

"Warm in here, isn't it?" Nick said.

"That looked like jealousy," Erin exclaimed. "Pure, naked jealousy. Do you think Joe—"

"Please don't say it," Nick begged. "I can't stand it."

"Why shouldn't he be in love with her? Isn't she entitled to some personal happiness? She needs someone who cares for her as a woman, not a political robot—"

"The last thing she needs is a campaign manager who's so besotted he can't think straight."

"Politics and love don't mix?"

"Well, I wouldn't necessarily insist on that. . . . How about a little more champagne?"

"I've had enough. I'm saying stupid things." Erin dabbed

delicately at her upper lip with the handkerchief Kay had insisted on giving her.

"A breath of fresh air, perhaps?" Nick suggested. "You won't need your scarf; the terrace is heated."

"The terrace is what?"

"Electric coils under the flagstones. I read about it in some magazine."

They threaded their way through the crowd, which seemed to have increased. The celebrities, including Rosemary, were surrounded; a flourish of the fan betrayed her presence and suggested Joe's lecture hadn't had much effect. Erin caught a glimpse of Jeff in deep discussion with a tall slender female swathed in emerald-green taffeta—the Style editor of the *Post*, according to Nick.

Electric coils notwithstanding, the terrace was cooler than the drawing room, and the fresh breeze felt good on Erin's feverish cheeks. People were seated at the tables scattered along the expanse of flagstones. A woman who had been pointed out to Erin as the wife of an influential Democratic senator looked deep into the eyes of a man who was not the influential senator; at another table a group of men had their heads together in a discussion whose intensity appeared to be financial rather than romantic. It was a good place for a private conversation. The musicians were making such a din that Nick had to yell in order to be heard.

"Let's get out of this!"

A glare of blue-white light drew them along a winding path that ended in another flagstoned terrace fronting the swimming pool. It was enormous, heart-shaped, and of course heated. Erin was not surprised at any of these features; what did surprise her was the extremely artificial and pricey scent that permeated the air. Juliet must have dumped a couple of gallons of Musky Lust into the water.

Farther along the terrace a rumba band, ruffled from wrists to waists, performed while laughing couples made rough stabs at the intricate steps. There were murals along the sides and bottom of the pool; dolphins, mermaids, Father Neptune complete with beard and trident, and other interesting accoutrements. Erin gasped. "That man—there—he hasn't got on any—"

"Neither does she," said Nick, indicating the second of the two intertwined bodies. Slowly, hieratically, the writhing forms sank toward the bottom of the pool.

"They'll drown!"

"No such luck," Nick said. "How about a refreshing dip?"

"No such luck."

"My dear young woman, I was not proposing anything improper. I'm sure those engaging little cabanas are fully equipped with bathing attire in every possible size and shape."

Erin supposed the structures in question were cabanas. What they looked like was a row of ancient Roman houses, with terra-cotta facades and red-tiled roofs. She stared at them incredulously.

"She had them copied from the ruins of Ostia," Nick said. "But I understand the murals on the inside walls are from Pompeii. You know the ones I mean."

"Oh, those murals. I've heard about them." In fact she had seen a set of purportedly bootlegged postcards. Italian guides made a big deal of showing the paintings of Pompeii's whorehouse only to men, but it was said that a bribe—even a modest bribe—would remove their moral principles.

"Heard about them? If you haven't seen them—"

"No." Erin resisted his attempt to draw her toward the restored ruins. "God, this is disgusting. It's not that I object to orgies per se, but a political fund-raiser. . . . And for Rosemary!"

"It's not that I object to orgies or to any means of raising dough; I just hate tacky orgies," Nick said laughing. "Let's take a turn in the garden. 'Where every prospect pleases, And only man is vile.' "

The gardens of Magnolia Hill were famous, tended lovingly for generations. The lighting, it was safe to assume, had been added by Juliet. But even the garish spots and clusters of colored lanterns could not destroy the classic elegance of the landscaping. The waxy white magnolia blossoms were long since gone, but the glossy leaves glimmered with a more austere beauty; azaleas and rhododendrons formed masses of soft foliage; and the fall flowers put on a brave show. There were shadowy alcoves along the winding, carefully manicured paths. As they moved farther from the house the music faded, allowing them to hear softer sounds—rustles and muted laughter and heavy breathing. They had to go some distance before they found a bench that was unoccupied, probably because it was brightly illumined by overhanging lanterns.

The garden it faced had been laid out in formal French style, with angular strips of low plantings outlining squares and circles of earth. A few roses still struggled to bloom; the circular pool in the center of the bed was as still as a dark mirror.

The lanterns were red, yellow, and blue—bright red, yellow, and blue. They turned Nick's face into a bizarre patchwork of color. Erin knew hers must look just as odd, but Nick didn't seem to notice. "Are you cold?" he asked softly. She shook her head, but Nick took off his jacket and draped it around her shoulders. She leaned against the warmth of his arm and shoulder; when his other hand touched her cheek and turned her face toward his she protested.

"We're absolutely spotlighted, Nick. Anyone can see—"

"So what?"

The distant beat of the music was drowned out by the rush of blood in her veins as his lips found hers, gently at first, then with growing insistence. Her arms went around him, hands moving slowly across the hard muscles of his back until they found a resting place, and she felt his response in the pressure of his mouth and the rhythm of his pulse.

She had forgotten about the lanterns overhead and the possibility of being observed. It was Nick who ended the kiss with a final soft touch on her parted lips. He guided her head into the curve of his shoulder and rested his cheek against her hair.

It was all very sweet and harmless and romantic, and Nick's kisses aroused her in a way she had never experienced, not with such intensity. There was no reason why she should have felt a gradual, rising unease. It might have been the soft sounds in the trees behind them: sounds that could have been wind, or night animals . . . or something else. The sensation was as difficult to define as it was increasingly peremptory. Erin stirred, and Nick's arms tightened.

"No," she said reluctantly. "Let's go back, it must be late."

"Not that late." His fingers curled around her cheek and turned her face toward his. The warmth of his breath brushed her mouth.

"No. don't. Nick, please."

"What's the matter?"

"Your forehead is blue."

Nick chuckled softly. "Yours is red. It looks wonderful. You look wonderful. You taste wonderful—like strawberries, and roses, and—"

"Nick." She knew now what the trouble was. "Somebody is watching us. I can feel them—eyes, staring, leering. . . ."

"Oh, for God's sake!" Nick let her go so abruptly that she swayed backward. He jumped to his feet. "If you don't want me to kiss you, just say so. You don't have to invent horror stories to turn me off."

He loomed over her, arms crossed, face set in a scowl. Erin scowled back. "One of these days, Nick McDermott, you are going to believe me when I tell you something. It will probably be the same day hell freezes over. Until then . . ."

"I get it. Sure, I get it! I don't need a brick wall to fall on me!" Nick raised his arms in an appeal to the starry heavens. "Women!" he told them.

"Men!" Erin shouted after his retreating form. There was no reply.

As soon as he was out of sight, the discomfort she had forgotten in her anger fell on her with the force of an avalanche. She started up and turned, scanning the clustered shadows. There was no sign of life or of movement, but she knew IT was still there, watching and waiting. She said weakly, "Nick?"

No answer. He really had gone, gone and left her alone in this place of murky shadows and lurid lights. . . . At that moment the lights flickered and went out.

Erin picked up her skirts and ran. Never mind common sense, never mind dignity; the fear that gripped her was primitive and primeval, as reasonless as it was compelling. She wasn't even surprised when something long and dark snaked out of a shrub alongside the path and wrapped around her throat.

The hand that clamped over her mouth as she was dragged into the shrubbery was a little slow. She got out one shrill cry before her breath was cut off, not only by the fingers squeezing her face but by the arm pressed against her throat. She kicked and squirmed and tried to bite. When the deadly grip suddenly released her she thought for a moment that her struggles had succeeded. Then she heard him.

"Erin? Where the hell are you? Erin, answer me. . . . Oh, damn!"

He had fallen over her feet, which were stretched across the path.

The ensuing interval was a wild fumbling in the dark that ended with both of them kneeling, their arms around one another. Nick's conversation consisted solely of profanity and self-recrimination. "I never should have gone off like that . . . damn it, damn it, oh, shit, are you all right? Oh, damn it to hell!"

Finally they composed themselves, and still embracing, staggered along the path until they found light. Nick stopped, held her off at arm's length, and inspected her.

"No blood," he said, his voice wavering. "Are you . . ."

"I'm not hurt. Just shook up. What about my dress? It's torn, isn't it? I can feel a breeze down my back."

"Never mind your goddamn dress. I should be kicked from here to Florida and back. Leaving you alone with this place full of drunks and dirty old men—"

"Dirty old . . . Oh. Are you suggesting—"

"I'm not suggesting anything, I'm too busy despising myself." Nick groaned and smote himself heavily on the brow. "And after you told me, begged me—you said there was somebody there. . . . How about if I lie down and you jump on me a few times? Then we'll go over to the pool and I'll quietly drown myself while you watch."

"Don't go to all that trouble just for me," Erin said.

He grabbed her, holding her so tightly she squeaked in protest. "I've never been as glad to see anyone as I was to see you," she admitted. "But my dress—"

"Women," Nick said, grinning sheepishly. "Turn around and let's have a look. Hmmm. Seems to be a slit or a hole or something down the back. Very sexy. However, you might care to resume my coat until you can wend your way to the ladies' room and make repairs."

"Your coat! I had it. . . . It must be back there in the bushes."

"I'll go look. You wait here." It was evident from Nick's expression that he hoped to find something besides his coat in the bushes, but Erin refused to be left behind, and Nick didn't argue with her. He was doomed to disappointment; the coat was there, crumpled and dusty, but there was no sign of anyone.

Nick held her hand tightly as they retraced their steps. He was silent, having used up his stock of expletives, and Erin was absorbed in her thoughts. No doubt Nick was right, her attacker must have been one of Juliet's guests, too drunk to know what he was doing or too drunk to care. But there had been nothing even remotely sexual about that hard grip. She couldn't even be certain that it had been a man's arm and hand.

The majority of the guests had left but a few remained— the serious eaters and drinkers, and the journalists, hanging grimly on for fear of missing some titillating news item. They had some reason to hope for a damaging statement or embarrassing display; a goodly number of those present were far from sober, including the hostess, who was notorious for her after-hours performances.

The latter clung limpetlike to Rosemary. "You can't leave yet, dahling, I haven't had a chance to talk to you. Now that those other boring people have gone home, we could . . . dance, maybe? Or have a good old-fashioned sing-along. Where's that damned piano player?"

"Things appear to be getting out of hand," said Erin, as the distinguished actress lifted the damask tablecloth and bent to peer under it—looking for the vanished pianist. "Where's Joe?"

"He's given up," Nick said, indicating the weary figure propped against a bookcase. From Joe's expression of satisfaction Erin deduced that the take had been even better than he had hoped.

"Poor Rosemary," she said. "She looks exhausted."

Nick squared his shoulders and straightened his tie. " 'Once more into the breach, dear friends. . . .' "

The distraction proved effective, though it took the famous thespian a few seconds to recognize Nick. The contact lenses she wore to intensify the color of her famous sapphire-blue eyes seemed to be irritating them.

He succeeded in distracting her from Rosemary, but not from her determination to prolong the life of the party. "Dolls," she murmured, gazing into Nick's eyes.

"Uh," said Nick. "I don't think—"

"No, honey, you're right. Dollhouses. That was it. I was gonna show you my . . . Hey, Rosie! You haven't seen my collection." Her coordination was better than it appeared. Without loosing her hold on Nick she made a grab for Rosemary, who was edging away. "Come on. We'll all go see my collection!"

Nick went with Juliet—it was that, or have the sleeve of his rented suit ripped off. Erin joined Rosemary, who had waved away a proffered tray filled with brimming glasses. Rosemary's cheeks had a grayish tinge and her smile was as rigid as concrete.

"You must be ready to lie down and die," Erin said.

Rosemary studied her thoughtfully. Erin was suddenly conscious of her disheveled state—smeared lipstick, tumbled hair, and, most damning of all, Nick's jacket, which she still wore because she had not had a chance to examine the damage to her dress. That Rosemary observed these phenomena was obvious; that she misinterpreted them became clear when she tactfully refrained from comment.

"On the whole, I think I'd rather kill Juliet," she said. "Oh, well, such are the vicissitudes of politics. Maybe she'll pass out on the dolls."

It was a long walk, down crossing corridors, to the rooms where Juliet kept her collection. The rooms were unlocked but not undefended. A guard had been posted in the corridor. He saluted Juliet respectfully; she paid no more attention to him than if he had been a suit of armor.

No doubt the dolls were beautiful, rare, and expensive. Erin was too tired to give them more than a passing glance, or pay much attention to their hostess's lecture. Juliet admitted she couldn't remember all the names, but she knew what each had cost, down to the last penny.

Most of the dolls were in glass cases, along with various accessories—clothing, doll furniture, and so on. In the center of the room, on long tables arranged in an open square, were a number of dollhouses. They ranged from an elaborately detailed Victorian mansion inhabited by a large family of blank-faced dolls to a reproduction of a Tudor cottage with a real thatched roof and an attached garden of tiny dried flowers. Erin stood swaying gently, her eyes half-closed, until a voice murmured, "You appear as animated and as charming as these dolls. I'm about to escape; I presume if I offered to drive you home, you'd mistake my intentions again."

Erin forced her eyes open and looked up at him. "Mr. Laurence, if this is your idea of an amusing game, get someone else to play with you. And if it's supposed to count as an apology for your boorishness, don't trouble yourself."

A faint but perceptible flush stained Laurence's high cheekbones. "I deserved that," he said with unexpected humility. "If you'd just give me a chance to explain why I behaved so badly . . ." He broke off with a hiss of annoyance. "Joe, as I live and breathe. Have you no tact? Didn't you observe I was trying to make my peace with a justly offended lady?"

"Is that what you were doing?" Joe yawned till his jaw cracked. "Do me a favor and work on turning Juliet off. I can't stand this much longer. Dolls, for Christ's sake!"

"Juliet is one of those unfortunate individuals who can't endure her own company," Laurence replied. "Small wonder; no one else can endure it for long. Very well, old chap, since you ask me, I'll see what can be done."

But Rosemary had taken matters into her own hands. Erin observed the technique admiringly; it consisted of talking without drawing breath or allowing the other person to get a word in, while moving inexorably toward the exit. "Dahling Juliet, it's been so unbelievable, I cannot tell you; I'll call, write, bless you; come along, Erin, everyone, it's been so-o-o-o-o stupefying. . . ."

She glided out of the room, followed by her hostess. Joe let out a sigh of relief. "Thank God. Hurry up, Erin, before Rosie has to stop for breath."

They were in the vestibule collecting coats and wraps when they heard the hoarse shouts and the pound of heavy running feet.

Joe swore long and loud, but they had no choice but to retrace their steps. One could hardly desert the ship without at least asking what had caused the alarm.

They were in time to catch one quick, unforgettable glimpse of the disaster. The cottage was burning, with a miniature fury as delicate as the flaming flowers in its garden. A golden lacework of fire covered the thatched roof. One of the doll-dwellers, dressed in flowered farthingale and tiny ruff, lay face down across the threshold as if it had fallen in a futile attempt to escape. Then the guard ran in with a fire extinguisher and a fountain of white foam buried the ruins.

Chapter
Eight

BY THE TIME Erin finally got to bed she was so tired she thought she could sleep through a hurricane. But some part of her mind must have remained alert and on watch; when the sounds from the adjoining room began, she woke instantly.

Every limb felt as if it were encased in iron, and for a while she argued sleepily with the warning mental voice. "It's just Kay going to the bathroom, she doesn't need me...." But the footsteps didn't cross the hall, they passed her door and went on. "She can't sleep, she's going down for a book or a glass of milk...." The silent sentry didn't believe that either. There was something about the footsteps.... They were too loud, they clicked emphatically, with no consideration for other sleepers in the house.

Erin struggled out of bed and ran to the door. She had opened her window and the night air was chilly, but she didn't stop to put on robe or slippers. Kay's footsteps, still unmuted, made it clear that she was heading for one of the rooms on the second floor. Erin followed. The light on the landing, which was left burning at night, showed her that Rosemary's door stood wide open, though the room itself was dark.

Erin's alarmed imagination boiled with theories she would have been ashamed to voice aloud. But surely there was something wrong. No one would waken a weary friend except in a dire emergency, and if Kay were bent on a private conference she wouldn't make so much noise, or leave the door ajar.

Noiseless, on bare feet, she crept toward the door, not entirely certain of what she intended to do. As she stood in brief hesitation, a light went on within; and in its glow Erin beheld an eerie sight: Kay, standing at the foot of the bed, perfectly perpendicular and totally unconscious. Her staring eyes looked past Rosemary at some vision only she could see, and her hands fumbled across the blankets like those of a blind woman.

Rosemary's face was crumpled and sallow. The muscles in her throat contracted as she swallowed. "Kay," she said hoarsely. "What is it?"

Kay's hearing was as distorted as her vision. She did not respond. Bending stiffly, she raised the ruffled flounce and looked under the bed. Then she straightened, crossed the room, and went into the closet.

"I'm sorry," Erin whispered from the doorway. "I heard her moving around, and there was something odd. . . . She's sleepwalking, isn't she?"

"It would seem so." Rosemary showed no surprise at seeing her.

"Has she done this before?"

Rosemary shook her head. "Not for years. . . ." She started violently. A voice—obviously Kay's, but eerily unlike her normal tones—echoed from the depths of the closet.

"Nobody. Nobody here. Have to make sure. Where else? . . . The dressing room? Have to look. Make sure he is all right. . . ."

Rosemary threw back the covers. Her nightgown was an astonishingly flimsy feminine concoction of ruffles and lace and ribbons, but she didn't seem to be aware of the cold.

Kay was groping among the garments hanging on the racks. She had not turned on the light, and Erin shivered with a chill that had nothing to do with the temperature of the room. Could a sleepwalker see in the dark? Impossible. There was nothing supernatural about the phenomenon, it was a purely explicable, if not exactly normal, aberration. . . .

"It's all right, Kay," Rosemary said quietly. "There's no one here."

She had to repeat the reassurances over and over before they penetrated Kay's sleeping and obsessed mind, but when Rosemary finally took her gently by the arm she went along, docile as a child. Between them they got her up the stairs and into bed. The moment she lay down, her eyes closed and she began to snore.

Rosemary let out a long, shaken breath. "She'll be all right now. Try to get some sleep."

"But what if she—"

"She won't. At least . . ." Rosemary fell silent; every strained muscle in her face mirrored her thoughts as she grappled with the problem, considering alternatives, and decided on a course of action.

"I'll lock her door," she said finally. "If she wakes before I can unlock it—well, that can't be helped, I'll have to tell her anyway. . . . Take action to prevent this from happening again. Perhaps you had better lock the connecting door as well. Don't worry, it's extremely unlikely that she would repeat the performance twice in one night. I'd appreciate it if you didn't mention this, not even to Kay. I'll tell her she woke me when she came into my room and that I got her into bed without disturbing anyone. She'd be distressed and humiliated to think anyone else knew about her weakness, as she would view it."

She had it all figured out. "I'll do whatever you want," Erin said.

Rosemary put an affectionate hand on her arm and exclaimed, "Good heavens, child, you're cold as ice. Hop back into bed. Don't give this another thought, it's not your responsibility."

Whose then? Erin wondered, as she curled up under the

covers and tried to defrost her frozen feet. Rosemary's, of course. How long had it been since Kay stopped being a prop on which Rosemary could lean and started to become just another burden? Days—or years? Jeff had mentioned Kay's increasing inefficiency, but that was only part of the problem. Kay was devoted and dedicated to someone—but that someone wasn't Rosemary. The single revealing pronoun that had slipped from her subconscious gave her true feelings away. "He" could only be Edward Marshall—long dead, but still the object of her fanatical concern. Erin could only wonder that she had been so slow to recognize the truth. Kay never referred to Rosemary by the title she had won; "congressman" was reserved for Edward. And whose idea had it been to preserve his office like a shrine?

It must have been sheer hell to live like that, Erin thought drowsily. To be, not just the shadow of your predecessor, but the shadow of a ghost.

She fell asleep before she could decide what, if anything, she could do about the situation. The sentry went off duty; she didn't wake until sunlight stroked her closed eyelids.

Her first thought was for the occupant of the adjoining room. Jumping out of bed, she went to the connecting door and turned the key.

Kay's room was unoccupied. The bed was neatly made. Rosemary had been as good as her word.

From the strength of the sunlight Erin realized it must be late morning. Her watch had stopped; she had forgotten to wind it the night before. She put on jeans and a sweatshirt emblazoned with "Rosemary White Marshall for Senator" and ran downstairs.

There was no one in the commons room—not even Will. Erin remembered he had said something about having to go to Charlottesville. She was filling a cup from the coffee urn when Christie came in. "Good morning, Cinderella. Or should it be Sleeping Beauty?"

The tone was less provocative than the words, however, and Christie went on, "I guess you're entitled to sleep in. What happened last night? I tried to worm it out of Jeff, but you know him, he just primped his mouth and looked stern."

She splashed coffee into a cup and sat down next to Erin. The latter took her time about answering. If she had learned one thing since she started working for Rosemary, it was to think before she spoke. Not that she always succeeded in following the rule. . . .

The brilliant scarlet and mustard-yellow stripes of Christie's skirt made her eyes ache. Christie also wore a sweatshirt, they were standard issue, but she had added a few strands of bright beads and shoved the sleeves up to her elbows. On her, the baggy garment looked like a designer creation.

With an effort Erin forced her memory back past the sleep-walking episode—which Christie couldn't possibly know about—to the reception. How much did Christie know—how much should she be told? Was she only curious about the life-style of the rich and notorious, or had she heard of the evening's blazing conclusion?

"It was a great place to visit, but I wouldn't want to live there," she said cautiously.

"Then you're crazy. Who was there? Did you talk to Juliet? What was she wearing? How was the food? Did you get to meet Paul Newman and Stevie Cortlandt?"

"Stevie . . . oh, the singer. I didn't get to meet anybody," Erin admitted regretfully. "The famous names were surrounded all evening."

Christie didn't bother to conceal her contempt. "Why didn't you walk right up and introduce yourself? I can't imagine being in the same room with Robert Redford and not having the gumption to meet him."

"It was a rather—confused evening," Erin said humbly. Knowing Christie wouldn't give up until she had squeezed some vicarious excitement out of the event, she launched into a description of the buffet, Juliet's gown, and the guest list. "I gather it was a success financially," she added. "At least Joe implied it was."

"Yeah, he is even talking about hiring a direct-mail company. How was Nick?"

"Haven't you seen him?"

"No. He left you a message."

"With you?"

"How could he leave a message with me when I didn't see him?"

Erin bit back a sharp retort. She didn't blame Christie for resenting her evening out; in Christie's place she would have felt the same. Passing over a highly placed worker in favor of a newcomer still wet behind the ears wasn't just or kind. It was not the first time Erin had wondered why she was so extraordinarily favored.

"He left a note," Christie said, rising. "It's on your desk. You do remember where your desk is?"

That didn't deserve a reply either. Erin followed Christie into the office, where she found Nick's note lying on her desk blotter. It was brief and to the point: "Had to go out, see you lunchtime. We need to talk."

An emphatic black slash underlined "need." Erin slipped the note into her pocket. She "needed" to talk to Nick too. They had barely spoken on the drive home.

She worked steadily until twelve. Nick hadn't shown up, so she went looking for him and found him in the commons room browsing among the cold cuts. On the table next to him was a fat green-eyed calico cat devouring a piece of salami.

Another tribute to the memory of Edward Marshall. . . . Erin picked the cat up and carried it out, the salami still dangling from its mouth. When she returned, Nick looked at her sourly. "If you are quite finished playing with the kitties," he began.

"They aren't supposed to be in here, much less eating off the plates. Are you too hung over to notice such minor details?"

"I am not hung over."

"Preoccupied, then. Your note was somewhat peremptory—"

Nick cleared his throat loudly and gestured. "You haven't said hello to Will."

"I didn't see him. Hello, Will."

"Hello," said Will.

"I thought you were in Charlottesville."

There was no answer from Will; by his standards none was required, since it was obvious he wasn't in Charlottesville.

"He just got back," Nick said. "Want to go for a walk?"

"I haven't had lunch.",

"Oh." Nick slapped a piece of ham between two pieces of bread and handed it to her. "Here."

"Thanks," Erin said. There were other things she might have said—yearned to say, in fact—but Nick didn't give her the opportunity. "Nice day for a picnic," he mumbled, nudging her toward the door.

It was a nice day. Jackson and Jan had taken advantage of the sunshine and were sitting on the porch eating their sandwiches. Instead of lingering to talk as he usually did, Nick replied to their greetings with an abstracted wave and kept walking.

He had made it clear that he wanted a private conversation, so Erin waited till they were some distance from the house before she spoke. "Has something happened?"

"Has something happened?" Nick directed his query to the unheeding sky, arms flung wide in appeal. "Listen to the woman! You saw what happened. Too many things have happened. Doesn't anyone but me wonder why they're happening and who is making them happen?"

Erin came to a stop. "Nick, if you want to talk, I'll listen. I can't concoct sensible answers to incoherent cries of woe. Let's sit down. This isn't much of a lunch, but I want to eat it."

Nick stared. "My God, you sounded just like Rosemary. Aren't you going to yell at me for treating you like an object?"

"No, but I may throw something. There's a lot to be said for Rosemary's methods. She seems to get more respect from you guys than I do."

"I'm sorry. I lay awake half the night brooding about this, and I've got to get it off my chest before I explode."

Two cats joined them on the bench under the pines—one gray Persian, one tabby of questionable ancestry—and Erin fed them bits of the sandwich while Nick sat in silence scowling at his dusty shoes. Finally she said, "For a man who threatened to explode if he wasn't allowed to talk, you aren't being very vocal."

"I'm trying to find a good lead." Nick ran his fingers through his hair. "How does this grab you? 'What lunatic has been setting all the goddamn fires?' "

"Too wordy. If there is such a word as 'wordy.' "

Nick wasn't listening. "Politics is a weird business and a lot of weird things can happen during a campaign. Hate mail, demonstrations, even assault and battery. But I've never heard of anything like this. Taken singly, the incidents are meaningless and nonthreatening. When you add them up. . . . And please don't utter the word 'coincidence.' "

"I wasn't going to. You seem to have forgotten that we discussed this same subject a week ago. You were the skeptic then. You laughed at me when I suggested—"

"Laugh! I did not." Erin fixed him with a steady stare. After a moment Nick's eyes dropped. "Anyhow, things were different then. The fire last night was one coincidence too many."

"He's slow but he's sure," Erin informed one of the cats, who opened its mouth as if to reply but yawned instead. "Why don't you admit it, Nick? You didn't want to see a pattern in these incidents because it was Laurence who proposed the theory."

"Er—never mind that. Laurence's theory is off the wall, Erin. Even in sensational fiction it's against the rules to make the criminal a homicidal maniac."

Erin protested. "Don't use that word. Nobody has been killed, or even hurt."

"Not yet."

The dry sandwich stuck in Erin's throat. She divided the rest of it between the drooling cats.

"These incidents are not the work of a lunatic, homicidal or otherwise," Nick went on. "The first two fires could have been accidental. The third, in the cemetery, was no accident; but its significance, insofar as Rosemary is concerned, was questionable. Any anonymous loony could have done it, for any one of a hundred reasons. Last night . . . That could have been an accident too. The material of that dollhouse was highly flammable and there were a lot of drunks wandering around brandishing cigars and cigarettes. But that makes four fires in a row, four in less than two weeks, and all of them connected in one way or another with Rosemary. There's a recurrent theme, isn't there?''

"You're forgetting something," Erin said reluctantly. "The doll, or poppet, or whatever you want to call it."

"I hadn't forgotten. I was waiting for you to bring it up. Same theme, Erin. It was smeared with ashes."

Erin sighed. "Fire again."

"Yeah."

"What about the attack on me last night?"

"Obviously I considered that. But it doesn't fit the theme. Unless there was something you forgot to mention."

"No lighted matches or smell of smoke," Erin said wryly. "I guess it was just your common garden-variety rapist. That's a relief, in a way; I'd rather not be part of your pattern. But Nick, what's the point of it all? Without some logical connection—some common, underlying motive—the incidents don't fit together. Are they meant to be threats—warnings of worse to come? Like, for instance, setting fire to the house?"

"I don't think so. It would be too difficult to start a fire that could cause serious damage, much less bodily harm. There are smoke detectors in every room, people coming and going all day, the dogs patrolling at night. It seems more likely to me that the fires aren't portents of future events, but reminders of a past event."

Erin felt a cowardly sense of relief. She and Kay would be most vulnerable to an attack by fire; the rooms on the second floor had wide windows and a relatively easy drop into thick shrubbery below.

"That's ingenious," she said. "Rosemary's past, you mean?"

"She's the focus," Nick insisted. "Maybe I'm unduly influenced by the political angle, but that's the nightmare of every campaign staff—the fear that the candidate has something nasty lurking in the closet, disclosure of which could wreck his chances. Rosemary has run for office before, but those were shoo-ins, virtually uncontested races. This is different. This could lead . . . all the way to the top. Buzz Bennett isn't the only one who would pay any price to get something damaging on Rosemary.''

"Agreed. But Nick, if Bennett knew about the skeleton in the closet, he wouldn't play cat and mouse, he'd just leak it to the press. Wouldn't he?''

"I would think so. I've been over this again and again, and I can't make sense of it either. But I'll be damned if I'm going to sit here like a toad on a rock and wait for the next fire.''

"Have you discussed this with anyone else?''

"Who, for instance?'' He turned to face her, his eyes narrowed and his lips tight. "You're too intelligent to miss the logical conclusion, Erin; you just don't want to admit it. The arsonist isn't an outsider. It has to be one of us.''

Erin was unable to produce a convincing counterargument. Not only had she reached the same conclusion, she had carried it one step farther; to an unbiased observer, she must be high on the list of suspects, if not at the top.

Luckily for her, Nick was not unbiased. She saw no point in mentioning this little aberration, since it would only have hurt his feelings; and anyway, he could undoubtedly come up with a convincing rationalization for his naive trust in her.

She edged closer to him and he responded at once, draping his arm around her shoulders and smiling as cheerfully as if the ominous scenario he had produced were only a plot for a novel he planned to write. If she had cheered him, he had done the same for her; bad as it was, his theory wasn't as grisly as some of the ones that had occurred to her.

"Do you suppose Rosemary knows?'' she asked.

"Well, she'd have to, wouldn't she? She hasn't given anything away, but that's only to be expected; these days a politician has to cultivate a poker face and outperform Gielgud. But did you see her face last night when we burst into the room and saw the blazing dollhouse?''

"No.''

"I did. All I can say is, I'm glad she's never had occasion to look at me that way. Now it's not Rosemary's style to remain passive; sooner or later, she'll act—confront her adversary, if she knows who it is, or take steps to find out, if she doesn't. That's why I decided to get you in on this. I can't be with her all the time—''

"Wait a minute." Erin stiffened. "You don't mean . . . spy on her? On Rosemary?''

"I wouldn't exactly put it like that. . . .''

"I would." She moved away from him, to the farthest end of the bench. It was depressing to discover the real reason why Nick had confided in her—not blind, doting trust, but brutal necessity. And the idea of spying sickened her. "Maybe I should get one of those Groucho Marx masks with a big nose and a mustache," she added bitingly.

"You look ridiculous when you're mad," Nick said, grinning.

"Why don't you say I'm cute when I'm mad, and be thoroughly offensive? If a man took offense at your behavior, you wouldn't tell him he was cute—"

"He wouldn't *be* cute. Okay, I'm sorry. Look, Erin, I don't like the idea any better than you do, but it has to be done. For her own good.''

"I'll bet that's what the boys in the CIA tell themselves," Erin grumbled; but when he put his arm around her and pulled her back to his side she didn't resist. "It's impossible, Nick. Aside from the moral issue, how are you going to keep up with Rosemary's activities? She's always on the go these days.''

"Ah, but most of her activities are public," Nick said. "It's her private time that interests me, and God knows she has little of that. I'm not suggesting you should listen at doors or anything like that, just keep an eye on her, and try to let me know if she makes an attempt to sneak off on her own. That would be significant; she almost always has someone with her during the day, Joe or Jeff or Kay.''

"All right, I'll try. But it's a far-out chance, Nick.''

"Admitted. There is one other thing we could do.''

"Like what?''

"Try a little detective work on our own." He was so obviously pleased at the idea, Erin knew better than to laugh. She fixed a bright, interested look on her face, and Nick went on with mounting enthusiasm, "We'll start with the theory that these incidents refer to something in the past involving Rosemary a d maybe her husband. It couldn't have happened recently or someone would have dug it up. Nor could it have occurred more than thirty years ago, because it would be irrelevant.''

"Not necessarily. I've seen so-called exposés about college careers of candidates—something as seemingly trivial as cheating on an exam.''

Nick's answer was a triumph of inverted logic. "Right. So most likely the Marshall name was never mentioned in connection with this unknown event—''

"Then how the hell do you expect to identify it?''

"Ouch." Nick rubbed his ear. "You don't have to yell.''

"Sorry. But you really are . . . Let me try that again. You said yourself that the press and political opponents would love to get something on Rosemary. If skilled investigators haven't found this mysterious crime, how do you think you're going to succeed?''

"We have a clue they don't have," Nick said. "Fire. This has something to do with a fire, not just a little backyard bonfire but something serious. Arson, perhaps. It may have been serious enough to rate newspaper coverage, at least in the local rags. The Marshalls have lived in Virginia since prehistoric times; we won't have to check every newspaper in the country, just those in the state.''

"Oh, great. That shouldn't take more than a month.''

Nick glanced at his watch and then jumped up. "I've got to go. Is there any way you can get to a library in the next few days?''

To call Nick single-minded was to understate the case. None of her reasoned arguments had had the slightest effect, or dimmed his manic enthusiasm one whit. She shook her head. "I don't have a car, remember?''

"Maybe you could ask Kay. . . . No, I guess that won't work. Okay, I think I can get away Friday. Ask for the day off. In the meantime—watch Rosemary. I'm late. Gotta run.''

He planted a quick, forceful kiss on her mouth, hugged her till her ribs creaked, and dashed off.

Erin stood watching him. She was reminded of an antique

movie advertisement for a now-forgotten film—''Will She Kill
Him or Kiss Him?'' She didn't really want to kill him—not
more than once or twice a day, at any rate. His volatile personality took a little getting used to, but really, his outbursts
and subsequent apologies were easier to live with than days
of sulking. As for kissing him . . . Nobody was perfect, especially Nick, but in that particular area he came very close.

The next few days passed quietly, insofar as mysterious
fires were concerned. In every other way they were chaotic.
With Election Day almost upon them, the pace began to pick
up, though Erin would not have believed it to be possible.
Sunday was a working day like any other; no mention was
made of going to church. At least Kay was sleeping through
the night. The bottle of sleeping pills Erin found on her bedside table when she tidied the room might have had something to do with that. Rosemary indulged her old friend and
secretary in a lot of ways, but she could put her foot down
when she had to.

Erin could almost have wished Kay's nights had been more
disturbed; rested and refreshed, the older woman had plenty
of energy during the day, and she kept the others hopping.
Between her household duties and her office chores Erin
barely had time to snatch food at irregular intervals, and Kay's
temper was so short she drove the entire office staff to the
verge of revolution. Yet no one wanted to complain to Rosemary, who had more than enough on her mind as it was. She
was on the go from morning till night, and claimed to be so
full of coffee, tea, and other liquids that she sloshed when
she walked.

''I just wish people wouldn't insist on feeding me,'' she
groaned. ''It can't be because I look undernourished. I can
hardly fasten this skirt.'' She demonstrated, trying to insert
a finger into the waistband.

''Food is a traditional symbol of hospitality and of approval,'' Will explained seriously. ''The psychological implications of offering and accepting sustenance—''

''Don't use that word in my presence, Will,'' Rosemary
said.

Will smiled gently. "Which one? Psychological or implications?"

"Both. Either. None of the above. I'm so sick of jargon."

Passing through the commons room on her way from the kitchen, Erin overheard the last part of the conversation. Rosemary gave her a severe look. "You aren't going to offer me that cup, are you? I don't care what's in it, I don't want it."

"It's for Kay," Erin explained. "She's working on that speech, and she wanted—"

"Working? It's almost midnight. Tell her . . . No, I'll tell her myself. Give me that cup and go to bed."

When Rosemary used that tone, nobody argued with her—except possibly Joe. Erin handed over the coffee. "Oh, great," Rosemary muttered, inspecting the dark liquid. "I don't suppose it's decaffeinated? No, I thought not. That woman . . . She is sleeping, isn't she? No more alarms and excursions?"

She had not lowered her voice. Erin glanced at Will, who had turned his back and bent his head over his papers. "No," she said. "I mean—yes, she's sleeping through the night."

"Good. I told you not to worry about it. You aren't, are you?"

"No."

"Any problems? Anything you want to unload?"

"Nothing," Erin said firmly. "Everything is just fine."

"Liar." Rosemary rose on tiptoe and gave her a quick kiss on the cheek. "Nice, kind, thoughtful liar. Good night, Erin."

The kiss burned like the conventional coals of fire. I can't spy on her, Erin thought, as she beat a hasty retreat. Not even for her own good. Damn Nick anyway. He had gotten her all stirred up and worried, and then disappeared; she hadn't set eyes on him for days. Just like a man . . .

She was awakened at what felt like the crack of dawn by Kay's knock and call: "It's after seven, Erin. Rise and shine."

Rise and shine indeed. It was a phrase Erin particularly loathed, having heard it only too often from her aunt. Nothing else was shining. Fog pressed at the window like a huge gray face, an accidental arrangement of branches without forming slitted eyes and a sullen slash of mouth.

Erin pulled the blanket up over her head. But it was no use; Kay's tone had been of the variety that might be characterized as pleasant but firm.

Sarah's placid, cheerful face and one of Sarah's excellent breakfasts improved her spirits a little, but from then on things went from better to worse. Rosemary was in a bad mood; Joe, never one to take criticism amiably, snapped back at her when she took exception to something he had said; and even Jeff was glum and silent.

The general malaise came to a head later that morning, during a strategy meeting in Rosemary's office. The raised voices and sound of fists pounding furniture were audible in the outer office. Finally the door burst open and Rosemary came out. Her face was crimson with fury. She was followed not by Joe but by his voice which would have carried clear to Middleburg: "Get your butt back in here! We haven't decided—"

"Oh yes, we have!" Whirling around, Rosemary delivered the defiance at top pitch. "I'm not going to do it, and that's final! Who the hell do you think you are?"

A crash from within the office was probably Joe's chair going over. He appeared in the doorway waving his cigar. "I'm the stupid ass who's trying to run this campaign, that's who! I must have been crazy to take on the job. If I can't get the slightest degree of cooperation from you—"

Jeff's anxious face appeared at Joe's shoulder. "Hey, Joe, calm down. Rosemary, why don't you come in and sit down and we'll have a nice quiet discussion—"

This conciliatory speech was drowned out by Joe and Rosemary yelling at once. Rosemary ended the discussion by groping blindly for the nearest loose object on the nearest desk and pitching it straight at Joe.

The results were horrendous. The coffee mug had been half full, but the amount of brown liquid that spattered wall and floor looked like a gallon. Rosemary's aim wasn't too good—or perhaps it was excellent. The cup hit the wall next to the door and shattered, sending fragments flying.

Joe's head came back into view. "Now that you've got that out of your system, come back in here," he said mildly.

"No." Rosemary's voice was just as calm. "I said I won't, and I won't. I'm going upstairs for a while. Leave me alone."

"You're supposed to be on the Hill at two—" Joe began.

Jeff cleared his throat. "We've got a meeting at noon, Joe. In D.C. Maybe we ought to postpone this. The weather is bad and if we don't get started pretty soon. . . ."

"Oh, all right," Joe said ungraciously. "Maybe Rosemary will be through sulking by the time we get back. Honest to God, talk about childish, irrational behavior—"

Jeff reached around him and pulled the door shut.

Rosemary swept the room with a long, sober survey. "Joe is right. That was a childish, rude performance, and I apologize to all of you." Then a broad smile spread across her face. "But, by gosh, it sure felt good!"

She knew how to play an audience. Erin felt her lips stretching into an answering grin, the same look that transformed all the other faces. "Christie, I've made a mess of your office and disgraced myself," Rosemary went on. "I'm afraid you aren't going to respect me in the morning."

She could have spattered the office with Joe's blood and Christie wouldn't have said a word. She murmured a bemused disclaimer. Rosemary gave her an affectionate pat on the back and announced, "I am going into seclusion to meditate on my sins—and maybe get a little work done. See you all later."

She had scarcely left the room when the door of the inner office opened and Nick slithered out. He came straight to Erin. "I need you to help me with something."

"What?"

His back to the others, Nick made a hideous face. What he was trying to convey Erin did not know, but the effect was so grotesque she decided she had better not ask any more questions. He hadn't even answered the first one.

She followed him into the hall. "This is it," Nick hissed theatrically. "Hurry up!"

The hall was quiet and gloomy. There was no one in sight. "This is what?" Erin demanded. "Hurry up where?"

"Jesus H. Christ, do I have to spell everything out?" Nick waved his arms wildly but kept his voice low. "This is a setup. She picked that fight deliberately, to get some time to herself. We have to be ready to follow her."

"It's raining," Erin protested, as he towed her toward the door. "Why can't we wait inside?"

"Because there are five different ways out of this house, and also because when you are trailing someone the idea is to keep them from noticing that that's what you're doing. Here—take this."

He snatched a garment at random from the coats hanging on the hall tree and flung it at her.

Nick's car was parked by the front door, along with several others. Erin struggled into the coat; from its length and its brilliant crimson color, she deduced it must belong to Christie, and she hoped devoutly that that wronged woman would not decide to leave the house before they returned.

Nick fought his usual battle with the recalcitrant car door, finally got it closed, and slid behind the wheel.

"Hunker down," he ordered.

"She couldn't see me if I were outlined in neon," Erin said crossly. "The windows are all fogged up. How long do we have to sit here before you admit you're wrong? Rosemary isn't going anywhere."

"This is the first chance she's had to get away since the last fire," Nick replied, squinting through the rain-streaked windshield. "And that argument was a fake. I know Rosemary; she and Joe are always yelling at each other, but she never walks out on a fight."

"What was the argument about?"

"Joe wanted her to plan a series of speeches and visits to the southwest. That's Bennett country, and we're down in the polls in that part of the state. She said there wasn't time—"

"That's true, isn't it? Her schedule is impossible already."

"There's always time for what has to be done," Nick said. "Then she said— Hey, look! Was I right or was I right? Squat down!"

The figure he had indicated had emerged from one of the side doors and was walking quickly toward the garage. It wore a nondescript flapping raincoat and carried an umbrella; but the brassy gold of its hair was visible even through the falling rain.

"That's not Rosemary. It must be one of the girls who—"

"That's Rosemary. Haven't you ever heard of wigs? I recognize her walk." The keys were already in the ignition; his fingers played with them but did not turn them. "Hunker—"

"Shut up."

Before long they heard the sound of a motor, and a vehicle came into sight. It was the old pickup truck; through the window Erin saw a glint of brassy hair. The driver's head did not turn as the truck passed them and lurched along the rutted driveway, sending sprays of water from under the wheels.

Nick turned the key. The engine whined and coughed and died. "Goddamn battery," he muttered. The truck reached the gate, paused briefly, and turned left. Nick swore and pounded the dash with his left fist; the engine caught, stuttered, and settled to an uneasy roar.

Erin was thrown forward, then back, as Nick went in hot pursuit. His natural resiliency had asserted itself and he was beaming with satisfaction. "We can't follow too close anyhow," he explained. "I should have taken one of the other cars, I guess, but there wasn't time to borrow . . . Oops, sorry, you'd better buckle the seat belt, I may have to make some quick stops and turns."

Erin rubbed her forehead. It had contacted the windshield rather forcibly when Nick hit a large-sized pothole. He continued to drive with more panache than care until they caught sight of the pickup a few hundred yards ahead. Rosemary— if it was Rosemary—was driving under the speed limit, keeping carefully in her lane and slowing on every curve. Rain had soaked the fallen leaves into slippery masses and visibility was poor; but Nick, characteristically, found another interpretation for the other driver's caution.

"She doesn't want to get stopped by a cop," he muttered. "Wonder where she's going?"

"Home, I shouldn't wonder. If that's one of the maids—"

"It is not one of the maids, none of 'em have hair that color. Nobody has hair that color. . . . They wouldn't take the truck, it belongs to the estate."

"Maybe they—she—got permission to borrow it. Maybe she's going home to get lunch for her husband, or on an errand for Sarah."

"You have a very vivid imagination," said Nick, banging on the windshield in an ineffectual effort to speed up the wipers, which seemed to suffer from the same lassitude that affected all the other parts of the car.

"*I* have a vivid imagination? If that's Rosemary, why didn't she use her own car? Or Kay's?"

"Obviously because she doesn't want to be recognized," Nick said smugly. "Sam won't even notice the truck is missing; he's deaf as a post and right now he's absorbed in his soaps. No reason for him to go out on a day like this."

Ominous noises from under the dash implied that the heater had been turned on, but the air blasting Erin's legs was ice cold. She turned the collar of the coat up and shivered.

Her own theory received a blow when they passed through Middleburg without stopping and headed east on Route 50. Most of the kitchen workers were local people, and 50 was the most direct route to Washington. Nick grunted with satisfaction as the pickup increased its speed. "I knew it. She's meeting someone. If she turns north at the crossroads, she could be going to Leesburg."

The pickup turned south, onto Route 15. "Not Leesburg," Nick muttered. "The Virginia suburbs? Route 15 to 66, I'll bet. She should have stayed on 50."

There was a good deal of traffic; Nick let several other vehicles get between them and their quarry. The wipers wheezed and stuttered.

Some distance ahead a stoplight glowed green, where a state route intersected the highway. Without signaling, the truck moved into the left lane, catching Nick by surprise. He stamped on the brake. "Now where the hell is she going? Come on, one of you guys, get in that left lane, I don't want to be right behind her. . . ."

The truck had to wait for oncoming traffic to clear. The

light turned yellow and it completed its turn, followed, illegally, by the car behind it. Nick pulled into the left lane and sat quivering with frustration while the pickup disappeared into the distance. "That is Route 234. Maybe she's going to take 29 east to Fairfax. Unless she spotted us and is trying to lose us. . . . Damn! She's going to do it, too, if I don't get moving!"

He made an illegal turn on the red; the car veered sickeningly as the balding tires skidded on wet pavement.

"Nick, for God's sake," Erin groaned.

"It's okay, I'm a good driver," Nick assured her. Water rose in a mighty spray as the car roared through a puddle.

After a frenzied mile or so they caught up with the pickup, whose driver was proceeding at a sedate pace. Nick grunted with satisfaction and slowed down. In good weather it would have been a pleasant drive, for the road wound and curved through the countryside, and the fall foliage was muted by mist into soft pale shades of umber and topaz, like a time-faded tapestry. Gradually the rain slackened to a drizzle and the sky brightened.

Nick paid no attention to the scenery or the weather, he was still theorizing. "Wherever she's going, it's this side of the Beltway. Fairfax, maybe, or west Falls Church. She'll have to turn on 29."

She didn't. A stoplight marked the intersection. Instead of turning, the pickup crossed the highway.

"Manassas," Nick said blankly. "She's heading for Manassas. Why would anyone want to go there?"

Erin huddled into the folds of the coat. The question was obviously rhetorical, so she didn't answer it, though she could think of a number of reasons why a number of people might want to go to Manassas. It contained as many potential voters as any other town of its size in Virginia, and it was large enough to rate a temporary Democratic campaign office. However, she was becoming a reluctant convert to Nick's theory. A worker on a legitimate errand to local headquarters would take his or her car, not Sam's pickup.

The imminence of the town was announced by the usual sprawl of commercial clutter—gas stations, fast-food chains, motels. Traffic had thickened; there were several other vehicles between them and the truck when it made a sudden turn into a small shopping center and pulled into a parking place next to a fast-food restaurant with a familiar arch. Nick followed suit, picking a spot from which he could see but not easily be seen. The driver got out of the truck and trotted toward the restaurant. She was not carrying an umbrella, but she had tied a brown scarf over her brassy curls.

By this time Erin was thoroughly infected with the thrill of the chase. Height, shape, and walk were definitely Rosemary's and the choice of a rendezvous was unexceptionable if her aim was to pass unrecognized. No one would expect to see Rosemary Marshall lunching in a McDonald's on the outskirts of a town forty miles from home, and the chance of accidentally encountering a colleague was almost nonexistent.

"Now what?" she asked.

"We can't go in," Nick said. "She'd see us for sure. Are you hungry?"

"Not especially. Are you?"

"I'm always hungry. Have you got any money?"

"Not a cent. You dragged me out of the house before I could get my purse."

Nick shifted position and dragged a worn wallet out of his hip pocket. It bulged, but not with cash; sorting through a motley collection of business cards, scribbled notes, and receipts, Nick finally located a few bills. "Seven bucks. Hey, not bad. What would you like?"

"Just coffee. You said we couldn't go in—"

"We are about to make use of that marvelous modern invention, the drive-in window. And, not so incidentally, case the joint as we do so."

The front and side of the restaurant had large windows. Heedless of the fine drizzle, Nick rolled his own window down and peered intently as they glided slowly past. "I don't see her, do you?"

"No. Wait—there she is, on the other side. I recognize the scarf."

"Where? Oh—yeah." Nick's voice rose in a howl of triumph. "Who's a genius? There's someone at the same table. A woman. Do you recognize her?"

"She's got one of those plastic rain hats shielding her face. You're going to hit that post. . . ."

The car swerved and managed to avoid the post. Nick drove on around the restaurant and turned into the drive-in lane. He was ingenuously delighted to learn there was a special on hamburgers and ordered three, with fries and coffee, receiving a jingle of change in return. Then they went around again, with little more success; both women were leaning forward, heads together, and Rosemary's scarf hid the face of her companion. Nick backed into a parking place near the door of the restaurant and turned off the ignition.

Nick ate two of the hamburgers and all the french fries, munching vigorously without taking his eyes off the door of the restaurant. Erin found she was hungry after all and accepted the other hamburger. It was lunchtime; the door of the restaurant kept opening and closing as customers crowded in. A few came out. Nick had barely finished eating when Rosemary appeared. Without pausing or looking around, she walked to the truck and got in.

It was unquestionably Rosemary, though Erin wouldn't have recognized her if she had not been expecting to see her. A thick layer of bright-red lipstick had altered the shape of her mouth, and mascara practically dripped from her lashes. She looked like an aging but optimistic go-go dancer, and the brilliant red mouth wore a wide familiar smile.

"There she is," Erin exclaimed. "Aren't you going to follow her?"

The truck backed out of its place and jolted toward the exit. Nick shook his head. "I know where she's going. Home. She has to be at her office on the Hill at two, and if she doesn't drive like a bat she won't make it. It's the other one I'm interested in. Come on, lady, come on; I haven't got all day."

Another five minutes passed before he got his wish, and at first Erin wasn't certain the plump little woman who came out was their quarry. A couple of other women had worn the cheap, ubiquitous plastic rain hat and she had seen only the shoulders of a tan coat, the commonest variety of bad-weather clothing. This woman had a round, healthy pink face and pink-tinted glasses. Masses of fluffy white hair had been flattened by the plastic cap.

Nick let out a startled exclamation. "My God! It can't be!"

"Who? Who?"

"Don't you recognize her?"

"She looks vaguely familiar."

"It's her all right," Nick said, neglecting grammar in his excitement.

The woman trotted across the parking lot and got into a long, sleek black car—a Cadillac. "Yep," Nick said. "She favors Cadillacs. Jesus, look at that! They tell stories all over the state about her driving. When the word goes out that she's on the road, everybody stays home."

The big car shot forward in a series of jerks and starts, skimmed a post, forced the driver of an oncoming Camaro into a wild sideways swerve, and turned into the line of traffic on the highway without pausing or signaling. Horns blared.

"That's her," Nick repeated.

"Who, damn it?"

Nick turned to face her. His face was awed. "That, my dear, was Miz Marylou. The much-loved, loyal wife of our incumbent senator, Bill the Buzzard Bennett."

Chapter Nine

THE DISCOVERY stupefied Nick so completely that he didn't even swear when his car refused to start. Calmly extracting a set of jumper cables from the trunk, he talked a boy in a car almost as decrepit as his into assisting in the restoration of power and presented him with a campaign button as a thank-you gift. Not until they were back on the road heading home did he condescend to discuss the matter, and with less than the exuberance Erin would have expected. She was the one who peppered him with questions and speculations.

"I suppose they've known each other for years, haven't they? Would you say they were friends? Because if they are, then it would be a little difficult for them to get together, with things as they are. Maybe they have a mutual godchild or friend who's in trouble, and they wanted to confer."

"That's stupid."

"You think everything has a political orientation. It doesn't, you know; there are some people in this world who go right on sleeping and eating and worrying about the mortgage without giving a damn whether Rosemary Marshall wins an election. There are matters of greater importance—'' Her voice rose to a shriek as Nick cut across Route 29 on the last split second of the yellow.

"Sorry," Nick said. "If I stop, the damn engine may conk out for good. The battery is shot."

"Why don't you buy a new one?"

"Can't afford it,"

"Oh. Maybe if you asked Rosemary—"

"No!" Nick added less vehemently, "It was my decision to quit my job, she didn't ask me to. I'll make out all right. Rosemary has done enough for me already—and believe me, she doesn't have any money to spare. Do you know how much it costs to run a political campaign these days?"

"Yes, I know. If I've heard that once, I've heard it a hundred times."

"I'm sorry I yelled," Nick said. "Don't say anything. . . . I mean, *please* don't say anything to Rosemary about my cash flow. Or about following her."

"Oh, all right."

"I don't know how to figure this," Nick muttered, scowling at the streaked windshield. "Is it a side issue, or is it connected with the other business? It has to be! Supposing Miz Marylou found out Buzz is paying somebody to harass Rosemary. . . ."

"Would she betray her own husband?"

"Hard to say. She's known for her good works and general saintliness; Buzz's constituents adore her, she's been one of his biggest assets. She's stuck to him through thick and thin and forty years of adultery. I mean, hell, everybody knew what he was up to, the Shady Lane Motel deal only made it public. It couldn't have come as a shock to her unless she's as stupid as she is noble."

"It might have been the last straw."

"Yeah, I suppose. You never know what will tip someone over the edge."

They were approaching the stoplight at the intersection of 234 and 15. Erin braced herself and involuntarily closed her eyes. They made it through on the green, with only a little skid.

"Something else could have been the last straw for Miz Marylou," Nick said. "If she's the saint everyone believes her to be, she wouldn't stand by with folded hands if Buzz were planning something that goes beyond the normal dirty tricks of politics—something criminal or life-threatening. She'd warn the intended victim, wouldn't she?"

The conversation went downhill from there. Erin argued that even if Nick's surmise was true, Rosemary had now been fully informed about the danger. "Forewarned is forearmed," she insisted.

"Don't throw that tired old cliché at me," Nick snarled, hunching over the wheel. "Women always seem to think they've solved a problem by quoting a proverb."

"And men are always making wild generalizations," Erin snarled back.

"Like that one?"

Neither spoke again until they reached the house. Patches of blue sky were visible to the west through rents in the clouds, and the sun burst through, sending sparks winking from wet branches and waking the autumn colors to dazzling brilliance.

"What did you get for Jeff?" Nick asked.

Erin was still sulking and his sudden cheerfulness annoyed her. "Why should I get something for Jeff?"

"There's a birthday party today, isn't there?"

"Oh, damn, I forgot. What time is the party?"

"Around six, I think." Nick glanced at his watch. "I'd offer to drive you to town, but I'm already late. Tell you what, you can go halves with me. I spent more than I could afford."

"How much?"

"It'll cost you fifteen bucks."

"No wonder you're broke. What is it?"

"You have to see it to appreciate it fully." Nick grinned. "Take my word, it's sensational. What do you say?"

"Oh, all right. I suppose you want me to pay you now."

"That's okay. I trust you." He opened the screen door. A cat walked out, stopped directly in their path, studied the weather, and decided it would pass. It stood there, tail erect and twitching, and Erin preceded Nick inside. He headed for the commons room with a casual "See you later."

Nick had an admirable if irritating ability to forget all about an argument once it was over. It was a habit almost essential to anyone involved in politics. Erin wished she could do it. Not that it was easy to stay angry with Nick. He was such a cheerful character. His penniless state didn't seem to bother him, and he was generous to a fault. Imagine spending thirty dollars on a present for someone who was not a close friend, when he couldn't afford a new battery for his car.

Christie was at her desk when Erin entered the office. She stopped working long enough to skewer Erin a cool stare but didn't speak, so Erin decided she was in bad odor for taking a long lunch hour, but that the theft of the coat had not been discovered. She settled down at her own desk, but found it hard to concentrate. It was difficult to think of a reason why Rosemary and her archenemy's wife would put their heads together in private. There were a lot of holes in Nick's theory; if Erin hadn't been so annoyed with him, she would have pointed them out. She was quite willing to believe that a politician might consider winning an election a sufficient motive for murder—but only if he believed he had no chance of winning otherwise. Bennett was still ahead. Possessing even more than the average politician's share of ego, he surely must be convinced he would win. If he knew something that would damage Rosemary's chances, he would publicize the fact, not kill the opponent.

None of it made sense, not even political sense, which was only distantly related to the real world. Erin was relieved when Kay called her into her office and gave her a pile of papers to be copied and mailed out.

She saw nothing of Rosemary until late afternoon. The sight of her, smiling and composed and elegantly garbed in a softly tailored wool suit, was so at variance with the brassy-haired conspirator and the mug-throwing virago, Erin could only stare.

Rosemary greeted the group with a cheerful "Another day, another vote for the right—sorry, make that left." She stopped at Erin's desk; the latter braced herself. There was no reason why she should feel guilty, but she had an irrational feeling that her knowledge was printed on her face.

"How are you at blowing up balloons?" Rosemary asked in a conspiratorial whisper.

"It's one of my prized skills."

"Go help Nick with the decorations, then. I'll keep Jeff occupied."

She looked as if she had nothing on her mind but surprising her aide. Humming under her breath, she went on her way.

Erin found Nick hard at work, aided and abetted by Will. Sarah stood in the doorway, hands on her hips and a broad smile on her face, watching Will drape crepe-paper streamers from the chandelier. "That's enough," she called. "Save some for the table."

"This goes on the table." Nick ripped the plastic envelope from a gaudy paper tablecloth covered with cavorting bears dressed in party clothes and a glaring HAPPY BEARTHDAY in bright red.

"Rosemary sent me to blow up balloons," Erin said.

"The balloons are my province," Will said, removing a package of them from a brown paper bag. His expression was as solemn as ever. "I happen to have an extremely capable set of lungs. I don't waste my breath shouting idle threats and insults at other people, the way the rest of these neurotics do, so I have more to give to balloons."

"How are you going to hang them up?" Nick asked.

Will looked blank. "I don't know. Scotch tape?"

"You can't put tape on a balloon. How about if we tie a piece of string around each one? Sarah, got any string?"

"There's a ball of it in the drawer beside the sink. You put that back when you're through with it, and my scissors too!"

Leaving the balloons to the two self-appointed experts, Erin spread the cloth on the table, laid out napkins and paper plates, and went to help Sarah in the kitchen. The cake was a masterpiece that deserved the hearty praise she heaped on it: a huge angel food piled with whipped cream and filled with strawberries. She sneaked a sandwich from under the damp cloth that covered the plate and took a bite. "Mmmmm, that's wonderful. Tuna—but what else?"

"A smidge of that Dijon mustard and sour cream, along with the mayonnaise."

"You went to a lot of trouble, Sarah."

"Rosemary said to, but I would've anyhow. I get the feeling that boy don't have much family life, or if he does, it's the wrong kind. He never talks about his folks."

"Maybe he's an orphan. Or just a very private person. I haven't heard anybody talk about family, it's all politics around here."

"They talk to me," Sarah said.

Erin paused with another sandwich halfway to her mouth and considered Sarah's placid face and round, comfortable figure. "Yes," she said. "I can see why they would."

"It's the kitchen, honey," Sarah said. "Not me. People come in for a cup of coffee or a snack, and sit down, and put their elbows on the table; and there I am, stirring something on the stove or mixing batter—it's like being back home with your mama, you know what I mean?"

"You're an archetypal figure," Erin said.

Sarah gave a rich laugh. "If you say so, honey."

"You know what it means. Don't kid me."

"Sure, I know. I just don't hold with fancy words. Hear too many of 'em around here all the time." She took another plate from the refrigerator and filled in the empty spaces Erin had left. "Have some more, Erin, there's plenty. Then tell me how many candles."

"Gosh, I don't know. I'll ask Nick."

Nick knew. According to Rosemary, Jeff was thirty-one. Erin retreated to the kitchen to report, adding, "You should see what those two characters are doing to that room. They've got crepe paper hanging from every hook; it looks like a jungle."

"Good to see 'em enjoying themselves," Sarah said. "Everybody needs a little break. Things have been pretty tense around here lately."

"You noticed it too?"

"It's natural, I guess." Sarah brooded over the cake, her

face unusually serious. "Means a lot—this election. High time we had somebody like Rosemary up there in the Senate. She stands for—well, for a lot of things. Here, Erin, open that jar of nuts and put 'em in a bowl."

"Could that be why Rosemary decided to throw Jeff a party? To give people a chance to relax and be silly?"

She expected Sarah would deny this and claim Rosemary's reason was purely altruistic; but Sarah's answer had more than a touch of ambiguity. "She usually has a couple of reasons for doing what she does."

The other guests straggled in over the course of the next half hour. By six o'clock they were all present, stealing sandwiches, laughing and talking, and making rude remarks about the decor. Nick defended his work heatedly; Will simply blinked and remarked that the detractors obviously lacked the barest rudiments of artistic taste.

Nick was enjoying himself. His face beamed, and his eyes shone as he rushed around the room, rearranging his balloons, listening at the door to see if Jeff was coming, distributing party hats and noisemakers. His suggestion that they all hide behind sofas and draperies and jump out shouting "Surprise" was unanimously hooted down, but when Jeff came in, following Rosemary and followed by Joe, the chorus of "Happy Birthday" was heartfelt, if somewhat ragged.

Jeff registered the proper emotions—surprise, pleasure, embarrassment, appreciation—but Erin suspected he had not been completely unwitting. There had been a dozen people in on the secret; perhaps one of them had let something slip. At any rate, Jeff's pleasure seemed to be genuine. He let Nick put a cardboard party hat on his head, and when Sarah carried in the cake ablaze with candles, he directed the chorus of "Happy Birthday," beating time with his tin noisemaker.

The sight of the stack of brightly wrapped gifts obviously disconcerted him. "Whose idea was this?" he demanded. "I didn't expect . . . You shouldn't have done this, Rosemary."

"What makes you think it was her idea?" Joe asked in an injured tone. "I am known all over Washington for my benevolence, my constant care for others, my—"

A chorus of jeers and laughter drowned him out. Christie handed Jeff a glass of wine. "You'd better wait till you see the gifts before you start thanking people."

"I guess that's right." Jeff smiled. "I shudder to think what Nick's idea of an appropriate gift might be."

"You wound me to the heart," Nick exclaimed, clapping his hand to his chest. "Since you're so suspicious, you can open mine first. It's from me and Erin, actually; we expect a groveling apology when you see what it is."

Erin still had no idea what was in the box; she braced herself, hoping Nick had not selected anything too vulgar. The gift was certainly vulgar, though not in the sense she had feared. It was a cheap copy of a British barrister's wig, curls, queue, and all. Jeff's amusement and delight were unfeigned; he clapped it onto his head and wore it while he opened the remainder of the gifts.

Most of them were funny or friendly or both: a box of homemade cookies from one of the girls in the office, a five-foot-long scarf from another ("considering you get paid about the same as Bob Cratchit"), a hideous plaster kitten with oversized eyes, and so on. Joe's offering was different: a leather wallet and matching key case, of rich and obviously expensive morocco. "I noticed you'd lost your key chain," Joe grunted, when Jeff turned to him in speechless surprise. "Anybody else want something to drink besides me?"

He wandered off before Jeff could say anything, and Rosemary shook her head. "Don't thank him, he doesn't know how to accept graciously."

She had saved her own gift for last. The others crowded around, laughing and conjecturing, while Jeff undid the pretty wrappings and opened the plain white box. His face went absolutely rigid, a carving in mahogany.

"It's an antique," he said in an odd, strained voice. "A family heirloom. You can't. . . ."

"It's no heirloom," Rosemary said casually. "My dad loved it, though; it was the only thing he never hocked."

"Your father's?" Jeff's clenched fingers relaxed; carefully he placed the box on the table. "I can't take this."

"Sure you can. There's a chain too." Rosemary lifted the

watch and draped the chain across Jeff's flat stomach. "Now I ask you—is that class or what? It goes with your three-piece suits and your image of aristocratic intellectuality."

Joe had joined the group, a glass of bourbon in his hand. "You may as well take it," he advised. "If you don't, the damn thing will keep turning up. In your soup, or your underwear drawer, or the glove compartment of your car."

Rosemary had replaced the watch and chain in the box. Jeff eyed it as if it were a snake coiled to strike. "Don't tell me your father would have wanted me to have it, Rosemary. I can't imagine. . . ."

"And you'd be right." Rosemary accepted the implicit challenge head-on, as if she refused to insult Jeff by pretending there was no problem. "My father was the biggest good-ol'-boy bigot in Virginia. The only reason he didn't join the Klan was because he was such a famous drunk they wouldn't take him."

"I can't imagine the Klan turning anybody down on those grounds," Nick said.

If he was trying to lighten the tension he failed. Jeff looked around the circle of sympathetic faces and then fixed an unsmiling stare on Rosemary. "I don't get it."

"I didn't want to embarrass you," Rosemary said quietly. "But if you insist, I'll make a speech. You gave up a good job to join a campaign that appeared to be doomed from the start. God knows I'm not paying you what you're worth, and if we lose, which is quite possible, you'll be out of a job. You've worked outrageous hours and put up with my tantrums and Joe's rudeness, and tried to keep the peace—"

Jeff stopped her with a brusque gesture and turned away, his face averted. After an aching pause Rosemary went on, "Don't make a big deal of it, Jeff. What the hell, it's not a family heirloom, Pop won it in a poker game. I should apologize for insulting you with a secondhand present. Look at it as a gift from one gambler to another. Or . . . as a token of esteem and affection from a friend."

The voice was the one she used in public, every inflection controlled and skilled. Erin had heard it before, mouthing the

common catchwords of modern politics. Even so, she had a
lump in her throat and two of the girls were frankly sniffing.

But the one who appeared most affected was Kay. She had
participated in the festivities with the pained smile of someone who is ill-adept at friendly foolishness; her gift had been
appropriate and unimaginative—a handsome fountain pen.
Like all the others, Erin had been focusing on Rosemary and
Jeff during the little drama and she was caught by surprise
when Kay suddenly rose and blundered out of the room. The
silly party hat looked grotesque above her strained face and
haunted eyes.

Chapter Ten

ERIN WENT TO BED early and dreamed she was trying to climb a tree whose upper branches burned like a giant torch. On the tip-top branch perched Miz Marylou; and though the flames curled all around her, her clothes didn't even smolder and the expression on her plump pink face, as she peered down at her would-be rescuer, was one of amused interest.

Erin found it hard to get back to sleep after that. As she turned and squirmed, trying to find a comfortable position, the disquieting ideas Nick had planted in her head took on new and more alarming dimensions.

Kay had returned to the commons rooms after only a few minutes, perfectly composed; she had made no reference then or later to her precipitate departure from the party. Erin might have supposed she had imagined the look of strain and horror if there had not been other evidence that something was bothering Kay.

If Rosemary knew the reason for the campaign of harassment, Kay surely must know too. The relationship between the two women was much more complex than Erin had originally supposed; undercurrents of jealousy and resentment blurred what had appeared to be a long-standing, easygoing friendship. But the one thing the two undoubtedly had in common was their familiarity with intimate details of Rosemary's life with Edward Marshall.

Kay must know why these things were happening. Either she knew more than Rosemary, or she was less skilled at concealment. Her reaction to the poppet, her sleepwalking . . . What could have happened to upset her at the birthday party? Something about the watch? Had it really belonged to Edward, and not to Rosemary's father?

No, that was impossible. Erin didn't doubt that Rosemary could lie like a trooper when she had to—she would never have succeeded in politics without that skill—but not even Rosemary would produce so flagrant a falsehood in the presence of someone who knew the truth. If the watch had been Edward's, though, Kay's reaction would be understandable. She would feel that Edward Marshall's possessions ought to be preserved like holy relics, not given so casually to a mere acquaintance.

Erin rolled over and pounded the pillow. The whole situation was impossible. Perhaps she and Nick were both losing their minds. Infectious insanity . . . Nick was such a smooth talker, he could hypnotize a listener into believing anything he said.

She hadn't mentioned the sleepwalking incident to Nick. Rosemary had asked her not to. It was a confidence not to be violated lightly, especially since she couldn't see that it added anything to their understanding of the problem. So Kay was upset. Nick must know that; he had seen her collapse at the sight of the poppet, he was fully aware of her relationship with Edward and with Rosemary. Why hadn't he suggested spying on Kay? What did he know that she didn't? What did either of them know, in fact?

She finally did fall asleep, but the matter was still on her mind when she woke next morning, and when she heard the soft sounds from the next room she went at once to the door and knocked. That was her job, after all, to be of assistance to Kay.

Kay was sitting on the edge of the bed. She had pulled the sheet around her, and her bra lay beside her on the bed.

Kay's modesty had surprised and annoyed Erin at first; it made the task of helping her dress doubly difficult. She was beginning to understand that a woman may not enjoy baring sagging breasts and lumpy thighs in the presence of a girl who is still some years away from those disasters, and now a certain degree of sympathy tempered her impatience.

"Let me help you with this," she said, picking up the brassiere. "It takes a contortionist to fasten one of the darned things, even with two good hands."

Kay turned her back and let the sheet fall. "Thank you," she said in a muffled voice. "I've been wearing the ones that fasten in the front, but my—my arthritis is bad this morning, and I couldn't reach. . . . Thank you. I guess I'll wear slacks today. Putting on panty hose is beyond me."

Erin knew better than to offer assistance with the last-named garment. Kay had been crimson with embarrassment the first and only time Erin had smoothed and shaken her into them.

"You look just fine in pants," she said tactfully, turning and plumping up a pillow while Kay got into the pants. "Can I . . ."

Kay submitted to having her blouse and pants buttoned up. "I hate depending on people," she grumbled.

"I don't blame you. Surely it won't be much longer, though."

"I hope not. My hand feels much better."

After Kay had gone downstairs, Erin made a whirlwind toilette and set to work straightening up the rooms. The maids—a fancy title for the two local girls who came in three days a week—had enough to do keeping the rooms on the lower floors clean. She stripped Kay's bed and wrapped the sheets around a bundle of her own clothes that needed washing.

When she entered the commons room with her armful of linens, she found Rosemary with Kay. Dressed for the day in one of her soft pastel suits, the congresswoman leaned forward at an acute angle to avoid dripping coffee on the immaculate white bow at her throat. "Good morning," she said. "What on earth is that?"

"Laundry," Erin said. "Is it okay if I use the machine?"

"Of course. But those look like sheets. You don't have to change the beds; ask Mary to do it."

Kay's lips pursed and she made clicking sounds of disapproval. "Now, Rosemary, you know I've always taken care of my own room. Those shiftless girls barely get through their work as it is. If you ask them to do something extra, they'll sulk and scamp the downstairs rooms. If I could do it myself—"

"I don't mind," Erin said quickly. She hoped to avert an explosion from Rosemary, whose countenance betrayed her annoyance, but she only succeeded in making matters worse.

"You interrupted me, Erin."

"I'm sorry—"

Rosemary banged her empty cup down on the table. At least she didn't throw it, though she looked as if she would have liked to. "For God's sake, Kay, don't pick on her! It's damned nice of her to do this dirty work; you should thank her instead of lecturing her about her manners!"

Kay did not reply. Eyes lowered, mouth a drooping curve, she radiated hurt feelings. Rosemary drew a long breath. "Sorry, Kay."

"That's quite all right, dear. Better you should shout at me than at a voter."

"Huh," said Rosemary. "We're all a bit edgy. Have you been taking those sleeping pills, Kay?"

"I don't believe in them." Kay's mouth set stubbornly.

"Honestly, Kay! The doctor said—"

"Excuse me," Erin said, and left them to it.

She stopped for a little gossip with Sarah and ended up sitting at the kitchen table pigging out on toast and homemade strawberry jam while she told Sarah how her mother used to make jam every summer—until this last year.

"I worry about her. She just sits around and mopes and feels sorry for herself, and my aunt is no help, she's five years older than Mother, and she loves to run other people's lives for them. She's babying mother instead of encouraging her to take control of her life.''

''That's not so easy to do when you've always had somebody to look after you,'' Sarah said soberly. ''There are a lot of women like your mama, Erin, and the men the age of your daddy, they wanted it to be that way.''

''You're absolutely right. He did everything for her—balanced the checkbook, took care of the cars, argued with repairmen—and kidded her about how sweet and inefficient she was. She ate it up, she'd giggle and smile at him. . . .''

''So she let him do it to her,'' Sarah said, passing the toast.

''She not only let him, she collaborated with him. She liked being . . .'' Erin's voice caught. ''Being a little girl. Daddy's little girl. Just like me. And I collaborated too, I loved it. Why did it take me so long to see. . . . Sarah, you're a witch. Or a closet psychoanalyst. How did you do that?''

''You're making an awful mess with that piece of toast,'' Sarah said. ''I didn't do nothing, you did it. Things boil around in your insides long enough, they finally have to come out.''

''Poor mother,'' Erin murmured. She had squeezed the toast in her clenched hand; absently she smoothed it out and took a bite. ''What's going to become of her? I should have seen it happening. I should have done something.''

''No, I doubt you could have, honey. Sounds like your mama's all right. She's got a roof over her head and enough to eat and somebody to look after her like your daddy did. There's plenty not so well off. You can't change her now. You can't really change anybody, you got to take them the way they are. All you can do is love them.''

Erin made a face, and Sarah laughed. ''Or hate them. Nothing wrong with some good healthy hate. Just don't waste any on your daddy. He didn't mean to do wrong. He didn't even know he was doing it.''

''You scare me sometimes,'' Erin said with a smile. ''You're right; for a while I almost did hate him, without realizing it. I've stopped dreaming about him.''

''That's a good sign.''

"I think so. And I know it's foolish to waste time regretting what might have been. But I wish I had been more forceful, and more aware those last months of his life. I might have made it easier for him if I had insisted on knowing more about his business affairs. There was something on his mind, I'm sure of it. But whenever I asked him a question, he'd just laugh and—and lie. He was going to be fine, he'd be on his feet again in no time, no need for me to worry my pretty little head; one of these days I'd find some nice young fellow who would take care of me. . . . Oh, damn it, Sarah, I'm dumping on you, like everybody else around here. Why don't you tell me to shut up?"

"I'll send you my bill," Sarah said placidly.

When Erin opened the kitchen door she saw Kay standing a short distance away. Her face was a trifle flushed, and there was something awkward about her pose, as if she had come to a sudden stop, or had stepped back instead of forward.

"Were you looking for me?" Erin asked.

"Yes. No. . . ." Kay's laugh had a strained note. "I've got so much on my mind I don't know what I'm saying. I came—I came to tell Sarah we are having extra people for supper. And I wanted . . . I wondered if you could do a few errands for me later. There's cleaning to be picked up, and a prescription to be filled. . . ."

"I can go now, if you like."

"No! That is . . . the cleaning won't be ready until after noon."

"Whenever you say."

"I'll talk to you later." Kay passed her and went into the kitchen.

Erin tried to remember exactly what she had said to Sarah. If Kay had been eavesdropping . . . But of course she hadn't, Kay wouldn't do such a thing, and anyway she wouldn't have heard anything important. Just family worries, some intensely personal, to be sure, but nothing she need be ashamed of.

It was slightly before noon when Kay called her into the inner office. "I'm leaving for a luncheon appointment," she said. "I'd like you to—"

"Drive you? I'd be glad to."

Kay's forehead creased. "That is a very exasperating habit, Erin. Please allow me to finish my own sentence."

"I'm sorry. I thought you wanted me to run some errands."

"I've changed my mind." She looked challengingly at Erin. Having been slapped down once, Erin was not about to venture an opinion, but Kay knew what she was thinking. "I am perfectly capable of driving," she said firmly. "What I want you to do is sit here and wait for a call I'm expecting. Actually, I don't believe it will come through today, but there is a possibility that Mr. . . ." She hesitated for a moment and then went on, "Mr. Brown will call earlier. Take notes of the information he gives you—"

"Shall I turn on the recorder?"

Kay's frown deepened. "I could do that if I wanted the information recorded. I said, take notes. On paper. Put them into this drawer, and close the drawer. It locks automatically."

"Yes, ma'am."

Kay reached for her suit jacket. Erin moved to help her.

"I apologize," Kay said, her face averted. "I didn't mean to snap at you."

"That's all right."

"I have a lot on my mind," Kay said, half to herself. "Make sure that drawer is locked after you close it, Erin. But as I said, it's unlikely the call will come through before I get back."

"I'll make sure."

Kay started for the door. Then she turned. "You understand, I'm sure, that this information is confidential. I don't want you to mention the call to anyone."

"I won't," Erin said shortly.

"Of course not." Kay forced a smile. "You're a good girl, Erin. I have every confidence in you. This information I'm expecting isn't important except—except to me. It's a—a personal matter. Don't even mention it to Rosemary. She has enough on her mind, and I don't want her worrying about my problems."

"Whatever you say."

After Kay had gone, closing the door carefully behind her, Erin allowed her face to relax. What was that all about? she wondered. Kay's compliments had been as unconvincing as her stammered explanation. She didn't have to explain an order; the very fact that she had done so suggested that there was something peculiar about this task. Erin had no doubt that the call was political in nature and that she had been selected to receive it because she was too ignorant to understand implications that would have been immediately apparent to Christie and the others. The idea only whetted her curiosity.

By one o'clock it seemed unlikely that her curiosity would be satisfied. That was when Nick found her, bursting into the office with an exasperated "What are you doing in here? I looked all over for you. Christie said—"

The phone chose that most inconvenient moment to ring. Erin's hand hovered over the instrument. Then she picked it up, said, "Hold, please," and covered the mouthpiece with her hand. Not only was Nick standing in the doorway, Christie was right behind him, remonstrating with him.

"Nick, you can't go in there; Kay said Erin wasn't to be disturbed till she—"

"Oh, for God's sake, what is this, the War Room at the Pentagon?"

"Five minutes," Erin said, hoping she was right.

The door slammed. Erin made a wry face. At least the caller didn't resent having to wait; from the earpiece came a mellifluous crooning. "Bringing in the sheaves . . . " Mr. Brown must be a member of a church choir.

"Hello," she said.

"Who's this?" asked a gruff male voice.

"Is this Mr. Brown?"

"Yes. Miss Goodrick?"

"This is her secretary," Erin said. "I was instructed to take down the information you have for her."

"She didn't say nothing about a secretary."

"She had to leave for an appointment, and she wasn't really expecting you to call until later."

"So I'm efficient. She told me—"

"See here, Mr. Brown. This number happens to be private and unlisted. Here I am, and there you are; how would I know your name unless Miss Goodrick had told me?"

A gruff chuckle vibrated against her ear. "Okay, sister, it's no skin off my nose anyhow. Got a pencil?"

"Go ahead."

It didn't take long. A few names, a few dates.

"That's all?" Erin asked.

"That's it. I'll send my bill. In a plain envelope like she said." Another hoarse chuckle, and then a click. Mr. Brown had hung up.

Erin looked at the sheet of paper in front of her. It told her nothing. Five first names—two male, three female—eight dates. As she studied them, a pattern began to emerge. Each name was followed by at least one date; these ranged in time from March 19, 1957 to December 10, 1966. All but two names had a second date following the first. And all the second dates were identical: July 4, 1967.

Birth and death? Juxtaposed pairs of dates almost demanded that interpretation, but the more Erin studied the figures, the less she liked it. If it was correct, the three people who had died were children; the youngest had been less than a year old. And surely three children wouldn't die on the same date of natural causes. Had they been members of the same family? No last names had been supplied. There had been two survivors; a boy, the firstborn, and a younger girl.

As she had been instructed, Erin put the paper into the drawer and slammed it shut. Kay's assumption had been correct, she had not the slightest idea what the information might mean. If Kay was engaged in some underhanded attempt to discredit Senator Bennett, she was glad she didn't understand.

She had only time to exchange a few words with Nick before he was off again; he invited her to come along for the ride, an invitation she was forced to refuse. "There's too much to do, Nick."

"Yeah, okay. I have to go to D.C. and I thought maybe . . ."

She knew what he meant, but she didn't say it either; they

were standing in the hall and there was too great a chance of being overheard. "I can't," she repeated, "Kay's not in the best of all possible moods these days, and if she came back and found me gone—"

"Okay, okay. But don't forget to ask her about Friday."

Kay returned a short time later. She had been gone for less than two hours, so obviously her appointment had not been in D.C. But of course she wouldn't risk driving that far, in heavy traffic, Erin thought idly.

To judge from Kay's expression, she had not enjoyed her outing. She darted a quick unsmiling glance at Erin, who was at her own desk, and hesitated for a moment, but went on without stopping. Erin half-rose and then sat down again. The situation was one Will would have considered self-explanatory; when Kay looked, she would find the notes of Mr. Brown's call, and would know why Erin had abandoned her post. She decided, however, that this might not be the best time to ask for a day off. She would wait until she could catch Kay in a better mood—if that eventuality ever occurred.

The opportunity did not arise until they stopped for supper, and before she had a chance to talk to Kay, the others began drifting in—Christie and Jan; Anita and Jackson; Joe, annoyed because Rosemary wasn't back from the Hill yet; and finally Rosemary herself, accompanied by Jeff and sputtering angrily over the defection of a colleague who had promised to support a bill she favored.

"Somebody got to him," she exclaimed, tossing her bag onto the couch. "He won't tell me who, or what he was offered in exchange, but I swear—"

"Never mind all that stuff," Joe interrupted.

"Stuff? What do you mean, stuff? That stuff is what I was elected to do, Joe."

The arrival of Nick broke up the argument. Erin tried to catch his eye, but he took a seat next to Rosemary and became intent on what she was saying. Erin joined Jeff at the table. He offered her the glass he had just filled.

"Have some Madeira, m' dear? It's Chablis, actually."

Erin shook her head. "I thought you didn't drink."

"I didn't used to." Jeff raised the glass to his lips.

"Bad day?"

"No worse than usual."

"You look exhausted. Have you had anything to eat? I'll bet you skipped lunch again. Have some cheese. Supper is almost ready."

She put a chunk of Brie on a cracker and held it out to him. Jeff smiled, and he accepted the tidbit. "Have I mentioned lately that it's very nice having you here?"

"You can't say it too often to suit me," Erin said cheerfully.

"You could return the compliment."

"Haven't I?" She handed him another cracker and watched soberly while he ate it. "I guess I haven't. This has turned out to be a fantastic experience for me, Jeff; a growing time, in a lot of different ways. But it's been difficult at times. You've made it much easier than it might have been. So often when I've been depressed or resentful or beleaguered, it was you who came to the rescue. You've defended me, encouraged me, taught me—"

"Hey, wait, this is embarrassing." Jeff actually did look embarrassed; his eyes avoided hers. "You make me sound like some kind of saint."

"No, actually I sound like one of Rosemary's early speech drafts," Erin said, laughing. "The kind she edits because, as she says, it oozes with sloppy sentimentality. But I meant it, Jeff."

"Thanks."

"Thank you. Have another cracker."

He laughed and accepted the offering. They stood nibbling and sipping in silence, comfortable in one another's company.

Night had fallen; the windows framed a sprinkle of stars, and the breeze carried the scent of burning leaves. The atmosphere had mellowed. Nick and Joe talked quietly, Rosemary was laughing over something Will had said. . . . Will? He must have been there all along; Erin hadn't seen him come in. His chameleonlike talent of blending with the background would have been very useful to a spy or undercover agent.

More likely, Erin thought charitably, it was simply the habit of a shy, reserved man.

The night was so still that the sound of gravel crunching under the wheels of a car carried distinctly to the two, who were standing near the window. Jeff turned to look.

"I wonder who that is."

"Kay said something about company for supper."

"News to me," Jeff said. "Maybe she meant Christie and Jan; she treats the office workers like outsiders. . . . Oh, no."

How he had deduced the identity of the newcomer Erin did not know. Perhaps it was the distinctive sound of the car's engine, or just the pricking of his thumbs.

Laurence didn't knock or ring the bell, he simply walked in. He stopped in the doorway looking them over like an actor counting the house, or a predator picking his prey from a herd of grazing deer. His eyes were as cold and opaque as those of a lion studying a potential kill, and Erin wondered how she could ever have felt the faintest stir of empathy for him.

She expected Jeff would speak, if only to warn the others their conversation was being overheard, but he seemed to be struck dumb. Kay was the next to see Laurence.

"Why, Philips," she exclaimed. "I didn't expect to see you this evening."

To Erin her surprise seemed exaggerated, but then so did the reactions of the others—Joe's unconcealed annoyance, Rosemary's forced civility. Laurence had that effect on people.

He greeted them with a casual flip of his hand and said coolly, "I knocked, but you were having such a jolly time you didn't hear. Please go on with what you were doing; I wanted to have a word with Rosemary, but I'm in no hurry, and I would hate to disturb such a pleasant gathering."

"I was just leaving," Christie murmured.

"Me, too." Jan edged toward the door.

Erin tried to join the exodus, but Laurence exclaimed, "Don't run away, Erin, or you'll force me to believe you are trying to avoid me. Oh, hello, Will, I didn't see you. Still hiding behind a stack of books?"

Will smiled vaguely and adjusted his glasses. Laurence's vulturine eye moved on to the next victim. "Nick, dear boy! You made quite an impression the other night; Juliet is still raving about your charms. Joe, how are you? You look a bit the worse for wear, old chap, you really ought to get more exercise, you know. And those cheap cigars aren't good for you. I speak only out of concern for your health, old fellow. With the campaign at such a crucial stage it would be a pity to lose you."

Rosemary put a firm hand on Joe's arm. "Would you care for something to drink, Philips?"

"Thank you, a glass of wine would be nice. No, don't get up, Rosemary. I'll help myself; or perhaps Jeff . . ."

He sauntered toward the table. Erin realized that this time he wasn't concentrating on her. If Jeff was aware of Laurence's speculative gaze he didn't show it; he poured the wine with a steady hand.

"Thank you." Laurence accepted the glass, his eyes never leaving Jeff's face. "I understand you celebrated your birthday recently, Jeff. I'm sorry I wasn't invited to the party, I'd like to have presented a small token of my esteem."

"It wasn't a formal affair," Jeff said quietly.

"No? I regret all the more having missed it then. I enjoy informal arrangements. And I love giving presents to deserving individuals."

He didn't look at Erin, but she knew the remark was directed at her. Nick had been right; Laurence would never forgive her for returning his gift so publicly. She was pleased to discover that she no longer cared what he did or said; she had a delightfully childish desire to put out her tongue, or thumb her nose.

"I've already had more than I deserve," Jeff said, with a glance at Rosemary.

"No, no, dear fellow. You deserve the best, and if you go on as you've begun, you will get what you deserve. Your future unquestionably lies in politics. I foresee a brilliant career." He lifted his glass in a toast.

Joe lit a cigar and blew a thick cloud of smoke in Laurence's direction. "I'm always suspicious of you when you're laying on the compliments, Laurence; are you trying to lure Jeff away from us?''

"Now why would I do a thing like that?'' Laurence asked innocently.

"Rumor has it that you have a few political aspirations yourself,'' Joe said. "Forget it, Laurence, or establish residence in another state. Sarbanes and Mikulski have got Maryland sewn up, and Montgomery County is solidly Democratic. You won't have a prayer.''

"I cannot imagine how these rumors start,'' Laurence said.

Rosemary's fingers beat an impatient tattoo on the edge of the table. "Come into my office, Philips,'' she said, rising. "These people have things to do. We can talk privately.''

"I had hoped to persuade you to have dinner with me,'' Laurence said. "I made reservations at the Red Fox, but if you prefer another restaurant . . .''

"No, that would be fine.'' Rosemary sounded less pleased than resigned; apparently she had decided it was easier to go along with Laurence's plan than get rid of him. "I can't take long, Philips. I have work to do this evening.''

"I'll make it worth your while,'' Laurence promised, smiling.

They went out together, Laurence's hand possessive on Rosemary's arm. "What do you suppose he's up to now?'' Joe demanded.

"We'll soon find out,'' Kay said. She had raised no objection to Rosemary's defection, but it was obvious she didn't approve.

Erin was the only one who heard Jeff's murmur. "Will we? I wonder.''

Chapter
Eleven

THERE WAS NO COMMENT from Nick, for the simple reason that he was no longer there. Erin turned in time to see the door close behind him. She took off in pursuit, heedless of the stares and amused speculation of the others.

Nick was at the front door. "Are you trying to avoid me, or what?" Erin demanded. "I haven't had a chance to talk to you for days. . . . Wait a minute. Where do you think you're going?"

Nick tried to shake her off. "Let me go or come with me. I'm going to lose them!"

The taillights of Laurence's car dimmed and brightened as he made his careful way along the rutted drive. Erin released her grip. "You're going to follow them? Nick, you are absolutely the most—"

"No time. Talk to you later."

He plunged out. Erin stood watching. The taillights had disappeared before Nick's balky engine finally caught; undaunted, he pulled a screeching turn and went in hot pursuit.

Torn between amusement and exasperation, Erin returned to face Kay's visible disapproval and Joe's jokes. "Never chase a man, kiddo, let them do the chasing. Especially when the man is Nick."

Will's head popped up over the books. "And above all, never take Joe's advice on matters of the heart. He doesn't have one."

Jeff's description of politics as stumbling from one crisis to the next became more apt with each passing day. Erin came downstairs the following morning to find a fresh domestic crisis awaiting her. Kay had fallen during the night and reinjured her hand; she and Rosemary were in the midst of a hot debate on the subject when Erin walked into the commons room. Her appearance ended the argument; Kay got up and walked out, leaving Rosemary flat.

"Oh, shit," said the latter, slamming her fist onto the table. "I'm sorry, Erin—"

"You know you don't have to apologize to me."

"Not for bad language, at any rate." Rosemary drew a long, steadying breath. "I shouldn't have lost my temper with her. She denies she was walking in her sleep, claims she was on her way to the bathroom when she fell."

"I didn't hear her," Erin said. "I should have been listening—"

"No, I'm guiltier than you, guiltier than you," Rosemary chanted. A haggard smile warmed her face. "Did you ever read *Pogo*? Remind me to lend you my collection sometime. She's trying to lay a guilt trip on me, says she was so groggy from the sleeping pills I made her take that she lost her balance. Which is a bunch of baloney—like your feeling that you ought to have been lying awake all night. In the next breath she insisted she had run out of sleeping pills. I think she flushed them down the john."

"Would you like me to take her to the doctor? I know you don't have time."

"I do like a person who makes practical suggestions," Rosemary said approvingly. "Unfortunately it won't work. Kay says she's fine, her hand just needs rest and time. And that old fake White—her doctor—is no damned help. I've already called him, he just said to refill the prescription for the pain medication and call him in a few days if it doesn't improve. I'll tell you what you could do, though—run into town and pick up the prescriptions. Sleeping pills and pain-killer. Would you mind?''

"Of course not. That is, if Kay will let me drive the car."

"I'll make sure she does." Rosemary glanced at her watch. "Damn, I'm late. Thank you, Erin. I keep saying that—believe me, it's from the heart."

It was shortly before noon when Kay called Erin into her office and handed over the car keys. She spoke about the errand as if it had been her idea; Erin was careful not to say anything that would indicate she knew better. Kay had a list of other errands as well: the cleaning that had never been picked up, a few groceries. She didn't look well; her face was gray under her heavy makeup.

It was a warm, bright day, with a brisk wind blowing the fallen leaves into multicolored clouds. Erin lingered to stroke a cat that came to rub itself against her leg. She wasn't look-ing forward to the drive. Accidents could occur even with the most skilled and careful of drivers, but she knew Kay would hold her personally accountable for any dent or scratch. Things like that always seemed to happen when you were using someone else's car. . . . She was tempted to ask Sam if she could borrow the pickup. She'd feel quite comfortable in that battered vehicle; nothing short of a major collision could worsen its condition.

Since she hadn't seen Nick's car parked out in front, she had assumed he was off somewhere. The car was in the stable-yard, and Nick was in it—literally, for the hood was up and only the lower half of his body was visible. He didn't hear her coming; when she greeted him, he started and he banged his head on the hood, which promptly collapsed on him.

"I'm so sorry," she exclaimed, helping him extract him-self from the metal jaws. "Are you hurt?"

Nick rubbed his head. "Happens all the time," he said cheerfully. "I should have propped it with something. Where are you off to?"

"Errands for Kay." She dangled the keys.

"How about a lift to town? I was trying to recharge the battery, but I'm afraid it's a hopeless cause. I'll have to buy a new one."

"I thought you were broke."

"I may be able to squeeze one more charge out of my Visa. Worth a try, anyway."

He plucked the keys from her hand and led the way to the Mercedes. This high-handed maneuver would have prompted a caustic comment from Erin if she hadn't been glad to be relieved of the responsibility of driving. She allowed herself one mild warning: "For God's sake, drive carefully, will you? Kay will kill me if anything happens to this car."

"No, she'll kill me." Nick backed the car out and proceeded with exaggerated slowness down the driveway. "Anything new to report?"

"About what?"

"Anything."

"I don't know why you're asking me, you're the great detective. I presume Rosemary and Mr. Laurence went to the Red Fox last night, just as he said they would?"

"Uh-huh. Then home again, home again, jiggety-jog. Any comment?"

"No."

"Good. Then I needn't mention that although tailing them turned out to be an idle exercise, I had no way of knowing that until I did it."

"I can't argue with that," Erin said agreeably. "Did you find out what he wanted to talk to Rosemary about?"

"Oh, that." Nick didn't stop at the end of the drive; after making the turn he put his foot down and the car picked up speed. "He's invited her to appear on his show Sunday."

"Firing Squad?"

"Hey, that's a good one," Nick said, with a sputter of laughter. "Where'd you hear that?"

"It's Fran's name for it. She says Laurence is as bad as Buckley when it comes to snide comments and unanswerable questions—and since it's not taped, but live, a lot of his guests have had a rough time."

"Shot down in flames, no survivors," Nick agreed. "Most of the guests are politicians, you'd think they would have learned how to lie and equivocate; but Laurence really knows how to needle people."

"That's why it's so popular, I suppose. It has all the ghoulish fascination of stock-car racing; the viewers hope someone will crash right in front of their eyes."

"A few people have. Remember the time he goaded Senator Willis into admitting he was gay?"

"Fran told me about it. Maybe it wouldn't be such a smart move for Rosemary to go on."

"That's what Joe says. He doesn't trust Laurence any farther than he can throw him, says he. But it's first-class exposure, free media to the max, and Rosemary says she'd be a fool to pass it up."

"He certainly seems to be an ardent fan of hers," Erin said doubtfully. "Slow down, Nick, this hill—"

"The trick," said Nick, over the squeal of tires, "is to get up enough speed going down so that you don't have to pump so much gas going up the next one. I dunno, though. I'm like Joe, I don't trust the skunk. He may be fond of Rosemary, but he loves his precious self and his precious show more."

"Nick, the stop sign is there, just around the curve."

"Yes, darling, I know. If there's anything that gripes me more than a woman who is smarter than I am, it's a woman who tries to tell me . . ."

"What's the matter?" Erin asked.

Nick leaned forward, peering through the windshield. "Is that smoke?"

"Where?" Then she saw it. "Oh, God. It's coming from under the hood. The engine must be overheating. Stop, Nick."

Instead of stopping at the sign, Nick made an abrupt right turn onto the shoulder of the highway and slammed on the brakes. "That's not steam, that's smoke. Out. Get the hell out of the car."

There was no shoulder on the narrow road they had just left, no place to pull over without risking being rear-ended by another car coming around the curve. She understood his reason for turning, but she didn't understand his urgency, nor why, instead of opening the hood, he ran to the back of the car and unlocked the trunk. Not until she got out and saw that the vaporous extrusion was black, not the pale shade of steaming water.

Nick came running back, carrying a blanket. "Get the hell away from here," he yelled. "Move it!"

He had released the hood latch before he got out of the car. When he lifted the hood, a tongue of flame licked out at him; instead of drawing back he threw the blanket and himself onto the engine.

It had happened too quickly; Erin had no time to react to his orders, even if she had wanted to. When she saw him disappear under the hood, she ran—not away from the car, but toward Nick. "Get out of there," she screamed, tugging at his coattails. "Are you crazy? Let it blow up, let it burn!"

Nick said something. She didn't catch the words, she was screaming too loudly, using words she had never expected to hear from her own lips, calling him every name she could think of. Not until a pair of hands grabbed her by the waist and swung her aside did she realize another vehicle had stopped on the shoulder ahead of them. A pickup—of course. Rusty blue, of course. . . .

"It's okay, lady, you can stop yelling," said the Good Samaritan, a tall, towheaded youth in jeans and a visored cap. "He's got it out. You wanna dump dirt on it, buddy, just to make sure? I got a shovel in the back. . . ."

Erin staggered out of the way and sat down on the ground, while Nick and the other man evaluated the situation. For a while both of them had their heads together under the hood, and she bit her lip to keep from shrieking at them. After an amiable and hideously prolonged discussion, they nodded at one another, and Nick came toward Erin. "He's going to give us a lift back to the house. Are you okay?"

"Am I . . ." She took a long, steadying breath. "You stupid, bullheaded, thoughtless, arrogant, cocky . . . man!"

"Now that stung," Nick said, grinning from ear to ear. "Kindly select a less offensive epithet."

"You're all covered with soot!"

"And I have a blister on my thumb," said Nick. "Hold

on, honey, you can faint or do something interesting like that after we get home.''

"I am not going to faint!" She glared at him. "I am going to kill you. What do you mean by scaring me like that?''

"That's better. Here we go. . . . This is real nice of you, pal.''

The young man dropped them at the gate and brushed away their thanks with a casual "No sweat." Erin thought she was in perfect control of her emotions until Nick plucked the campaign button from his lapel and pressed it on the Good Samaritan. She collapsed onto the ground and laughed till she cried.

Nick sat down beside her and put a tentative arm around her.

"Don't touch me!" A hard shove emphasized the words.

"What are you mad at me for?" Nick demanded aggrievedly. "I didn't do anything.''

"Except risk your stupid neck for a hunk of machinery, and push me out of the way like some doddering little old lady, and—''

"Oh, gee whiz, I apologize for all those terrible things.''

"You could have been killed!''

"If I had let that car blow, Kay would have killed me.''

"It's not funny! You never take me seriously. What's a rotten piece of machinery compared to death or serious injury?''

"There was no danger of that," Nick protested. "Luckily Kay had a blanket in the trunk. She read some newspaper article about keeping the car stocked with survival equipment; there's even a bag of kitty litter for icy conditions. . . .''

"Shut up! You're doing it again, talking down to me. Why won't you take me seriously?''

"I do, believe me I do. You scare the hell out of me when you act like this. I can't understand why you . . .'' A new and apparently pleasing idea dawned and was reflected on his face. "Could it be that you're all shook up because you thought I might've been hurt? My mother used to scream at me when she—''

"You bastard!''

"Leave my mother out of this.'' There was nothing tentative about the hands that drew her into a hard embrace. He smelled of oil and smoke but Erin didn't care; it was an aroma as sweet as perfume to her. Not until much later did she realize that his lips were crusted with ashes, and that she had absorbed them into her mouth with the eagerness of someone participating in a ceremonial rite.

"We look kind of silly squatting here by the side of the road," Nick remarked some time later. "I know a pretty little spot back in the woods—"

"Certainly not. At least . . . not now. Talk to me."

Nick helped her to her feet. "About fires?"

"About this fire. What was it?"

Nick hesitated, but only for a moment.

"It looks as if one of the fuel-injection lines came loose."

"Fuel? You mean gas? But if gas was leaking, wouldn't we have smelled it?"

"No. That's the thing." Nick picked up a stone and began to draw in the dust. "See, the fuel-injection lines go into the fuel distributor—here. Gas doesn't flow through them until the fuel pump starts up. Then, if there's a loose connection, some of the gas will spurt out onto the engine, and when the temperature rises to a certain point, the gas will ignite."

"I see. Do I have to ask the next question?"

Nick sighed. "I wish I knew the next answer, Erin. If you ask a Mercedes dealer whether the line could work loose, he'll deny it with his last breath; but there's always a possibility of a faulty connection. A good mechanic will check things like that as a matter of routine when the car is serviced; and if I know Kay, it has been serviced regularly. We can find out when she had it in last, and we can ask the mechanic whether he checked the fuel connections. He will, of course, say he did."

"How hard would it be to loosen it?"

"All you'd need is a wrench and a couple of minutes—and the necessary know-how."

"So anyone could have done it."

"Not you." Nick produced a rather wan smile. "You aren't even sure gas is fuel."

Like Queen Victoria, Erin was not amused. "I wouldn't

have known how to do the job. But you don't know that I don't know.''

Nick rose lithely to his feet and helped her to rise. ''Your syntax is a little confused, but I get your meaning. Anyone could have had what I am pleased to call the know-how. Even Kay, I suppose. You pick up odd bits of information here and there. Like, a mechanic might have pointed out that the connection was loose, and warned her always to have it checked.''

''Yes, let's not be sexist in selecting suspects. More to the point is why it was done.''

''That's obvious, isn't it?'' Nick kicked a pebble and watched it dribble off into the grass. ''Another fire. Only this one could have been dangerous.''

''How dangerous? You said it wasn't.''

''I lied. Or let's say I exaggerated a trifle. To put it in the simplest possible terms—''

''In deference to my stupidity?''

''In deference to your charming ignorance of the internal combustion engine. If the driver kept his or her head, it is extremely unlikely that he or she could have been killed or seriously injured. If you see something boiling out from under the hood, your first impulse is to open it and find out what's going on. An inexperienced driver might assume, as you did, that the car had overheated. I knew that wasn't the case, but I thought—if I thought at all—that oil had slopped over onto the engine, or a rag or paper towel had been left inside. If I had known it was gas . . . Oh, I suppose I'd have done the same thing, most people would—try to put out the fire by smothering it. Opening the hood admits air, and that fans the flames, so you've got to move fast and hope the fire hasn't taken serious hold.''

''But you are an experienced driver,'' Erin said slowly. ''If I had been alone . . .''

''Don't think about it,'' Nick said gruffly.

''We have to think about it. What's the worst that could have happened?''

''The damned car could have blown up, that's the worst that could have happened!'' Nick shouted. They walked on in silence for a while, and then Nick said in a calmer voice,

"But not right away; long before that happened, even a moron would have taken alarm, and backed away. If you're thinking attempted murder, forget it. Not only was the method inefficient, but the perpetrator couldn't have known who would drive the car next. Up until this morning, Kay's hand was improving—"

"She did drive it," Erin said. "Yesterday."

"You've driven it recently," Nick pointed out. "So has Jeff. She'd lend it to Rosemary, I suppose."

"Or Will?"

"I don't know. Maybe."

"Joe?"

"He's the last person she'd allow behind the wheel of her precious," Nick said. "Next to last, I should say; I'm the ultimate. No, it has to be a piece of random malice, Erin, like all the others. Ask Kay if you can take tomorrow off."

The fire had shaken her nerve more than she had realized. At first she didn't understand what he was driving at. "Why?"

"You haven't had a day off since you started work, have you?"

"No, but I can hardly complain. Here I am mixing with the glamour guys and gals of politics, studying the inner workings of the greatest game on earth. It's all so—so stimulating."

"Isn't it, though. Nothing like being scorched periodically to add zest to life. . . . You've never visited the Hill, or had a power lunch. Yeah. That should work just fine. I think it's time our hardworking little novice got shown the sights of Washington. Duke Zeibert's for lunch, maybe."

"Nick—"

"Or The Monocle. It's not far from the Library of Congress."

*   *

KAY DIDN'T FAINT when they told her what had happened, but for a few alarmed seconds Erin thought she was going to. Her face turned a sickly shade of greenish white, and Nick had to help her into a chair. Her first coherent words were, "How bad is it?"

Nick crossed his fingers and lied like a rug. "Not bad, Kay. Really. It could have been a lot worse."

"Oh my God." Kay hid her face in her hands.

"It would have been a lot worse if Nick hadn't risked himself to put the fire out," Erin said. Kay hadn't even had the decency to ask if either of them had been hurt.

"I wasn't referring to the car," Kay said in a shaking voice. "Are you all right, Erin? When I think what could have happened . . ."

"Nothing happened," Erin said quickly, regretting her first assumption. "I'm fine."

"I have a blister on my thumb," Nick whined, holding the digit in question out for inspection. "Kiss it and make it well."

Kay's lips quivered; for a moment it was questionable as to whether she would laugh or cry, but Nick's foolery had the desired effect. "Well, thank goodness that's all," she said. "What were you doing with Erin, Nick? I am glad you were with her, and I'm very grateful to you for your quick thinking, but . . ."

"I hitched a ride," Nick said, looking as innocent as any saint.

"I see. Well, I'm grateful you did. I should never have asked Erin to drive that car."

"It wouldn't have mattered who was driving," Nick said. "It could have been you. Or me."

Kay shook her head. "That will be the day, young man. There aren't many people I'd trust with that car. . . ." Her voice trailed off and her face took on the blank, listening look of someone considering a new and not too pleasant idea. "Never mind. The important thing is that no one was hurt."

Nick went off to borrow the pickup and make arrangements for the Mercedes to be towed to a garage. He offered to do the errands while he was in town; when Erin handed over the list, he twisted his face into such hideous contortions she thought he was having a fit, until it dawned on her he was reminding her of what they had discussed earlier.

The color had returned to Kay's face, but she sat where Nick had placed her, hands limp and eyes abstracted. When

Erin asked if she could take the next day off, Kay nodded. "Yes, that will be quite all right."

Erin couldn't believe she had heard correctly. No argument, no discussion. "Are you sure?"

"Yes, why not? You deserve it; you've worked very hard and you've just had a very unpleasant experience. Run along now; I have things to do."

Nick returned with the cleaning and Kay's medicine, but without a battery. As he described it, the machine had emitted strident jeers of laughter when his credit card was inserted.

"I think mine might run to a battery," Erin offered. "Just as a loan, of course."

She wasn't sure how Nick would take the offer, and his first reaction was to stiffen and look haughty. Then he grinned sheepishly. "Save it. We may need it for something else."

"How are we going to get into town tomorrow?"

Nick waved an airy hand. "I'll think of something."

They ended up riding in with Joe, who had spent the night, as he was doing with increasing frequency. He and Rosemary had taken to working late; but according to Nick, fatigue wasn't the primary reason why Rosemary insisted on his staying over.

"Why, then?" Erin asked. "Do he and Rosemary have something going?"

Nick's brows drew together. "Have you got some kind of hang-up about Rosemary's sexual activities? First you had her hopping into bed with Laurence, now you're suggesting she and Joe—"

"Why, Nick, you're blushing," Erin said maliciously. "I didn't mean to shock you."

"I am not blushing!"

"But you're shocked. Yes, you are! Talk about hang-ups—you have a blind spot where Rosemary is concerned, and you're not the only one—you all do it, treat her like a piece of damp clay you can pummel into any shape you want." A poignant memory of Rosemary's lament on the night of her granddaughter's birthday came back to her, and she added with equal vehemence, "She's not a series of platitudes and a two-dimensional campaign poster, she's a human being, with human needs and, I daresay, a few human weaknesses."

"Okay, okay." Nick considered the idea. "So maybe you have a point. But Joe . . . He's not her type."

"How do you know?"

"I don't." Nick smiled reluctantly. "There's no accounting for tastes, as the old lady said when she kissed the pig."

"Cow."

"What?"

"When she kissed the . . . Oh, never mind, I don't think the comparison is very nice either way. Rosemary's private life is none of our business, so long as she's discreet about it. She seems to have been very discreet indeed, or you wouldn't be hanging on to this fantasy that she's as pure as Caesar's wife. You're probably right about one thing, though; she wouldn't carry on an affair with Joe here in her own house, under Kay's very nose."

"Kay's the worst offender, in your terms," Nick said. "She'd throw a fit if she thought Rosemary were betraying the sacred memory of Edward Marshall."

"So why does Rosemary insist Joe stay overnight?"

"What? Oh, that. It's just that Joe's drinking is getting a little heavy. She doesn't want him to have an accident, or get picked up for DWI. Listen, you're here at night, have you ever noticed—"

"Oh, grow up," Erin exclaimed.

Joe showed no ill effects when he appeared for breakfast. In fact, he was turned out with unusual smartness; suit pressed, shoes shined, shirt spotless. When Erin complimented him on his appearance he tugged self-consciously at his tie, a conservative paisley print on a dark background.

"Is this tie okay, do you think? Rosemary gave it to me; she says my others look like I'd closed my eyes and picked 'em off a rack at a discount outlet."

"It's perfect," Erin said. She caught Nick's eye. He blushed.

Joe dropped them at the Capitol. "How are you going to

get home?'' he asked, leaning across Erin to open the door for her—a mark of distinguished favor.

"Jeff said he'd pick us up at three, if we could be here on the dot," Nick answered.

"You'd damned well better be here on the dot. When Jeff says three, he means three, not three-oh-five or even three-oh-one."

Nick grimaced. "I know. He's in a foul mood lately, isn't he? Almost bit my head off when I asked him for a lift."

"Wait a minute." Joe fumbled for his wallet. "You better pick up a battery for that wreck of yours. Get Jeff to stop someplace on the way home."

Nick stepped back, his hands behind him. "No, thanks," he said stiffly.

"Don't be a goddamn jerk," Joe shouted. "We need more vehicles. I'm renting yours for the campaign, okay? It's perfect for our humble, lower-middle-class image. So take the money and shut up."

He dropped the bill at Nick's feet, slammed the car door and took off. Erin jumped on the money and caught it as it started to flutter away. It was a hundred-dollar bill.

Nick watched the car weave a path between the concrete barricades that had been set up in the hope of discouraging terrorists. "He's in a *very* cheerful mood this morning, isn't he?"

Erin burst out laughing.

"What's so funny?" Nick demanded.

"You. Are we going to stand here all morning?"

"Wait till he's out of sight. Turn around, admire the Capitol, and try to look impressed."

That wasn't difficult. Erin had become accustomed to the sight of the massive dome crowning the city, but she had never taken the time to go sightseeing, and she was surprised at how light and well-balanced the building appeared at close range. The capitals of the Corinthian columns looked like frozen lace, and the lofty flights of marble stairs, one on either end and one in the center, raised the eye to the swelling curves of the dome.

"You've been inside, haven't you?" Nick asked.

"No."

"You haven't? I wish we had time for a real sightseeing tour of Washington. If I say it as shouldn't, you won't find a better guide. I'm hooked on this town. I used to spend all my spare time wandering the streets and poking into odd corners. I'll bet I'm one of the few people who can identify every single one of the statues."

"It is a beautiful city," Erin agreed. "Too bad about those barricades; trying to disguise them as planters didn't work very well."

"Life in the twentieth century," Nick said wryly. "Okay, he's gone; we can be on our way."

As they walked, Nick gave her a sample of his talents as a guide. "The Senate side of the Capitol is on the north, and the House is on the south, ahead of us. Those are the House office buildings across the street, facing the House side, as the Senate buildings face the Senate side. There are three House buildings—Cannon, Longworth, and Rayburn, the newest. Rosemary's office is there, in the Longworth Building."

"They're so big," Erin said, studying the long white marble facades that seemed to stretch for blocks.

"Well, there are over four hundred representatives. They all need offices, plus offices for secretaries and staff, meeting rooms, places to eat, restrooms. . . . As a matter of fact, this business of staff has gotten out of hand. Did you know that each congressman is allowed up to twenty-two staffers? Senators get more, depending on the population of the states they represent—as high as eighty in some cases. All salaries courtesy of the taxpayers."

"That seems reasonable. The more constituents, the more work, right?"

"It isn't the proportions, it's the sheer numbers. At last count there were 20,000 staffers serving the 535 members of Congress, and that doesn't include the staffs of legislative agencies. It's become a matter of prestige—how big your offices are, how many serfs you have attending upon your needs. Taxpayers' money shouldn't be spent puffing up the egos of their representatives. The worst part of it is, a lot of work the staffers do is either unnecessary or self-serving. One of the reasons why it has become so difficult to get legislation passed, and accepted by the administration, is that the bills are packed with special-interest provisions cooked up by staff representatives. The process is getting so complicated it can't work.''

''Very interesting.''

''Was I lecturing? Sorry, the subject gripes me. Of course,'' Nick added with a grin, ''there has to be room on Rosemary's staff for a few more worthy souls. Next year— God willing and cross your fingers—Rosemary will be moving a couple of blocks north, to one of the Senate office buildings. Now look over there—on the west lawn. See that big oak tree? It's over a hundred years old. You've seen it on television, it's where the correspondents do their stand-ups. One of these days . . .''

'' 'This is Nick McDermott, reporting from Capitol Hill.' ''

''Maybe. Or, 'This is Joe Schmoe, speaking with Senator McDermott.' ''

''Is that what you want?''

''I'm not sure what I want right now. Just to be part of this, somehow, some way.''

The gleaming white of the buildings, the emerald-green lawns and brilliant fall foliage shone in the sunlight as if freshly painted. But it wasn't only the beauty of the scene, it was what it signified. The reality might be tarnished and stained, but the vision somehow endured.

Nick tugged at her arm. ''Hurry up, let's make that light.''

''What's that big white building over there with the columns?''

Nick gave her a pitying look. ''That's the Supreme Court, you sweet little hick. What have you been doing with your time since you arrived in D.C.?''

''Not sightseeing.''

''Why not? People come from all over the country—the world—to see this town.''

''I don't know. I wasn't much interested back then. And it's no fun alone.''

''You poor abandoned child. Take a good look then, while we're here.''

Erin squinted at the stately white building. ''What does the

inscription read? 'Equal justice . . . under law.' Nice senti-
ment.''

"That's what this is all about." Nick gestured grandly.
"At least that's what it's supposed to be about. Now this
structure on your left, with the squatty green cupola, is the
original Library of Congress, conveniently situated near the
Cápitol to make it easier for the legislators to improve their
teeny little minds. That's the old building, named after
Thomas Jefferson. There are two others—the Adams, over
that way, and the newest, the Madison, where we're headed.
You have to see the inside of the Jefferson, it's impressive as
hell—long red curtains at the windows, paintings and marble
floors and all that jazz. Maybe next time . . .''

The architecture of the Madison building was in striking
contrast in that of its ornately adorned elder sibling. A stark
cube of pale-gray marble, polished till it glistened, its entrance was lined with square unadorned columns of the same
material. A number of redwood picnic tables added a pleasantly homely touch. Many were already occupied by students
and tourists enjoying the fall weather.

Nick had obviously been there before. Without hesitation
or questions, he led her past the guard and along a bare white
corridor to a door labeled "Newspaper Room." After filling
out a request form and handing it in at the Circulation Desk,
they found a pair of empty places and sat down to wait for
the microfilm to be delivered.

"You know how to operate these gizmos, don't you?" Nick
spoke in a low voice, out of deference to the researchers
occupying the other desks.

"Yes, I think so. Why did you ask for the Richmond newspaper?"

"Do I have to explain everything?"

"If you want my cooperation, you do. The main thrust of
this enterprise is of coursę clear to me, but I cherished a
forlorn hope that you had concocted some sensible way of
carrying it out.''

Nick gave her a pained look. "You had better pray we find
what we're looking for in the Richmond paper, because if we
don't, there are dozens of local rags we'll have to check. And

the Washington *Post*, which covers the Virginia suburbs."
Erin groaned and Nick went on, "The Richmond paper is
the best bet for a couple of reasons. First, it's the biggest one
in the state. Second, the Marshalls lived in Richmond for ten
years, while Ed Marshall was in the state legislature. His
mother still lives there, in the family home."

"His mother?"

"Most people have mothers."

"Hard to be born without one," Erin agreed. "I didn't
know she was still alive."

"She and Rosemary don't get along. She thought Eddie
Boy married beneath him. Point is, the Marshalls have Richmond connections. It seemed a logical place to start. So, if
you have no further objections . . ."

She had a number of them, but the arrival of the microfilm
put an end to the discussion. The sheer number of boxes was
daunting; Erin watched despondently as Nick divided them
into two stacks and shoved one at her.

He hadn't explained what she was to look for, and in a
way she was flattered by his assumption that she had sense
enough to figure it out for herself. The dates on the film she
had been given began with January 1, 1956, and ended with
1969. Nick had taken the lion's share; his presumably began
where hers left off, and went up to the present. The beginning
date was not as arbitrary as it might seem. In 1956, Rosemary
had been newly married. Nothing that had happened to her
before then would have much bearing on her career, which
was closely connected with that of her husband.

Erin sighed and extracted the first spool of film from the
box. It went faster than she had expected, once she got the
hang of it. Skip the sports section, the classified, the pages
devoted to entertainment and style, look for the key words:
"Fire, Blaze." They occurred only too often. "Two Children
Killed in Fire." "Blaze Destroys Warehouse." "Arson Suspected in Downtown Blaze." She had to read each of these
stories carefully, looking for anything that might connect them
with Rosemary, even indirectly. As she plowed doggedly on,
a pattern emerged, but not the one for which they were
searching. Most of the fires had occurred in low-rent dis-

tricts, and in winter. "Defective Space Heater Blamed for Blaze in Apartment Building." "Police Suspect Child Playing with Matches Started Tenement Fire."

She had to stop every now and then to rest her eyes and change the film. The third of these interludes coincided with one of Nick's. They stared gloomily at one another over the scattered boxes. "How far have you gotten?" Nick asked.

"Fifty-nine."

"That's pretty good."

"No, it's not. At that rate, it will take all day to finish this lot, and how do we know we've even got the right time period? Or the right paper, or the right slant? Maybe the fires have an entirely different meaning."

"I know." Nick knuckled his eyes. "It's so damned depressing. Did you notice how many kids are killed in fires?"

"That appears to be one of the hazards of poverty." Erin's lips twisted. "There was no such thing as decent, cheap day care—there still isn't—so single parents had the choice of going on welfare or leaving the kids alone in the apartment. I can't stand—"

She broke off. Nick said awkwardly, "Try not to let it get to you. Can you stand a little more of it?"

"What? Oh, sure. It's okay."

The stories had affected her painfully, but that was not why her breath had caught and her voice had stopped. After Nick returned to his reader she sat staring at the lighted screen in front of her, wondering why she had been so slow to make the connection. Children, that was the catalytic word. Children killed in fires. . . . Kay's list of names, Mr. Brown's list. Three children, three identical dates. And the poppet—the doll. A child's toy.

She sorted through the boxes looking for the date. It was an easy one to remember: July 4, 1967.

There was only one fire mentioned in the newspaper of that date. Carelessly handled fireworks had started a small blaze in a field, no harm done, no injury to man or beast. Erin was about to relax when she realized an incident later in the day might not have made that edition. She went on to July 5.

And there it was. Front page.

The name Marshall was not mentioned, but she knew she had found what they were looking for. The names had rooted themselves in her subconscious; they were instantly familiar. Raymond, the eldest; Mary Sue, Allen, Alice, Linda. And their mother, Josephine Wilson, age twenty-seven.

The police had gotten the names from the boy, Raymond. There was no other record; the family had been squatters, illegal residents of a building that had been condemned and was due to be demolished. The boy had tried to get back inside. . . .

Erin pulled back from the reader. "I found it," she said.

"What? Where? Let me see." They exchanged places. After he had read the story, Nick looked up with a puzzled frown. "There's nothing abut Rosemary in this."

"It's the one," Erin insisted. "It has to be. I'll explain in a minute. See if there's a follow-up. They said police were investigating. . . ."

Nick gave her a curious look, but did as she asked. After an interval he said, "Yeah, here it is. There was another body found—that of a man. Downstairs, in the room under the one where the family was staying. They think he was a bum, a wino, who passed out and let a cigarette fall into a pile of old newspapers. The weather was hot and dry, it hadn't rained for days. . . . Statement by an official of the company that owned the building. . . . Blah, blah, sad tragedy, blah, blah, said Mr. Roy—Roy. . . ." His voice trailed off.

"Well?" Erin said impatiently. "Roy what? Marshall?"

Nick raised his head and looked at her. His face was that of a stranger. "Not Marshall. Hartsock. Roy Hartsock, attorney-at-law. Your father?"

Chapter Twelve

ERIN HAD ONLY the vaguest recollection of the succeeding half hour. She sat in a stupor while Nick finished the job with silent, tight-lipped efficiency. After he had collected the copies of the articles, he had to lift her bodily from the chair and lead her out.

It was not until they left the building and the fresh air brushed her hot face that she fully recovered her senses. One of the picnic tables had just been vacated; she dropped onto the bench with a thud that made her whole body vibrate.

"I didn't know," she mumbled. "I didn't. I really didn't."

Nick sat down beside her. He couldn't take his eyes off the pages he held—or else he was reluctant to look her in the eye.

"Then how did you know this was the right story?" he asked reasonably.

"I'll tell you. I was going to tell you. Just listen. . . ."

Her narrative was not a model of coherence but Nick had no trouble following it. "Brown," he repeated. "He didn't say who he was?"

"No. But it's obvious, isn't it? Kay hired him to find that information. Birth and death dates. He must be a private detective."

"So Kay knows about this."

"But I don't. I didn't. Nick, you've got to believe me!" She grabbed his lapels and tried to shake him. Nick sat like a rock, his eyes moving slowly over her face, feature by feature. Then he took her head between his hands and pressed his lips to hers.

When he raised his head she saw he was smiling. "Sure, I believe you. Whoops, there go the papers—grab them. . . ."

Erin let him chase the papers; she was so weak with relief she felt giddy. "Do you really, Nick? Not just because I kiss so well?"

"That doesn't hurt." Nick sat down again. "No, but seriously, as someone once said—you should have seen your face. If you were faking that wide-eyed horror you ought to try out for Arena Stage. And besides, if you had known about your father's involvement, you wouldn't have shown me the story."

"I can't believe it. I had no idea—"

"You're repeating yourself, love." Nick pushed a lock of hair away from his face; the breeze had stiffened. "I'm feeling somewhat bewildered myself. To be honest with you, and myself, I never really expected to find anything. The odds were so against it. It's like stumbling over a genuine dead body when you're playing cops and robbers. Why didn't you tell me about that phone call?"

"I didn't make the connection till now. There are so many underhanded, undercover things going on—I assumed it had to do with the campaign."

"Fair enough." Nick's eyes returned to the copies. "So what have we got? A tenement fire in which several members of a family were killed. They were there illegally. The building was owned by a corporation whose nominal head was your father. But we know the Marshalls were involved—"

"No, we don't. Not yet. Has it occurred to you, Nick, that this business might be aimed, not at Rosemary, but . . ." She swallowed. "At me? Unless there are earlier incidents of which I am unaware, the first fire happened the day I came to Middleburg for my job interview.''

''Jesus, I never thought of that.'' He thought about it, and Erin was guiltily pleased to observe that the possibility of a threat against her distressed him more than danger to Rosemary. Then his face cleared and he shook his head.

''I admit some of the incidents are ambiguous, like the one involving Kay's car; but except for you getting mauled at the fund-raiser—which I still believe was unrelated to the other things—nothing has been directed at you. Whereas the fire in the graveyard was a direct hit at the Marshalls—specifically Ed Marshall. I think he was the owner of that building. Your dad was just the owner of record, or whatever the term is.''

''Why should Marshall want to conceal the fact?''

Nick shrugged. ''I don't know anything about corporate law, or finance, or any of that stuff. If I did, I'd be a rich entrepreneur instead of an impoverished journalist. There may not have been anything fishy about the corporation itself, but I can think of a lot of reasons why Marshall might not want his name on record. Tax evasion, maybe. And don't forget he was running for office. 'Slumlord' isn't a name politicians enjoy.''

''That's not good enough, Nick. I only read the first story; it said the police were investigating. What did they find?''

''The police always investigate fires,'' Nick began. Erin reached for the papers; he gave in with a sigh. ''Okay, don't bother reading it, I'll tell you. The police found no sign of arson. They concluded the poor drunk downstairs started the fire. But it happened at a very convenient time for the owners of the building. It was heavily mortgaged and due to be demolished. It was also heavily insured.''

''I see.''

''Erin, honey, there's no evidence that your father had anything to do with that fire. He says in one of the stories that the corporation plans to set up a trust fund for the surviving children, even though there was no legal liability. They had ignored the 'Condemned' signs, broken through boarded-up windows, and sneaked in.''

"That sounds like a guilty conscience," Erin said dully.

"Any decent person would feel terrible about a thing like that, even if he hadn't been responsible."

"It was the year after the fire that Dad broke connections with the Marshalls and moved to Indianapolis," Erin said. "He never saw them again, never had anything to do with them, except for an occasional letter or card—and that was Mother's doing. . . ."

"Well, doesn't that suggest that if there was something fishy about the fire, your father didn't know about it beforehand? Maybe it was disgust and abhorrence that prompted him to break relations. Maybe it was just the way his career ball happened to bounce. Either way he's in the clear."

"Isn't there something called accessory after the fact?"

"Forget about your old man," Nick snapped. "Oh, hell, I know you can't, but at least try, for the moment, to concentrate on the issue at hand. Somebody knows about this incident and is holding it over Rosemary's head. Who?"

"Well, it isn't me. But . . . but—oh, Nick! Rosemary probably believes it is. Kay, too. I can hardly blame them. Look at the facts. I show up, out of the blue, asking for a job, and the very first time I set foot in the place there's an unexplained fire. I could have done everything that has been done—I was there. They made sure I was there, they invited me, so they could keep an eye on me—"

"Wait a minute, you're going too fast and too far. The only reason you were asked to move in was because Kay—"

"Yes, don't you see? That accident came at a very convenient time, didn't it? Kay is the only person who could have planned it. She deliberately injured her hand. Only it turned out to be more serious than she had expected, she only meant to bruise it."

"So Kay knows the whole story."

"Of course she knows. She worked for Mr. Marshall even before Rosemary came on the scene, she was his business assistant as well as a personal friend. And think of the time schedule, Nick. My father died over a year ago. He had plenty of time to straighten up his affairs, destroy any documents that might have incriminated the Marshalls—or hand them over to his heirs. I made good and sure everybody knew Mother was incapable of dealing with business matters; if Dad had passed the information on, it would have been to me."

Nick nodded reluctantly. "And the guilty parties would be only too ready to smell blackmail in everything you said or did."

"Could something like that really damage Rosemary politically?"

"That would depend. How deeply was she involved? Was she an officer of the corporation—is her signature on the legal papers? Remember the flap about Ferraro's involvement in her husband's business, and what that did to her career. And this has sensitive side issues. The slumlord image wouldn't go over well, especially for a candidate who's made a big moral issue of supporting poverty programs and civil rights. Hypocrisy is the operative word, and a damned dangerous one in politics. Yes, I'd say Rosemary would go to some lengths to keep it under wraps."

"Who's doing this, then? I swear, Nick—"

"I said I believed you. And what's more," Nick added thoughtfully, "Rosemary and Kay aren't certain about you either. If they were, Kay wouldn't have bothered looking up those names. You want to talk about motives for harassment, the surviving members of that family have good cause to resent the Marshalls. Did you happen to notice—"

"I could hardly help noticing, it was right there in the paper."

"Yeah. The Wilsons were black. If the oldest boy was ten in 1967, he'd be about the same age as . . ."

"Jeff," Erin murmured.

"Jeff came to work for Rosemary about a year ago. Gave up a good job, just as she said. When was it, exactly, that your father died?"

"May. It's been more than a year—almost eighteen months."

"Let's assume the trust fund for the kids was set up," Nick said. "Your father would have been the logical person to handle it; but the money had to come from Marshall, or from the corporation itself. They would take every possible precaution to keep Marshall's name out of it, but transactions of that sort can be traced, surely, by someone who knows the tricks of the trade.''

"A lawyer, for instance. And Jeff is a lawyer. Oh, damn.'' Erin bit her lip. "It looks bad, doesn't it? Jeff could be Raymond Wilson. He was born in 1957. . . . Nick! Raymond's birthday was in March! Nick, it can't be Jeff. We just celebrated his birthday, remember?''

"Hey, that's right!'' Nick looked as relieved as she felt. "Are you sure about the month?''

"Pretty sure. We can find out.''

"Do the same thing Brown did,'' Nick said excitedly. "I'll bet he just went to the courthouse and looked up birth and death certificates.''

"We don't even have to do that. Mr. Brown is probably listed in the Richmond classifieds. I'll call him back, tell him I mislaid the data.''

"Good thinking, Erin.''

"I'm so glad,'' Erin said. "I don't want it to be Jeff.''

"You don't want what to be Jeff?'' inquired a mild voice.

Nick jumped a good two inches. Standing behind them, looking at them with a benevolent smile, was Will.

"If I ever saw guilt writ large upon a pair of human faces, I see it now,'' Will went on. "Don't worry, I won't tell Joe I found you canoodling instead of working.''

"I've never canoodled in my life,'' Nick said, recovering himself. "Canoodled! Where do you find words like that? And don't tell me in the dictionary. We are not neglecting our duty, we've got the day off.''

"Hell of a place to spend it,'' Will said.

"Uh—just part of the sightseeing tour. What are you doing here?''

Will raised his eyebrows. "I work here. Where do you suppose I get the information I give Rosemary?''

"I always thought you made it up,'' Nick said. "Well, I guess we'd better get moving, Erin, right? We've got to see the White House, the monuments, the . . . the . . . See you later, Will.''

Without moving or changing expression, Will somehow managed to look smaller. Abandoned, forlorn, lonely . . .

"Join us for lunch?" Erin suggested. As soon as the words were out of her mouth she could have kicked herself—and so could Nick; he gave her a look of bitter reproach.

"I'm brown-bagging it." Will indicated his bulging, shabby briefcase. "I only brought one sandwich, but if you'd care to share it . . ."

"I wouldn't deprive you for the world," Nick assured him. "It's probably a peanut-butter sandwich, isn't it?"

"Why, yes. But you're more than welcome—"

"He lives on peanut butter," Nick explained. "Prolonged infantilism. No, thanks, Will. See you tonight?"

"Yes, indeed."

"You could have asked him for a ride home," Erin said, trotting to keep up with Nick's rapid strides. "If we miss Jeff—"

"We won't. Why'd you ask him to have lunch with us? We've got a lot of things to talk about."

"I don't know why. It was idiotic of me; the words just said themselves."

Nick's steps slowed. He looked back. "He's standing in front of the building watching us. You know, I wonder about Will. That absentminded professor shtick of his doesn't quite make it. Could he have been following us?"

"He has a logical reason for being there."

"Oh, yeah? There's a fairly decent library at the University of Virginia, and Charlottesville is only an hour from Richmond. Why does he have to come to Washington to work?"

"To be near Rosemary."

"Oh, God, you're not going to start that again, are you?"

"No, I was just suggesting one possibility. There are others."

"Indeed there are. He could be in on this, Erin. He and Rosemary go back a long way."

"So do a lot of other people and Rosemary. How long has she known Will?"

"Dunno. We're going to have to investigate the whole

crowd. Would your Visa run to a private eye's pay, do you suppose?''

''I don't suppose, I know. It wouldn't.''

''At least we can check on the surviving Wilson kids without too much effort,'' Nick said thoughtfully. ''Jeff's out; let's hope we can eliminate Christie and Jackson on the same grounds.''

''Jeff is only out if the arsonist is one of the Wilsons. There are other motives.''

''Damn, there you go again, being logical. And, what's worse, being right. Once you admit a political motive, the field is wide open. Three people certainly knew about the Richmond fire—Rosemary, Kay, your father. And one of *them* could have told others. Ed Marshall could have confessed, before he died. And if we managed to track this down, a trained investigator might well be able to do the same. This is the first really dirty campaign Rosemary's ever fought—the first one where she faced an opponent without scruples. It would be worth a lot to Buzz to get something on her.''

''But if he knows, why is he playing cat and mouse?''

''Yeah, well, I've been thinking about that. I doubt Buzz knows. What this looks like to me is a setup for blackmail. 'Pay me, in cash or in favors, or I'll take my information to Bennett.' When she balks, he lights another match.''

''Bennett's wife doesn't fit into that scenario.''

''I can't think of any way to make her fit,'' Nick admitted. ''So maybe the scenario is wrong. That meeting between Miz Marylou and Rosemary has to be connected with this somehow, there can't be two conspiracies going on.''

''Two? Why not six or seven? Washington is a city of conspiracies, big and small. Everybody's hiding something, everybody is up to something.''

''Now, now, don't exaggerate,'' Nick said. ''What you need is a little nourishment. And perhaps a drop of the cup that cheers and inebriates. Down this way.''

The building was of cream-colored brick, with dark-green shutters and a canopy of the same color. Window boxes held bright displays of crimson geraniums. Erin hung back, and Nick said, ''What's the matter? Aren't you hungry?''

"I am, actually. But Nick, isn't this place awfully expensive?"

Nick flung the door wide. "My dear, think no more of mundane matters. This is one of the few places in town where my credit is still good. At least I hope it is. . . . Please look impressed when the maitre d' greets me by name."

The maitre d' did greet him by name, and led the way to a table at the rear, behind a free-standing fireplace that occupied the center of the room.

"You notice I'm not important enough to rate a table where I can see and be seen," Nick explained.

"This is nice and secluded," Erin said politely. "Nick, was that Senator Kennedy?"

"Uh-huh. The guy with him is the majority leader. And that couple . . . I'll be damned. There's Philips Laurence. I wonder what he's doing here, this isn't his usual ambience."

"Who's that with him?"

"I don't know. Damnedest hat I ever saw, it's like a limp funnel." The deep-brimmed navy hat hid the woman's face, and most of her body was concealed by the table and by her companion. Nick twisted around to get a better look. Erin poked him.

"Don't stare, he'll see you. He's looking this way—"

"Oh, everybody stares in places like this. It isn't the food that brings people, it's the clientele. Damn, I think he's spotted us."

Laurence said something to his companion, rose, and came toward them. "Hello there," he said, smiling.

Nick gave a theatrical start. "Oh—hello, Mr. Laurence. I didn't see you. Would you care to join us?"

Laurence recognized this piece of bravado for what it was. His closed lips stretched wider. "What a lovely idea. Unfortunately, I'm lunching with someone else. Why don't *you* join *us*?"

"We haven't ordered yet and you're almost finished," Nick said.

"That's true. How clever of you to have observed that without seeing me."

There was nothing Nick could say to that, so he remained silent.

"I'd like to get your input on Rosemary's appearance on my show Sunday," Laurence went on.

"You got my input, such as it was, the other day," Nick said. "What's to say? It's your show, you have your own way of handling things."

Laurence tired of baiting him. "Quite. I understand; when you are entertaining a beautiful young lady, you don't want to share her. Enjoy your lunch, children."

"Smug son of a bitch," Nick said, glowering at Laurence's retreating back.

"Nick. That's—"

"I don't care if he does hear me. He is a smug SOB. Did I tell you about the meeting we had, to discuss Rosemary's appearance? He told me—"

"Nick, that's not what I was going to say. Just shut up and listen to me. That's your trouble, you know that? You never listen—"

The waiter glided up to ask if they were ready to order. Nick waved him away.

"Look at the menu," he growled.

"I'm looking at the woman with Mr. Laurence. Nick, it's Kay. That's what I was trying to tell you."

"The fish is good," Nick muttered. "Might as well . . . What?"

"Don't turn around."

"Why not?"

"Because if she had wanted us to know she was here, she would have waved or nodded or something."

Nick pretended to drop his menu. The performance wouldn't have deceived a child. "Are you sure?" he asked, straightening. "I can't tell."

"Yes, I'm sure. I got a better look when he was away from the table. Look at her hand—it's bandaged."

"Lunching with the enemy," Nick muttered. "And in disguise—"

"It's a pretty feeble disguise and a pretty public place for a secret meeting. And Mr. Laurence is an ally, not an enemy.''

"Hmmmm. So why doesn't she wave or something?''

"I don't know. I'll have a chef's salad,'' Erin added, as the waiter approached.

Nick insisted she look at the menu, and persuaded her to change her mind. Breast of Chicken Rosemary was too appropriate to resist. She paid no attention to the prolonged discussion about food and wine that ensued. She was watching Kay and Laurence—and thinking.

The Pandora's box she had unwittingly opened might yet contain a small sprite of Hope, but right now she couldn't find it. All she could see were the sins and mischiefs. The discovery had made clear a number of things she had vaguely wondered about—Rosemary's financial generosity to her, Kay's inappropriate questions during the purported job interview—and cast a cloud of doubt on others she hadn't considered. It was like a spotlight, distorting by its very brightness and casting of shadows. The conversation with Joe, in which he had expressed such a kindly interest in her and her father; Christie's antagonism; Laurence's dislike; Will's habit of turning up when she least expected him.

How many of these insights were real and how many were only distortions?

After Nick had dealt with the wine steward, enjoying every nuance of tasting and approving, he shook her out of her unhappy thoughts by demanding that she report on Kay and Laurence.

"They're still talking,'' Erin said. (And what about the innumerable combinations of people? Kay and Laurence, Jeff and Kay . . . Stop it, she told herself.) "Now she's handing him something. . . . The headwaiter is bringing the check. . . . Laurence is smiling in that patronizing way of his. . . . He's signing the check. Didn't even look at it.''

"Adding up the bill is uncouth,'' Nick remarked. "Remind me not. . . . Now what?''

"Don't turn around! She's coming this way.''

Kay's face was darkly shadowed by the drooping hat brim but a vagrant ray of light reflected from her eyeballs so that she seemed to be peering slyly out at them like a fox from its lair. Even her voice echoed oddly. "I didn't expect to see you two."

Nick had risen, napkin in hand. "Didn't Erin tell you I was going to show her the sights?"

"Oh, yes. It slipped my mind, I guess. Well—enjoy yourselves."

She walked toward the door, where Laurence was waiting.

"That was short and sweet," Nick said, sitting down and reaching for his wineglass. "I was too well-mannered to say so, but I wasn't expecting to see her either. I thought she was going to Norfolk with Rosemary."

"I'd love to have overheard that conversation," Erin said, watching Laurence gallantly usher Kay out the door.

"You wouldn't have heard anything interesting. If they have secrets to exchange they'll do it in Laurence's car, or on a park bench. Lunching together in a public place, openly and innocently, could be a cover-up for the real reason why they had to meet. But Kay sure as hell didn't think she would run into us. I'll bet she'd have tried to sneak out without speaking if Laurence hadn't convinced her she was bound to be recognized—"

"Stop it." Erin put her hands over her ears. "I feel as if I've wandered into a scenario about secret agents and the CIA. Their reason for meeting was probably quite innocent. I wouldn't be too surprised to learn that they had had an affair once upon a time, and perhaps the old flame still smolders. . . . Oh, damn. What's the use of speculating when we don't know what we're talking about?"

"That's all we can do—speculate. Hmmmm. That's an interesting idea. It hadn't occurred to me; but then I lack your fine insight into romantic matters. Laurence used to have something of a reputation along those lines. Seems to have reformed lately. AIDS has affected a lot of life-styles."

"It doesn't seem to have inhibited Senator Bennett."

"I refuse to discuss AIDS or Buzz Bennett," Nick declared. "Or anything else that might upset my stomach. Have some more wine."

By the time they finished the prolonged and expensive

meal, they had to hurry in order to meet Jeff. Nick had consumed most of the bottle of wine—"I'm not driving, and at these prices I'll be damned if I send any of it back"—and he called for the check with a flourish whose insouciance undoubtedly owed something to the alcohol. The waiter bent down and murmured something in his ear. The change in Nick's expression verged on the ludicrous.

"What is it?" Erin asked apprehensively, as the waiter glided away. "I've got some money, if there's any problem—"

Nick had to swallow twice before he could speak. "No problem. None at all. That bastard Laurence already paid it. Can you believe the chutzpah of that—"

"It was a nice gesture."

"Nice? Why is it that when Laurence offers me something, I want to snap at his hand like a mad dog?" Nick's lowering brows lifted and the corners of his mouth twitched. "If I'd known he was going to pick up the check I'd have had dessert."

A faint autumnal haze hung over the city, mellowing the afternoon sun. Nick sniffed the air appreciatively. "I suppose it's loaded with ozone and other yucky substances, but it smells good, doesn't it?"

"I keep thinking I smell smoke," Erin said.

Nick gave her a sharp look. "You do. Everybody's burning leaves this time of year. Don't let it get to you, Erin."

He left her no breath to answer, but took her arm and hurried her along. Even at the best pace they could set, they were a few minutes late. Jeff was waiting for them. He didn't look pleased.

"You know what the traffic on the bridge is like. I want to get the hell out of town before it starts."

"We were only three minutes late," Nick protested. "For me that's damned good. I wouldn't have done it for anybody but you, pal."

"I believe that." Jeff shifted into drive and slid the car deftly into the traffic. "But only because you know I won't wait for you. Punctuality isn't just a virtue, you know, it's a necessity in this business, especially for small-fry like you and me. One of these days you're going to cook your goose keeping some big shot waiting—''

"Okay, okay." Nick, in the backseat, stretched his legs out and relaxed. "What are you so grumpy about these days? Is something bugging you?"

"What's not to bug me? The polls are slipping, the paperwork is piling up, the flyer that should have gone out last week is still on your desk—"

"That's because the printer screwed up," Nick retorted. "Did you want me to send out the first lot, the ones that called Rosemary the candidate of the asses?"

"That's a rotten phrase anyway. Sounds like the Communist Manifesto."

Nick sat up. If looks could have killed, the glare he directed at the back of Jeff's neck would have felled him on the spot. "Oh, yeah? Well, for your information—"

"Boys, boys, don't fight." Erin mimicked Kay's prim voice. "We must all pull together and overcome these little difficulties."

The only response she got was a pair of grunts, one tenor and one baritone, but Nick leaned back and the tight line of Jeff's lips relaxed. In an effort to find a noncontroversial subject, Erin said, "I see you're using your new key case, Jeff. It's really good-looking."

"Yes." After a moment Jeff said awkwardly, "I—uh—I enjoyed the party. It was nice of you. Thanks."

"But you never wear your bee-you-tiful wig," Nick complained.

His high-pitched, whiny falsetto won a reluctant smile from Jeff. "I'm saving it for election day," he said.

"Good. We'll have a big drunken bash. We are going to win, you know."

"Yes," Jeff said. "We are."

Chapter
Thirteen

KAY DID NOT refer to their meeting in town. In fact, if Erin had not known she was suffering from a tendency to find undercurrents where there were none, she would have suspected Kay deliberately kept her hopping from one task to another so she wouldn't have an opportunity to talk with anyone. It was almost eleven before Kay finally dismissed her. By that time the others had left. Rosemary was not expected back that night. She had gone directly to Charlottesville, where she was to make several appearances the following day.

Erin waited until Kay had gone upstairs before she headed for the commons room and the telephone. She didn't place the call until she had looked into every corner to make sure Will was not lurking.

Her mother was delighted to hear her voice, and brushed aside her apologies for calling so late. "It's cheaper after eleven, darling; there's no need to run up Rosemary's phone bill."

Getting her mother to talk about the good old days at U. Va. wasn't difficult. The hard part was turning the flood of nostalgia in the direction she wanted to go. She listened patiently to a long, rambling description of Rosemary's first meeting with the man she was to marry—a story she had heard dozens of times.

"She looked so sweet in that blue dress I loaned her. Her family was dirt-poor, you know, the poor girl didn't have hardly a stitch of decent clothes. Fortunately we wore the same size. She was a tiny little thing— Well, I was too, if you can believe it! She was going with some other boy, and I had a hard time persuading her to double-date with Edward and your daddy and me, but I knew she wouldn't be able to resist him. He had everything—good looks, money, a fine old family name. And he fell for her like a ton of bricks, if you know what I mean. Your daddy and Edward were fraternity brothers. . . ."

"Yes, I know. It's a pity you had to move away and break up a friendship. And a partnership—weren't Dad and Mr. Marshall partners?"

"Oh, no, honey, they were never in business together. Your daddy did some legal work for him, that was all. Yes, it was too bad, I hated to leave Richmond, but by that time Rosemary and Edward were living at Fairweather, and the offer was one your daddy just couldn't refuse. He never regretted it, I know. He was so happy in Indianapolis. We were both so happy. . . ."

Tears choked her voice; in the background Erin heard another voice, that of her aunt, demanding to know what Erin had said to make her poor mother cry.

She managed to get in one more question. Desperation made her frame it less subtly than she would have liked, but the word "fire" obviously struck no nerve with her mother. "Fire? At Fairweather? Oh, no, honey, there wasn't any such thing, not that I knew about. Nor at our house, I'd certainly remember that! Where did you get the idea? . . ."

"I must have got it wrong," Erin said quickly. "Mother, how are you feeling? Is your leg better?"

It was and it wasn't. The pills the doctor had prescribed helped some, but it still hurt when she walked too much. Erin listened, making sympathetic comments at appropriate intervals. That was the least she could do, listen sympathetically; but her heart sank as her mother kept referring to Ann's ideas and Ann's opinions and Ann's medical theories. I've got to get her out of there, she thought. But how? I can hardly support myself, much less another person, and I couldn't live with her, we'd drive each other crazy.

Finally her mother remembered Rosemary's phone bill. "It's been wonderful talking to you, darling."

"Me too, Mom. I love you."

After she had hung up she sat slumped in her chair for a long time, fighting discouragement. It appeared there was nothing she could do for anyone. She certainly hadn't learned anything that might help Rosemary.

The following day was a torment of mounting frustration. Kay was crankier than ever; the Richmond telephone directory had no listing for a Brown Detective Agency, and neither did the directories for D.C., northern Virginia, or the Maryland suburbs; Nick had left at dawn, to join Rosemary in Charlottesville and escort her through her schedule before driving her home. The idea of calling assorted detective agencies, starting with A-1 Investigative Services and going on through the alphabet, was too depressing to consider seriously, even if she had had time and privacy, which Kay made sure she did not. The state offices in Richmond were closed for the weekend, including the Bureau of Vital Statistics.

The appearance of Jeff, late in the afternoon, was a godsend. His affectionate, teasing manner with Kay amused her and distracted her attention from her victim. Joe came in shortly afterward and commandeered Erin's services with a peremptory firmness that left Kay no chance to object. As soon as he got her into his office he told her to sit down and put her feet up and keep quiet. "I figured you'd about had it with poor old Kay," he explained gruffly. "Read a dirty book or something. Relax."

However, he was unable to supply a dirty book, so Erin had to content herself with Elizabeth Drew's commentary on campaign financing—several years old, but unfortunately still only too apropos. Some of the figures quoted shocked her so much she ventured to disturb Joe with a request for verification.

Joe snorted. "Kiddo, it's worse now. A Senate seat today

costs three million bucks, give or take a few hundred thou.
That means that if he wants to run again, a Senator has to
raise ten thousand a week for six long years. Doesn't leave
him much time to do his job, hmmm?''

"The best Congress money can buy," Erin said.

"Hey, that's not bad." Joe reached for a pen.

"It's not original. I read it somewhere. . . . In the *Post*, I
think."

"So what's a little plagiarism?" Joe tossed the pen aside
and picked up a cigar. "As for the cost of a presidential
campaign these days . . ."

"I don't think I want to hear about it, I'm depressed enough
already. It's funny," Erin added, "how little attention I've
been paying to the Big One. I know it's more important than
a Senate race, but . . ."

"Not to us," Joe said. "Oh, sure, the presidential race does
affect others, including ours, but in my not so humble opinion
it's a waste of time to worry about it, because the effect is so
unpredictable. Local loyalties often supersede party affiliation.
Look at Mac Mathias, and that seat in Maryland he owned for
so long—a Republican in a solidly Democratic state. And this
time we don't have to worry about those long Reagan coattails.
George Bush is walking around in a . . . what do you call those
cute little jackets like bellboys wear?''

"Those cute little jackets like bellboys wear."

"Smart-ass," Joe said, grinning. "You talk too much. I've
got work to do."

Erin knew he had enjoyed the discussion. If he hadn't, he
would have told her to shut up.

Thanks to Joe and Jeff—and Will, who had oozed imper-
ceptibly into his corner at some point—the evening passed
more pleasantly than she would have expected. They were all
in the commons room watching the eleven-o'clock news when
Rosemary came in, followed by Nick.

"How did it go?" Joe asked alertly.

Rosemary tossed her purse onto the couch and collapsed
next to it. "Mediocre. I told you I couldn't compete with a
football game, especially U. Va. and Maryland."

"Students." Joe dismissed the entire student body with a

flourish of his cigar. "I didn't expect much from that. Bunch of smug little yuppies."

"Rosemary, you look exhausted," Kay said. "Why don't you get ready for bed and I'll give you a back rub—"

She broke off, with a look of disgust. Rosemary laughed.

"Not one-handed, darling."

"I keep forgetting," Kay muttered. "Erin, could you—"

"I don't need a back rub," Rosemary said. "Stop fussing, Kay."

"The Chamber of Commerce talk went great," Nick said, drifting toward the coffee maker. "Rosemary nailed them on waste in the defense budget—reeled off a long list of examples without even referring to her notes."

"We should have Charlottesville in the bag," Jeff said. "Albemarle County has gone Democratic in the last umpteen presidential elections, even the Reagan landslide. Our own polls show a comfortable lead."

"Yeah, right. I think we should concentrate on fringe areas now. Rosemary, I know you're sick of hearing this, but you have got to make another swing through the southwest—"

"Keep your shirt on, Joe," Rosemary said. "I'm making an appearance there next week. A coffee. Roanoke. Tuesday. How about that?"

"You didn't tell me." Joe's formidable eyebrows sloped into a V. "Why didn't you tell me?"

"Because I knew you'd try to set up a couple of dozen other appearances. I haven't time for that. I'm only doing this one because the subject is so important to me."

"What subject?" Joe demanded.

Rosemary's smile was seraphic. "Gun control."

"Gun—gun—gun control! Jesus Christ, Rosemary, are you out of your mind? There are five shotguns per household in that part of the state. Some of 'em have never tasted store-bought meat. What are you—why . . ."

It dawned on him that he was being set up, and he sputtered to a stop. Rosemary's dimple had put in an appearance, and Nick was grinning—though there was a touch of sheepishness in his expression. It was Will who caught Erin's attention, however. His silences had begun to fascinate her;

they were not simply an absence of speech, they varied in intensity and type and carried an astonishing variety of unspoken messages. Catching her curious gaze, he lowered one eyelid in a wink.

"You didn't ask who was sponsoring the coffee," Rosemary said.

"Okay," Joe said warily. "So I'm asking."

"Remember the story in last week's Roanoke paper, about the eight-year-old who shot and killed his little brother while he was playing with daddy's .45 Magnum?"

"There are stories like that all the time," Joe muttered. "How do you expect me to . . . Oh my God. Don't tell me. It isn't . . ."

"The mother," Rosemary said.

Erin gasped, and even Joe, the cynical old campaigner, looked shocked. But only for a split second.

"Did you set this up?" he demanded of Nick.

"Will suggested it," Nick said. "He found the clipping. We talked it over, and I made a quick trip to Roanoke the other day." He glanced at Erin and added defensively, "She suggested it. I swear she did. She talked. . . . Did she talk! Said the other women in the area, and a lot of the men, were sick of seeing kids getting blown away, sick of watching the NRA buy votes of congressmen whose constituents overwhelmingly favor some form of handgun control."

"Some of that was in the newspaper story," said Will in his soft voice. "The last part, as you probably realize, was Nick."

"Some of it was in the story, but believe me, it wasn't like actually hearing her." Nick's face was bleak. "It wasn't one of the happiest visits I've ever paid to a voter. I think it did her good, though. She . . . she broke down and cried, finally. All over my best tie."

"I had already written her a letter of condolence," Rosemary said. The dimple was long since gone and her voice had the note of crisp efficiency that often covered strong emotion. "I always write to the families in cases like that. That's one of Will's jobs, to find relevant stories. He didn't tell me

what he and Nick were planning until after it had been ar-
rangéd, but I approved wholeheartedly.''

"I guess even an old dog like me can learn something from
beginners," Joe said handsomely. "Good work, guys. I suppose you've arranged for full media coverage, Nick? Hey—
how about '20/20,' or 'Nightline?' I could call Koppel—''

"I already did. His assistant said he'd pass the idea on, but
everybody has done the gun-control bit. The Washington stations are all sending crews, though.''

"Great." Joe rubbed his hands and beamed like Scrooge
after his reformation.

"Pray for good weather," Will said. "She's arranged an
open-air meeting, in the park.''

Joe looked doubtful. "She's arranging it? Listen, Nick,
you better keep an eye on her. Tactfully, of course—like I'd
do it. Amateurs don't know how—''

"She's no amateur," Nick said. "You haven't heard the
kicker yet, Joe. Mrs. O'Malley happens to be the president
of the County Right-to-Life Chapter. She's an old pro at organization; ran a couple of the marches on Washington.''

Joe seemed less bemused by this information than Nick
himself. "People," he said with a shrug. "So now she's
endorsing Rosemary? Fantastic! Great publicity!''

"It's not so surprising," Rosemary said. "She just decided
that the right to life applies to children as well as fetuses.''

Erin was the first to say good night. As she had hoped he
would, Nick followed her out of the room and caught up with
her at the foot of the stairs.

"Are you mad at me?" he asked.

"What about?"

"Taking advantage of that woman's personal tragedy for our
own purposes. It may seem like a rotten thing to do, but—''

"Oh, that." Erin leaned wearily against the banister. "Either I'm becoming hardened to political reality, or I've learned
that moral issues are seldom as simple as they seem. Does it
bother you?''

"Yeah, some." Nick propped himself against the opposite
wall, like a matching bookend. Even his eyelids sagged.

"God, I'm tired. Well, I'm glad you don't think any the less of me for being a lousy opportunist. You looked as if you had bitten into something spoiled."

"I did. Yesterday."

Nick began. "Moral issues aren't always—"

"This one is. Was my father a criminal or wasn't he? You can't get much simpler than that."

"It's a lot more complicated than that and you know it. The point is not whether your father was a crook. The point is that he's dead and buried." Erin gasped. Nick passed a weary hand over his mouth and then went on, "I'm too tired to think what I'm saying. I didn't put that very well. Look at it this way: Your father can't be hurt, he's out of it. But Rosemary . . ."

"Always Rosemary! All right, what about her? Not long ago you were all gung ho about saving her from scandal. What have you done for her lately?"

"You know what I've been doing. The campaign—"

"May come to a crashing halt if what you suspect is true."

"All right, all right. I know. But I can't take time off at this stage without arousing a lot of curiosity. Be fair, Erin, you haven't had time either. I'm sure Kay has had you on the run—"

"I found time to look through a couple of dozen phone books. Brown isn't listed."

"Brown. Oh, you mean that . . . I can't think what to do next, then."

"You can't think, or you prefer not to discuss it with me? My father is dead—and buried, as you so nicely put it—but I'm alive, and it would be naive of you to trust me. You just can't trust anybody these days, can you? Especially where something as important as Rosemary's career is concerned."

"You know that's not true. Erin . . ." He reached out for her.

The commons room door opened and Kay emerged, followed by Rosemary. Caught by surprise, Nick moved clumsily, tripping over his own feet and presenting a perfect picture of an awkward swain.

Kay frowned disapprovingly; Rosemary broke into a broad grin. Nick stepped aside to let them ascend the stairs. As

Rosemary passed him she muttered, "Carry on," and Nick turned red.

"I wish she wouldn't do that," he whispered, watching them disappear around the turn of the stairs.

"She was just kidding," Erin said. She added pointedly, "But I wasn't. I shouldn't have blown up the way I did, Nick. But everything I said was true. Maybe you have cause to question my motives; but you've got to do something, you can't just sit back and—"

"Nick! Goddamn it, where is that kid? Nick!"

Joe's voice was only slightly softened by the closed door. Nick groaned. "Talk about being caught between a rock and a hard place. . . ."

"Which am I?" Erin inquired sweetly.

"I refuse to answer on the usual grounds. Erin . . . Honey, darling, sweetie pie—give me a break, okay? I trust you, esteem and honor you. . . . Hell, I think I love you. I swear—"

"Nick!"

"Damn it! Just give me a little time, Erin. We'll talk later, I promise."

                    *   *

"LATER" TURNED OUT to be a stretch of three days. Nick spent a good deal of the time in Roanoke, "tactfully" helping to organize the gun-control rally. His brief visits to the house never coincided with Erin's free time.

No further incidents occurred, but Erin was always expecting something to happen and her nerves stretched tighter and tighter as the days passed. The smell of burning haunted her dreams. The smoke was actual and real; after the driest October in over twenty years, brush fires had broken out across the southeastern states. Weary fire fighters, their faces soot-blackened and drawn, appeared on the evening news broadcasts; weather forecasters reluctantly admitted there was no hope of rain in the immediate future. Police claimed that two of the largest blazes, one in western Virginia and one in South Carolina, were the result of arson. As far east as Baltimore and Washington the sun shone dimly through an overhanging haze of gray smoke.

"The fire won't come anywhere near here," Joe said, as they watched one such broadcast. "Just don't throw a lit cigarette away when you're walking in the woods."

Kay sniffed. "You're a fine one to talk. You and your cigars."

"Ah, but I don't walk in the woods," Joe said complacently.

"You don't walk anywhere," Kay snapped. "And you drink too much. You're a prime candidate for a heart attack, Joe."

Joe took the criticism good-humoredly. "At least I'm having a good time while I'm alive. Loosen up, Kay baby. There's no danger from those fires, they're miles away, and we may get rain by the end of the week."

Kay's hands moved restlessly, picking at the fabric of her skirt. Her favorite knitting bags were piled untidily on the bookshelves gathering dust. It was a pity she was unable to relieve the tension that stiffened her body and lined her face, Erin thought, reluctantly sympathetic. She suspected she knew why Kay was so sensitive to the mention of fire.

The only notable occurrence during Nick's absence was the change in Christie's attitude. She and Erin had been the only ones in the office Sunday afternoon; even Joe had taken time off to watch the Redskins play their longtime rivals from Dallas. His whoops of alternating triumph and rage, as the score fluctuated, could be heard even at a distance, and after one outburst Christie laughed and said, "That had to be an interception. You can almost tell what's happening on the field by the intensity of Joe's yell."

Erin wasn't sure how to react. Christie had made tentative overtures before, and then slapped her down when she responded. She leaned back in her chair and flexed her stiff fingers. "You sound like a fan yourself," she said. "Why aren't you watching the big game?"

"Not me, kid. I hate football. My ex–significant other used to be glued to the damned TV all weekend every weekend. Like a nice feminine female, I kept him company, worked hard to learn about his hobby. . . . Why are women such fools?"

"It's hard to break early training," Erin said. "Even if

you were brought up by a liberated mother—which I certainly was not—you're barraged by messages from other sources. Movies, TV, aunts and friends. Be nice, be kind, don't hurt people's feelings, no matter what they do to yours. . . ."

"He sure didn't do much for mine," Christie said sourly. "You should have seen me hauling beer and sandwiches at him and apologizing when there wasn't enough mayo on the bread. Apologizing when supper wasn't ready when he got home, apologizing for talking about my work instead of listening to him bitch about what a hard day he'd had. . . . I'm sorry, you don't want to hear this, it's so damned boring."

"If you feel like talking, I feel like listening. I think that's one area in which women have an edge over men; we can give each other support because we aren't ashamed to admit we make a mistake now and then."

Christie studied her expressionlessly for a moment. Then her lips parted in a flash of even white teeth.

"You a mind reader, or what?"

"Huh?"

"I was trying to work up to admitting I made a mistake with you. I took you for one of those sweet-faced ruffly-blouse-type females that was looking for a free meal ticket and a cushy job."

Erin winced. "I may have been heading in that direction." Then she added with a flash of temper, "But at least I didn't judge you, or anybody else, by some stupid stereotype."

Christie's eyes narrowed. Before she could reply, Erin went on hotly, "Did you think I was after your job? Oh, I see that amuses you; the very idea of a nobody like me undermining your position—"

"It's been done. By people less qualified than you, to people better qualified than I."

"Yes, I suppose so. That wasn't what I had in mind when I came here, Christie; I'll be damned if I know what I did want. But I know now: not necessarily your job, but one like it. I won't sneak in by the back door, I'll earn it fair and square. So watch out. From now on I'll be snapping at your heels."

Leaning against the desk, arms folded, Christie studied her without expression. Then her lips parted and she let out a whoop of uninhibited laughter. "Girl, I sure did you wrong. Fair enough; from now on it's a fight to the finish, no holds barred, but no hitting below the belt."

She held out a strong, slim hand and Erin grasped it. "We don't have to fight."

"Yeah, but we probably will. I'm competitive as hell, and apparently you are too. I'm all for a good honest fight now and then." She stretched, yawning, and Erin watched her lean grace with admiration not unmixed with envy.

"I think we're entitled to a break," Christie said. "I'm going for a run."

"Is that how you keep that gorgeous figure?"

Christie laughed, but looked pleased. "That's how I keep from going crazy in this madhouse. The conditions aren't ideal—there's no regular track, just a path through the woods—but it's sure relaxing. Do you run or jog or anything?"

Erin realized she had received an invitation. She said doubtfully, "I couldn't keep up with you, I'm really out of condition. And I don't have the right clothes."

"Nothing wrong with jeans and a sweatshirt. Let's see your shoes."

Erin stretched out a sneakered foot. Christie frowned. "Well, it doesn't matter, we'll just take it easy. That is—if you want to come."

To refuse might have weakened the tenuous new relationship. Besides, it offered a chance to ask questions. . . . Erin stood up, stretched. "Sounds like a great idea."

As they crossed the stableyard the not-too-muted sounds from Sam's cottage indicated that he was also glued to the big game. Fields and wooded hills dreamed in the hazy sunlight. Fallen leaves crackled dryly under their feet.

The path opened up between a stand of cypresses. It was in better condition than Erin had expected; when she commented on the relatively smooth surface, Christie said, "Thanks to Nick. You know the way he grabs hold of an idea and runs with it; I happened to mention it would be nice to have a place to run, and the next day he was out here with a rider mower. The weeds were waist-high! He even dug up a roller someplace and ran it up and down.'' She bent to check the laces on her shoes. "I kept him company when I could; it was a pretty sight, I can tell you. Ever see Nick without a shirt, and sweat gleaming on all those muscles?''

"No."

"Oh, really? There's a general impression—"

"It's wrong." After a brief hesitation Erin added, "Give me a little more time."

It was the right response. Christie laughed. "Good luck. He's a sweet guy. Not my type, though. He's too intense. I need somebody who can keep his cool."

"Like Jeff?"

"From one extreme to the other." Christie's smile faded. "There's something about Jeff . . . I don't know, it's like he's built a wall around himself a hundred feet high and two hundred feet thick. I'd like to be there if he ever tears it down, but I haven't got the time or the energy to fight something as strong as that. Ready? Watch your feet, the surface isn't as smooth as it looks. You could sprain an ankle."

She took her running seriously. The pace she set might have been slow for her, but it left Erin gasping. When they stopped for a brief rest she didn't have enough breath to ask questions. Christie did all the talking; her breathing was scarcely quicker than normal.

"I love this place," she said, the sweep of her arm indicating the panorama of meadow and forest stretching westward, framed by the outline of the distant mountains. The setting sun washed their slopes with apricot, and burned on the tops of the trees behind them.

"You wouldn't think there was a house or a human being for miles," Christie went on dreamily. "Even Fairweather is hidden by the trees. If you come up here at twilight and sit quietly, after a while you start hearing little rustles and movements in the grass. Once a doe walked right past me, not ten feet away, with her fawn following—"

A sound like that of a dry branch cracking interrupted her. Christie turned to look, shading her eyes with her hand.

"Was that a shot?" Erin asked uneasily.

"Some jackass hunter," Christie said. "Deer season

doesn't start for another month, but there're always a few heroes who can't wait to start killing things.''

Erin struggled to her feet. Her lungs still ached. "It sounded close."

"Sound carries a long way on a quiet day like this. He's not on Rosemary's land, at least not with her permission. We'd better start back, though, it's getting late. You don't mind if I go ahead, do you? You can't get lost, just follow the trail."

Erin dropped back onto the fallen tree trunk they had used as a bench. "I'll just rest a few more minutes."

Christie gave her a friendly slap on the back. "It gets easier with practice. You did fine for a beginner."

She took off, running with a grace and ease that made Erin feel eighty years old. Within moments she had disappeared among the trees.

As soon as she was out of sight, the strangeness began, as if her presence had held something sly and ugly at bay. Nothing in the landscape changed, but now it conjured up different images: loneliness instead of peace, isolation rather than solitude. The air was acrid with smoke, and the swollen, sullen sun sent long, blurred shadows sliding across the grass—shadows without definition or substance, like the thoughts in Erin's mind. She had reached a point where every statement, every look was distorted by her suspicions. Christie had been awfully anxious to make friends all of a sudden. And what had she said about Jeff. . . . "It's like he's built a wall a hundred feet high." Perhaps she had misremembered that vital date of birth, because she didn't want it to be Jeff. If he was the survivor of that tragic family, he had good reason to hide behind a wall of deception.

Was Nick avoiding her because he still entertained doubts about her, or for other reasons? He had personal and family connections with Rosemary that went back into the past; hadn't he said something about his aunt working for the Marshalls? A housekeeper had plenty of opportunities to discover the personal secrets of the people who employed her.

Erin jumped to her feet. The heavy dusk was making her morbid. Time she was getting back. She must be at least a mile from the house; the path had twisted and turned all the way. She should make better time going back, since it was downhill, but soon the sun would set, and considering her total ignorance of woodcraft, there was a distinct possibility that she might lose her way. She got to her feet. As she started toward the trees she heard a second, far-off echo of gunfire.

It was already dusky under the branches, but a long finger of sunlight kept her company for a short distance as she plodded through the fallen leaves. Then a turn in the path cut off the sunlight; shadows sprang at her like enemies from ambush. The leaves crackled under her feet as she broke into a trot. The distance seemed much longer than a mile, and it was with considerable relief that she emerged into the open and saw the roofs and chimneys of Fairweather below.

With the darkening woods behind her and an evening breeze dispelling some of the smoke, she felt rather foolish about her panic. That was what it had been, irrational terror, in the ancient sense of the word. The faint haze in the air only mellowed the pastoral beauty of pasture and field and clustered dwellings; she stood still, waiting for her breathing to slow and her weakened knees to regain their strength.

A rustle and snap of shaken branches behind her startled her, but at first she did not connect that sound with the other, the now familiar crack of a rifle. The next bullet came close enough to whine before it smacked into a tree trunk.

It was instinct rather than reason that sent Erin into headlong flight. She didn't stop running until she had reached the shelter of the stables.

A high-powered rifle could carry . . . how far? Miles, she believed. The hunter probably hadn't even known she was there. He had fired at some miserable animal, and missed. No one could have known she would walk in the woods that day.

But if someone had been out with a gun, hanging around in the hope of finding her out of doors . . . There were such things as telescopic sights.

No, and again no. That was too farfetched. Delusions of persecution, that was what she was developing.

And anyway, gunfire wasn't . . . fire.

*   *

IT IS A WELL-KNOWN FACT of life in Washington that the mood of the entire city is colored by the results of the Sunday football game. When the Redskins lose, especially to Dallas, eyes are downcast and voices are surly. When they win, even Monday morning can be endured.

Whether the 'Skins thrashing of their traditional rivals affected Joe's mood was unproved, but he was certainly in excellent spirits next morning. A meeting with the State Democratic Committee Monday afternoon proved to be the first crack in his good humor, but that wasn't unusual; he always managed to pick a fight with someone in that despised group. The final blow came at six o'clock, when Buzz Bennett's latest campaign plug was aired. Bennett had hired the most prestigious group in the country to produce the commercial, which lasted for a full three minutes, and they had earned their money; he kissed old ladies on their wrinkled cheeks and promised to introduce a bill doubling Social Security benefits; he hugged babies and promised their beaming parents he would make certain every child in Virginia had a chance to attend college, not to mention medical school; he stood stiffly at attention, hand pressed to his heaving chest, as a line of fighter planes shot across the cloud-strewn blue sky, and swore America would never bow the knee to tyranny. It was noticed by some that he conspicuously refrained form kissing, hugging, or even speaking to pretty girls. The overall effect—music, production, and Buzz's craggy, sincere face—was so skillfully calculated that Erin felt her throat tighten, even though she knew her response was as mindless and irresistible as the salivation of Pavlov's unfortunate dogs.

Joe was moved only to rage. "Why the hell isn't our new spot ready?" he roared, pounding on the table with both fists. "Where the hell is that lazy swine Nick?"

"You sent him to Roanoke," Will said. "He told you he couldn't—"

"We're shorthanded, that's the trouble," Joe snarled. "Short on people, short on money. It's Rosemary's fault. Goddamn prudish, overly fastidious broad—we could have got half a million more from PACs if she hadn't been so goddamn fussy. Where is she? Why isn't she here?''

"As you yourself told me not twenty minutes ago, she and Kay are dining with the Morgans," Will reminded him. "Probably trying to smooth over the insults you handed him this afternoon.''

"If the man can't take honest criticism he doesn't deserve to be party chairman," Joe said, chewing on his cigar. "All I said was that if we depended on the support of the party we'd be dead in the water. What's wrong with that? When is Nick due back? I want to talk to him about lighting a fire under those media morons.''

At midnight Nick still had not returned, and Erin decided to give up and go to bed. She was pleasantly tired after an afternoon walk—not run—in the woods. She had had to force herself to return to the scene of her panic, but the effort had been worthwhile; there had been no repetition of that odd, senseless fear, only peace and beauty, without so much as a distant echo of gunfire.

Rosemary and Kay had returned shortly after eleven. Both looked drawn and tired, and Rosemary lost no time in telling Joe what she thought of his performance earlier in the day. "Harry was seething. He said you called him an ignorant nincompoop.''

"I did not. When have you ever heard me use a bland, innocuous word like 'nincompoop'?''

"I suppose he was too well-bred to repeat what you really said." Rosemary waved away the coffee Jeff offered her. "Thanks, Jeff dear, but I dare not insert another drop of liquid into this bloated body. And none for you, either, Kay," she added, turning to her secretary. "You hardly spoke a word this evening. That hand is giving you a lot of pain, isn't it? There must be something wrong. An infection, maybe? You're going to Dr. White tomorrow, and I don't want to hear any arguments.''

"Not tomorrow," Kay said. "Tomorrow is Roanoke, re-member?''

"Damn, I forgot. All right, Wednesday, then. Without fail. And take those sleeping pills tonight, do you hear?''

"I don't have any," Kay said.

"Surely you do," Erin exclaimed. "You gave me the prescription to be filled just last week. Nick picked it up for you, after the . . . after . . ."

Her voice faltered as Kay transfixed her with a furious scowl. She had spoken without thinking and without any intent except reassurance; why was Kay so angry?

"Good Lord," Rosemary exclaimed. "You haven't taken a whole bottle?"

"No, of course not," Kay said. "I do have them. I just didn't . . . I guess I forgot."

*   *

THE HOUSE SEEMED very empty next day. The inner circle had accompanied Rosemary to Roanoke; Christie was downtown, liaising, as the phrase went, with Democratic headquarters. As Erin typed the date on a letter she realized that election day was two weeks away. Two weeks to determine the outcome of Rosemary's bid for the Senate, and the futures of those who depended on her for jobs, patronage, support. Two weeks for her to find out the truth about her father. Assuming, of course, that the whole ugly business didn't blow up in their faces before then, wrecking Rosemary's reputation and career and the hopes of those who had supported her.

Erin wasn't even sure any longer what mattered more. Nick had been right; nothing could hurt her father now, though a disclosure of his complicity might have a devastating effect on her mother. But then her mother would probably just refuse to believe it. Erin wished she could do the same. She couldn't, and she could not share Nick's hope that nothing more would happen—that their theories had been wildly, melodramatically wrong, or that the unknown had, for reasons known only to himself, abandoned his campaign of intimidation.

It hadn't occurred to her before that she might search for clues in the house itself. The idea went against every moral principle she had learned. Besides, this was the first real opportunity she had had; there wasn't a soul around who would interrupt or interfere. It might also be her last chance.

One way or the other, win or lose, everything would come

to a crashing halt on November 8. Rosemary would finish out her House term, a few office workers would clean up the debris, financial and physical; but staff would be cut and Kay would no longer need her assistance. Even if Rosemary won and even if she offered Erin another job, that job would be in Washington; the offices here had been set up especially for the campaign. The others would disperse as well; she would never again have as good a chance to watch them and question them, search. . . .

Hands idle on the keys of the word processor, she stared into space and fought a battle with long-accepted values. What she had said to Christie was only too true; women were trained to be law-abiding, gentle, considerate of others. Ladies didn't pry. Neither, in fact, did gentlemen; that moral maxim had no sexist overtones. Something Nick had quoted came back to her; some government official, she had forgotten who, decrying the efforts to break foreign codes. "Gentlemen don't read one another's mail," he had loftily proclaimed. A noble attitude like that one could lose a war, cost thousands of lives. She could lose her own personal war by following an equivalent ethical code. "Moral issues aren't as simple as they seem." She had said that herself. It seemed the most appropriate guide at this particular moment.

But where to look? Kay's office and Rosemary's were out of the question; she couldn't spend the necessary amount of time in either without one of the other workers' noticing. Besides, damaging, secret information was more likely to be concealed in one's private quarters. Too many people had access to the offices, and some—Joe, for example—would consider no locked drawer or safe out of bounds.

Rosemary's room, then. Or Kay's. Fine, Erin thought wryly. Now if I only had the faintest idea what to look for. . . .

That wasn't the only problem, as she discovered when she found herself in Kay's room. "The guilty flee where no man pursueth," and they also quake in their boots or sneakers even when no one is watching. She had taken the coward's way out by going first to Kay's room. No one could climb the bare, squeaking stairs or walk along the uncarpeted wooden floor without her hearing them approach, and even if she was found in the room, she had a valid excuse for being there. There was absolutely no reason why her hands should be icy and trembling, except her own guilty conscience.

She started by straightening up the room, plumping pillows—and feeling them to make certain nothing had been hidden inside—and remaking the bed. (Nothing under the mattress, nothing tucked in the springs, no locked box or briefcase under the bed.) Nothing under the rug, either. Lying flat on her stomach with the dusty stiffness over her head and shoulders, she swept the entire area with her hands, feeling at the same time for loose boards.

She had taken the precaution of arming herself, not with a weapon, but with a dustcloth. Next she tackled the mantel and the table, looking in every vase, opening every little box and jar. A crystalline tinkle of music broke out when she lifted the lid of a porcelain casket and her guilty start of alarm almost caused her to drop the fragile thing. She recognized the tune: "Tales from the Vienna Woods." A memento of a trip to Austria, or just one of Kay's collectibles? She seemed to collect everything—porcelain, pottery, crystal; stuffed cats, wooden owls; objets d'art and just plain junk. Erin's unsteady fingers tipped over an earring holder. It was of brass, in the shape of a cat with several tails, and couldn't be damaged, but the earrings flew in every direction and she had to crawl around before she found them all—and had to pray she had restored them to their original places.

The closet came next. She could always say she was checking to see if any garment needed mending or pressing. . . . Nothing in the pockets of coats and dresses, no betraying crackles or lumps in the linings. Nothing in the purses lined in a neat row on the shelf—navy, black, brown, white, beige— or the shoes, in a hanging holder. She got a chair and climbed on it to examine the topmost shelf. The boxes there contained hats, plus a few odds and ends of old accessories Kay seldom wore and couldn't bear to throw away.

The clock ticking on the mantel told her she had been away from her desk too long. Actually, it wasn't so much the clock as her own discomfort that urged her to complete the search or abandon it. Every quivering nerve argued for the second alternative, but she forced herself to continue. This might be her best, her only, opportunity. But the next part of the search was one she abhorred. Opening drawers seemed—was—an even greater violation of privacy than what she had done thus far.

Underwear, gloves, scarves, cosmetics. A paperback book, tucked under a pile of bras. Erin's compressed lips slipped into a half-smile at the sight of the title and the cover—an impossibly beautiful, artfully half-clothed female clasped in the ardent embrace of a handsome bare-chested hero. At least Kay's tastes were normal. This was just your average, acceptable bodice ripper. Poor prissy woman, why did she bother hiding it?

There were two more books of the same type in the drawer of the bedside table, along with three of the tiny gold boxes of candy Laurence had said were Kay's favorites. So Kay—poor Kay—hoarded chocolates as well as lurid novels. Erin flipped idly through the pages of one of the books, picturing Kay propped up in bed reveling in the passionate adventures of Raven, Countess of Woodbridge, as she munched raspberry creams. If Kay would just relax and admit her harmless weaknesses, laugh over them, enjoy them . . . There were several more of the little gold boxes, emptied of their contents, in the wastebasket.

On the top of the nightstand was an assortment of bottles—vitamins, aspirin, sedatives. The bottle labeled "Dalmane" was almost full.

Only one piece of furniture remained to be investigated—a low bookcase beneath the west window. Erin had put it off till last, almost hoping something would interrupt her search. In some ways books were more personal than souvenirs and accessories, even more personal than clothing. They were reflections, not of the body but of the mind and the heart. And the books people kept in their bedrooms were the most intimate of all—old favorites turned to for comfort when one was sick in bed with a cold, or wakeful during a long lonely night.

She recognized only a few of the titles. *Gone With the Wind*. . . . She might have expected that one, a whole generation of women must have yearned for Rhett Butler. Most of the other novels appeared to be old-fashioned historical romances; flipping quickly through the pages, she didn't see a single word that would have shocked the primmest censor. Kay had hidden the "dirty books" in her dresser drawer.

The majority of the books on the shelves were not novels. They were albums—some cheap plastic, some bound elegantly in leather. Photograph albums. And that too she might have expected.

She started with the last one and wasn't surprised to find that most of the clippings and photographs featured not Kay, but Rosemary. All of Kay's adult life had been lived vicariously, through someone else. She had no husband, no children, no life of her own.

The albums had been arranged in chronological order. Erin took out the one farthest to the left. Old family pictures, black and white originally but yellowing with age. One of the children might have been Kay, she couldn't tell. She returned it to the shelf and took out the next. School pictures, junior high and high school. The clothes had the archaic humor of past fashions not old enough to be quaint—bobby socks and saddle shoes, pleated skirts, baggy sweaters. Kay with her bike, her dog; standing in front of a narrow frame house. Erin didn't linger over these. Kay's youth was no business of hers.

She found the first pictures of Edward Marshall in the third album. Seated behind a desk, he had raised his head to smile at the camera, and the photograph was labeled in Kay's neat hand. "My new boss, Mr. Marshall, Virginia State Senator. An exciting job!"

Exclamation points proliferated thereafter. Mr. Marshall and his "sweet little bride" soon became "Edward" and "Rosemary," and family snapshots mingled with publicity pictures. "Rosemary and I making pancakes Sunday morning. Taken by Edward. We weren't very good cooks!" A coy "First pictures of the new baby" accompanied by a snapshot of Rosemary sprawled gracelessly in an easy chair; an arrow indicated her bulging maternity smock.

So by that time Kay was family friend as well as personal secretary. She had been with Marshall almost from the start of his political career. Most of the pictures were of him and Rosemary, of the baby, of the handsome mansion in Rich-

mond, of Fairweather. Several depicted Edward with his favorite cats—holding them, stroking them, dangling ribbons
for them to play with. Rosemary was also shown playing with
the cats. Her antipathy—or, more accurately, her indifference—must have developed after Edward's death.

Erin hurried through the other volumes. The search not
only made her uncomfortable, it had had another result she
had not anticipated—a profound if unwilling pity for Kay. No
wonder Kay was so fiercely devoted to Marshall's memory
and Rosemary's success. They were all she had.

All at once a familiar picture caught Erin's eye. She had
seen the same one in her mother's album. It had never interested her before; now she stared intently, as if she could will
the miniature faces to speak to her.

Her mother and father, Rosemary and Edward, and two
other people, dressed in evening clothes and standing beside
a limousine. Kay had labeled it, but the names of the third
pair struck no chord of memory. On their way to a ball at the
governor's mansion. . . . Her mother cherished that photograph, one of the few mementos of her participation in the
social life of the state capital.

At the end of the book, tucked into a pocket in the back
cover, she found a tattered business-sized envelope. Inside
were a few newspaper clippings, brown and frayed with age.
They were from the Richmond *Times-Dispatch* and they described a fire in an abandoned tenement. Tucked into the
envelope with them was a single sheet of paper. A list of
names and dates.

Chapter
Fourteen

NICK CALLED shortly after four. He didn't have to tell her there were other people in the room with him; his formal tone and message made that clear. "Rosemary wants you to tell Sarah we'll be later than we expected—not to wait, just leave a casserole or something in the oven."

"How did it go?" Erin asked in the same tone. She was at her desk; the others made no pretense of not listening.

"Fantastic. Watch the six-o'clock news. We're leaving shortly, but it will take us at least two hours."

He rang off, and Erin turned to her audience. "He says it was fantastic; watch the six-o'clock news."

She went to the kitchen to pass on the message to the cook, who nodded as she tore lettuce into smaller pieces. "I figured that. My famous gourmet Chicken à la Sarah is in the fridge; I'll finish making the salad and then run along home in time for the news program. There's an apple pie too, you might want to warm it up before you serve it. Make sure Rosemary eats, mind."

Christie was just coming in the front door when Erin entered the hall. "Wooo, what a day," the tall girl groaned, running her hand over her tightly clustered curls. "Anything happen while I was gone?"

Erin passed on Nick's message. "That's great," Christie said. "Guess I'll stick around—catch the news here."

She gave Erin a sidelong look, and Erin said shortly, "You don't have to ask me—or even announce your intentions."

"My, my, aren't we touchy today. I just thought I'd be polite—seeing as how you're in loco housekeeper around here."

The hit was too close to home. Erin knew her face must have betrayed her, but Christie took guilt for resentment. "I told you we'd fight," she said.

"It takes two to fight. I'm not in the mood."

Christie laughed. "You're no fun. Want to go for a run? I need to stretch my legs. Been hunched over a desk or fighting city traffic the whole day."

"I guess not. I went out earlier."

She didn't tell Christie what had driven her out of the house—or why she had gone only a short distance before the stench of wood smoke sent her running back.

Christie sent the others home at five-thirty, though they obviously wouldn't have minded staying to watch the news. Erin went to the kitchen to check on the food situation and found, as she had expected, that Sarah had everything under control, including fresh-made coffee. She returned to the commons room to find Will adjusting the television.

"I thought you'd gone to Roanoke," she said.

"Not me. I don't make public appearances. Prefer my role as power behind the throne."

"But you weren't here—"

"Yes, I was. All day."

"I didn't see you."

Will lowered his voice to a sinister drone. "No one sees the Shadow. But the Shadow knows . . . ."

He knelt to adjust the controls of the VCR. Christie came in, saw what he was doing and nodded approval. "Good idea, Will. What are you going to do if it's on all the stations?"

"The best I can," said Will, inserting a blank tape.

Christie went to the kitchen and came back with a beer. "I deserve this," she announced, dropping heavily into a chair. "I don't know where the hell the committee finds these people. Half of them don't know what they're supposed to do and the other half don't do it."

She went on grumbling; Will responded with polite murmurs of sympathy, and Erin only half-listened. The slip of paper in the pocket of her jeans burned against her skin. She had copied the list of names before replacing it in the envelope and returning the album to its place. She was trying to figure out a subtle way of asking the date of Christie's birth when the news came on.

How much of the spectacle was due to Nick and how much to Mrs. O'Malley, Erin did not know, but it wasn't hard to understand why the event had rated such extensive media attention. The emotions of the crowd, most of them women and children, overwhelmed the small screen. The music was performed by massed church choirs, black and white joining in the old hymns: "Amazing Grace," "Abide with Me," "A Mighty Fortress Is Our God." And Rosemary—dressed not in black, but in a soft-gray print that made her the symbol of all grieving mothers, her eyes luminous with unshed tears. She began with a message of love and sympathy, but ended with a call to arms. "The time has come—the time is long past—to end the slaughter of the innocents. I'm not going to tell you that if I'm elected I'll make this my first priority. You know I will; you know I have. What I *am* telling you is that, win or lose, in the Senate of the United States or out of it, I will continue the fight till it's won—as a woman, as a citizen, as a mother!"

The choirs burst into "The Battle Hymn of the Republic," and the cameras panned to the audience—singing, swaying, faces streaked with tears.

The screen went black; Will switched channels in time to catch the same ending on another station. Christie turned to Erin. "You're crying," she said accusingly.

"So are you."

"Am I? Jee-sus! Is she fantastic, or what?"

"She is," Will agreed calmly. "But the setup couldn't have been more ideal. Any politician could have milked it, but Rosemary does it best because she—"

"Because she's a bigger ham than the rest of them?"

They hadn't heard her come in. She had left her coat in the hall and was still wearing the soft-gray dress, a grandmotherly ruffle of lace framing her face. Deep lines bracketed her level, unsmiling mouth.

"Because she really means it," Will said.

The brackets shivered, curved, disappeared. "Thanks," Rosemary said. "Hello, Christie—Erin."

"Where are the others?" Will asked.

Kay came in, followed by Jeff, who answered the question. "They're right behind us, unless that jalopy of Nick's broke down. Did you tape it?"

"Yes. Pretty impressive."

"We knocked 'em dead!" That was Joe, accompanied by the usual thick cloud of cigar smoke. "Sockerino!"

He tossed his topcoat over the back of the sofa. Kay clucked and carried it to the coat rack. Nick was the last to enter. Joe turned to him, beaming. "Good job, kid. I'm glad you listened to me and held off on our commercial. I want to incorporate some of that footage. Rosie, what do you— Hey, where are you going?"

Without speaking, Rosemary left the room. Joe started after her.

"No," Will said, his voice uncharacteristically sharp. "Leave her alone. She's going to call Jannie." Joe stared at him, and he added, "Her daughter—remember? She always calls Jannie when she's . . . Give her a break, Joe."

"I know who Jannie is," Joe grumbled. "Oh, well. Yeah. Now, Nick, as I was saying . . ."

Erin slipped out of the room and went to the kitchen. She had lit the oven and taken the casserole from the refrigerator when Nick came in.

"Need some help?"

"You can put the plates and the silver on the table. It will take twenty minutes or so to heat the casserole."

"Good. That will give Rosemary time to unwind." Nick

opened the cupboard doors. "Did you see her? Was that sensational, or what?"

"Sensational," Erin said.

Nick put the stack of plates down on the counter. "Something's bugging you. What happened?"

"I searched Kay's room this afternoon."

Nick crossed the room in two long strides and clapped his hand over her mouth. "Not so loud!"

Erin pried his fingers away. "Nobody's eavesdropping. They're all too full of their latest triumph. Including you. I found a set of those clippings—you know the ones I mean—hidden in an old photograph album. Along with the list of names. I was right about the boy. Jeff is in the clear."

"Wait a minute. I have to get my mind back on track, I've been so busy with other things. . . . Jeff's okay? Good. The clippings . . . That means she knows. She's always known."

"We assumed that," Erin said. "The search was wasted effort, actually. I didn't find out anything we didn't already know."

"Nothing happened while I was gone?" He lowered his voice to a conspiratorial whisper. "No fires?"

"The whole goddamn state is on fire," Erin snapped. "You can smell the smoke everywhere."

"Yeah, I know, but . . . You're mad at me, aren't you?"

Erin opened the oven door.

"Here, let me do that." Nick took the casserole from her. He put it in the oven, burned his hand on the rack, swore, and closed the door. "I'm sorry, Erin, honest. I'm still in a state of shock. I mean, I knew Rosemary was a pro, but after today . . . She had that crowd in the palm of her hand, it was pure magic, and she's got nowhere to go but up. We're going to win; I never really believed it till now. And after that—anything is possible."

His eyes were dazed by visions. Erin knew what he saw, heard the music that played in his inner ear. "Hail to the Chief"—brasses blaring, full military band. Even the secondhand echoes of it stirred her blood like bubbles in champagne, but it could not overcome her sense of foreboding.

She said harshly, "Not if someone is holding a dirty secret over Rosemary's head."

Nick came back to earth with a painful thud.

"But nothing has happened lately. Maybe it's over."

"It will never be over," Erin said. "Not for me. Not until I know what happened."

"Erin." He reached for her hand. She tried to pull it away, but he held on, closing hard, warm fingers over hers. "I know we can't just drop this business; I don't intend to. But insofar as your father is concerned, it's your personal problem. Either he had guilty knowledge of that fire, or he didn't. Nothing is going to change, except your perception of him."

"And that's not important?"

"Sure it is. But Rosemary's father was a lush and a bigot. My mom found Jesus a few years ago and now she sends every penny she earns to some slimy TV evangelist, and reads me long lectures about my sins every time I put my face in the door. She thinks Rosemary is an instrument of the devil because she refuses to fight abortion or condemn those dirty homosexuals."

"Is there a point to these rambling reminiscences?" Erin inquired.

"Oh, hell, you know what I'm driving at. You're responsible for yourself, not for anybody else—mother, father, brother, husband. Nobody's perfect—"

"Oh, Nick, what a stupid cliché!" She threw her arms around him and hugged him hard. "You always know just what to say, you silver-tongued devil, you."

The swinging door banged open. "Ha, caught you," Joe said cheerfully. "Can that wait till after supper? I'm starved."

"Twenty minutes," Erin said. "We were just about to—"

"I can see what you were just about to." Joe picked up a plate of rolls, popped one into his mouth and left, chuckling deep in his throat.

"Shit," Nick said, untangling himself. "This place is like Georgetown on Halloween. Look, honey, we'll keep at it. I promise. I just don't know what to do next."

"You don't have time to do anything. I understand. And

it's going to get worse before it gets better. I guess all we can do is wait.''

"I'll think of something,'' Nick promised. "I'd better put some food on the table before the rest of the crowd busts in here.'' He picked up a bowl of chips. "One good thing,'' he said with a grin. "If Rosemary makes it to the White House she'll be able to afford some servants.''

He kicked the door open and passed through, balancing plates in one hand and the bowl of chips in the other. He was still on an emotional high, unable to believe anything could cloud the glorious future he envisioned. Erin wished she could believe in it—see herself opening the door of the Oval Office and telling the President (the President!) that the Prime Minister and the Premier were arriving at the East Portico. She lacked Nick's natural ebullience, his ability to bounce back from depression.

By the time the food was on the table, Rosemary was back. She had changed into her baggy jeans and campaign sweatshirt, but it wasn't the comfortable clothes that made her look twenty years younger.

"I think my granddaughter is a little confused about the election,'' she reported with a chuckle. "She wants to know when she can come visit me in the White House and meet Mr. Lincoln.''

"Tell her to wait a few years,'' Joe grunted. "By that time she'll be old enough to settle for sleeping in Lincoln's bed.''

Rosemary's performance had impressed even blasé Washington. The phones rang all evening with inquiries and messages of congratulation, and florists' vans made repeated visits. An arrangement of long-stemmed red roses moved Joe to a cynical comment. "That's a good omen; he never jumps on a bandwagon till it's at the finish line.''

Most ostentatious of all the offerings was a basket of delicate, rare green-and-white orchids. Kay read the card first and handed it to Rosemary. Rosemary glanced at it and tossed it aside without comment. Later, when she was tidying the room, Erin found it and was unable to resist reading it. "To two beautiful women, and a bright future for both of them and their most faithful admirer.'' That was so typical of Lau-

rence, she thought, to include himself in the good wishes—
and not so typically tactful of him to include Kay. What was
the nature of the bond between that particular odd couple?
Erin was no longer certain that her original theory explained
the relationship. Former lovers could remain friends, but
Laurence didn't strike her as the sort of man who would
bother making, or keeping, a friend.

*   *

THIRTEEN DAYS to election. Everyone was counting down.
As she trotted around the house answering phones, helping
with mailings, and running errands, Erin wondered if anything short of a major conflagration would be noticed in the
general frenzy. Yet she couldn't dispel the feeling that something was going to happen; that the temporary lull was only
the calm before the storm.

Shortly before noon Jeff appeared, looking even more im-
passive than usual. He paused at Erin's desk to ask when Nick
and Joe were expected back.

"I think they said around two. They're finishing the commercial. Aren't you supposed to take Kay to the doctor?"

Since the accident Kay had not used the Mercedes or allowed anyone else to do so, though it was back from the shop
and the mechanic had assured them it was perfectly safe. He
couldn't understand how such a freak accident could have
happened. He had personally checked those connections when
the car was last serviced, only a few months earlier. It
wouldn't happen again, not in a million years. . . .

"I did," Jeff said. "I took her in, but she told me not to
wait. Said she had errands to do, and she'd call or get a ride
from someone."

He seemed to expect a response, though she couldn't think
why. "There's bound to be someone around who can go and
get her, Jeff. Don't worry about it."

"I'm not. I just . . ." Erin looked at him more closely and
saw the fine parallel lines between his brows. He leaned
closer. "She was acting kind of strange. Said some peculiar
things."

"Like what?"

Jeff hesitated. "Quoting Scripture. The word 'sin' kept recurring."

A trickle of cold touched Erin's spine. "That is odd. I've never heard Kay quote from the Bible."

"Suggest anything to you?"

"No."

"Well." Jeff straightened. "It isn't important, I guess. See you later."

The word had suggested something to her, though—a well-known phrase that had a grim, personal application. "The sins of the fathers . . ." With an effort, she forced herself to concentrate on her work. There were a lot of other mentions of that word in Holy Writ. She wished she had dared ask Jeff what Kay had actually said.

Later she got a call and recognized a voice she hadn't heard for some time. "Oh, hell, Fran. I'm sorry, but I can't tie up this line; we've had so many calls—"

"I know, I got busy signals all morning. Things are pretty lively around here, too."

"At the office?"

"No, I'm at Democratic headquarters in Arlington. I called in sick this morning. I figure I'm entitled to a few days off, and right now is when I'm really needed. Boy, you should see this place, Erin. That speech of Rosemary's yesterday—"

"I'll tell her you were impressed," Erin said. "I'm sure she'll appreciate it."

"Impressed? I was bawling so hard I got my popcorn all wet. How's that hunk of a manager?"

"I presume you're referring to Nick," Erin said, unable to repress a smile; the description certainly didn't fit Joe. "He's not the campaign manager, he's consultant for media affairs."

"Oh, right. He's doing a great job."

"I have to hang up," Erin said, knowing the usual polite evasions wouldn't work with Fran.

"What's his sign?"

"His what?"

"His sign. What's the matter, can't you hear me? My horoscope says a Libra will surprise me with a romantic gesture that could lead to a long-lasting affair.''

"Oh, his astrological sign. Honest to God, Fran, of all the idiotic questions!''

"Don't you know? I always ask guys, it's one of the first things—''

"No, I don't know. You really believe that nonsense?''

Fran giggled. "I believe it when it's something I want to believe. He's probably a Leo—or maybe Gemini. Libras are calm and well-balanced. Maybe that gorgeous Jeff—''

"Do you have anything sensible to say?'' Erin demanded. "If not, I'm going to hang up.''

"Yeah, okay; some millionaire could be trying to get through to offer Rosemary lots of bucks. Call me when you get a chance, will you? I want to hear everything. By the way, are you going to spend election evening there at the house, or are you coming home? I'd love to have company while I watch the returns. . . .''

The hint was so blatant it ended Erin's fading patience. She said, "Good-bye,'' and hung up without giving Fran a chance to reply. She couldn't have said why the call had left her feeling cross and on edge. She ought to be used to Fran by now.

That evening she ate alone and spent the evening watching television. The others were all out on campaign business, scattered across the state from Arlington to Charlottesville. Apparently she had not been needed. Rosemary's commercial had its first airing; though she meant to study it critically and impartially, Erin had a lump in her throat and tears in her eyes when it ended, even though she had learned enough about media techniques to understand how the effect had been produced. She picked up the book she was reading, on the running of a presidential campaign, but it failed to hold her attention; she didn't want to read about it, she wanted to do it. She knew she had a long way to go and a lot to learn, but she ached to be in on the action instead of being relegated to typing lists and washing dishes.

In that sullen mood of self-pity she went to bed. Voices and the sound of car doors slamming roused her; she pulled the blankets up over her head and went back to sleep. She did not hear Kay come up the stairs and enter her room. She heard nothing more till the birds woke her at dawn.

Down the stairs at a dead run, stumbling over the hem of her robe, catching herself with a desperate grab at the banister. Into the commons room and through the kitchen. No smell of coffee brewing, no comforting, calm presence . . . it was too early, the sun was barely over the horizon, Sarah wouldn't be there for another hour.

It seemed to take forever to turn the key and release the chain. Her fingers kept slipping. Out the door finally; there was frost on the ground, it burned like hot coals on her bare feet. They left dark prints across the whitened macadam of the stableyard. She pounded on the door with both fists and kept pounding till she heard a gruff, resentful voice grunt out a sleepy question. She would have answered it if she could, but when she opened her mouth no sounds came out. She beat on the door again.

It opened with an abruptness that sent her stumbling forward into Nick's arms. He was wearing only a pair of skimpy shorts, and she clung to him, grateful for the warmth of bone and muscle.

"Jesus, Erin! What happened?"

"Kay. She's dead. I just found her."

He made her sit down while he put on jeans and shirt and slipped his feet into sneakers. "Take deep breaths," he instructed. "Put your head down."

"It's all right. I'm all right now. I just can't . . . seem to catch . . . my breath."

"Are you sure?"

"About . . . Kay? Yes, I'm sure. I tried . . ."

"Okay. Let's go."

He didn't notice she was barefoot until she stepped on a sharp-edged pebble and cried out in pain. He picked her up, barely pausing, and carried her into the kitchen, where he deposited her in a chair.

"Stay here. You could make some coffee, if you feel up to it."

"Sure. That's a good idea."

The familiar domestic routine steadied her, as Nick had anticipated. He was back down before the liquid had finished dripping, his face visibly paler.

"She's dead, all right. Was that how you found her—lying on her back, with the covers down to her waist?"

"No. She was on her side, curled up—peaceful. I thought she was asleep. Then . . . I don't know what it was that alerted me. . . . Yes, I do. I couldn't hear her breathing. Usually I can hear her through the closed door. She snores. . . ."

"Yes, okay. So you turned her over—felt for a pulse?"

"I don't remember exactly what I did." Erin's brow wrinkled painfully. "Pulse, yes. I felt for a heartbeat. Then I tried mouth-to-mouth—"

"Jesus Christ, Erin! She was cold! Not ice-cold, but definitely chilly."

"I noticed that," Erin said dully. "That was when I lost my head and ran out of the house."

"Why didn't you wake Rosemary, or Joe?"

"I didn't know Joe was here. And I couldn't go to Rosemary, Nick—not at that unearthly hour, not just rush in and blurt it out." She pushed the tangled hair from her face and pressed her hands to her head. "I was looking for Sarah, I suppose. Someone warm and solid and unflappable. The rock in the storm. She wasn't here, so . . ."

"You mean I was your second choice?" Erin stared blankly at him, and Nick's feeble attempt at a smile never made it past his lips. "I should take that as a compliment. Let me think. I don't like to leave you alone—"

"I'm perfectly fine," Erin said.

"You're in shock, that's what you are." He filled a cup with coffee and poured in half the sugar bowl, waving aside Erin's protests. "Drink it. All of it. I'm going to wake Joe, and then one of us will have to break it to Rosemary. Hang on till I get back."

"No problem." Her hand was rock-steady as she reached

for the cup. Maybe I am in shock, she thought coolly. If so, I hope it lasts. This is no time to break down and blubber. We were wondering what would happen next. Well, now it's happened.

As the dreadful day wore on she could only marvel at the calm efficiency with which the others dealt with Kay's death. For Joe it was easy. Nothing mattered to him now except the election; his only concern was how the tragedy would affect Rosemary and her already overcrowded schedule. His attitude seemed horribly calloused to Erin, but when she said as much to Will, he shook his head.

"Joe isn't calloused, he's just honest. It may make you uncomfortable, but don't misjudge him. He didn't know Kay well, and he wasn't particularly fond of her. The pressure he's putting on Rosemary, to get on with her work, is the best possible thing for her. Don't worry, she can handle it. She's handled worse."

Later that morning Rosemary called her into her office. She was not alone. Standing beside the desk was a tall, raw-boned man with graying hair and a long, large-featured face. "This is Harry Blair, our local lawman," Rosemary said. "He wants to ask you a few questions."

She was pale but quite composed; the only trace of tears was the faint pinkness of her eyelids.

Blair's attitude was almost paternal. Erin told her story; when she started to explain why she had gone running out of the house, instead of notifying one of the occupants, he cut her off with a kindly, "Yes, I see. Perfectly natural thing to do. I don't suppose you happened to notice anything out of the way, anything unusual? Not that you'd be likely to, the way things were. . . ."

"*Was* there anything out of the way?" Erin asked.

Blair appeared a trifle disconcerted. Sweet little young ladies in a state of shock weren't supposed to ask leading questions. He ignored the question and asked one of his own. "Did you see the bottle of sleeping pills on the table by the bed?"

"No. I mean, I suppose it was there, I just didn't . . . Was that how she died? An overdose?"

"Suppose you just let me ask the questions, miss."

"You don't have to treat her like an idiot, Harry," Rosemary said with some asperity. "Naturally she would wonder. Yes, Erin, that's the assumption. The bottle was almost full. Didn't you pick up a refill of that prescription last week?"

"It was Nick who picked it up, actually. I was going to, but the car—"

"Yes," Rosemary said quickly. "The point is that it was a refill. The original prescription was filled only the week before. I have explained that we can't be certain Kay took the medication as prescribed; if she didn't, there are fifteen or twenty of the capsules unaccounted for. Obviously you can't account for them. . . . Is there anything else you want to ask her, Harry?"

Blair's expression showed that he knew he was being manipulated, but he seemed more amused than resentful. "Just the usual things. Whether you noticed anything unusual in her behavior—signs of depression, confusion, anything abnormal?"

Rosemary's hands were folded on the desktop; her eyes were fixed on Erin. The message came across loud and clear. "I didn't know her that well," Erin said slowly. "I only met her a couple of weeks ago. She was annoyed because of her hand—not being able to do the things she normally did, it was frustrating for such an active person."

"Yes, we know about that. Well, I guess that's it, then. Thanks, Mrs. Marshall. I'm sorry about this. We'll make it as easy on you as we can."

"I appreciate that, Harry. If you want to talk to anyone else, ask Joe. He's in his office, I expect." Her gesture at Erin kept the latter in her chair; after the sheriff had left, Rosemary said, "I'm so sorry, Erin. I never imagined when I asked you to come here that you'd be faced with anything so dreadful. If there's anything I can do—"

"I'm the one who should be saying that," Erin broke in. "You've already done a great deal and I expect you'll be

called on to do more. If you stay. If you choose to bow out—
for a few days, or forever—I won't blame you in the least.''

"I'll stay. Of course I'll stay."

"Good." Rosemary's quick smile reshaped every feature,
warming her eyes, smoothing out the lines of weariness and
tension. It was the smile known and loved by millions of
voters; Erin suspected she could turn it on and off like a light
switch, but it had the same effect on her that it did on Rosemary's audiences.

"I was hoping you'd say that," Rosemary went on. "I just
want to tell you what has happened and what to expect. I
think you're like me—you'd rather know the worst than imagine things. There will be an autopsy. Depending on the results of the autopsy, there may or may not be an inquest. If
it is determined that Kay died of an overdose, the verdict will
almost certainly be accidental death."

"I see."

"Yes. You're a clever little thing, aren't you?" Rosemary's
hands twisted. "I have one more thing to say. I'm going to
be candid with you, not only because you are intelligent
enough to figure it out for yourself but because I don't want
to leave you with any lingering doubts or feelings of regret.
I had known Kay for a long time. Our friendship was based
on shared experiences and memories and interests, rather than
emotional commitment, but it was very real. And yet her
death came as something of a relief. You look shocked. Please
don't. You were very tactful in your answer to Harry Blair,
but you must have noticed her memory lapses, and you, of
all people, have suffered from her increasingly short temper.
Sooner or later, it would have been necessary for me to replace Kay. She could not have accepted that. This is so much
kinder. To go out, painlessly and quickly, before your ambitions and hopes are shattered . . ." Her reddened lids lowered and she bowed her head. "It's what I'd want for myself,"
she whispered.

Erin's eyes filled with tears, the first she had shed that day;
but even as she nodded in sympathetic agreement, some separate section of her mind told her that she had just witnessed

one of Rosemary's more impressive performances. Nick was absolutely right, she was getting better all the time.

*   *

"THE INQUEST is Monday?" Erin exclaimed. "So soon?"

"That's what happens when you are a big shot, on your own turf," Nick said. "Everybody is cooperating. Get it over with, out of the way, so the important people won't be inconvenienced."

They were sitting on the tree trunk watching the sun set from Christie's favorite spot on the hill. Christie wasn't with them; she wouldn't get a chance to run that day, except to run herself ragged. Erin ought to have been in the office trying to help, but she had felt a desperate need to get away from the house. Nick had caught up with her along the path, scaring her half to death when she heard his pounding footsteps behind her.

Nick poked moodily at the ground with a stick he had picked up. Its rough point made little impression; the ground was baked hard. The stick cracked across, and Nick tossed it aside. "It's all wrong, Erin," he said. "Cover-up is the name of the game in politics, but this stinks. Joe is counting on a verdict of accidental death."

"The sleeping pills."

"Uh-huh."

"I don't believe it."

"Neither do I."

Nick shifted position. The log was certainly not the most comfortable of seats. "The police are thinking suicide," Erin said. "If the autopsy shows she had Alzheimer's or cancer, or some other horrible disease, that will confirm their theory. If it doesn't . . . well, everybody knows menopause is tough on these old ladies, they get funny ideas. So make it accidental death, spare the feelings of the survivors, don't dig around for dirt that might hurt Rosemary's campaign."

"Nasty, logical way you have of looking at things," Nick muttered. "Maybe she did kill herself. Maybe she was the arsonist."

"Menopause?" Erin suggested caustically.

"Blackmail, pure and simple. To remind Rosemary she knew the truth, and intended to hang on to her job."

"Then she got religion and repented? That would be a nice neat solution, wouldn't it? Criminal and judge in one; crime wave ended, punishment meted out."

"I'm afraid it's too neat," Nick admitted gloomily. "The other possibility is that she found out who was persecuting Rosemary, and the criminal silenced her."

"That would suggest that she confronted the suspect instead of going to Rosemary or the police. So it was someone she knew and liked?"

"Say rather someone she feared. That's the whole point about blackmail; the victim can't go to the police. So why should he kill her? It's usually the other way around."

"But we keep coming back to the same group of people," Erin argued. "It wouldn't have been difficult for any one of them to arrange for Kay to get an overdose."

"And it would have been almost impossible for anyone outside that group to have pumped the pills into her." Nick brooded. "Damn. That lets Laurence out. He was my favorite suspect."

"I don't like him either, but I can't think of any reason why he'd want to threaten or blackmail Rosemary. It all goes back to that fire in Richmond. Who else could have known about it?"

"Everybody and his kid brother," Nick said despondently. "We've been down that track before. However, I want you to know I'm finally getting my act together. I ran a few checks on some of our suspects today. Better late than never, right? If I hadn't sat on my butt dreaming dreams of glory, Kay might—"

"No, don't ever think that." Erin put a comforting arm around him. "It's unfair, untrue, and unproductive. If we had known what was going to happen, we'd all have behaved differently. But we didn't know. At least you were nice to her. She liked you."

"Mmmmmm." Nick returned the compliment physically and verbally, drawing her close before he said, "She liked you too."

"No, she didn't. And—and I really didn't like her very much. I wasn't as nice as I should have been."

"I expect everyone feels the same," Nick said gently. "You know something? I don't think Rosemary really liked her either. She's probably feeling guiltier than anyone."

"She has no reason to feel guilty. She put up with a lot more from Kay than most people would. Oh, Nick, what are we going to do?"

"How about a little canoodling? No, don't give me that reproachful look; as the man said, life goes on. The more love in it, the better."

She responded, not in words, but by raising her face to his. His kiss was warm and sweet; less than passionate and more than kind, both a fulfillment and a promise.

"Now, then," he said, "where were we?"

"Checking on suspects?"

"Right. I think we have to eliminate Joe. Not only does he have every reason to pray for victory, but he didn't know Rosemary until last winter, when he joined the campaign. I found no connection between them before that, except for casual encounters in the course of political business.

"Will she's known since college. Dated him a few times before she met the great Edward Marshall and was swept off her feet. He was married; got a divorce last year. Three kids. I couldn't find any evidence that he saw much, if anything, of Rosemary after she married Marshall. It's not likely that he would, you know."

"Not likely, but you can't be sure."

"True. I didn't have time for in-depth investigations. As for Laurence, he was Ed's friend originally, not Rosemary's. They met at Hah-vahd as undergraduates. We know Jeff is clean, but I looked him up anyway; he comes from Arizona, went to law school in LA, where he aced everything—law review, the works—and then went to work for the State's Attorney's office in Sacramento. He joined the campaign in April. Said he wanted to get into politics, and he liked Rosemary's style—"

"Isn't that an inadequate reason for giving up his job and

traveling clear across the country to work for a woman he'd never met?''

"No more inadequate than my reasons for giving up *my* job and scrounging scraps from Sarah to keep body and soul together. He may have met her casually, for all you know, and been swept off his feet. She has that effect on people. Where was I? Oh, yeah. Jeff's parents are both living, and he has two younger brothers.''

"Good work," Erin said. "How'd you find that out?''

"Personnel file. Same for Christie; mother's dead, father's married a second time, they live in Petersburg. Her birth date is May fourteenth.''

"That lets her out.''

"Right. Sarah—''

"Oh, Nick!''

"A sleuth has to keep an open mind. The woman who died in Richmond could have had a sister. If she did, it wasn't Sarah. Background is an open book. Same for Jackson. He's a native Washingtonian.''

"So where does that leave us?''

"Right back on square one," Nick said. "Any suggestions?''

"We can't take this to the police.''

"This tangled web of surmise and guesswork? No, dearie, we sure as hell can't. There's only one thing we can do. Confront Rosemary.''

"I didn't think you'd agree to do that.''

"Nothing else we can do without more time and a helluva lot more resources than either of us can command. But we've got to do something. Even if we're wrong, even if we end up looking like a pair of horses' behinds, we can't sit on our hands and wait for the next incident. If Kay's death was murder, we've got ourselves a whole new ball game.''

He jumped to his feet and began pacing up and down, his fists clenched. Erin got up too. "I agree. Completely. But we don't know how Kay died, not yet. Let's wait till after the autopsy.''

"I don't know if I can wait that long," Nick groaned. "Something else is going to happen, Erin. I can feel it.''

"Yes." A shiver ran through her. Nick stopped pacing and put his arm around her. "Cold?"

"No. Somebody walked over my grave."

"Don't say things like that!"

*   *

WHEN THEY NEARED the house Nick let out a grunt of disgust. "Damn, there's Laurence's car. I might have known that ghoul would be on the scene."

"How did he find out so quickly?"

"He has informants all over town. The word has gone out; I sent the obituary to the paper a couple of hours ago, and Christie called some people; Rosemary canceled her appointments for this afternoon, you know."

"I should know; I made several calls myself." Erin rubbed her forehead. She had had a dull headache all day, on which the aspirin she had taken had little effect. "I'm not functioning at peak efficiency."

"Me neither. Let's sneak in the back door. The mood I'm in right now, I don't think I can listen to Laurence ooze sympathy and advice."

"Rosemary doesn't seem to mind," Erin said thoughtfully. "And there are times—"

"Oh, for God's sake, not that again!"

"No, not that again. I was going to say that I have a feeling there's more to him than meets the eye, that his languid air is only a facade." She broke off with a laugh. "For instance . . ."

Laurence had just come out of the house. As usual, there were several cats waiting to sneak in; as soon as the screen door opened, a lean calico darted between his feet and he executed a complex, graceless stagger to avoid stepping on the animal. They heard his comment; it was profane but amused, and he paused to stroke one of the losers in the race. "Sorry, old chap, better luck next time."

It was too late for the guilty pair to retreat. Laurence caught sight of them and wove a tortuous path around the cats on the steps and the porch. "Hello, young Nick. I dropped by to discuss Sunday's show, but this is obviously not the time. Perhaps we can set up another appointment.''

"I don't know," Nick began.

"Nor do I, as yet." Laurence took his gloves from his pocket and carefully drew them on. They were of fine morocco and fit like a second skin. His face was sober, with no trace of its habitual mockery. "Rosemary said the funeral will probably be on Tuesday. You'll let me know? I'll be there, of course."

"I'm very sorry," Erin said. "You were old friends, I know."

Laurence sighed. "Yes, I probably knew Kay as well as anyone—except Rosemary, of course. I believe . . . You were the one who found her, Erin? How dreadful for you."

"It was a shock, of course. But she looked very peaceful. I'm sure she didn't suffer."

"Thank you for telling me that." He smiled at her. "Take care of her, young Nick. She's a treasure."

He got in the car and drove away.

"That's a switch," Erin remarked. "He didn't think I was a treasure last week."

"Patronizing bastard," Nick muttered.

"He did seem to be genuinely distressed about Kay."

"Or putting on a good act. Why does he always have to call me young Nick?"

"Maybe he doesn't realize how it annoys you."

Nick made a rude noise through pursed lips. "Well, anyhow, things are back to normal," he said, as they approached the commons room and heard the voices within raised in strident argument. "You'd think Joe could keep off her back—now, of all times."

He opened the door and Joe's voice boomed out. "For once I agree with Laurence. Why the hell did you insist on an autopsy?"

Rosemary stood with her back to him. She was holding one of the knitting bags. "That's the proper procedure in a case of sudden death," she said.

"Yeah, but it wasn't . . . Doc White was perfectly willing to sign the death certificate. Heart failure."

Rosemary was dressed to go out, in a black wool jersey dress with a wide lace collar. The full skirt swung out as she turned. "Jack White is a smug snob. He wants to put me in his debt by sparing me the embarrassment of an inquiry, and a lot of media attention. He thinks Kay had too much to drink, and that she overdosed on those wretched pills."

"So maybe she did. What's wrong with a kindly cover-up? Spare her, you, her family—"

"She had no family, only distant cousins. We—I was her family. That's why I owe her, at the least, the dignity of the truth." Rosemary's makeup was heavier than usual; it gave her face the smooth matte surface of a porcelain figurine. The glaze cracked momentarily, as she said, "Kay could not have taken an accidental overdose, Joe. Her sleeping pills were the mildest-possible prescription sedative. She'd have had to swallow every capsule in that bottle to get a fatal dose, and she hated taking pills, you know how she resisted it."

"Nembutal and alcohol—"

"She didn't drink that much. And she knew the danger of mixing drugs—who better than careful Kay? No, Joe. Either her heart gave out or she took those pills deliberately. One way or the other, I have to know."

"So you can wallow in guilt—one way or the other? For failing to notice she was ill, or depressed? Haven't you paid your dues to Kay, Rosemary? I don't give a damn how devoted she was to Ed Marshall, or how much she'd done for you, you stopped owing her a long time ago."

Rosemary's lips took on an ugly shape, but it was Will, watching from his corner, who spoke.

"Shut up, Joe. What's the point of arguing? We'll know tomorrow."

"That's right," Rosemary said. "We'll know tomorrow. I must go now, or I'll be late. Jeff. . . ."

Erin hadn't seen him. Slouched in a chair by the window, he had been as motionless as a statue. He started violently when Rosemary spoke his name, and rose to his feet.

"Yes, right. I'm ready."

He picked up her coat and held it for her. Instead of slipping into it she put her hand on his cheek and forced him to look into her eyes. "My dear—you look exhausted. Joe can drive me, you stay here and rest."

"No, it's okay. If you can do it, I can. Don't be . . . don't coddle me, Rosemary."

"All right, if you say so. Come on, Joe."

They went out together. Rosemary took Jeff's arm; it was questionable as to who was supporting whom.

"So she's keeping her appointment," Erin said. "Just as if nothing had happened."

"This dinner was scheduled months ago," Will said mildly. "The governor will be there. He's a very popular man, and his active support means a lot to the campaign."

"You sound just like Joe," Erin muttered.

Will's gray eyes brightened, but not with amusement. "I take it that is not a compliment. Would you prefer Rosemary to lose the election, as a gesture of respect for her secretary?" Erin started to protest, but Will went on in his even, inexorable voice. "Kay was Ed's protégée and devotee. Rosemary inherited her along with a lot of other things, good and bad. Kay transferred her loyalty to Rosemary, and she has clung like a leech. Do you realize how tiring, how infuriating, that secondhand devotion can be? Always demanding perfection that can never be attained because nobody could possibly measure up to the standard of the great Edward Marshall? If Rosemary weren't the decent person she is, she'd have dumped Kay years ago. She doesn't deserve your jejune criticism."

He had risen to his feet and looked even taller than his real height.

"I'm sorry," Erin mumbled.

Will seemed to shrink inside his shabby gray cardigan. "My fault. I didn't mean to get so heated."

"All the same," Nick said, "Jeff seems a lot more upset than Rosemary."

"Yes," Will said. "He does, doesn't he?"

Chapter
Fifteen

IF THAT DAY had been mad, the next was sheer chaos. The obituary appeared in the morning *Post*, along with a short, factual story that described Kay as Rosemary's secretary and friend. Calls of genuine condolence and curiosity veiled as condolence started pouring in, and florists' vans beat a steady path to the house. Receiving one such offering—another of the twenty-dollar tasteful sympathy ensembles featured by "Flowers by Wire"—Christie was moved to plaintive protest. "The house is starting to smell like a funeral parlor. You know we'll have to acknowledge every single one of these damned bouquets."

"Who's it from?" Erin asked, watching Christie wrench the tasteful card from the flowers.

"A constituent, I suppose. Never heard of her." Christie tossed the card into the drawer in the hall table that had been designated as a temporary receptacle. "No address, of course, that wouldn't be tasteful. Her name is probably on file, one of our constant correspondents. That'll be a nice little job for someone—looking up all these names."

"Do you want me to—"

"Not today, for God's sake. I need you on the phones."

During her lunch break Erin walked to the gate to stretch her legs and see what Sam thought of it all. He had been pressed into service to screen callers, and she broke into a broad grin when she saw his arrangements. There was no doubt that Sam had taken his assignment seriously. He had set himself up with a folding lawn chair and a matching table. On the table was a thermos of coffee, a lunch pail, and a clipboard. Leaning against the chair was a shotgun; and pinned to Sam's jacket was an enormous "Rosemary Marshall" button.

"I came to ask if you wanted some coffee or a sandwich," she began.

"No, ma'am, I'm all set here, but I sure thank you for thinking of it." He bounded to his feet, alert as a hunting hound; a car had pulled up by the gate. "Can't you see the sign?" he shouted, making a megaphone of his withered hands. "No admittance 'cept on business."

There were two women in the car. The one on the passenger side put her head out the window. It was crowned with pink curlers; a cheap rayon scarf failed to conceal these ornaments.

"That's a helluva nice way to greet people," she yelled back. "We brought Rosemary some flowers. Came to tell her we're sorry about her friend."

"She ain't here." Sam limped to the gate. "I'll tell her. Thank you," he added.

"I'll get them," Erin said, unhooking the gate. She took the flowers—a brilliant if unmatched bunch of homegrown chrysanthemums—and offered effusive thanks and explanations. The women received both amiably enough, but as they left, the one in the curlers called, "Better get the grouchy old nigger off the gate, honey, he's got no more manners than a monkey."

They were gone before Erin could think of a sufficiently stinging reply. Flushed and furious, she hooked the gate after her. She couldn't look at Sam; she was suffused with the guilt decent people feel when faced with the indecency of others. She dropped the gaudy chrysanthemums on the gravel and stamped on them.

"You hadn't ought to do that," Sam said reprovingly. "What if she seen you? She's a voter, you know."

"She's a horse's ass," Erin said.

"And you hadn't ought to use words like that, neither, you been goin' around with that boy Nick too much." The old man's face creased into a hundred wrinkles. "Felt good, though, didn't it?"

"Felt great," Erin said. She planted her feet firmly on the flowers.

"Well, okay this time, but you gotta learn to be polite no matter how you feel," Sam said firmly. "That's what politics is all about." He scratched his head and looked sheepish. "Partly my own fault. She got on my nerves, was all; I seen her around, heard her talk. . . . Then she turns up here with them flowers she yanked outta her front yard, nothing better to do than nose into other people's business, and calling Miss Rosemary by her first name like she was a friend. I won't do that again. You don't need to worry."

"I'm not worried. You're better at it than I am." Erin grinned at him. "But don't you think the shotgun is a little excessive?"

Sam grinned back. "It ain't loaded. But it sure is a powerful moral inducement."

Later that afternoon as she sat at her desk trying to find a gracious way of ending a conversation with a caller who insisted on recounting every detail of every occasion on which she had shaken Rosemary's hand, the outer door opened and a man entered. Of medium height and lean, wiry build, he was so astonishingly handsome, Erin stopped listening altogether and gaped. He was a stranger to her, and apparently to Christie as well; the office manager bore down on him with the obvious intention of evicting him. A low-voiced conversation ensued; then Christie shrugged helplessly and after hesitating for a moment let him into Kay's office. She returned to her desk without comment, avoiding the curious stares of the others.

She didn't have to explain to Erin. The man's sleek cap of black hair and chiseled features didn't resemble even a conventional TV cop—producers have decided upon the tough, rugged, and homely stereotype—but there was something about him that shouted his profession aloud—the confidence of his carriage, the keen, watchful eyes, the way he walked.

Erin hung up on the caller. Her palms were damp; she wiped them on her skirt. For a wonder the phone didn't ring again the instant she put it down, and she got quickly to her feet. She had to find Nick.

He was in the commons room with Will. "The police are here," she announced breathlessly. "One policeman, anyway. Plainclothes."

"Is that so?" Will adjusted his glasses. "Well, well. How interesting."

"Sometimes your cool drives me crazy," Nick growled. "You act as if you expected this."

"I was prepared for such a contingency," Will replied sedately. "Weren't you?"

"I—uh—what contingency? Does this mean the autopsy was—"

Will didn't let him finish. "Let's get back to work, Nick. Philips will be along shortly, and he'll expect you to be ready for him."

"Mr. Laurence?" Erin exclaimed.

"He wants to discuss Sunday's show," Will said. "Nick, will you . . . Nick!" He nudged Nick, who was glaring off into space as if at some profoundly distasteful vision.

"What? Oh, hell, I can't concentrate on this, Will."

"We've covered most of it." Will nudged his papers into a neat stack and stood up. "I need to look up some figures. Give you time to get your wits together. Talk to him, Erin, knock some sense into him. Oh—by the way, a friend of yours called a while ago. I don't know how she got this number—"

"I do, and it wasn't from me," Erin said. "What did she want?"

"Nick talked to her. After that, at my suggestion, he took the phone off the hook." Will's eyes widened in a look of innocent surprise. "It made the most alarming noises for a while, but finally they stopped. I trust the instrument has not been permanently disabled. If you should wish to return the call—"

"Thanks, Will, but I've no intention of calling Fran. She just wants to get in on the action, and she goes on and on, about . . . about . . ."

Will took her silence as an indication that she had finished a conversation in which he had minimal interest anyway; with a genteel nod, he ambled to the door and went out.

"She is a talker," Nick agreed. "Damn it, Erin, it looks as if we were right about Kay. It's funny, but you know I never quite believed our theory, even when—"

"Nick." She turned on him, caught him by the shoulders. "Nick, I just remembered. I know what it was Fran said that bugged me. Astrology. Signs. He's a Pisces, Nick, and that means—"

"Wait a minute." The emotion in her trembling voice and horrified expression made sense to him, even if her words did not. "We can't talk here, too many people around. Come outside."

The weather had turned gray and gloomy. Not a breath of wind stirred; the dismal sky sagged like a heavy blanket, trailing ragged clouds.

A rapturous chorus of barks heralded the arrival of the dogs; Nick picked up a stick and waved it threateningly at Tiny, who settled back onto his haunches and looked as if the idea of jumping up on people had never occurred to him. "Cut it out, guys. I'm not in the mood today."

The older dog was more sensitive. When they sat down on the bench he laid a graying head on Erin's lap and stared at her with melting, sympathetic eyes.

"Is it about Jeff?" Nick asked.

"Yes. Nick, where did you get those birth dates?"

"I told you. The personnel files."

"And where did the information on those files come from?"

"Why—from the people who filled out the application forms. You had to do one, didn't you? Name, address, educational and business experience . . ." Nick's jaw dropped. "Oh, shit. Oh my God. How could I have been so stupid?"

"I didn't think of it either. No one ever checked that information?"

"No, why should they? This isn't a security agency. Joe must have called Sacramento, he mentioned the raves he got from Jeff's boss. But he wouldn't ask about Jeff's birth date, any more than he'd question his height or his weight."

"There was no reason why he should," Erin agreed. "Or why we should think it odd that Jeff 'happened to let it slip' that his birthday was last week. But that's out of character, Nick; Jeff never talked about his family or his personal life. And then there was the fish. On his key chain," she added impatiently, as Nick stared at her in bewilderment. "I noticed it the first time he drove me out here. It was heavy silver, stylized, very handsome. Then it disappeared. Remember, Joe said something about Jeff losing his key chain, that was why he got him a new one for a birthday present. Jeff never mentioned it; and wouldn't you think he'd question people, ask whether they had seen it, if he had simply misplaced it? It looked expensive—a gift, maybe. But it was Fran rambling on about horoscopes that put the idea into my head. The fish is the astrological sign for Pisces. Depending on the system you follow, that's late February into March."

She didn't have to go on; she could tell by his stricken face that he remembered those fatal dates as well as she did. "Oh my God," he said hoarsely. "It all spells Merry Christmas, doesn't it? If he planned this from the start—if he came here looking for revenge—sure, he's a smart guy, he'd know the true date of his birthday would be a dead giveaway. It was perfectly safe for him to lie about it on that personnel file, nobody would think of questioning it or even notice it, until the incidents began. He'd be one of the first to be suspected by anyone who knew about the Richmond fire. A falsified record would probably dispel suspicion—it sure as hell dispelled ours. Then just to hammer the point home he mentioned his birthday was coming up. . . ."

"It's guesswork, though," Erin said. "No proof."

"No problem about that," Nick said. He dropped his head onto his hands. "One phone call is all we need."

"To California?"

"Right. The correct birth date is probably on his personnel file at the state offices; he wouldn't have any reason to lie about it at that point."

"We'd better do it, then. Before he comes back."

"Yeah," Nick said, not moving.

"Where is he?"

"Going the rounds with Rosemary and Joe. Coffee with the Friends of Virginia Wildlife, lunch with the DAR, a strategy meeting at headquarters. . . . Geez. I hate this."

"Me too. Let's get it over with. Maybe we're wrong, Nick."

"A happy thought," Nick said gloomily.

They headed down the hall toward the offices. "No, not Kay's," Erin exclaimed. "The policeman is in there."

Nick stopped short. "Damn, I forgot about him. One disaster at a time is about all I can handle. Christ, Erin, he wouldn't be here unless the autopsy—"

"We'll cope with that when we're sure about Jeff. Come on." She tugged at him, seized with a fierce, sick impatience. It was like going to the dentist; you knew it would hurt, and you knew you had to do it, you just wanted to get it over with as soon as possible.

They went into Rosemary's office. Nick settled behind the desk and switched on the computer. "I hope I can remember. . . ." He pressed keys. "Yeah, here it is. Surveys, polls . . . personnel files."

Erin came around the desk and looked over his shoulder. "That's Jeff's?"

"Right. Jefferson Andrew Ross, male, age 31, born Prescott, Arizona, October 13, 1959."

"It looks so convincing, doesn't it?"

"That's the power of the printed word. Doesn't mean a damned thing. Let's see. Present employer, State's Attorney's Office, Sacramento, California, immediate superior . . . There's even a phone number. Okay, here goes."

His air of grim fortitude changed to annoyance as he was put through the conventional bureaucratic shuffle. "Oh, I want personnel? What a surprise. Switch me, will you, this is an out-of-state call. . . . Damn it, you gave me the wrong extension, operator, I want 367. . . . I know you can't give out information to unauthorized persons, lady, I'm calling from the office of Rosemary White Marshall, United States Congresswoman; what do you want, a security clearance? I'm not asking for his medical records, I just need a couple of vital statistics. Okay, I'll hold on."

Erin didn't have to hear the answer, she read it on Nick's face. "Thanks," he said slowly, and hung up.

"We were right?" she asked.

"You were right. It would be a pretty wild coincidence, wouldn't it, for two different men to have the same birth date?"

"Damn." After a moment she said reluctantly, "There's a convenient cop right down the hall."

The palely lit screen of the computer glared at them, with its damning evidence of deliberate misrepresentation. Nick slapped his hand down on the keyboard, and the square went dark. "No," he said. "Goddammit, I'm not going to turn the guy in without giving him a chance to defend himself. It could be a setup."

"Not very likely."

"Maybe not. I can see Jeff doing the other things—hell, I can even sympathize with him, if he really thinks Rosemary had a hand in the death of his family. But murder?"

"We're the only sickos who have considered murder," Erin muttered. "The autopsy might show Kay had taken a lethal dose of something, but there's nothing to prove it wasn't self-administered."

"Not yet, there isn't. There will be an investigation, count on it. And if anything funny turns up, and Jeff is known to have set the fires, he'll be in deep trouble."

"Okay, I'm with you. We talk to Jeff first."

"I talk to him. I may be a naive bleeding-heart sucker, but I'm not taking a chance with you."

"You're a naive bleeding heart and a male chauvinist to

boot. Don't you dare give me that 'women and children into the boats' crap!''

"For God's sake, don't yell!''

"I'm sorry." Erin clapped her hand to her mouth.

Nick got up. "We'd better get out of here before someone wanders in. They're due back anytime now. We'll have to play it by ear—get Jeff off for a private conversation, find out what the autopsy showed.''

By mutual consent they avoided the offices and the commons room. It was impossible to think of working; Erin felt as if she were catching the flu; her face was hot and her stomach was queasy. Nick kept cracking his knuckles. They settled down on the porch steps, where they were immediately swarmed over by cats. Fortunately for their nerves they didn't have to wait long. A hazy swollen sun still hovered over the treetops when the Olds rolled along the drive and stopped in front of the house.

There were only two people in the car, both in the front seat. "Rosemary and . . . who is it?" Erin asked.

"Jeff. Joe must have stayed in town."

Nick cracked another knuckle. Erin flinched and bit her lip. Not so much a visit to the dentist as pure stage fright. . . . She hoped Nick had some idea of how to introduce the subject, for her mind was a total blank.

Jeff got out of the car, gave them a curious look, and went around to help Rosemary out. She stood quite still for a few seconds, twisting her shoulders and her head as if her neck were stiff. Then a determinedly bright smile curved her lips and she started toward them.

"Taking a break?" she asked. "It must have been pure hell today.''

Nick got to his feet. "The police are here," he blurted.

In the strange dull light, all the faces were shaded and sallow. Jeff's cheeks were a muddy grayish-brown; his color did not change, but his body jerked slightly, as if he had been struck by an invisible missile. Rosemary only nodded and went up the steps, automatically avoiding the cats.

Jeff turned toward the car.

"Where are you going?" Nick asked.

"What's it to you?" The slam of the screen door as it closed behind Rosemary shot Nick forward as if propelled by a spring. Jeff spun around. "Get your hands off me!"

"Give me the car keys." Nick grabbed for them. Jeff caught his wrist; they stood locked in straining struggle, Nick's teeth bared in a snarl, Jeff's lips a tight line.

"Stop it." Erin ran toward them. "Don't, please don't. Jeff, you can't run away, that won't do any good. Nick, let him go."

"I'll let go if he will," Nick gasped.

They fell apart, both panting, not with exertion but with anger and tension.

"We know," Nick said. "Don't you get it? We know who you are. We haven't told anybody. I'm sorry I jumped you, I lost my head, I . . . Say something, damn it!"

Jeff leaned back against the fender. Every bone in his body slumped. "In a way, I'm glad," he said quietly. "I'm glad it's over."

* *

NICK SWITCHED ON the lights. His small cottage was almost as dark as night, the two narrow windows closely curtained. Jeff turned slowly, studying the room and its furnishings with the cool appraisal of a decorator trying to decide what should be done.

"What a dump," he said.

"A humble spot, but mine own." Nick indicated a shabby overstuffed chair, one of two that flanked the tiny, boarded-up fireplace. A couple of rickety tables, their tops stained with white rings, and a worn rag rug were the only other furniture. "Sit down."

"Sure you don't want to do a strip search?" Jeff asked pleasantly.

"Well, now that you mention it . . ." Nick advanced on him.

"Assume the position," Jeff muttered. Turning, he braced his hands on the mantel and spread his legs. Nick felt him over, from underarms to ankles; when he rose, his face was dull red.

"Sorry, I had to."

"Naturally. I'd do the same. Finished?" Jeff sat down and crossed his legs. He was much more at ease than either of his inquisitors, and as he contemplated their embarrassed faces he smiled faintly.

"How'd you find out?"

"That your name is really Raymond Wilson?"

Jeff's smile froze; Erin realized that until that moment he had not abandoned the forlorn hope that they were talking about something else. Then he shrugged. "I guess it doesn't matter now. I'm glad it's over, but I'm not sorry I did it. The only think I'm ashamed of is what I did to you, Erin. Until you turned up, I had confined my activities to a few anonymous letters. I was afraid to be more direct, because I knew I was the first person she'd suspect if anything happened right there in the house. I had to avoid suspicion at all costs, because I hadn't covered my tracks too well; the first serious investigation would show I had lied about a number of things. Then you appeared, like a sign from heaven—the obvious culprit. They couldn't prove anything, you were innocent— who knew that better than I—but it was a low-down trick all the same, and I regret—"

"Shut up!" Nick shouted. He clutched his head. "Damn it! You sit there chatting idly, like some high-class thief talking down to the dumb cops. . . . Why'd you do it? Why?"

"You know I'm Raymond Wilson and you ask me that?" Jeff said quietly.

"I know. It was horrible. But why Rosemary? She had nothing to do with it. It was an accident, a ghastly, tragic accident—"

"It was no accident," Jeff said.

Nick and Erin exchanged glances. Jeff saw the exchange, saw the sick look on Erin's face. "I'm sorry, Erin. If it's any consolation, I don't believe your father knew ahead of time what was planned. But he sure as hell knew or suspected afterward. That fire was set deliberately, for the insurance. And for another reason. Two birds with one stone. Such a convenient way of getting rid of all the excess baggage in a man's life."

He had them now, and he knew it; the faces that stared back at him were masks of horrified repugnance. His words stung like drops of acid. "I'm only sorry I couldn't do more. What sort of punishment would you inflict on a man who tried to burn his child and its mother alive?"

* *

"No, THERE'S NO WAY I could be mistaken. I was ten years old—old enough to understand and ask questions, old enough to worry about what the hell was going to become of us. When you're poor and on the streets, you grow up fast.

"The man I thought was my father had been killed in an accident at work the year before. He was working construction, part-time; there was no pension and no insurance—and no compensation, they said he was drunk on the job. It was a lie. He didn't drink. He couldn't afford to.

"She was pregnant when it happened. She couldn't get a job, even if she had been able to find someone to take care of us. Cheap day care in those days wasn't just bad, it was nonexistent. Welfare? Oh, sure, it's such a munificent sum. All those welfare queens driving around in their Cadillacs. . . . Try to find some place to live that isn't infested with rats and roaches and perverts on what a benevolent society doles out to you.

"We struggled along for a while on the welfare and the little they had saved. I did odd jobs after school when I could get them. Everything came to a head one day in the summer. It had been so damned hot we were all sick with it, the baby was ailing, there'd been some bureaucratic foul-up about the welfare that month, and the landlord said we had to get out. That was the day Mary Sue came in, with her clothes torn, crying, because some man had pulled her into a doorway and tried to . . . She was six.

"It was that night she told me. My mother. She was at the end of her rope, there was nothing else she could do but turn to the man who'd gotten her pregnant—with me. She'd never asked him for a cent or a favor before, and all she wanted then was a place to stay where her kids wouldn't be raped or turned to drugs. He was rich, he owned property. Surely he could find some job for her. Maid, cook, scrubwoman, she didn't care, so long as it was honest work and we were safe. She wouldn t have asked for herself, but she'd lower herself for us.

"I tried to talk her out of it. I was sick with shame and rage. But two days later, when we got evicted, there wasn't much I could do; it was hot, and the baby was worse—we had to have someplace to go. We waited till after dark before we went to the place he'd told her about. 'Just till I can find a permanent home for you,' he'd said. 'Just for a few days.' She accepted his demand for secrecy; she'd never have betrayed him, even if he had refused to help. She pounded that into me—telling the truth could hurt him, and we weren't the kind who did low-down things like that.

"When we got to the place, one of the boards on the window was loose, just like he said it would be, and there was some furniture in an upstairs room. Just a couple of mattresses and a beat-up old table—and a broom and some rags. Wasn't that a cute touch? He wouldn't have the place cleaned up for us, but he knew her well enough to realize that damned broom was a symbol as well as a necessity to her.

"He'd left food, too, and a cooler with water and soft drinks, even some ice. The kids fell on those sandwiches like starving animals, they hadn't eaten all day. Neither had I. I can still taste that bologna sandwich. . . .

"I remember how she looked when she saw it. 'He's a good man,' she said. 'I told you, Raymond, he's a good man really. We'll be all right now.' "

He looked at Erin, whose face shone with the tears that slipped unchecked down her cheeks. "You don't want to hear the next part," he said. "I managed to get hold of Mary Sue and lead her out. The smoke was pretty bad; she fell down and I had to drag her most of the way. I thought the others were right behind me. When I got over coughing and being sick, and realized they were still inside . . . I tried to go back in, but the fire department had come by then, and they held me back."

Nick cleared his throat. "The paper—the newspaper—said the police found no evidence of arson."

"I heard one of the firemen say the building wouldn't have gone up so fast if it hadn't been torched," Jeff said calmly. "And there was one other thing. They said it started in the room under ours. Quite likely it did. It was an inferno when I saw it, on my way out. But it wasn't the only part of the building that was burning. There was another, separate fire on the stairs. The lowest flight. I pushed Mary Sue off the landing and jumped after her. If I'd been a minute later we wouldn't have made it."

Nick shook his head dazedly. "Jesus."

"It took me a long time to figure it out," Jeff went on in the same icy, dispassionate voice. "Years. It was several years before I could think about it or remember it. Sometimes I almost convinced myself it had never happened—that it was just a recurrent nightmare. Because afterward, everything was completely different. Like a new life—born again, right? There we were, Mary Sue and I, in a fancy hospital, with everybody treating us like paying patients; and after we got out, we went in different directions—Mary Sue to a family in Wyoming, me to Arizona. The Rosses were respectable, middle-class folks; he was manager of a hardware store, and she taught school. Two kids, both younger than I. At first I was in such a numbed state I didn't question what was happening. I had a room of my own, plenty to eat, clothes that fit, with no holes or patches—and a nice, kind mother-type who came in and held me at night when I woke up screaming. Mary Sue got on better. She was younger. I see her every now and then. She's married, with a couple of kids. I didn't tell her what I was planning. She doesn't know anything about . . . anything."

His voice was calm as ever, but when he talked of his sister his hands twisted and curled, with a horrible life of their own, tearing at each other like small animals. "I was in high school before I started asking questions. That's the rebel time, I suppose, the time when you question everything. God knows I had plenty to wonder about. Like where the money was coming from. A couple of years of psychiatric treatment costs a bundle. And there was my college fund, they kept talking about graduate school or med school as if there'd be no problem about paying for it. I finally asked her point-blank. She didn't lie to me, I'll give her that. The money was part of the deal—every month till I was twenty-one. She tried to tell me they'd have taken me anyway, even without it, but I knew it was a lie; I remembered enough to know what I must have been like when they got me, a sullen, shivering, bed-wetting, screaming idiot. I knew the money must be coming from him, and I figured he must have something pretty heavy on his conscience to lay out such a big sum. I remembered those two separate fires—one of them cutting off our only means of escape. And I knew what I had to do.

"That took more years. Getting a fancy education so I could compete in whitey's world and find out what I needed to know. I was in my second year of law school before I had the expertise to trace it back, the complex pattern of interlocking companies that had been designed to conceal the real ownership of that building. I figured it was your father, Erin, who had handled the trust for me and Mary Sue, but I knew he wasn't the one I was after. My daddy, the one who owned the building, was a rich man, an important man. Some daddy, huh? So I followed the trail and there it was in black and white—his name, and hers right next to it.

"You can't imagine how I felt when I found out he was dead. I was so disappointed I got stinking drunk. Then . . . well, for a while I just let it lie. I probably wouldn't have done anything if Rosemary had been . . . oh, you know, sick or poor or miserable, or anything but what she is. But then last year she announced for the Senate, and I saw her on some television program, and she looked so young and successful and everybody was bragging on her and saying maybe the White House someday, and I thought of my mother, and how she'd died, and how she'd looked like an old woman, what with worry and hard work and all. She was twenty-seven years old. Twenty-seven! And I couldn't—I couldn't . . ."

The even voice finally broke. He hid his face in his hands. Erin started impulsively toward him, but Nick caught her and held her back. He knew, as did she after a moment of thought, that sympathy would have been an affront just then. Lines from a poem she had once read came to her with stinging poignancy:

> *What voice can my invention find to say*
> *So soft, precise, and scrupulous a word*
> *You shall not take it for another sword?*

Jeff lowered his hands. His eyes were dry, and his voice rose to a pitch of almost childish indignation when he spoke. "And you know what's really funny? I had decided to call it off. You probably won't believe me. If I caught a burglar red-handed, and he swore he had changed his mind and didn't intend to rob me, I'd fall down laughing. But it's true. The crowning irony was that it was the damned birthday party that did me in—the party I set up, in my infinite cleverness, to dispel suspicion. I hadn't been feeling too fond of myself anyway. Rosemary treated me so . . . ah, hell, I knew it was professional habit, she turns it on and off without even thinking about it, but it's awfully effective, you know? I started wondering whether maybe she didn't know about the fire. Maybe she was a victim of that swine too. She never once showed any sign of doubting me, but it seemed to me Kay was looking askance. She had been Marshall's confidential secretary and I felt sure she was in on the whole thing; at least she must have known about the trust, and about me. So I made a point of casually mentioning my birthday coming up, just in case it occurred to her to check up on l'il ole Raymond Wilson. And then she—Rosemary—that goddamn watch . . . I mean, of all the cornball, manipulative stunts. . . . And it worked, just the way she intended it should; I felt like a piece of shit. I had a couple of other things planned, but I couldn't . . ."

He got up and turned his back to them, his arm resting on the mantel, his head bowed on his arm.

"What do you mean, you couldn't?" Nick looked as forbidding as a Grand Inquisitor, but Erin knew he was fighting unwilling sympathy. "You did. I could almost overlook the other things, nobody was endangered by them; but the Mercedes was different. If Kay had been driving—"

"That wasn't me." Jeff did not raise his head. "There's no reason why you should believe that either, but it's true. If I hadn't already made up my mind to pack it up, that would have done it; it scared the hell out of me. I felt like Frankenstein, creating a monster and losing control of it. Only I didn't mean to . . . Leave me alone for a while, will you?"

Nick had to clear his throat before he spoke. "Yeah, all right. Look, Jeff, you stay here. If you try to run—"

"You've got the car keys," Jeff said, not turning.

"Oh, yeah. Okay. I'll just . . . We'll be back."

They tiptoed out, as from a sickroom. The sun was setting in a horror of dull flame; the crimson light made Nick's face look as if it had suffered a bad sunburn. They retreated to "their" bench before either spoke.

"Jesus," Nick said, wiping his brow. "That's the worst thing I've been through in a long time."

"It was awful, wasn't it?" Erin collapsed beside him.

"I can't decide whether I've just had my heartstrings lacerated by the most tragic story I've ever heard, or been conned by a consummate liar."

"Nick! You don't really believe he was lying!"

"No, I don't, but then I'm the biggest sucker on two feet. Hell, I cry over lost puppies. Everything he said about Rosemary applies to him, Erin. He's learned political tricks from the pros, and there are no bigger con men in the world."

"He meant every word he said," Erin insisted.

"Okay, so he meant it. That doesn't mean it's true. He's sick, Erin. Possibly psycho. Did you notice what he said about Kay—that she was getting suspicious? If he thought she was about to blow the whistle on him—"

"No. I don't believe it."

"I feel sorry for him too," Nick said gently. "One part of his story is certainly true, and it was horrible enough to turn anyone's brain. We'd better get back inside and find out what the cops are doing. Then we'll decide whether to tell Rosemary, or talk to Jeff again, or . . . Let's get away from this god-awful sunset. Your hair looks like it's on fire, and although it is astonishingly beautiful, the imagery doesn't exactly soothe me right now."

Nick's afflictions were only beginning. They arrived at the front of the house in time to see a car pull up and park by the steps with superb disregard for the convenience of others.

"Oh, God, it's Laurence again," Nick groaned. "I forgot he was coming. No use trying to duck, he's seen us."

Erin expected to hear a joking comment about their habit of playing hooky but the columnist was in no jesting mood.

"What a hellish evening," he said, contemplating the lurid sunset. "The sky looks like one of Turner's more frenetic efforts."

"Uh—yeah," Nick said. "Coming in?"

"Naturally. You hadn't forgotten our appointment? But then," Laurence added, as they climbed the steps, "I suppose you might be excused for doing so, you've had other problems on your minds."

"You don't know the half of it," Nick said under his breath.

Laurence was reputed to have the hearing of a bat, among other, even less attractive characteristics. "I do, though," he said. "I've seen situations that were a lot worse. This will blow over in time, don't worry."

As they entered the hall, a man rose from one of the chairs. He looked perfectly at ease, and Erin felt a flash of déjà vu that had nothing to do with her earlier sight of him. A memory older and less direct . . . That was it—a fifties film, colorized, of course—featuring one of the suave, sophisticated leading men who specialized in urbane comedies about the upper classes.

Nick stopped. "Who's that?" he hissed. "Not . . . he doesn't look like a cop."

"Ssssh."

Laurence showed no sign of surprise. He stepped forward with all the aplomb of the master of the house.

"Cardoza, isn't it? What is the D.C. criminal investigation department doing in the wilds of suburbia?"

"You've got a good memory, Mr. Laurence," was the smiling reply.

"You are a memorable individual," Laurence said. His eyes lingered on Cardoza's face just long enough to suggest that it was his good looks, not his professional talents, that made him so memorable.

"Let me see," Laurence went on. "It was five—no, six years ago we last met. The Martin case. Quite a remarkable series of events. You handled it admirably, as I recall. But you haven't answered my question. Aren't you out of your jurisdiction?"

"I'm not with the D.C.P.D.," Cardoza said. "I'm living in Leesburg now and working for the county sheriff's office."

"How delightful. You must find it a pleasant change."

"In some ways. If you'll excuse me, Mr. Laurence, I'd like to have a word with this young lady. You are Miss Erin Hartsock, aren't you?"

"Yes, I am."

Cardoza smiled at her. His teeth were as perfect as his other features, they all but shone with their own light. He was obviously trying to put her at ease. "The description was a good one. I won't take much of your time, Miss Hartsock, I know you people are pretty busy. Perhaps you wouldn't mind coming upstairs with me."

"Not without me," Nick said. He took Erin's arm. She glowered at him and tried to shake him off, to no avail.

"You must be Mr. McDermott," Cardoza said. "Certainly, come along if you like. I have a few questions for you too. Excuse us, Mr. Laurence."

The hint had no effect. Laurence followed them up the stairs and into Kay's room. "What's this all about, Cardoza?" he asked.

"I'm surprised you should have to ask, Mr. Laurence. The feeling around town is that you know everything before it happens."

Laurence leaned against the door and folded his arms. "It doesn't require clairvoyance to conjecture why you are here. What was the result of the autopsy?"

Cardoza looked him over from head to foot, in silence. "Come, come," Laurence said impatiently. "This child isn't going to answer any questions until you tell her what has happened."

"Just what I was going to say," Nick added.

Erin finally managed to detach herself from his grasp. "I would prefer to speak for myself, if you don't mind. Naturally I'm anxious to find out what is going on, but I'm chiefly interested in—in getting this over with. What is it you want to know, Mr. Cardoza?"

Cardoza's attractive smile seemed to be reserved for her. "A very sensible attitude, Miss Hartsock. I'd like you to try to remember yesterday morning. I'm sure it was a very shocking experience for you; no doubt your memory is somewhat blurred. But did you notice anything that struck you as unusual or unexpected?"

"Except for Kay being dead? No."

"Cardoza, I must insist," Laurence began.

"Oh, do be quiet, Mr. Laurence," Erin exclaimed. Laurence blinked. He looked, as Nick said later, almost human in his surprise.

"I think I know what you want," Erin said. "As Mr. Laurence has said, it doesn't take much intelligence to figure out what must have happened. If Kay had died of natural causes, you wouldn't be here. And you know about the sleeping pills; so you must be looking for something else. A bottle, or a container of some kind. I didn't see anything like that. I didn't see anything unusual."

"Oh, we found the container," Cardoza said calmly. "At least we found an empty bottle with a few grains of white powder in the bottom. The pharmacist's label had been torn off. It was in the medicine chest in the bathroom."

"White powder?" Nick repeated.

"Yes, the conventional, sinister white powder," Cardoza smiled. "It may turn out to be something as harmless as aspirin. We won't know until it has been analyzed."

"I never saw any unlabeled bottles," Erin said. "Not on her bedside table, anyway. We did share the bathroom, but I didn't put anything in the medicine chest; I can't remember ever opening it, in fact. I tried to be as unobtrusive as possible."

"The perfect guest. Was it you who cleaned the room after . . . afterward? I noticed the bed has been stripped, the wastebaskets emptied."

"No. It was one of the cleaning women, I think. I offered to do it, but I was needed elsewhere."

"I see. Well, I think that does it—for now. Thank you, Miss Hartsock."

"Aren't you going to ask me anything?" Nick demanded.

Cardoza's placid gaze rested on him. "No, Mr. Mc-Dermott, I've changed my mind. Is there something you want to tell me?"

"No. No, I guess not."

"Then I'll be going. Give my regards to Mrs. Marshall, will you please?" A sudden, unexpected grin lit his face. "Tell her she's got my vote."

Instead of following Cardoza downstairs, Laurence stayed with them. Not until they heard the distant sound of the front door closing did he speak.

"Where is Rosemary?"

"In her office, I suppose." It wasn't the question Erin had expected. "I'm sorry, Mr. Laurence, I shouldn't have spoken so rudely."

"I had it coming." The columnist smiled ruefully. "If people would slap me down more often I might not be so obnoxious. Look here, you two, developments have taken a nasty turn. I know Cardoza, he used to be one of the best homicide detectives in Washington."

"But he said he was working with the sheriff's office," Erin objected. "He didn't say anything about homicide."

"It's either homicide or suicide," Laurence replied curtly. "You displayed commendable acumen in your analysis, my dear. Cardoza wouldn't be looking for other drugs if Kay died from an overdose of medication she was known to have possessed. He let you off too easily. He didn't ask any of the obvious questions. So he'll be back. The next time, he'll be just as charming—that's one of his trademarks—and a lot more persistent. Sooner or later, he'll find out about the fires. Perhaps he's already made the connection; the incident in the graveyard was well publicized."

Nick had been fidgeting like a bored schoolboy, cracking his knuckles, shifting from one foot to the other. Erin knew why he was so nervous; she sympathized completely. But she wished he would control himself. He looked like a guilty felon. Laurence's reference to the fires was too much for him.

"With all respect, Mr. Laurence, I wish you'd get the hell out of here," he burst out. ".'All this intellectual speculation is a waste of time, and there's something—there are a lot of things I ought to be doing."

Laurence gave Nick a look that was almost affectionate. "I know you don't like me, Nick. Can't say I blame you. But with all respect to *you*, you are unaware of certain matters that make this situation very frightening and potentially dangerous. I'd like to take you wholly into my confidence. I would do so if I could; but is isn't my secret."

"Secret?" Nick repeated, his eyes widening.

"I have to talk to Rosemary."

Rosemary was nowhere to be found.

"I've no idea where she is," Christie insisted. Unlike the others in the office, who were visibly wilted after a long day, she appeared as fresh and well-groomed as ever. Her black eyes snapped as she responded to Laurence's insistent questions. "She left me in charge, told me to field questions and calls for the rest of the evening. If you think I can't handle it—"

"That was the farthest thing from my thoughts," Laurence's attempt at a smile produced only a grotesque grimace. "Rosemary is fortunate to have such a splendid deputy. I'm worried about her, that's all. This has been a ghastly experience for her."

"Yes." Christie's lips clamped together. She wasn't going to say anything that might appear in print.

Rosemary was not in her room, or in the commons room. The latter was unoccupied and dark until Nick turned on the lights. "Where the hell is everybody?" he asked.

"Good question." Laurence thought for a moment. Then he said crisply, "I'm not concerned about Will. I presume he's gone home; even a workaholic has to relax sometimes. Joe was in town this afternoon; he had a dinner appointment, so he's accounted for. Where is Jeff?"

Erin had expected the question and had believed she was braced for it, but Laurence shot the words at her like bullets, and the startling change in his manner had weakened her defenses. She had never seen him like this—curt, direct, all his irritating mannerisms in abeyance. Worst of all, he was afraid. She could feel his fear, like a cold, clammy aura.

She said, "I don't know," but her voice was breathy and unconvincing. Nick said nothing.

Laurence's eyes shifted from her to Nick and back again. "You do know something," he said. "What? Damn it, this is no time to play games. He's supposed to be here. Rosemary is supposed to be here. She's disappeared too. Do you see a possible connection?"

Nick's eyes fell before the older man's piercing look. "No."

He sounded as unconvincing, and unconvinced, as Erin had. They were amateurs at this game, both of them—a game of deception and duplicity, equivocation and downright lies. And Laurence was a master at his trade. Erin knew how his guests on "Firing Squad" must feel, pilloried and mercilessly stripped naked, down to the depths of their souls.

"No," Nick repeated. "She's gone off on one of her mysterious expeditions—"

"Ah." Laurence almost smiled. "You know about those, do you? You're a clever pair."

Nick flushed with chagrin. He had fallen for one of the oldest but most effective techniques of interrogation, admitting a lesser charge in his effort to deny one that was more serious.

"What else do you know?" Laurence demanded. "Come, come. Are you aware, for instance, that Jeff is your pyromaniac? Ah, I see you are. You two have a lot to learn if you intend to succeed at politics or poker. Your faces are as transparent as glass. Don't feel bad, you've done quite well for amateurs. Perhaps investigative reporting is your métier, Nick. All you need is a little more experience and the kind of network I've built up over the years."

He had them in full retreat now, reeling from one unexpected blow after the other, alternating firmness and flattery in the good-cop, bad-cop routine. Now his voice hardened.

"Jeff was to drive Rosemary home this afternoon. The car is here. Rosemary was here. Now she's gone. Where is Jeff?"

The facade, the mask, of indifference and cynicism were gone. His lean face was haggard, drawn not by fear but by pure desperation. "You don't trust me," he said. "There's no reason why you should, so it's up to me to convince you, even if, in order to do so, I must violate a trust I've held for more than twenty years, and dishonor the dead. Do you know who Jeff is?"

Their very failure to respond was an admission. If they had not known, the question would have produced curiosity and further questions instead of silence. By the time Erin realized this, it was too late. Laurence turned to her.

"The boy is out of his mind," he said earnestly. "Psychotic. If you recall, I suggested early on that the perpetrator of those tricks must be mentally disturbed. I blame myself, I ought to have acted earlier. I hoped to keep this business under wraps, get Jeff the help he needed without bringing criminal charges. The acts he had committed were, at worst, malicious mischief. I saw no sign of homicidal mania. I miscalculated. Badly. Fatally, in fact."

"Fatally," Nick repeated. "Are you accusing Jeff of . . . You mean Kay?"

"Kay would never have taken her own life. I talked to her the day she died, she was . . ." Laurence's eyelids fell. "It's too late for Kay. Rosemary is the one I'm concerned about now. We've got to find her. Or Jeff. If you know, or even suspect, where he may be, you must tell me."

The next seconds were the longest Erin had ever experienced. "He's right, Nick," she said finally. "We can't take the chance."

"He wouldn't hurt Rosemary," Nick said. "Oh, this is crazy! She's in no danger, she's gone haring off on one of her—" He broke off, paling, and Erin knew he was remembering what he had once said. If Rosemary knew who was playing the tricks on her, she would confront the perpetrator. And if she confronted Jeff, in his present state of mind . . .

"He said she was a victim too," Nick insisted. "It was Marshall he hated. Edward Marshall. His own father—"

"What?" Laurence turned on him like a tiger. "Ed? Jeff told you Ed was . . ."

"I'm sorry," Nick stood his ground, though Laurence loomed over him, fists clenched and face distorted. "I don't blame you for wanting to protect your friend. And Rosemary, if she didn't know . . ."

"Rosemary." The columnist passed a shaking hand over his face. "No. She knew nothing. She was a demure little housewife in those days, shy and insecure. Ed would never . . . Angels and ministers of grace defend us. This is worse than I feared. Give me a minute to think. . . ."

His control was incredible. It was no more than sixty seconds before his twisted features smoothed out. "So Jeff knows. Josie told him, I suppose."

"You knew her?" Nick asked.

"She was one of the maids at the Richmond house. I used to spend holidays with Ed when we were in college. Pretty little thing, with a very flirtatious manner. Ed used to joke with her, but I never imagined . . . Ah, well, there's no use trying to deceive you. He boasted about his conquest, as young men will. When I read about the fire, years later, I recognized the name—and I thought what a ghastly coincidence it was. So Jeff . . . No wonder the poor devil is demented. Nick. I have to talk to him. Maybe it's not too late. Maybe I can explain . . . Where is he?"

Nick was beyond resistance. The suggestion that Rosemary might be in danger had destroyed his last doubts. "He's at my place—the overseer's cabin. At least he was half an hour ago."

"Is the door locked?"

"No. Maybe I should have locked him in, but I didn't think—"

"It doesn't matter. You acted for the best. Let me talk to him. All we can do now is minimize the damage and the pain—especially to Rosemary. I think I see a way. . . . Give me fifteen minutes alone with him."

He left the room, almost running. Nick took an uncertain step after him. "Why do I have the feeling I've made a horrible mistake?" he demanded.

"Probably because anything we do is going to end in disaster," Erin said dismally. "Shall we go after him?"

"He can take care of himself," Nick said. "Damn it, I still can't believe Jeff is a threat to anyone, much less Rosemary. Let's see if we can figure out where she might have gone."

Christie, now alone in the office, was in no mood for idle conversation. "What am I, the nursemaid?" she demanded. "I don't know *where* she's gone, or *if* she's gone. She could be in her room. I don't know where anybody is except you two, and I wish you were someplace else. I've got a heavy date tonight and a couple of things to finish before I can leave."

Chastened but no less alarmed, they retreated. A search of Rosemary's room revealed no message and no clue. They were about to leave when Nick stopped. "Wait a minute. Where's that god-awful wig?"

The wig was not in the closet or the dressing room. An empty hatbox, its lid askew, might have contained it. "That's it," Nick said, looking considerably more cheerful. "She's off on another escapade. I'm tempted to call Buzz Bennett and ask to speak to Miz Marylou."

"That's stupid," Erin said; she was far too worried to be tactful. "If Mrs. Bennett is at home we're right back where we started, and if she isn't, we haven't the slightest idea whether she's on her way to meet Rosemary or at the movies. Furthermore—"

"The pickup!" Nick slapped his forehead. "Why didn't I think of it before? If it's missing, we can stop worrying."

"That's not so stupid," Erin agreed. "Let's look."

The pickup truck was not in its usual place. A lighted window and the sound of the TV set made it clear Sam had not taken it. Nick sagged against the open garage door. "What a relief. I'd give a couple of my back teeth to know what the hell Rosemary is up to, but at least we know she's not having her throat cut by Jeff. I don't know why I let that louse Laurence con me—"

"Speaking of Laurence," Erin said. "He's been gone a lot longer than fifteen minutes."

"Maybe he's waiting for us in the commons room."

"We just came through that way. We'd have met him if he had been on his way back."

They turned, like puppets pulled by the same string, to stare at the door of Nick's cottage, only a few hundred feet away.

The curtains were drawn, as Nick had left them, but slits of yellow light showed at the sides. There was no other sign of life; and as they slowly approached the place they heard no sound whatever.

"I guess I ought to knock," Nick said, when they stood before the door.

He proceeded to do so. There was no answer. "Oh-oh," Nick said softly. The door was not locked. He threw it open.

"They're gone," he exclaimed. "Both of them. Unless . . ."

But the bathroom, the only closed-off cubicle in the one-room structure, was dark and deserted. "They must be at the house." Nick's voice was shrill. "We missed them somehow."

"No," Erin said. "Look at this."

She held out the piece of paper she had found on the table, weighted down by a book. Nick snatched it from her.

"Dear Nick [it read]. *Jeff has explained everything. We were all wrong about him. I've decided he should lie low for a while till we get this business straightened out. Better for you that you shouldn't know where he is, in case the police question you. I'll call you as soon as I get him settled. Don't worry, everything is going to be all right."*

They stared at one another for a moment. Nick let out a long, breathy sigh. "Things seem to be looking up," he said. "We don't know where Rosemary is, but we know where she's not—namely, and to wit, in the clutches of a homicidal maniac. Laurence has taken charge of the Jeff mess, and assures us all will be well. Maybe I misjudged the guy after all. Everything is hunky-dory, right?"

Erin didn't answer. "So why," Nick demanded, "are alarm bells jangling in my skull? You don't look too happy either."

"Those bells are deafening me. But I don't know why."

"We're in over our heads," Nick said. "I'm ready to scream for help, if that's okay with you."

"I'll join you. But who do we scream at? The cops?"

"I'm not quite ready to throw Jeff to the wolves yet. I want to talk to somebody with good sense and a clear head, who isn't as close to this as we are."

"Who, Joe?"

"Mr. Temper Tantrum? No, thanks. I was thinking of Will. Don't know why I didn't think of him before."

"Nobody thinks of Will," Erin said. "He works at being invisible. But until a few minutes ago we weren't sure he was innocent."

"We're sure now." Nick worried his lower lip. "Erin, did anything about that note strike you as odd?"

"Aside from the fact that it wasn't written in Laurence's pseudo-literary style—"

"That's it! I knew there was something, but I couldn't put my finger on it."

"He was in a hurry . . . concerned . . ."

"Yeah, maybe. I still want a consultation."

"But Will isn't here. What if he's on his way back to Charlottesville?"

"As it happens, Will is not in Charlottesville. He moved up here a few days ago, so he could be on the spot during the last days of the campaign. He's got a room at some hotel. . . . Damn, he told me the name, but I can't remember it. Wait a minute."

He grabbed the phone and punched a few numbers. When he spoke his voice was soft and wheedling. "Yes, ma'am, I sure hope you can. I'm looking for a hotel or a motel on fifty west, near Gilbert's Corners. Could be a Middleburg number, or maybe . . . Well, you see, ma'am, I had an accident a few years back, and both my eyes . . . Oh, thanks, ma'am, I sure would appreciate it. No, it wasn't a Ramada or a Sheraton. It had a name like . . . no . . . hey, right! That's it! May God bless you, ma'am, for your kind heart."

Erin pressed both hands over her mouth. She was afraid that if she started laughing she wouldn't be able to stop. "You ought to be ashamed," she hissed, as Nick dialed again.

He ignored her as she deserved. "Windy Hill Hotel? Yes, will you please connect me with Mr. William Gates? What? The hell you say! Listen, mister—"

He stared incredulously at the telephone.

"He hung up on me!"

"I don't blame him."

"Mr. Gates is not taking calls," Nick said, in savage mimicry of the clerk's refined tones. "Here, you call back and ask how to get there. He probably won't tell me."

Scenting a possible client, the clerk was happy to supply the information. "I didn't dare to ask for Will's room number," Erin began.

"That's okay, we'll find him." Nick towed her toward the door.

It should have taken longer than ten minutes to reach the motel. Nick's driving exceeded his best, or worst, effort in maniacal speed; either he had a sixth sense for police cars or their luck had turned, for they were not stopped. They almost missed the Windy Hill Hotel. Its small, discreet sign was half concealed by trees. Nick pulled a screeching turn and slammed on the brakes.

"Looks like a classier version of the Shady Lane Motel," he muttered as they cruised along the line of small cabins. The trees and shrubs that landscaped the grounds were losing their leaves, but they still provided a high degree of privacy for the occupants of the isolated buildings, which were designed to look like Swiss chalets. "Look for Will's car."

"I don't think I would . . . Is that it?"

"Yep." Nick glided to a stop beside the brown Ford. "He is at home, the bastard."

"That belligerent attitude won't get you any farther with Will than it did with the desk clerk. He deserves an evening off, he's probably reading or napping—"

"That's too damned bad." Nick slammed his door and strode purposefully to the cottage. A tiny porch enclosed the entrance; Nick began pounding on the door.

At first there was no reply. Nick continued the fusillade and finally a voice demanded he identify himself.

"It's me, Nick. Open up."

"I might have known." Will's voice was resigned but firm. "Get lost, Nick. I'm off duty and I intend to remain so."

"I've got to talk to you. We're in a real mess, Will. We need help."

"I know about the autopsy."

"No, you don't understand. That's the least of our problems. Let me in."

"No way, buddy. Whatever it is can wait till tomorrow."

"It can't wait," Nick bawled, rattling the door. "Rosemary has disappeared and Jeff's gone too, but it's worse than that, he's flipped his lid, gone crazy, and he's taken Laurence—"

"Stop bellowing," Will said sharply. "Wait a minute."

Nick pressed his ear to the door. After only a momentary hesitation Erin followed his example. Will must be watching television. She couldn't made out the words, but there were at least two voices, one higher in pitch than the other. . . .

The truth was beginning to dawn on her when the door opened, so suddenly that both eavesdroppers were caught in flagrante delicto. Nick had been too distracted to make the logical deduction from what he had heard; when he saw who it was, he literally staggered back.

Rosemary had let her hair down. It flowed loosely to her shoulders. She was wearing an astonishing negligee of chiffon and black lace and—as the light behind her made evident— nothing else.

Chapter
Sixteen

"WHAT'S THIS about Jeff?" Rosemary demanded.

Nick choked. "I—uh—I guess we'd better go."

Rosemary shaded her eyes. "Erin too? Come in, both of you." Nick didn't move. Rosemary poked him. "In, I said. Don't stand there gawking. What's happened to Jeff?"

The motel room had a certain charm, if your tastes ran to ruffles and chintz and heart-shaped ornaments. At least it was new and clean, and although the queen-sized bed was the most prominent piece of furniture, there were chairs and a table in an alcove. On the table stood a bottle of wine and two glasses, one half-full.

"Sit down," Rosemary ordered, pointing to the chairs. Nick dropped into one as if he had been shot. "Now talk. What about Jeff?"

"Listen," Nick began, cracking a knuckle. "I'm really sorry. I was looking for Will—"

"Oh, for goodness' sakes," Rosemary snapped. "You're a big boy, Nick, stop squirming. I don't advertise my extracurricular activities, but I'm not ashamed of them. Or of my feelings for Will.''

Will had retreated to the bed. Half-sitting, half-lying against plumped pillows, glasses askew on the tip of his nose, his lips were quivering with repressed laughter. "Didn't you ever see a sex object before?'' he inquired.

A look passed between him and Rosemary, conveying such warmth and tenderness, such shared amusement and sheer delight in one another that Erin's self-consciousness vanished. If that was how it was for them, she was glad—and a little envious.

Then Will said briskly, "Enough of this persiflage. Suppose you eschew journalistic hyperbole and try a straight narrative form, beginning at the beginning and continuing until you reach the end.''

Rosemary listened to the first part of Nick's story in silence. The soft tapping of her fingers on the tabletop was her only sign of impatience, and her face betrayed nothing. But when Nick explained—choking with embarrassment—about Jeff's discovery that Edward Marshall was his father, Rosemary sprang to her feet. "That's impossible.''

"I'm sorry, Rosemary, I know it's hard,'' Nick began.

"Hard, my eye. It's impossible. Ed was . . . Never mind that, just take my word for it. Where did Jeff get this crazy idea?''

"His mother told him,'' Nick said. "It couldn't have been a lie, or a delusion of Jeff's, Rosemary; there's too much confirmatory evidence. She said his father had agreed to help them. They were in desperate straits, or she never would have appealed to him. He had arranged for them to stay temporarily in that building, one he owned, until he could make better arrangements. That was the clue—the ownership of the building—that enabled Jeff to trace—''

"I get the picture,'' Rosemary broke in. Her pupils were so widely dilated, her eyes looked black. "Enough of the orderly exposition, Nick. What was that about Jeff going off with Philips?''

Nick only got a few sentences out before she interrupted him again, even more dramatically. Her hand went to the neck of her robe and yanked. Erin had a flashing glimpse of bare skin before Rosemary dashed into the bathroom. "Go on," she yelled. "He left a note? Did he say where they were going?"

"No. He thought it would be better if we could tell the police we didn't—"

Rosemary emerged from the bathroom wearing jeans and buttoning her shirt.

Will was on his feet. "Better put on some shoes," he suggested, picking up his coat and shrugging into it.

Rosemary grabbed her sneakers but didn't stop to put them on. "Where?" she asked.

There might have been no one in the room but her and Will. "He wouldn't risk taking him to his apartment. They're probably still on the property. That would be the most logical—"

Rosemary flung the door open and ran out. Will paused in the doorway, car keys in his hand. "If you two want to join us, you'd better move," he said.

Will's headlights went on as they ran toward the car and piled into the backseat. Rosemary, in the passenger seat, bent over to slip on her shoes.

"Maybe I should drive," Nick suggested.

"Hang on," Will said.

Erin never forgot that drive. It exceeded anything she had ever gone through with Nick. Will didn't stop for signs or red lights; he banged on the horn and barreled through. Rosemary leaned forward, every muscle tense, as if she could add a few more miles per hour to the frantic pace. They were almost at the house before Nick got his breath back.

"We goofed, didn't we?"

"No, not at all," Will said. "Whoops—sorry; I'm afraid that turn was a little abrupt."

Erin got off Nick's lap. "Yes, we did. But I still don't understand what we did wrong. Is Mr. Laurence—is he in danger?"

Rosemary spoke. "Philips can take care of himself. No one better. It's Jeff I'm worried about. Can't you go any faster, Will?"

"We're almost there. Are the gates open, Nick?"

"Jesus, I hope so," Nick said devoutly, as Will made another slashing turn with no diminution of speed.

They bounced along the driveway and came to a stop in front of the house. "The outbuildings first," Rosemary said, through clenched teeth. "We'll need a flashlight—"

"Glove compartment," Will said. Rosemary snatched the flashlight. They got out of the car, leaving the doors open and the headlights burning, as Will continued in the same unhurried voice. "Erin, get to a phone and call the police. Extreme emergency, missing person, possible hostage situation. We need all the personnel we can get. Nick—"

"What? What?" Nick danced up and down, too nervous to stand still.

"Wait a minute," Will said. "There's someone out there."

His hearing must have been abnormally acute. It was a few seconds before Erin heard footsteps—quick, heavy, uneven. Then a figure reeled into the glow of the headlights. He swayed to a stop and raised a hand to his head. "Rosemary?" he said uncertainly. "Rosemary, is it you?"

"It's me," Rosemary said. "Where's Jeff?"

"Out there." Laurence leaned weakly against the fender and gestured toward the dark belt of woodland. "He's gone crazy. He made me write a note and then he hit me over the head. . . . When I came to, I was tied to a tree. I managed to free myself. . . ." He held out his hands in mute witness and showed the reddened marks on his wrists. "I was afraid he had you too. Rosemary—"

She was gone, running as if pursued by demons.

"Stop her," Laurence cried. "Nick—Will—don't let her go after him. He has a gun!"

He turned as if to follow. Quickly as he moved, Will was quicker. He caught Laurence's arm. "Hold on a minute."

Laurence whirled, tried to free himself. "What the devil are you doing? She's gone after a—"

Will hit him. It was a classic right cross, precise and passionless as a diagram, but aimed with enough accuracy and force to topple Laurence backward onto the gravel. He lay motionless.

"No time for the police now," Will said, bending over the columnist's sprawled body. "I had intended to ask you to get another flashlight from the kitchen, Nick, but we haven't time for that either. Nor—I fear—will we need it."

The sky above the burning trees was a garish crimson. "We better hurry," Nick said, grim-faced. "What about him?"

Will straightened. "Leave him. I wouldn't have bothered decking him if I didn't have a prejudice against being shot in the back." Carefully he checked the safety on the automatic he had taken from Laurence before putting it in his coat pocket. "Straight down the path as far as we can safely go. I doubt Mr. Fastidious would venture into the underbrush, but if we haven't found them by then, we split up. You two stay together, go north. I'll go south."

Erin could only guess what it cost Will to speak so calmly and collectedly. It had required more patience than she had known she possessed to stand quietly awaiting orders instead of rushing off after Rosemary; but she was agonizingly aware of the fact that there was not the slightest room for error now, and no time to be wasted on false trails. A few seconds might mean the difference between life and death.

As soon as Will finished speaking, she ran as she had never run before, ably assisted by Nick, who pulled her along in a series of giant leaps; but Will had disappeared into the woods before they reached them. It was dark under the trees at first, but all too soon the glow of the fire brightened the path, and smoke began to sting their nostrils. When they caught up with Will he was hoisting himself to his feet; he had fallen heavily, his face and shirtfront were smudged with dirt, and blood trickled from his nose. "No, don't wait," he wheezed, as Nick went to help him. "They—they're up there. Listen."

They had gone a few feet farther before Erin heard Rosemary. She wasn't screaming, just yelling, steadily and wordlessly, in order to guide them. Erin could see the fire now—a solid curtain of flame—up ahead. Smoke coiled among the tree trunks like giant gray snakes.

Rosemary was on her knees beside Jeff, struggling with the knotted rope that held him bound to a tree. Her hair was smoldering, and she continued to shout, even after Nick dropped down beside her.

Erin slapped at the sparks in Rosemary's hair. She stopped yelling and looked up. "Where's Will?"

"Right here. Get out of the way, Nick." Will began sawing at the rope. Where he had gotten the knife Erin didn't know, but she wasn't surprised that he had one. Nothing Will did from that time on would ever surprise her.

The heat was so intense she felt like a piece of meat on the grill, but it never occurred to her to retreat. "He's unconscious." She forced the words past the smoke that clogged her throat. "Or is he—he isn't—"

Rosemary staggered to her feet. "No, he's breathing. Philips must have . . ." A fit of coughing interrupted her. "Hurry, Will."

"These damned Swiss Army knives aren't all . . . they're cracked up to be," was the reply. "Thank God for a southwest wind. If it had been blowing the other way—"

A dead pine went up like a Roman candle, showering them with sparks. Will straightened with a grunt of satisfaction, and Nick, who had been supporting Jeff's head, heaved the limp body over his shoulder. "Let's get the hell out of here."

As they fled down the path they heard the distant sound of sirens.

*   *

JOE HAD ARRIVED shortly after they entered the woods; seeing the flames, he had called the fire department. There wasn't much the fire fighters could do, or cared to do, other than contain the fire and prevent it from reaching the house and outbuildings. Thanks to the southwest wind Laurence had failed to take into consideration when he started the blaze, it would burn itself out on the far edge of the woods.

Aside from blisters, scorched skin, and minor smoke inhalation, the rescuers were uninjured. Jeff was still unconscious when they loaded him into the ambulance.

Rosemary had to be forcibly prevented from going to the hospital with him. It was not until Will dragged her into the house and put her in front of a mirror that she gave in. None of them was a specimen of sartorial elegance, but Rosemary was in worse shape than the rest; she had been closer to the fire for a longer time, and she wasn't wearing anything under the shirt that had been ripped half off her body by brambles.

After some cursory first aid they assembled in the commons room. Food and drink, especially the latter, were the first priority, far more important than appearance. Rosemary had gone upstairs to bathe and change. Joe, who had watched the proceedings in appalled silence, finally found his voice.

"If somebody doesn't tell me what this is all about, I'll have a heart attack!" he shouted.

"Have a drink," Will suggested.

"I have a drink. What I want is information."

Will cleared his throat professorially. His nose was swollen, his hair was scorched, and a blister was rising on his chin. "To begin at the beginning—"

"Not you," Joe said. "Him. No, her." His cigar moved from Nick to Erin. "I don't want a detailed piece of reasoned research and I don't want one of Nick's disorganized speeches. Erin?"

"It was Jeff," Erin said. "The pyromaniac. He's really Raymond Wilson."

"Who the hell is Raymond Wilson?"

Joe turned with obvious relief to Rosemary, who had just come in. She was wearing tailored slacks and a loose sweater, and she moved as if every muscle in her body ached, but she was smiling. "I just called the hospital. Concussion and smoke inhalation—but he's going to be all right."

"That's nice." Joe puffed savagely at his cigar. "I like the kid, whatever his name may be. Now, if you don't mind . . ."

Rosemary began with the long-past fire in Richmond. Joe's eyes bulged. "And your name was on those papers? Jesus, Rosemary! I asked you if there was anything—"

"It never entered my mind, Joe. Honestly. I had nothing to do with Ed's business affairs, I signed everything he put in front of me, like the young fool I was; and I had no idea there was anything sinister about that tragedy."

Erin glanced at Nick. They were sitting side by side on the

couch, but not touching; there was hardly an inch of skin on either of them that hadn't been scorched, scraped, or bruised.

"Some brilliant detectives we were," Nick mumbled.

Rosemary heard him. "I can't blame you for assuming I was involved, Nick. You don't realize—you can't possibly realize—how naive I was, and how different things were, even twenty years ago. 'Women's lib' was a dirty word to me and a lot of other docile idiots. I hadn't graduated from college when I married Ed; I didn't go back and finish my degree until several years later.

"It wasn't just a question of feeling inferior—I *was* inferior, in every measurable way—wealth, age, sophistication, education, family background. And in even more important ways that are not susceptible to measurement."

Her eyes met Erin's in a flash of empathy and understanding so eloquent they might both have spoken aloud. Erin knew she was the only one in the room who did fully understand, with her emotions as well as her intelligence—the only one who had been there herself.

Rosemary went on, "I knew one thing you did not know, Nick—that Philips was Ed's secret partner in that deal and in others. They had been friends since college; Philips's family had a lot more money than the Marshalls, but they were nouveau riche, not landed aristocrats. I think that was what attracted Philips to Ed; he's always been a first-class snob. I also assumed that was why Philips supported me—the old family name, plus a few sentimental memories. . . . I guess I'm still somewhat naive. He wanted my help; he did have political aspirations, he planned to run for Congress in two years. It wouldn't have done either of us any good if that story had been made public, but Philips stood to lose a lot more than I did. He could not have denied being involved; the funds for the trust must have come from him, Ed never had that kind of money."

"Doesn't sound like Laurence," Nick said cynically. "It would have been more in character for him to sneak into the hospital where the kids had been taken, and try to finish the job."

"For all we know, he may have tried," Erin said. "But I

think—I'd like to think—that they forced him to put up the money. Mr. Marshall and my father. If one or both of them suspected what he had done, but couldn't prove it, that was the only way they could make amends."

Rosemary's bloodshot eyes widened. "Is that what's been worrying you, Erin—that your father was involved? He handled the legal arrangements, yes, but I'm absolutely certain he was blameless. I wish I could be equally certain about Ed. He was in bad shape that year. Insomnia, nightmares . . ."

"To me that seems more indicative of innocence than guilt," Will said gently. "Put it out of your mind, Rosemary. If Ed had been hard up for money he might have gone along with the idea of burning the building for the insurance, but he would never have consented to the other thing. That was Philips. And I think Erin's point is well taken; there was no way Philips could have been indicted. He covered his tracks admirably. However, if the story had come out, the mere suspicion of arson would have wrecked his political hopes and perhaps his career. Not to mention the fact that he had an illegitimate black son."

Joe choked on his drink. "What? Son? Who—"

"It passed me right by," Nick said, slapping himself on the forehead. "Right through my thick skull. Jeff didn't know his father's name until he traced the records. All his mother told him was that his daddy owned that building. Laurence visited the house often when the girl worked for the Marshall family. He remembered her name—even knew her married name. He wouldn't be likely to, unless she had meant more to him than a pretty, flirtatious servant, twenty-three years dead."

"Laurence was . . . Jeff is . . ." Joe mumbled.

"Well, Rosemary is sure it wasn't Mr. Marshall," Nick said. "And she ought to know. Oh, damn—I mean—"

"Use your imagination, Nick," Rosemary said.

Nick's cheeks were crimson. "Anyway, the important thing—the charge we can prove—is that Laurence tried his damndest to kill Jeff tonight. You remember, Erin, how dumbfounded he was when I told him Jeff believed Mr. Marshall was his father? He didn't know whether Josie Wilson had told her son about his true parentage; he still didn't know, even after he had identified Jeff as the Wilson boy. And then to find, after all those years, that young Wilson had got it all wrong. . . . I guess his fans didn't exaggerate his intelligence after all, it only took him a few seconds to see how he could use that mistaken belief to his advantage.''

"He was like a juggler trying to handle too many balls at once," Will said. "But he'd have gotten away with it, if he could have disposed of Jeff. We might have had our suspicions, but we couldn't have proved a thing. Not even arson.''

"No," Nick agreed. "Jeff was the only one who could have testified to that. Laurence fingered Jeff as the pyromaniac right away. His conscience—if I may use the word loosely—was a lot more sensitive than Rosemary's; he understood immediately what the fires meant. And he figured the pyromaniac wouldn't be so bitter unless he knew the Richmond fire was not an accident. It took him a while to confirm Jeff's identity—''

"Fingerprints!" Erin exclaimed. "Remember that anonymous letter, Nick, the one about there being no statute of limitations on murder? Laurence made off with it—''

"As I said, he was more sensitive to allegations of murder than Rosemary," Nick agreed. "I'm sure that was on his mind—testing the paper for fingerprints—but I doubt he got anything useful from it. Jeff would have been smart enough to wear gloves. Anyhow, all Laurence needed was the information we finally found—the respective birth dates.''

"He must have figured that out early on," Erin said. "And yet for a long time he behaved as if he suspected me.''

"He did more than suspect you," Nick said, looking self-conscious. "Ten to one it was Laurence who mugged you in the garden. Me and my brilliant ideas about dirty old men . . .''

"Nobody's perfect," Erin said consolingly. "I had hurt his sensitive feelings by talking back to him; maybe he just lost his temper.''

"Talking back to Philips would be sufficient grounds for mayhem in his book," Will said. "He may well have believed at first that you and Jeff were both potential black-